I0772763

From Rebellion to Nation

The Flame of Liberty

Dr. Michael J. McDermott

Fiction Disclaimer:

"From Rebellion to Nation: The Flame of Liberty" is a work of fiction. Names, characters, businesses, places, events, locales, and incidents are either the products of the author's imagination or used in a fictitious manner. Any resemblance to actual persons, living or dead, or actual events is purely coincidental. While historical settings and public figures may be represented, the book's content should be considered a work of fiction and not a historical record. The historical information provided is for background purposes only and has been altered to fit the narrative requirements of the story.

ISBN: 978-1-964462-35-6 (sc)
ISBN: 978-1-964462-37-0 (hc)
ISBN: 978-1-964462-36-3 (e)

Rev. date: 06/20/2024

Contents

Dedication vii
About the Author v
Prologue vii

Chapter 1   A Philadelphia Morning....................1
Chapter 2   Duties and Doubts.......................12
Chapter 3   The Incident 21
Chapter 4   The Awakening 34
Chapter 5   The Crossroads of Conviction 46
Chapter 6   Echoes of Loyalty.......................55
Chapter 7   Shadows and Secrets 65
Chapter 8   The Spark Ignites 75
Chapter 9   Shadows and Whispers...................86
Chapter 10   Bonds Forged in Fire 98
Chapter 11   The Siege of Resolve.................. 110
Chapter 12   The Price of Liberty 122
Chapter 13   Shadows and Ashes......................133
Chapter 14   Bonds Forged in Battle 145
Chapter 15   Echoes of War..........................156
Chapter 16   The Fog of War........................ 169
Chapter 17   Aftermath..............................180
Chapter 18   Crossroads.............................193
Chapter 19   The Turning Tide.......................205
Chapter 20   Shadows and Whispers...................217
Chapter 21   The Eve of Reckoning 229
Chapter 22   Battle Lines...........................240
Chapter 23   New Beginnings.........................253
Chapter 24   The Fabric of Society..................264

Chapter 25   Trials of Leadership 275
Chapter 26   Legacy of War 286
Chapter 27   The Ties That Bind 298
Chapter 28   Toward a Brighter Dawn 311

Epilogue: Reflections on a Nation Forged 323
Historical Setting and Events Notes for "From
Rebellion to Nation" 327

Dedication

To our Lord Jesus Christ, the unwavering beacon in the tempest of life, whose love and guidance have shepherded me through valleys and atop mountains. In every word penned and every story told, Your grace has been the quill, Your wisdom the ink. I am eternally grateful for the inspiration drawn from Your boundless compassion and the courage kindled by Your sacrifice.

And to my cherished wife, Faye, who has graced my life with her love for going on 49 resplendent years. Our journey together has been the greatest adventure, a testament to the beauty of companionship God so graciously grants. In every shared sunrise, in every storm weathered hand in hand, you have been my heart's echo, a melody of joy, and a solace of comfort. Our love, crafted with threads of patience, kindness, and an enduring commitment, mirrors the very essence of divine love.

This book is humbly dedicated to both of you. To my Savior, for the gift of salvation and the promise of eternal life, for being my rock and my redeemer. To my loving wife, for the gift of your love, which has been my sanctuary, my muse, and the light guiding me home. Together, you embody the wellspring of my inspiration and the purpose behind my every endeavor.

As these pages unfold, let them serve as a tribute to the profound impact you both have had on my life. May this story resonate with the love and grace that you, Lord Jesus, have shown me, and may it reflect the beauty and strength of a lifelong partnership, as I have been blessed to share with my dear Faye.

About the Author

Michael J. McDermott's narrative is one of adventure, resilience, and profound transformation. Born under the wide skies of the Marine Corps Air Station in Cherry Point, North Carolina, in September 1949, Michael's early years unfolded against a backdrop of constant movement, shadowing his father's Marine Corps assignments across the United States. From the verdant landscapes of Millington, Tennessee, to the sun-drenched avenues of Anaheim, California, each relocation stitched a patch into the rich tapestry of his childhood, imbuing him with deep-seated adaptability and an enduring sense of curiosity about the world and its myriad stories.

As adulthood beckoned, Michael's journey became one of personal discovery and ambition. From the familiar confines of Anaheim to the bustling streets of Detroit and Richland, his path was anything but linear, eventually leading him to lay down roots in Perris, California. It was in Riverside, California, in the serendipitous aisles of a K-Mart, that destiny played its hand, introducing him to the woman who would become his lifelong companion. Their meeting in 1975 marked the start of an epic 49-year odyssey of love, partnership, and mutual growth.

Michael's career is a testament to his dual commitment to service and scholarship. His enlistment in the US Marine Corps in 1967 thrust him into the heart of the Vietnam conflict, where he confronted the harrowing realities of war. This chapter of military service extended through tenure with the California National Guard in 1981, a transfer to the US Army in 1990, and culminating in Desert Storm's aftermath. Parallel to his military endeavors, Michael's academic pursuits flourished. From graduating as Valedictorian from Barkley College with a Law Diploma to later achieving a Bachelor of Science in Computer Technology and a Master's and Doctorate in Theology and Eschatology at the age of 70, his intellectual journey reflects a lifelong dedication to learning and personal evolution.

The transition into the realm of writing marked a pivotal chapter in Michael's life, transforming a leisurely hobby into a fervent passion. His literary odyssey, chronicled in works such as "The Final Battle: A Journey Through End Times," "Divine Journey: Moments with the Savior," "Beneath the Egyptian Moon: The Odyssey of a Dreamer," and his latest opus, "From Rebellion to Nation: The Flame of Liberty," invites readers into vast landscapes of imagination, spirituality, and historical intrigue. Each narrative is a mosaic of his insights and experiences, lovingly crafted to engage, enlighten, and inspire.

In the aftermath of his military and entrepreneurial ventures, Michael discovered his true vocation in serving the disabled and elderly, dedicating over two decades to this noble cause. Yet, it's within the simplicity of everyday life that he finds the greatest joy—be it hosting family barbecues under the summer sun, cherishing quiet evenings with his wife Faye and their dogs, or losing himself in movies with a steaming cup of coffee and a bowl of popcorn in hand.

Michael J. McDermott's life story is a compelling saga of courage, change, and the unyielding power of dreams. Through his multifaceted career, his deep-rooted love story, and his ventures into the literary world, Michael embodies the essence of a life well-lived—a beacon for those who dare to explore, to love, and to imagine beyond the boundaries of the known.

Prologue

In the quiet before dawn, the world holds its breath. It is a time of shadows, when the past and the future blend in the dim light of emerging day, whispering of what has been and what is yet to come. On such a morning, Philadelphia stirs, not yet aware of the role it is to play in the birth of a nation, nor of the heroes and villains it will foster in the crucible of revolution.

Emerging from the mist that veils the cobblestone streets, a figure strides with a purpose that transcends the early morning chill. Margaret Hale, a name yet to be inscribed in the annals of history, carries with her a knowledge that could reshape the course of the war. She is a specter in the shadows, a beacon of hope for those who dare to dream of freedom in a land oppressed by tyranny.

Elsewhere, in the dim light of a concealed cellar, James Bradford, a man torn between loyalties, strategizes his next move. Once a devoted soldier of the Crown, his heart now beats to the rhythm of a different drum—a drum that resonates with the call for justice, for freedom, for a chance to rectify the injustices of a divided land.

As the city rouses from its slumber, so too does the spirit of revolution. It is an ordinary day, and yet, it is the genesis of everything. The air crackles with the potential of change, with the fervent whispers of patriots who dare to envision a world where all men are born equal, where tyranny is a distant memory, and where liberty and justice are not just ideals but the very bedrock of a new society.

This is the dawn of America's struggle for independence, a battle that will be fought not just on the open fields of conflict but in the hearts and minds of those who call this land home. It is a story of courage and conviction, love and betrayal, sacrifice and triumph.

Here, the story begins in the shadowy embrace of the coming day. With each step Margaret takes, with every decision James makes, the path to freedom is carved deeper into the heart of a nation yet to be born.

Welcome to "From Rebellion to Nation: The Flame of Liberty," where the past is a prologue to a future written in the fire of revolution and the enduring desire for a world made anew.

This section of your novel is considered outside the main plot story but will always be closely related to it.

You might use a prologue to introduce a character or setting or provide relevant background information for the main event to come.

Similar to an introduction, a prologue is typically placed in the main body content of a book before the first chapter and is, therefore, not technically front-matter.

CHAPTER 1

A Philadelphia Morning

As the morning light bathed Philadelphia in a soft glow, Margaret Hale moved through her family's home with a quiet sense of purpose. The Hales were well-known in the city, not only for their successful mercantile business but also for their unwavering loyalty to the British Crown. This loyalty set them apart in these turbulent times.

Thomas Hale Sr., the patriarch, was a staunch Loyalist, his faith in the Crown unshaken even as cries for independence grew louder around him. Elizabeth, Margaret's mother, shared her husband's views, and her social circles were filled with others who hoped for reconciliation with Britain. And then there was Margaret's brother, who, much like his father, could not fathom turning against the king.

Margaret, however, was the exception. The injustices levied by distant rulers had ignited a fire within her, a desire for change that raged against her family's loyalty. Her views were a secret she clung to, a constant source of internal conflict that threatened to tear her apart.

At breakfast, the tension was thick, a palpable presence that hung in the air. Conversations tiptoed around the issues that divided them, focusing instead on the safer ground of business and daily concerns. Yet, the undercurrent of political discord was ever-present, like a silent specter at the table, threatening to shatter the fragile peace.

After excusing herself, Margaret stepped out into the bustling streets of Philadelphia, the air alive with the sounds of a city on the brink. She moved with a resolute stride, leading her away from the world her family clung to towards a meeting of fellow patriots. This gathering would have been inconceivable to her father and brother, but Margaret was undeterred.

The bookshop that hosted these clandestine meetings was a sanctuary for Margaret. Here, she could voice her beliefs without fear of retribution. As she stepped inside, the familiar scent of paper and ink enveloped her, a stark contrast to the charged atmosphere of the streets outside.

Inside, the discussion was spirited, driven by the latest British acts and the Continental Congress's responses. Margaret listened, her resolve strengthening with each word. These were her people, her cause, and she was ready to do whatever it took to support the fight for independence.

As the meeting concluded, Margaret felt the weight of her double life more acutely than ever. She was a Hale, yet she stood in opposition to everything her family believed. The walk home was a journey back into a world where she must tread carefully, her every word measured, her true self hidden beneath a veneer of loyalty to the Crown.

Yet, as the spire of Christ Church came into view, Margaret felt a surge of hope. The church, with its history of gathering both Loyalists and patriots, symbolized the complex tapestry of American society. It reminded her that change was possible and a new nation could be forged from the crucible of conflict.

The Hale residence loomed ahead, its facade a mask of stability and respectability. Margaret steeled herself as she approached, ready to slip back into the expected role, even as her heart yearned for the freedom to express her true convictions.

Margaret's return to her family's home was met with the usual blend of warmth and underlying tension that had become a staple of their interactions. The Hale residence, with its solid brick facade and neatly trimmed hedges, stood as a silent witness to the internal struggles of a family divided by ideology.

Thomas Hale Sr., a man whose loyalty to the Crown had been unwavering, sat in the study, surrounded by ledgers and correspondence. Like many others in Philadelphia, his business had felt the strain of increasing taxes and trade restrictions, yet he remained steadfast in his belief that reconciliation with Britain was possible.

Elizabeth Hale, ever the peacemaker, greeted Margaret with a worried smile. "You're back late, my dear," she commented, her eyes searching Margaret's face for signs of trouble.

"I was caught up," Margaret replied, her voice neutral, careful to conceal the true nature of her delay. "The market was busier than usual."

Margaret's younger brother, Edward, barely looked up from his book, his own views a mirror of their father's, though tempered by a youthful optimism that conflict could be avoided. "You and your markets, Margaret. One day, you'll buy the whole of Philadelphia, and then where will we put it all?" he joked, attempting to lighten the mood.

The attempt at humor did little to ease the tension. Dinner that evening was a quiet affair, the clinking of cutlery against plates filling the silences that words left behind. Thomas Sr. eventually broached the subject that loomed over them like a gathering storm.

"The latest dispatches from the governor are disheartening," he began, his voice carrying the weight of his concern. "They speak of mobilization, of preparing for the worst. I fear our loyalties will soon be tested in ways we cannot yet imagine."

Margaret felt a surge of defiance at her father's words but tempered her response, knowing the futility of arguing. "Perhaps it is not loyalty that is being tested, Father, but our resolve to stand for what is just," she said carefully.

Thomas Sr. sighed, his gaze a mix of frustration and sadness. "And what of the cost, Margaret? What of the lives that will be torn asunder by this... madness?"

The question hung in the air, unanswered. Margaret knew all too well the cost of the path she had chosen, but she also knew the price of inaction. As the meal concluded and the family retreated to their respective corners of the house, Margaret felt the weight of isolation that her beliefs had wrought.

Yet, as she lay in bed that night, listening to the sounds of a city equally divided, Margaret's resolve only strengthened. She understood the sacrifices that lay ahead, the bridges she might burn, and the possibility that Margret could lose everything she held dear. Building a new nation founded on principles of liberty and justice was worth every risk for the cause of freedom.

Tomorrow, she would walk these streets again, a daughter of Philadelphia, a patriot in a divided house, ready to face whatever the dawn might bring.

Margaret's return from the bustling Philadelphia streets marked not just the end of her morning errands but also a return to the complex reality of her existence within the Hale family. The house, with its grand facade and the comfort it represented, also housed a silent battleground of ideologies.

As she stepped through the door, the familiar scents of beeswax and lavender greeted her, a stark contrast to the sharp tang of revolution that lingered in the air outside. Her mother, Elizabeth, was in the drawing room, embroidery in hand, the very picture of genteel calm. Yet, her eyes betrayed a hint of concern as she looked up at Margaret.

"Did you find everything at the market, dear?" Elizabeth asked, setting aside her embroidery. Her question, simple on the surface, carried an undercurrent of worry—not just for the day's provisions but for the safety and future of her daughter in these troubled times.

Though her thoughts were miles away from the market's mundane transactions, Margaret smiled reassuringly. "Yes, Mother. The city is alive with talk, but the market remains a place of commerce, first and foremost."

The sound of heavy footsteps announced Thomas Hale Sr.'s entrance. Thomas, the patriarch of the Hale family, carried his loyalty to the Crown not as a burden but as a badge of honor, a stance that increasingly set him at odds with the revolutionary fervor gripping Philadelphia.

"Talk in the city is cheap," he declared, joining them in the drawing room. "Actions, however, have consequences. I hope you remember that, Margaret."

Margaret felt the weight of her father's words, a reminder of the tightrope she walked daily. "I do, Father. I believe in the power of thoughtful actions to shape our future," she said, her words carefully chosen to bridge the chasm that had begun to form within the Hale family.

As it often did, the conversation shifted to the broader implications of the conflict between the colonies and Britain. Thomas Sr. lamented the disruption of trade and the impact on his business. At the same time, Elizabeth expressed her fears for her family's safety and their community's future.

Edward, Margaret's younger brother, watched the exchange with interest and apprehension. His beliefs, still forming in the shadow of his family's divisions, left him uncertain of his place in the impending conflict.

Dinner that evening was a somber affair, the meal's richness unable to mask the undercurrent of tension. Each clink of silverware against china echoed like a distant drumbeat of war, a reminder of the turmoil outside their door and within their hearts.

Later, Margaret retired to her room, the day's events heavy on her mind. She gazed out at the night sky. The stars were like a beautiful painting of light against the dark sky, each star a distant beacon of hope. In the quiet of her room, she allowed herself to dream of a future where liberty and justice prevailed, and her family could stand united, not divided by the ideals that had built their nation.

Yet, even as she dreamed, Margaret knew the path ahead would be fraught with challenges. The dawn of revolution brought not just the promise of freedom but the specter of loss and sacrifice. She was ready to face whatever the future held, her resolve as steadfast as the cobblestone streets of Philadelphia.

Tomorrow would bring new challenges, decisions, and perhaps new divides. But it would also bring new opportunities to fight for the ideals Margret held dear and contribute to the cause of liberty in whatever way she could. For Margaret Hale, the journey had only just begun.

As the night deepened over Philadelphia, Margaret lay awake, the moon casting silvery shadows across her room. The quiet conversations of the day, laden with concern and veiled warnings, replayed in her mind. Despite the comfort of her bed, rest eluded her. Once a distant rumble, the revolution had become the heartbeat of her existence.

Rising before dawn, Margaret decided to use the early hours for contemplation and preparation. She dressed quietly, choosing practical attire that belied her status. In the solitude of dawn, she felt a kinship with the city of Philadelphia—poised on the brink of monumental change.

Descending the stairs, she moved silently, not wishing to disturb the household's slumber. She found Hannah, the family's loyal cook, in the kitchen, already at work. The older woman's hands moved with practiced ease, kneading dough for the day's bread. Hannah looked up, her face breaking into a warm smile at the sight of Margaret.

"Miss Margaret, up with the larks, I see," Hannah said, her tone a mix of affection and mild reproof. "What drives you from your bed at such an hour?"

Margaret approached, helping herself to a slice of bread from the previous day. "I find the morning brings clarity, Hannah," she replied in a low voice. "And in times such as these, clarity is as precious as gold."

Hannah nodded, understanding in her eyes. She had watched Margaret grow from a spirited child into a determined woman, her transformation mirroring the tumult of the times. "Be careful, child," she said, her voice barely above a whisper. "The world outside these walls is changing, and not all welcome the change."

Margaret felt the weight of Hannah's words. With her ear to the ground, the cook understood Philadelphia's pulse better than most. "I will," Margaret assured her, her resolve firm. "But change is necessary, Hannah. We stand at the edge of a new era, and I must play my part."

Leaving the kitchen, Margaret stepped out into the breaking dawn. The city was slowly waking, the first rays of sunlight casting a golden glow over the buildings. She made her way to a secluded spot she had found months ago, a small garden hidden away from the bustling streets. It was here, among the whispering trees and blooming flowers, that she felt closest to the cause she held dear.

As she sat, a leather-bound journal in her lap, Margaret began to write. Her words flowed freely, a cascade of hopes, fears, and convictions. This journal, her secret repository, held more than just the musings of a young woman; it contained the fervent dreams of a burgeoning nation.

She wrote of liberty, of the rights of man, and of the vision she had for America. Each word was a commitment, a promise to fight for a future where all might live free from tyranny. Margaret knew the road ahead would be fraught with hardship, but in the quiet of the garden, her purpose was clear.

The sound of the city coming to life pulled her from her reverie. Closing her journal, Margaret stood, her spirit buoyed by the act of putting pen to paper. She knew challenges awaited her, that her beliefs would test her in ways she could scarcely imagine. Yet, as she walked back to her home, the rising sun at her back, Margaret Hale carried a sense of hope with her.

For in her heart, she carried the flame of liberty, which she would nurture and protect, come what may. Today, like every day, she would face the world with courage, ready to play her part in the unfolding story of America.

As Margaret made her way back to the Hale residence, the streets of Philadelphia began to thrum with the energy of its people. Shopkeepers opened their shutters, and the aroma of fresh bread mingled with the smoky scent of morning fires. The city, a mosaic of hope and apprehension, moved around her, each person playing their part in the day's unfolding drama.

Upon her return, the house was stirring, the morning's tranquility giving way to the day's routines. Margaret slipped her journal back into its hiding place, a small nook behind a loose brick in her room—a secret shared with no one. This journal, filled with her most private thoughts and revolutionary dreams, was her anchor in a sea of uncertainty.

At breakfast, the conversation took a cautious turn, as it often did, skirting around the issues that lay heavy on everyone's hearts. Thomas Hale Sr., with his unwavering loyalty to the Crown, spoke of the latest news from England with a mixture of concern and hope. "Perhaps reason will prevail, and this madness will end," he mused, more to himself than to his family.

Margaret listened, her spoon poised above her plate, her thoughts racing. She understood her father's fears, the dread of impending conflict. Still, where he saw the madness, Margret saw a fight for fundamental rights and freedoms. The tension between her beliefs and her family's loyalties was a chasm she navigated daily, each word, each silence, a choice laden with meaning.

Ever the observer, Edward watched the exchange between his father and sister with a furrowed brow. His own loyalties were torn, shaped by his family's influence yet drawn to the passionate cries for independence that filled the streets. "And if reason does not prevail, Father?" he asked, his voice betraying his inner turmoil. "What then for us, for Philadelphia?"

The question hung in the air, unanswered, as each member of the Hale family wrestled with their fears and hopes for the future. The reality of their divided loyalties, a microcosm of the more significant conflict engulfing the colonies, was a shadow that loomed ever larger over their lives.

After breakfast, Margaret excused herself, citing errands in the city. Her steps took her not to the market or any of the usual haunts of a young lady of her standing but to a clandestine meeting of the local Sons and Daughters of Liberty. These meetings had become the true purpose behind her daily excursions, a chance to engage with the burgeoning resistance movement to contribute to the cause in any way she could.

The meeting place was a nondescript tavern; its sign weathered by time and the elements. Inside, the air was thick with the smell of ale and woodsmoke, the patrons a mix of fervent revolutionaries and those simply seeking respite from the day's toils. Margaret found her way to the back room, where a small group had already gathered, their faces alight with the fervor of their convictions.

As the door closed behind her, shutting out the noise of the tavern, Margaret felt a surge of purpose. Among these determined souls, she found a sense of belonging, a shared commitment to a cause greater than themselves. The following discussions of strategy and support for the Continental Army, of spreading the message of liberty throughout the colonies, were a balm to her spirit.

Leaving the tavern, Margaret felt the weight of her double life more acutely than ever. The path she had chosen, fraught with danger and dissent, was a solitary one. Yet, as Margret walked back through the streets of Philadelphia, her resolve was unwavering. Armed with the knowledge that the fight for freedom was a just cause, she was prepared to face any challenges that lay ahead.

The day was drawing to a close, the sun dipping below the horizon, casting long shadows across the cobblestones. Margaret Hale, a daughter of Philadelphia, moved through the city's streets, her heart heavy with the cost of the coming conflict but buoyed by the hope of the new nation that might yet emerge from the ashes of revolution.

The sun dipped below the horizon, its fading light casting

long shadows across the cobblestones of Philadelphia. Margaret Hale moved through the city's streets, her steps sure yet heavy with the enormity of the conflict to come. In her heart, the weight of potential loss and the cost of struggle were balanced by the bright flame of hope for the new nation that might emerge from the crucible of revolution. Her journey, marked by courage, conviction, and deep personal stakes, unfolded with each step she took into the twilight of a city on the brink of change.

CHAPTER 2

Duties and Doubts

As the first light of dawn crept over Philadelphia, casting a soft glow on the cobblestone streets, Captain James Bradford stood by the window in his quarters at the Hale residence. The room, a courtesy extended by Thomas Hale Sr. due to their families' old ties and out of respect for his rank, felt more like a gilded cage with each passing day. Dressed in his redcoat uniform, the fabric seemed to weigh heavier than mere cloth, embodying the conflict between his duty to the Crown and the doubts festering in his heart.

The Hale household was stirring, the aroma of breakfast weaving through the corridors—a brief respite from the brewing storm outside. Sarah, the maid, announced that breakfast was ready, her voice a reminder of the day's routines that awaited him.

Breakfast was served in the quiet ambiance of the dining room, where Thomas Sr. was already seated, a fortress of newspapers and letters before him. The air was thick with the unspoken, the morning light doing little to dispel the shadows of division within the family.

"Good morning, Captain Bradford," Thomas greeted, his voice carrying a note of formality befitting James's military rank. The conversation that followed tread carefully around the edges of political discord, a testament to the Hale family's divided loyalties.

Margaret's entrance brought a shift in the atmosphere, her resolve palpable. The meal progressed with discussions of trade and tidings from the docks, a veil over the deeper tensions that lay beneath. It was Margaret, however, who broached the subject everyone else danced around.

After the meal, she approached James with a request for a private word. In the seclusion of the drawing room, with the morning sun casting a checkerboard of light and shadow, Margaret's directness cut through the formalities.

"Mr. Bradford, as a Captain in the British Army, you've seen the impact of the Crown's decisions on this city," she began, her voice steady but charged with an undercurrent of challenge. "Have you not questioned the righteousness of our path, of the suffering imposed in the name of loyalty?"

James, taken aback by her forthrightness, found himself at a crossroads. "Miss Hale, my duty, my oath, binds me," he confessed, the weight of his uniform suddenly oppressive. "Yet, I cannot ignore the truths before me, the voices of those who suffer. Your question touches upon doubts I've harbored in silence."

Their dialogue was interrupted by the arrival of a fellow officer, a stark reminder of the world outside the Hale residence's walls. As James excused himself, the seeds of change Margaret had planted began to take root. Her words echoed in his mind, a clarion call to reexamine his loyalties, his duties, and the role he was to play in the unfolding drama of revolution.

Stepping back into the streets of Philadelphia, Captain James Bradford carried with him not just the weight of his rank but also a burgeoning sense of purpose. The decision before him was clear but laden with danger: to follow his duty to the Crown or to forge a new path led by the principles of justice and freedom that Margaret Hale embodied. As the city awoke around him, James realized that the coming days would demand more than mere allegiance; they would require courage, conviction, and, perhaps, a sacrifice of the only life he had known.

That morning, the air in the Hale residence was charged with unspoken tensions as if the house itself bore witness to the seismic shifts occurring within its walls and throughout Philadelphia. Captain James Bradford felt this acutely as he descended to join the Hale family for breakfast, his redcoat uniform a stark emblem of his allegiance amidst a household where loyalties were divided.

Thomas Hale Sr., a figure of respect and authority, greeted him with a nod, acknowledging their shared adherence to the Crown, albeit strained by the currents of change. "Captain Bradford, unsettling news from the docks today. It's becoming increasingly clear that compromise may be beyond our reach," Thomas remarked, his voice tinged with regret.

The breakfast table became a theater of diplomacy, where words were weighed and meanings parsed. Margaret's arrival introduced a new dynamic, her presence like a spark capable of igniting the air. Her commitment to the revolutionary cause was an open secret that added layers of complexity to her interactions with Bradford.

After the meal, Margaret's request for a private word with James pulled him into an orbit he found dangerous and compelling. They retreated to the drawing room, where the early light painted shadows on the floor, a fitting backdrop for the conversation that unfolded.

Margaret did not mince words. "Captain Bradford, your position grants you a unique perspective on the events shaping our city. Yet, I wonder, does it not also offer you a view of the suffering these policies inflict upon our people?" she inquired, her gaze steady.

James, taken aback by her directness, grappled with an answer: "Miss Hale, I am not blind to the hardships faced by the colonists. My allegiance to the Crown does not preclude my empathy for those who suffer under its decrees."

The dialogue between them, measured and fraught with implication, veered into the territory of personal conviction and moral responsibility. "And what of your duty to justice, to the fundamental rights of mankind?" Margaret pressed her voice a blend of challenge and plea.

Their exchange was interrupted by the arrival of a fellow officer, a reminder of the world beyond the Hale residence's confines. James excused himself, his mind tumultuous with conflicting loyalties and a newfound respect for Margaret's fervor.

As he stepped back into the streets of Philadelphia, Captain James Bradford carried with him the weight of their conversation, a seed of doubt planted firmly in his mind. The city around him, alive with the day's hustle, seemed to mirror his inner turmoil.

The day's duties called, yet James found his thoughts returning to Margaret Hale and her impassioned arguments for liberty and justice. The divide between his professional obligations and personal convictions had never felt so pronounced.

Navigating the cobbled streets, James realized that the choices he faced were not just about allegiance but about the kind of man he wished to be. The battle lines were drawn across the fields of Lexington and Concord and within the hearts and minds of individuals like himself.

Captain James Bradford stands at the precipice of change, his subsequent actions poised to define his role in the unfolding revolution. As Philadelphia braces for the storm of conflict, so too does Bradford, caught between the duty he has sworn and the doubts that Margaret Hale has stirred within him.

As Captain James Bradford stepped out into the bustling streets of Philadelphia, the crisp morning air carried the mixed scents of woodsmoke and fresh bread alongside the undercurrent of tension that pervaded the city. His conversation with Margaret Hale lingered in his mind, her passionate words challenging his beliefs and stirring doubts about his role as an officer in the British Army.

James's morning duties took him through the heart of the city, past markets teeming with colonists preparing for whatever the day might bring, and down towards the docks where British ships loomed like silent sentinels. Along the way, he couldn't help but notice the wary glances cast his way, a stark reminder of the widening rift between the Crown and its American subjects.

His destination was a meeting with his commanding officer, a task that would have been routine on any other day. Today, however, James felt as if he were walking towards a precipice, each step taking him closer to a decision that might alter the course of his life.

The meeting, held in a commandeered warehouse near the waterfront, was tense. Reports of increased revolutionary activity, of stockpiled arms and whispered plans for rebellion, filled the air. James listened, his expression impassive, but his mind raced. The reality of the conflict, of the impending bloodshed between neighbors and between families, became oppressively clear.

After the meeting, James found himself wandering the city, the weight of his uniform heavier than ever. He observed the people of Philadelphia, their faces marked by determination, fear, and hope. It was a city on the brink, its fate hanging in the balance, and James felt the pull of its people's desire for freedom. This desire mirrored his own growing disillusionment with the Crown's cause.

It was in this contemplative state that James crossed paths with Edward Hale, Margaret's younger brother, whose loyalty to the Crown was as unwavering as his sister's commitment to the revolution. Their encounter, unexpected and charged with the unspoken tension of their divided loyalties, gave James a glimpse into the personal toll of the conflict.

"Captain Bradford," Edward greeted him, his voice calm. "I trust you're finding our city to your liking despite the current... unrest?"

James paused, carefully considering his words. "Philadelphia is a city of great promise, Master Hale. It's the unrest, as you call it, that troubles me. The cost of this conflict will be high for both sides."

Edward's expression hardened. "The Crown will restore order," he stated, though his certainty seemed to falter. "It's only a matter of time."

Their brief exchange, polite yet fraught with the complexity of their positions, ended as quickly as it began, leaving James to continue his solitary walk. Much like his earlier discussion with Margaret, the conversation with Edward highlighted the personal dimensions of the conflict and the way it had infiltrated every aspect of Philadelphia, including the Hale family.

As the day faded into evening and James returned to the Hale residence, he felt the isolation of his position more acutely than ever. Caught between duty and conscience, loyalty and truth, he realized that the path he chose would require a courage he was only beginning to understand.

The day had not brought answers, but it had clarified the questions that James needed to confront. In the privacy of his room that night, he reflected on the journey that had brought him to this moment, to a city pulsing with the heartbeat of revolution and to a crossroads that would determine not just his fate but perhaps the fate of a nation.

As the day faded into evening and James returned to the Hale residence, he felt the isolation of his position more acutely than ever. Caught between duty and conscience, loyalty and truth, he realized that his path would require a courage he was only beginning to understand. The day had not brought answers, but it had sharpened the questions James needed to confront. In the privacy of his room that night, he reflected on his journey to this moment, to a city alive with the spirit of revolution, and to a crossroads in his life that would determine not just his own fate but perhaps the fate of a nation yet to be born.

As the shadows lengthened and the bustling streets of Philadelphia began to quiet, Captain James Bradford found himself standing before the Hale residence again, the day's encounters heavy on his mind. The conversations with Margaret and Edward, the tense meeting with his superiors, and the silent appeals in the eyes of the colonists he passed on the street—all swirled together, painting a complex portrait of a city and a man on the brink of irrevocable change.

Inside, the Hale family gathered for the evening meal, a semblance of normalcy amid a brewing storm. Yet, for James, the familiar rituals of dinner felt distant, as if he were observing them from afar. Margaret's passionate arguments for liberty, Edward's staunch loyalty to the Crown, and Mr. Hale's attempts to navigate the treacherous waters of neutrality—each perspective now seemed to him like pieces of a puzzle, hinting at a larger picture he had yet to comprehend.

As the meal concluded and the family retired to the drawing room, James excused himself, claiming fatigue. But instead of seeking his bed, he wandered into the garden, where the night air offered a cool embrace. The garden, a place of peace and reflection for the Hale family, now served as the backdrop for James's solitary contemplation.

Under the cover of darkness, James allowed himself to consider a future untethered from the obligations of his uniform. What would it mean to stand on the side of liberty? Could he betray his oath to the Crown for a cause he believed to be just? The questions, once whispered doubts, now roared in his ears like the ocean's tide.

It was there, in the quiet solitude of the garden, that James's resolve began to crystallize. The ideals of freedom and justice, so eloquently defended by Margaret and so fervently desired by the people of Philadelphia, resonated with his own yearning for a world governed by fairness and respect for the inherent rights of all.

As the clock in the Hale residence chimed the hour, marking the end of another day, James Bradford made his decision. With the dawn, he would begin the delicate process of disentangling himself from the British Army, a path fraught with danger but illuminated by the light of conviction.

He understood the risks and potential for loss and betrayal, but the promise of contributing to something greater than himself—a new nation founded on the principles of liberty and justice—offered hope in the tumultuous sea of revolution.

Returning to the house, James felt a sense of peace that had eluded him since his arrival in Philadelphia. The path ahead would be challenging, but it was right. And in that certainty, he found the strength to face whatever challenges lay ahead.

Under the canopy of stars, James Bradford's resolve solidified, testament to his profound internal journey—not just through the streets of Philadelphia but within the depths of his own conscience. The decision to leave behind his allegiance to the British Crown and embrace a cause that spoke to the very core of his beliefs was not made lightly. Yet, as he stood in the quiet of the Hale family's garden, it felt like the only choice possible.

Tomorrow would bring the challenge of charting a new course, of navigating the treacherous waters of rebellion and loyalty. But for tonight, James found solace in the clarity of his purpose. The journey ahead would undoubtedly test him and demand sacrifices he could scarcely imagine. Still, the promise of playing a part in the birth of a new nation and fighting for a future grounded in liberty and justice imbued him with a sense of hope.

With a last look at the night sky, James turned back towards the house, the weight of his decision both a burden and a liberation. As he crossed the threshold, the closing door behind him felt symbolic, marking an end to the life he had known. Ahead lay uncertainty, danger, and the possibility of a new beginning.

Chapter 3

The Incident

In the heart of Philadelphia, amidst an evening of elegance at the Hamilton estate, the city's elite gathered, their laughter echoing through the opulent halls. Margaret Hamilton, draped in the finery of her class yet feeling increasingly alienated, navigated the crowd with a grace that masked her internal turmoil. The luxurious setting starkly contrasted with the restless spirit of the city beyond the estate's walls, a reflection of the conflict raging within her.

Among the guests, James Bradford, a British officer, stood with his comrades, his sense of duty clashing with a growing disillusionment. Margaret momentarily captured his attention, and their brief exchange of glances revealed a shared sense of unease amidst the festivities, a hint of the alliance that was yet to come.

As whispers of an impending protest seeped into the conversations, both Margaret and James felt the pull of the turbulent world outside. Seizing a moment of solitude, Margaret escaped to the garden, her thoughts racing with the possibility of the night's events sparking a significant change.

Meanwhile, the city's cobblestone streets buzzed with the energy of rebellion. Margaret, driven by a compulsion to stand with those demanding freedom, found herself amidst the chanting crowd. James, observing from a distance, was torn between his orders and his conscience when the command was given to disperse the protesters.

The situation quickly escalated into chaos. In the fray, Margaret's efforts to assist an injured protester marked her for confrontation. It was then that James, propelled by a sudden clarity, intervened, shielding Margaret from harm in a decisive act that blurred the lines of allegiance.

As the tumult subsided, they found refuge in the shadowed quiet of an alleyway, confronting the implications of their actions. Margaret's inquiry, "Why?" was met with James's simple yet profound response, "For justice," marking a turning point in their understanding of each other.

This shared ordeal under the tumultuous skies of Philadelphia fostered an unexpected camaraderie between them. As they parted, the promise of future collaboration lingered in the air, a testament to the transformative power of shared convictions. Their relationship, once defined by their opposing sides, had now evolved into a partnership forged in the fires of rebellion, a bond that could change the course of history.

The night's events left Philadelphia caught in a delicate balance, with the Hamilton estate's festivities a world apart from the streets' cries for freedom. Margaret, her determination fortified, and James, resolved to support the cause of liberty, faced the dawn of a new day in a city—and a nation—on the brink of change.

In the quiet aftermath of the night's upheaval, the city of Philadelphia awoke to a palpable tension, the events of the previous evening casting long shadows over the cobblestone streets. Margaret Hamilton, returning to the sanctuary of her family's estate, found the opulence that once comforted her now served as a stark reminder of the divide between her world and the cause she secretly championed. Each step through the familiar halls echoed with the weight of her double life, a burden she carried with a renewed sense of purpose.

James Bradford, meanwhile, faced the dawn with a heavy heart, his actions of the night before marking a definitive break from the life he had known. The British uniform he once wore with pride now felt like a chain, binding him to a cause he could no longer in good conscience support. The decision to aid Margaret and the revolutionaries was not made lightly, understanding the consequences could be dire. Yet, as he gazed out over the barracks, watching the sun rise over a city divided, he knew there was no turning back.

The day brought with it a flurry of activity as both sides of the conflict braced for what was to come. Margaret used her position within a loyalist society to gather intelligence, and her every interaction was laced with the risk of discovery. Her evenings were spent in hushed meetings with fellow patriots, planning and strategizing under the cover of darkness. Each message smuggled, and each plan laid brought with it a mix of fear and exhilaration, the stakes higher than ever, the uncertainty of their success palpable.

James, on the other hand, found himself increasingly isolated among his fellow officers, his skepticism and questions drawing suspicion. The regiment's camaraderie, once a source of strength, now felt hollow. In the quiet moments alone, he plotted his next move, knowing that his future lay not with the British army but with the burgeoning revolution. His thoughts often drifted to Margaret, her courage and conviction a beacon in the uncertainty that surrounded him.

Margaret and James's journeys cross paths again, united by their common dedication to the revolutionary cause. They are able to have a covert discussion, their words laden with hidden connotations, after a fortuitous meeting in the busy market square. In them, we hear optimism for what the future holds and the promise of a country unencumbered by despotism. A brief but meaningful connection that holds the potential for much more.

As dawn began to paint the Philadelphia skyline, the repercussions of the night's events lingered in the minds of all involved. Margaret, with a renewed sense of purpose, and James, now questioning the very foundation of his allegiance, found themselves at a crossroads. Their unexpected partnership, formed in the crucible of conflict, promised to be the catalyst for deeper involvement in the burgeoning revolution. The city, a microcosm of the larger struggle for independence, awakened to a day that held the weight of newfound alliances and the unyielding quest for freedom.

As Philadelphia settles into the night, the city is a landscape of contrasts, of light and shadow. And within its heart, two souls, once bound to opposing sides, now united in a common cause, face the uncertain future with determination and hope. Their journey is a reflection of the larger struggle, a narrative thread in the tapestry of a nation's fight for liberty.

As Philadelphia settled into the night, a landscape of contrasts emerged, painting the city in strokes of light and shadow. Amidst this backdrop, Margaret Hamilton and James Bradford, once bound to opposing sides, now found themselves united by a cause greater than themselves. The uncertain future lay stretched before them, a blank canvas awaiting the marks of revolution.

In the quiet aftermath of the night's upheaval, Margaret returned to her family's estate. Each step through its opulent halls echoed with the weight of her double life. The grandeur that once signified comfort and status now seemed a gilded cage, trapping her in a world at odds with the freedoms she yearned for herself and her city. The whispers of silk gowns and clinking of fine china, remnants of the evening's earlier elegance, were now drowned out by the resounding calls for liberty that pulsed in her heart.

James, too, faced the dawn with a heavy heart and a mind in turmoil. His uniform, once worn with pride, now felt like a shroud, concealing the truth of his shifting loyalties. The solidarity of the regiment, a comfort in the past, now suffocated him, each order a reminder of the chain of command that bound him to actions he could no longer justify. The decision to intervene on behalf of Margaret and the protesters was a line crossed, a definitive break from his past life. As he watched the sun rise over the barracks, casting long shadows over the ground, James knew his path lay divergent from the red-coated ranks he once called brethren.

The day's light brought activity to the streets of Philadelphia, a city caught in the throes of change. Margaret, using her social standing as a shield, ventured into the heart of loyalist society by day, her every move a calculated risk. Each conversation was a dance, her words carefully chosen to extract information without revealing her true allegiance. By night, she met with fellow patriots in secret, their plans whispered in the shadows of alleyways and backrooms. The thrill of rebellion was laced with danger; each successful message delivered a victory, each gathering a defiance of the oppressive order they sought to overthrow.

James's isolation grew with each passing day. His questions and doubts set him apart from his fellow officers, their suspicions a constant shadow. The regiment's camaraderie had turned into a facade, one he maintained with increasing difficulty. Alone with his thoughts, he plotted his next steps, the image of Margaret's determined face a beacon in his deliberations. Her bravery and conviction, set against the backdrop of their shared ordeal, illuminated the path he felt compelled to follow.

Their paths converged once more in the bustling heart of

the market square, a fortuitous meeting that allowed them a brief exchange laden with significance. Around them, the city pulsed with the life of commerce and conversation, but their words to each other, though guarded, spoke of deeper currents, of shared dreams for a nation unburdened by tyranny.

As they parted, the promise of their next meeting hung in the air, a silent acknowledgment of the bond forged between them. Margaret and James, navigating the dichotomy of their existences, stood as symbols of the burgeoning revolution, their individual journeys reflecting the larger narrative of a nation striving for its identity.

The Incident, now a catalyst for their awakened resolve, had set them on a path irrevocably intertwined with the fate of the revolution. Philadelphia, with its cobblestone streets and colonial charm, had become a stage for the unfolding drama of independence; its citizens, including Margaret and James, were key players in the pursuit of a future defined by freedom and equality.

The night descended once more on Philadelphia, the city a tableau of the ongoing struggle, its lights, and shadows a metaphor for the conflict that raged within and without. In its midst, Margaret and James faced the coming days with determination, their spirits undaunted, their purpose clear. The journey ahead was fraught with uncertainty, but their resolve was unshakeable, fueled by the transformative power of "The Incident" and the unyielding quest for liberty.

Margaret navigated the crowded streets of Philadelphia, her mind racing with plans and possibilities. As she turned a corner, she almost collided with James, who seemed equally preoccupied.

"James!" she exclaimed, steadying herself. "I didn't expect to see you here."

James offered a quick, tense smile. "Nor I, you. These streets are becoming more dangerous by the day. Especially for those of us with... divided loyalties."

Margaret glanced around before leaning in, lowering her voice. "I've been gathering intelligence. There's a shipment of arms due to the British garrison by week's end. It could change the balance if intercepted."

James's interest piqued. "That is valuable information. But acting on it could expose you further. Are you certain you want to take that risk?"

"It's a risk worth taking if it aids our cause," Margaret replied firmly. "But I can't do it alone. I need help, James. Your help."

He looked conflicted but nodded. "Alright. We'll need a plan. Let's find somewhere private to talk."

They slipped into a quiet alleyway, the noise of the city dimming around them.

"Margaret, you know this puts us both in great danger," James said, his voice low. "If we're caught—"

"I know," she interrupted, her gaze steady. "But think of what it means if we succeed. We could turn the tide."

James ran a hand through his hair, sighing. "Alright. I'm with you. For justice, for freedom. But we must be cautious."

Their conversation was interrupted by the distant sound of marching feet. James peered around the corner before looking back at Margaret.

"It's now or never," he whispered. "We'll need to act quickly. Meet me tonight at the old mill. We can plan further there."

Margaret nodded, her heart racing with the gravity of their decision. "Thank you, James. See you tonight."

As they parted ways, the weight of their impending action settled over them. This was more than a mission; it was a declaration of their commitment to the cause and to each other.

That evening, in the shadowed confines of the old mill, Margaret and James laid out their plan. They spoke in hushed tones, mapping out every detail, aware that the success of their mission—and their very lives—depended on their precision and caution.

"We'll need a diversion," James proposed, poring over a crudely drawn map. "Something to draw the guards away from the shipment."

Margaret nodded, adding, "I have contacts who can create a disturbance on the opposite side of town. It should give us the window we need."

As they finalized their plans, there was a sense of camaraderie between them, a bond forged in the fires of rebellion. Their partnership, once tentative, had solidified into something unbreakable.

"Once this is over," Margaret said, her voice tinged with a mix of hope and uncertainty, "Philadelphia will never be the same."

"And neither will we," James added, meeting her gaze. "For better or worse, we're in this together."

They shook hands, the gesture sealing their pact. As they left the safety of the mill, the night air felt charged with the promise of change. Margaret and James stepped back into the shadows of the city, their hearts set on the dawn of a new day for Philadelphia and for themselves—a day of revolution and newfound alliances in the quest for freedom.

In the days that followed, their meticulously laid plans began to take shape. The city of Philadelphia, usually vibrant with the hustle and bustle of daily life, was now the stage for a much more crucial endeavor. Margaret and James, now allies in the cause for independence, found themselves at the heart of a daring mission that could sway the momentum in favor of the Continental Army.

One evening, as they reconvened in the secluded alcove of a quiet tavern, the air around them thick with anticipation and the low hum of hushed conversations, they reviewed their strategy for the final time.

"Everything's set for tomorrow," Margaret whispered across the table, her eyes scanning the room for any sign of eavesdroppers. "The diversion will start at dawn. We'll have a narrow window to intercept the shipment."

James, looking over a small, folded piece of parchment detailing the garrison's layout, nodded. "And we have our insiders at the docks ready to signal when the shipment arrives. We must be swift; the moment we have what we need, we retreat."

Margaret leaned in closer, her voice a mere breath. "I still can't believe we're doing this. If we succeed..."

"When we succeed," James corrected gently, offering her a reassuring look. "We're making history, Margaret. For justice, for freedom."

Their planning was interrupted by the tavern keeper, who approached with a new round of drinks. "On the house," he said, a knowing glint in his eye. "For the brave souls who dare to dream of a better tomorrow."

Grateful, they acknowledged his gesture, aware that their cause had more support than they might have initially realized. It was a small reminder of the collective yearning for change that pulsed through the city. This silent bond united them with their fellow patriots.

As the night deepened, they finalized their preparations, carefully discussing each step and contingency. The mission was fraught with danger, but they were driven by a cause far greater than their individual fears.

The next morning, under the cover of predawn shadows, Margaret and James set out to their respective positions. The city was eerily quiet, the tension of the impending action palpable in the cool morning air. As planned, a diversion exploded into action on the opposite side of town, drawing the attention of the British forces.

With precision, they moved towards the docks, their hearts racing with adrenaline. James, leading a small contingent of trusted rebels, watched for the signal from their insiders. Margaret, using her keen understanding of the city's layout, navigated the maze of streets to approach the shipment from a different angle.

The signal came, a brief flash of light from the direction of the docks, and they sprang into action. The shipment, left momentarily unguarded, was quickly overtaken. But their success was not without confrontation; British soldiers alerted to the disturbance, engaged them in a skirmish.

Margaret found herself face to face with a redcoat, her determination clashing with the soldier's aggression. James came to her aid. Together, they managed to disarm the soldier, a symbolic victory that strengthened their resolve.

With the stolen arms secured, they made their escape, weaving through alleyways and back streets, the sounds of pursuit echoing behind them. Their hearts pounded not just with the exertion of their flight but with the exhilaration of their success.

As they reached the safety of their hideout, the first rays of sunlight breaking over the horizon, Margaret and James allowed themselves a moment of triumph. The shipment, now in the hands of the Continental Army, marked a significant victory for the rebellion.

"We did it," Margaret breathed, her eyes alight with the fire of victory.

James, equally exhilarated, responded, "Together. We're changing the course of this war."

Their success that day was more than a strategic win; it was a testament to their partnership, to the power of shared conviction and courage in the face of adversity. As they stepped back into the light of the new day, Margaret and James knew that their journey had only just begun. They were no longer merely participants in the revolution; they were leaders, shaping the destiny of a nation yearning to be free.

As the first light of dawn painted the Philadelphia skyline in hues of gold and amber, marking the end of a night that had tested their limits and fortified their resolve, Margaret and James found a moment of respite in the safety of their hidden refuge. The successful interception of the arms shipment was more than a strategic victory; it was a declaration of their commitment to the cause of freedom, a testament to the strength found in unity.

"We did it," Margaret whispered, allowing the reality of their achievement to settle in. Her eyes met James's, reflecting not just the exhilaration of their success but also the profound bond that had been forged between them in the crucible of shared danger and shared ideals.

James nodded, a smile breaking through the exhaustion that lined his face. "Together," he affirmed, his voice steady and sure. "This is just the beginning, Margaret. We've proven what we're capable of when we stand together."

In the quiet of the dawn, as the city around them slowly awakened, unaware of the night's clandestine activities, Margaret and James allowed themselves a brief moment to envision the future they were fighting for—a future where liberty was not just a whispered dream but a lived reality for all.

But with the rising sun came the reminder of the challenges that lay ahead. The British would soon notice the missing shipment and the repercussions could be severe. There was no turning back now; they had irrevocably committed themselves to the revolution and to each other.

Margaret stood, her determination renewed in the light of day. "We must prepare for what comes next. Today's victory is a step towards freedom, but the road ahead is long and fraught with danger."

James rose to join her, his resolve mirroring her own. "Let them come. We'll be ready. For justice, for freedom, for the future of our nation."

As they stepped out of the refuge and into the bustling streets of Philadelphia, the city seemed to carry on as if nothing had changed. Yet, for Margaret and James, everything had changed. They were no longer mere spectators to the unfolding history of their nation; they were now architects of its future.

The promise of their next collaboration hung in the air, a beacon guiding them forward. With each step they took, they carried with them the hopes of those who dared to dream of independence, their actions a ripple in the larger tide of revolution that sought to sweep across the colonies.

Philadelphia, with its cobblestone streets and colonial charm, was a city on the brink of change. At its heart were two souls, once bound to opposing sides but now united in a common cause. Together, they faced the uncertain future with determination and hope, their journey a reflection of the larger struggle for liberty—a narrative thread in the tapestry of a nation's fight for freedom.

C H A P T E R 4

The Awakening

In the days following the incident that had rattled the town, an uneasy calm had settled over the streets. The harshness of British rule, once a distant concept, had been brutally exposed. Margaret and James, like many others, were thrust into a whirlwind of emotions, grappling with the stark reality of their situation, the seeds of dissent sown by what they had witnessed.

That morning, as Margaret weaved her way through the cobblestone streets, the memory of the incident lingered in her mind, a stark reminder of the injustices being perpetrated against her people. The usually vibrant town, with its bustling market and lively chatter, felt eerily subdued, the air heavy with a palpable sense of tension.

It was then that she came upon a scene that would forever alter the course of her life. A young boy, accused by British soldiers of theft, stood trembling as he faced punishment for a crime born of desperation. The injustice of it, so soon after the recent incident, ignited a fire within Margaret. Without thinking, she stepped forward, her voice cutting through the morning air, challenging the soldiers.

James, who had been observing from a distance, felt a surge of conflicting emotions—as Margaret intervened, he was torn between admiration and concern. The incident they had witnessed together deepened his doubts about the British cause. Now, seeing Margaret's bravery, he was compelled to act, joining her side in a show of solidarity.

Though they were forced to step back, unable to alter the boy's fate, the event marked a profound transformation for both of them. For Margaret, it was the moment her passive discontent ignited into a fierce flame of active resistance. She could no longer stand idly by while her people suffered. For James, it crystallized his internal conflict, the growing rift between his duty as a British officer and his sympathy for the colonial cause. This transformation, from passive observers to active participants, is a testament to their courage and determination.

In the aftermath, as they walked through the now silent streets, Margaret and James shared a moment of profound resolve. The incidents, both the recent confrontation and the one that had preceded it, had awakened a shared purpose. They understood that the path ahead would be fraught with challenges. Still, the decision to stand against oppression and fight for freedom was irrevocable. Their shared commitment to the cause, their unyielding resolve, is a testament to the strength of their bond and the power of their cause.

As the day gave way to evening and the town slowly came back to life, Margaret and James found themselves among those who whispered of rebellion, of taking a stand. In the glow of the setting sun, they made a pact, not just to each other but to the cause they now knew they must join.

The days that followed saw Margaret and James taking their first tentative steps into the world of rebellion. Margaret's keen mind and James's strategic acumen quickly made them invaluable to the burgeoning cause. Each mission, each act of defiance, drew them deeper into the struggle, binding their fates together with the fate of the revolution.

Spurred by the cruelty they had witnessed, their awakening set them on a path from which there was no turning back. They were no longer mere observers of history; they were now its makers, determined to shape the future of their land.

The morning had dawned like any other in the colonial town, promising the simplicity of daily routines and the quiet hum of life as it was known. However, the unfolding events would mark a significant shift in Margaret's and James's lives, embedding a deep-seated sense of purpose and direction in their hearts.

Margaret's walk to the market was interrupted by a gathering crowd, their voices a blend of fear and outrage. Pushing through, she was confronted by a scene that would remain etched in her memory: a young boy, accused by British soldiers of stealing bread, faced harsh punishment. The moment's injustice resonated with a growing awareness within her and spurred Margaret to action despite the risks. She challenged the soldiers, her voice steady with conviction.

Witnessing Margaret's boldness, James felt a profound respect for her courage. His own experiences and growing doubts about the righteousness of the British cause found clarity in her actions. The resolve in Margaret's eyes and her willingness to stand up against oppression moved something within him, drawing him closer to a decisive stand.

Forced to step back under threats from the soldiers, Margaret and James were left with a lingering sense of injustice as the boy was taken away. This moment, layered atop the simmering tensions and the injustices witnessed previously, catalyzed a transformation in both of them. They could no longer remain passive observers of the unfolding tyranny.

In the following days, their conversations deepened, turning towards action and the role they could play in the burgeoning movement for independence. They sought out others who shared their convictions, drawing themselves into the clandestine networks of rebellion spreading like wildfire through the colonies.

Margaret's keen understanding of the societal undercurrents and James's tactical acumen made them invaluable to the cause. Their efforts, from covert intelligence gathering to the distribution of seditious materials, were fueled by a shared commitment to the fight for freedom.

As they navigated the complexities of their newfound roles, the risks they took brought them closer, forging a bond built on mutual respect, shared ideals, and the recognition of the sacrifices they were willing to make for the cause of liberty.

The culmination of these events, from the intervention on behalf of the boy to their active participation in the rebellion, marked a significant turn in their journey. Margaret and James, once content to live under the radar, now found themselves at the forefront of a fight for a new future.

Their days were now defined by the dual challenges of evading British scrutiny and contributing to the revolutionary effort, each successful mission fueling their resolve. They had witnessed the cost of standing up against oppression, yet it was a price they were willing to pay for the promise of a better world. This willingness to sacrifice, to put their lives on the line for the cause of freedom, underscores the depth of their dedication and the gravity of the situation they find themselves in.

With each passing day, the fabric of Margaret and James's daily lives became increasingly interwoven with the clandestine activities of the rebellion. The initial act of defiance that had seen Margaret stand up for a young boy against British soldiers had ignited a spark within them both. This spark, nurtured by their shared experiences and the injustices they witnessed, grew into a steadfast flame of commitment to the cause of freedom.

Margaret's ventures into the heart of enemy territory became more frequent and daring. Her ability to blend into the shadows and gather crucial intelligence without arousing suspicion made her one of the rebellion's most valuable assets. Each piece of information she brought back—a planned troop movement, a supply convoy route, the location of a British cache—provided the Continental Army with the means to strike more effectively and outmaneuver their adversaries in a war where every advantage counted.

James, for his part, found himself increasingly involved in planning sessions, using the intelligence Margaret gathered to devise strategies that maximized their limited resources. His leadership on the battlefield, characterized by a blend of bravery and prudence, earned him the respect and loyalty of his men. Together, they executed raids and ambushes that harassed British forces, disrupting their operations and boosting the morale of the Continental Army.

The successes they achieved, however, were not without cost. The risks they took left them exposed to danger, not just from the British but from loyalist sympathizers within their own communities. The shadow of betrayal loomed large, a constant reminder of the precarious nature of their fight.

During one such mission, as Margaret returned with critical intelligence regarding a British fortification, the actual cost of their involvement became starkly evident. They had been betrayed. A loyalist, pretending sympathy for the cause, had divulged Margaret's identity to the British. She walked into a trap.

James, learning of her capture, was faced with a decision that would test the very limits of his resolve and his abilities as a leader. Rescue missions were fraught with peril, often considered too risky given the resources required and the potential for loss. Yet, the thought of abandoning Margaret to her fate was unconscionable.

With the help of a small, trusted team, James embarked on a daring plan to rescue Margaret. The operation, carried out under cover of darkness, was a testament to their determination and the depth of their commitment to one another and to the cause. Against all odds, they succeeded. Margaret was brought back from the brink, her resolve undimmed but her awareness of the dangers they faced sharper than ever.

In the aftermath, as they recuperated from their ordeal, Margaret and James were forced to confront the reality of their situation. Their actions, driven by a desire for justice and freedom, had placed them in the crosshairs of a powerful enemy. Yet, even as they grappled with the weight of their choices, their resolve only strengthened.

The awakening they had experienced, born from a moment of injustice and nurtured through trials and tribulations, had irrevocably changed them. They were no longer merely participants in the struggle for independence; they were leaders, symbols of the resilience and courage that defined the revolutionary cause.

As they prepared for the challenges ahead, Margaret and James knew the road to freedom would be long and dangerous. But together, with a shared vision of a future where liberty prevailed, they stepped forward into the uncertain dawn, ready to face whatever came their way.

While harrowing, their ordeal had only deepened Margaret and James's resolve. The rebellion, once a cause they supported, had now become a part of their very essence. They understood that the path they had chosen was fraught with danger, but it was a path they walked willingly, driven by the belief in a cause greater than themselves.

In the days that followed their narrow escape, the pair worked with even greater fervor. Margaret, her close brush with capture still fresh in her mind, became more cautious, refining her methods of intelligence gathering. She began training others, sharing her skills and knowledge, ensuring that if she were ever compromised again, the flow of vital information would not cease.

Inspired by Margaret's resilience, James took on a more prominent role in planning the army's strategic moves. His natural leadership skills, honed through adversity, made him an invaluable asset. He led his troops with a clear vision, always mindful of the greater objective. He became a mentor to younger soldiers, instilling in them the values of courage, integrity, and dedication to the cause.

The bond between Margaret and James, strengthened by shared experiences and a mutual dedication to the cause, symbolized hope within the rebellion. Their comrades looked to them not just for leadership but for inspiration, seeing in their partnership an embodiment of the principles they were fighting for.

Yet, their journey was not without its trials. The rebellion faced setbacks as British forces, spurred by the threat of losing control over the colonies, launched a series of counterattacks. The Continental Army found itself stretched thin, fighting on multiple fronts, each victory hard-won and each loss deeply felt.

Amidst this tumult, a message arrived at camp, bearing news that would again test Margaret and James's resolve. A trusted spy embedded within British ranks had obtained information about a planned large-scale offensive that, if successful, could crush the rebellion in its infancy.

The gravity of the situation weighed heavily on them. The intelligence pointed to a vulnerability in the British forces, a weakness that, if exploited, could turn the tide in their favor.

However, it also required a bold strategy involving significant risk.

Margaret and James, understanding the stakes, presented the plan to General Washington. It was a daring proposal, requiring precise execution and a bit of luck. Still, it was their best chance at thwarting the British offensive.

Washington, recognizing the potential of their plan and the conviction behind it, gave his approval. The days leading up to the operation were tense, the camp abuzz with preparations. Margaret and James, at the heart of the planning, worked tirelessly, their roles as leaders never more critical.

The night before the operation, as the camp lay quiet under the cloak of anticipation, Margaret and James shared a quiet moment, reflecting on the journey that had brought them to this point. They spoke of the future, of dreams of peace and freedom, and of the life they hoped to build once the war was over. It was a fleeting respite, a brief escape from the weight of their responsibilities.

As dawn broke, signaling the start of the operation, Margaret and James took their positions. The battle that unfolded was fierce, a maelstrom of chaos and determination. Through it all, they remained focused, their actions guided by the belief in their cause and the trust they had in each other.

The operation was a success. The Continental Army's cunning and bravery thwarted the British offensive, unraveling their plans. It was a victory that would be celebrated, a turning point in the rebellion, but Margaret and James knew the war was far from over.

They returned to camp, weary but triumphant, ready to face the next challenge. The road ahead was uncertain, filled with dangers and difficulties. Still, they faced it together, united by a cause that had become their calling.

In the aftermath of the thwarted offensive, the Continental Army found itself not just buoyed by a tactical victory but also solidified in its resolve. Once a makeshift assembly of disparate souls, the camp had transformed into a cohesive force, bound by shared purpose and steeled by the leadership of figures like Margaret and James. Their success had become a beacon, illuminating the possibility of victory against overwhelming odds.

As autumn unfurled its colors over the landscape, Margaret and James, amid their duties, found moments to reflect on the journey that had led them to this point. The awakening they had experienced, catalyzed by acts of cruelty and a determination to seek justice, had guided them from the periphery of rebellion into its very heart. They had become not just participants in the fight for independence but architects of its strategy, embodying the hope and resilience necessary to sustain the cause.

In her quieter moments, Margaret penned letters to allies and coded messages to spies, her words weaving the intricate web of intelligence that kept the rebellion a step ahead. Her role had expanded beyond gathering information; she was now a key figure in the network that spanned the colonies, a testament to her skill and courage.

When not leading his men in drills or planning their next engagement, James took to mapping the terrain, his strategic eye envisioning the battles yet to come. His reputation as a tactician and leader had grown, earning him the respect of his peers and the trust of his superiors. Together, they planned for skirmishes and the larger campaign, envisioning a future where their fledgling nation could stand sovereign and free.

Yet, the path to that future was fraught with hardship. News of British reinforcements arriving in the colonies sent ripples through the camp, a stark reminder that the road to independence would be long and arduous. When faced with this new challenge, Margaret and James doubled their efforts, their resolve unwavering.

During this time of heightened tension, an opportunity presented itself—an audacious plan to capture a key British outpost, which, if successful, could shift the balance of power in the region. The plan required precision and daring, qualities that Margaret and James had repeatedly demonstrated.

The night before the operation, the camp was a study in controlled chaos, with soldiers preparing for the mission under the cover of darkness. Margaret and James, at the center of the whirlwind, shared a moment of calm amidst the storm. Their hands clasped, a silent pledge of their commitment to the cause and each other.

As they embarked on the mission, the weight of the moment settled over them. This was more than a military engagement; it was a statement of their defiance, a declaration that the spirit of the revolution would not be quelled.

The operation unfolded under the cloak of night, Margaret, James, and their chosen band of soldiers moving like shadows across the landscape. Their approach was silent, their movements precise, a testament to the months of preparation and training that had honed their skills.

The outpost, unaware of the storm about to break upon it, was secured with minimal resistance, its capture a critical blow to British operations in the area. The victory was celebrated in the camp, a tangible sign that their cause was just, their strategy sound.

In the days that followed, as the implications of their success became apparent, Margaret and James were lauded as heroes of the rebellion. But for them, the accolades mattered little. Their focus remained on the cause for which they fought, the vision of freedom that had first awakened them to action.

As autumn gave way to winter, the revolution continued to unfold, each day bringing new challenges and new battles to be fought. But through it all, Margaret and James stood firm, their leadership a guiding light in the quest for independence.

As the embers of their latest victory began to cool in the early hours before dawn, the camp around Margaret and James buzzed with a subdued yet palpable sense of achievement. This operation, bold and fraught with danger, had not only succeeded but had also significantly disrupted British plans in the region. The outpost's capture, a feather in the cap of the Continental Army, was a blow to British morale and a boost to the rebels' spirits.

In the aftermath, as the soldiers busied themselves to secure their new position and tend to the few wounded, Margaret and James found a quiet corner of the camp. They stood together, wrapped in cloaks against the chill of the night, looking out at the men and women who had become their family in arms. The bond of shared purpose and struggle was evident in the glances they exchanged, the nodding acknowledgments of respect and camaraderie.

"It's moments like these," Margaret said, her voice soft but clear in the quiet, "that remind me why we're fighting. Not for glory or for conquest, but for a chance at a better world."

James nodded, his eyes reflecting the flickering light of the nearby fires. "And it's having you by my side that gives me the strength to keep fighting, no matter how hard the road ahead might be."

They turned to look at each other, their eyes meeting in a moment of deep understanding and shared resolve. The journey that had begun with a simple act of defiance had brought them to the heart of a revolution, transforming them from observers of history into its makers. They had faced trials that tested their courage, faith in the cause, and faith in each other, emerging stronger with each challenge.

As the first light of dawn began to streak the sky with hints of gold and pink, signaling the start of a new day, Margaret and James knew that their struggle was far from over. The road to independence was long and uncertain, fraught with more battles, sacrifices, and moments of doubt.

But as they looked out at the breaking day, they also knew that they would face whatever came their way together, united by a cause that was greater than themselves. The awakening they had experienced, born from the cruelty and injustice they had witnessed, had ignited a flame within them that no adversity could extinguish.

Their journey would continue, marked by victories, setbacks, moments of despair, and flashes of hope. But whatever the future held, Margaret and James were ready to meet it head-on, their spirits buoyed by the belief in the possibility of change, in the dream of a free and independent nation.

With a final look at the camp, now stirring to life in the new day's light, Margaret and James turned and walked back to their duties, their steps firm, their hearts resolved. The chapter of their awakening had concluded, but the story of their fight for freedom—and the story of the revolution—was just beginning.

CHAPTER 5

The Crossroads of Conviction

In the early hours of a Philadelphia morning, the city awakens under a canopy of soft dawn light, its streets a labyrinth of shadows and emerging day. With the resolve of her convictions casting a long shadow, Margaret Hale steps out into the crisp air, her mind a whirlwind of strategy and purpose. Today, like many before, she is to meet with the architects of rebellion, their cause as dangerous as it is, just their meetings shrouded in secrecy.

Margaret navigates the cobblestone streets with practiced ease, her destination a tavern known only to a trusted few. Inside, the air is thick with the tension of whispered plots and the shared urgency of a revolution on the brink. She takes her place among her compatriots, her voice steady and her plans bold, revealing her growing role in a network critical to the patriot cause. The stakes are high, and the danger is ever-present, but Margaret's determination is unwavering.

Elsewhere in the city, Captain James Bradford walks a different path. His uniform, once a symbol of pride, now feels like a mantle of doubt as he patrols the streets that harbor the very rebellion he's sworn to quell. Today, his duty brings him unsettlingly close to the heart of the revolution—a discarded note, a planned action, a secret that could change the course of the war if it fell into the wrong hands. James stands at a crossroads, the document in his hand a tangible representation of his internal strife. Loyalty or conscience? The decision weighs heavily on him.

As the day draws to a close, fate—or perhaps a more deliberate force—brings Margaret and James together. Their encounter is brief, yet charged with an intensity that defies its brevity. James, driven by a compulsion he can't quite fathom, offers Margaret a cryptic warning. It's a moment of connection that transcends their conflicting loyalties, leaving both to ponder the implications of their brief but impactful meeting.

Margaret, her curiosity piqued and her caution heightened, grapples with the enigma that is the British captain. Meanwhile, James, in turmoil, confronts the complexity of his future path. In the stillness of the evening, each contemplates the choices that lie ahead. For Margaret, the encounter with James is a stark reminder of the intricate nature of war, where enemies can show kindness and allies can be found in unexpected places. For James, it's a pivotal moment, a crack in the facade of his duty through which the light of his convictions begins to shine.

Philadelphia slumbers, but the night is alive with questions and the stirrings of change for Margaret and James. The revolution beckons, its voice resonating in the silence, and both understand that their decisions will reverberate far beyond the confines of their own lives. The course of the war, the destiny of a nation, and the paths of their hearts hang in the balance, poised on the precipice of a tomorrow that offers nothing but the certainty of choice.

In this city of brotherly love amidst the brewing storm of revolution, Chapter 3 unfolds—a tapestry of conviction, conflict, and the subtle threads of connection that hint at a shared destiny yet to be realized.

Margaret's evening was consumed by the flickering

candlelight that danced across the maps and letters strewn about her desk. Each piece of parchment, a fragment of the larger struggle for independence, seemed to pulse with the lifeblood of the revolution. While focused on the tasks, her thoughts couldn't help but wander to the British captain whose warning had unsettled her day. What motivations could drive a man, sworn to the Crown, to offer aid, however cryptic, to the cause of liberty? It was a riddle wrapped in the enemy's uniform, compelling yet confounding.

In the solitude of his quarters, James faced a tumultuous sea of doubt. Now hidden away, the note symbolized his first tangible step towards defiance—a small rebellion against the orders that had governed his life. The moonlight streaming through the window cast long shadows across the room, mirroring the conflict that stretched before him. Margaret's image lingered in his mind, a beacon of the cause he was drawn towards, her resolve igniting questions about his loyalties and the future he wanted to build.

Philadelphia, a city ensnared in the clutches of revolution, is a mosaic of clashing loyalties and concealed battles. Its streets reverberate with the footsteps of those who dare to dream of freedom. For Margaret and James, the day has marked a turning point, a moment when their paths intersect and their destinies intertwine. Each is propelled by their convictions and haunted by the specter of what lies ahead, their lives now inextricably linked to the unfolding drama of the American Revolution.

Setting aside her plans, Margaret gazed into the night, the stars overhead a tapestry of light against the darkness. The fight for independence was more than a clash of armies; it was a battle for the soul of a nation, a struggle in which she played a vital part. The challenges were immense, but her spirit, bolstered by the knowledge that others, like James, might join their cause, remained unbroken.

Finally succumbing to exhaustion, James lay in his bed with the turmoil of his thoughts, a steady companion. The decision to keep the note's contents to himself was the first step on a path that diverged sharply from the one he had always known. The morrow would bring its duties and decisions. Still, for now, he allowed himself to ponder the impossible—a future where his duty to the Crown was replaced by a deeper, more profound allegiance to the ideals espoused by the rebels.

In Philadelphia, as in the rest of the colonies, the dawn of each new day brought the revolution closer to its apex, each individual's choices weaving together to form the fabric of history. For Margaret Hale and Captain James Bradford, their journeys were still unfolding, marked by the courage to challenge, question, and dream of a world remade.

As dawn breaks, Margaret and James find themselves under the weight of decisions made and yet to come, each haunted by the previous day's events and the uncertain path ahead.

Margaret rises with the sun, her thoughts immediately turning to the tasks at hand. The network she's helped to build, a lattice of secret messages and silent allies, is more vital now than ever. Yet, James's warning lingers in her mind, a beacon of unease in the steadfast resolve that guides her. She wonders about the man behind the uniform, about the conflict that must rage within him, mirroring the tumult that has gripped the colonies.

Her day is filled with covert meetings and the exchange of information that flows like an underground river through the city. With each interaction, Margaret feels the weight of responsibility resting on her shoulders, not just for the cause but for the lives intertwined with her own. The rebel spirit is resilient but also vulnerable, dependent on the secrecy and loyalty of its members. Margaret finds strength in this vulnerability, a reminder that the fight for freedom is grounded in its people's collective hope and courage.

James, meanwhile, navigates his duties with a growing sense of disquiet. The note symbolizes his burgeoning defiance and has set him on an inevitable and treacherous course. His interactions with fellow officers, once marked by camaraderie, now carry an undercurrent of suspicion. He feels his superiors' eyes upon him, questioning his loyalty and probing for signs of dissent.

In a quiet moment of reflection, James contemplates the vast gulf between the man he was and the man he is becoming. The ideals of the rebellion, once distant echoes, now resonate with a clarity that is both exhilarating and terrifying. He knows the road ahead will be perilous, not just from the battlefield but from within the ranks of his comrades. Yet, the thought of standing on the wrong side of history and denying the truth that has taken root in his heart is a far more daunting fate.

As the day wanes, Margaret and James's paths converge again, a clandestine meeting by the river that runs like a lifeline through the city. The water whispers of change, battles fought and yet to come, as they share information that could turn the tide of the conflict. At this moment, the barriers between them—rebel and soldier, woman and man—seem to dissolve, leaving only the raw honesty of their shared convictions.

They speak of possibilities of a future forged from the ashes of war, where liberty is not just a dream but a reality. It's a vision that feels both distant and achingly close, requiring sacrifices they are both prepared to make. As they part, the promise of what could be hung in the air between them, a fragile thread of hope in a world torn asunder.

The night brings no reprieve for Margaret and James, each

wrestling with the enormity of their choices. For Margaret, it is the realization that the path to freedom is as perilous as it is righteous, marked by loss and triumph. For James, it is the acknowledgment that his loyalty lies not with a crown or a country but with the ideals of justice and equality that the rebellion embodies.

As Philadelphia holds its breath in the quiet before dawn, Margaret and James steel themselves for the days ahead. The crossroads of conviction have led them to the heart of a revolution that will test their courage, faith, and commitment to the cause of liberty. The journey is uncertain, the stakes unimaginable, but they step forward nonetheless, bound by a shared belief in a future worth fighting for.

Under the cover of evening, the streets of Philadelphia took on a hushed tone, as if the city itself anticipated the undercurrents of change swirling within its boundaries. Margaret, her day spent weaving through the intricate tapestry of rebellion, found herself at the edge of the city, where the urban expanse gave way to open fields and the promise of freedom beyond.

Her thoughts, ever on the movement's next steps, were unexpectedly interrupted by the sight of Captain James Bradford. Different from their last encounter, this meeting was not by chance. Having wrestled with the tumult within, James sought her out, driven by a need to share his decision.

"I've been considering our last encounter," James began, his voice steady but carrying an undercurrent of uncertainty. "And your cause. I find that my loyalties... they are shifting. Not easily, mind you, but with a certainty I can no longer ignore."

Margaret regarded him with a mix of surprise and cautious optimism. His admission, vague as it was, hinted at a profound internal struggle. "And what does that mean for you, Captain

Bradford?" she inquired, her voice betraying none of the hope that fluttered within her chest.

"It means," James paused, searching for the words, "that I find myself aligned with the ideals of freedom and liberty your cause represents. I am still a soldier, but perhaps, it's time I reconsider for whom I fight."

The declaration hung between them, a fragile bridge over the chasm of war that divided their worlds. Sensing the gravity of James' confession, Margaret extended a tentative olive branch. "There's much to be done, and trust is hard won in times like these. But perhaps... there's a place for you among us."

Their conversation, held in the waning light, marked the beginning of an uneasy alliance. For James, it was a step into the unknown, guided by a moral compass that pointed towards a new north. For Margaret, it represented a glimmer of hope, a chance to bolster their cause with a defector from the enemy ranks.

As they parted ways, the night enveloping the city once more, both Margaret and James were acutely aware of their chosen path. It was one fraught with danger, lined with the potential for betrayal, but illuminated by the faint light of shared conviction.

In the following days, their tentative alliance would be tested, forged in the fires of conflict and the shared pursuit of a cause greater than themselves. Philadelphia, a city on the brink, would serve as the backdrop to their unfolding story, a testament to the power of conviction and the possibility of unity in the face of division.

In the days following their clandestine meeting under the cover of twilight, Philadelphia seemed to buzz with palpable energy as if the air was charged with the anticipation of revolution. Margaret Hale found herself at the heart of this maelstrom, her days a blur of whispered messages, covert meetings, and the relentless push toward an elusive freedom.

James Bradford, now walking a path fraught with peril and betrayal, navigated his new reality with a cautious determination. The decision to align himself with the rebels, to cast aside the red coat for a cause that spoke to the core of his being, was not without its consequences. Each day brought with it the risk of discovery, of being branded a traitor by those he once called brothers-in-arms.

Yet, amidst the uncertainty and danger, a fragile bond between Margaret and James began to strengthen. Their initial wariness gave way to a grudging respect born of shared secrets and the mutual recognition of each other's sacrifices. In stolen moments, between the chaos of their respective duties, they found solace in their burgeoning camaraderie, a beacon of light in the shadow of war.

Ever the pragmatist, Margaret was wary of placing too much trust in a former enemy. But as James repeatedly proved his loyalty, delivering vital intelligence and aiding in critical missions, her skepticism began to wane. In James, she saw not the British captain he once was but the ally he had become, his actions speaking louder than the uniform he had forsaken.

For his part, James was awed by Margaret's unwavering commitment to the cause. Her strength and vision for a free America inspired him in ways he had not thought possible. She was the embodiment of the ideals he had come to hold dear, a living testament to the courage and resilience of the fledgling nation they both sought to protect.

As the summer waned, giving way to the cool embrace of autumn, the revolution's tide began to turn. The rebels, bolstered by recent victories and the support of allies both expected and surprising, prepared for the next phase of the conflict. Margaret and James, now integral parts of this intricate tapestry of resistance, stood ready to face whatever challenges lay ahead.

Their alliance, once uncertain, had solidified into something unbreakable, a partnership forged in the crucible of revolution. Together, they faced the future, not as soldier and spy, but as comrades-in-arms, united by a common goal—the birth of a nation founded on the principles of liberty and justice.

As Philadelphia prepared for the trials to come, Margaret and James found themselves not at the end of a journey but at the beginning of a new chapter in the fight for American independence. The road ahead was fraught with uncertainty, but in each other, they had found a steadfast ally, a source of strength in the battle for the soul of their country.

The story of Margaret Hale and James Bradford, two unlikely heroes drawn together by fate and bound by conviction, was a testament to the power of unity in the face of adversity. Their courage, sacrifice, and unwavering belief in the cause of freedom lay the heart of the revolution, beating strong beneath the cobblestone streets of Philadelphia.

C H A P T E R **6**

Echoes of Loyalty

The dawn light filtered through the curtains of Margaret's modest room, casting a soft glow on the plans before her. Each document and note was a piece of the larger puzzle in the fight for freedom. Like every day, today was a battle not just against the British but against time itself. The recent victory had provided a much-needed boost to the rebels' morale. Still, Margaret knew it was only a matter of time before the enemy struck back.

James, his allegiance now irrevocably altered, found himself walking the cobblestone streets of Philadelphia with a new purpose. His uniform, once a symbol of pride, now felt heavier with each step, a constant reminder of the delicate line he tread between two worlds. His meetings with Margaret, once marked by cautious distance, had transformed into sessions of earnest collaboration and shared resolve.

Their recent success had not gone unnoticed. Whispers of a traitor within the British ranks stirred unease among James's fellow officers, casting suspicious glances his way. Yet, it was within the rebel community that James found his true test. The trust Margaret placed in him, mirrored by the wary acceptance of her compatriots, was a mantle he bore with a sense of honor and profound responsibility.

The challenge they faced now was one of cunning and guile. An informant, lurking in the shadows, posed a grave threat, ready to unravel the fragile threads of their operations. Together, Margaret and James crafted a plan to expose the traitor, a dangerous gambit that required them to blend seamlessly into the fabric of a city divided by war.

Under the cloak of night, they set their plan into motion. The streets of Philadelphia, usually vibrant with the sounds of life, were eerily silent, the tension palpable in the air. Margaret led the way, her confidence unshaken, with James a silent shadow at her side. Their mission was one of many threads in the larger tapestry of rebellion, but its success was crucial.

Once revealed, the informant would secure the safety of their operations and solidify the trust between them and their fellow rebels. It was a testament to the strength of their alliance, a bond forged in the crucible of shared conviction.

As the first light of dawn broke over the horizon, painting the sky with hues of orange and pink, Margaret and James found themselves again at the crossroads of history. The streets of Philadelphia, witness to their unwavering courage and unyielding determination, were more than just battlegrounds; they were the very heart of the revolution.

Their return to the rebel hideout was met with anxious faces, which quickly turned to relief as the success of their mission became apparent. The informant, a shadow no more, had been exposed, and with them, the immediate threat to their cause had been neutralized.

In the aftermath, as the city awoke to another day of uncertainty and struggle, Margaret and James stood together, not just as rebels but as beacons of hope for a future they dared to dream. Their journey was far from over, but they had found an ally, a confidant, and a friend in each other. The road ahead was fraught with danger, but with the echo of loyalty and shared purpose as their guide, they pressed on, united in their quest for freedom and justice.

As the rebellion's momentum surged through Philadelphia, Margaret, and James, found themselves at the heart of a growing movement, their destinies intertwined with the cause they now both championed. Their recent victory over the British supply line was not just a blow to the enemy, but a testament to their partnership, each triumph and setback a shared experience.

Margaret's role within the rebellion had become indispensable. With British forces reeling and mounting stakes, her strategic insight and ability to galvanize the rebels were crucial. Her days were filled with secret meetings and daring plans, each decision critical to the success of their cause. Yet, in the rare moments of solitude, she pondered the path that had led her to the forefront of a struggle for freedom.

On the other hand, James felt the full weight of his decision to defect with every step he took in his British uniform. It was a constant reminder of the life he had forsaken, a sacrifice made in the name of principles that had come to define him. His interactions with Margaret, once cautious, had evolved into a source of strength and understanding, their alliance a cornerstone of the rebellion's hope.

Their next mission targeted a vital British supply chain, an ambitious plan fraught with risk yet essential for the rebels' continued resistance. Huddled over maps in the dim glow of the hideout, the critical nature of their task was evident. Success could significantly alter the conflict's course, while failure would spell disaster.

Veiled by night, Margaret and James led their team through Philadelphia's silent streets, their mission clear. The tension of the impending ambush hung heavy in the air, each moment stretching into eternity.

The attack came swiftly, catching the British convoy off guard. The rebels, driven by a fierce determination, quickly overcame the enemy forces, securing much-needed supplies. The battle, though brief, was intense, showcasing the rebels' growing capabilities and the strategic prowess of their leaders.

As dawn unveiled the new day, Margaret and James assessed their victory. The seized supplies were a boon for the rebels, a tangible outcome of their efforts, and a significant setback for the British. The victory was not without cost but underscored the rebellion's potential and leadership effectiveness.

In the aftermath, the impact of their success resonated throughout the city and among the rebel ranks. Margaret and James, their connection deepened through conflict and triumph, looked toward the future with a shared resolve. The struggle for independence was ongoing, but their actions demonstrated the power of unity and strategic action against seemingly insurmountable odds.

Their journey, marked by loyalty, sacrifice, and a steadfast commitment to freedom, unfolded amidst a nation striving to define itself. For Margaret and James, the fight confirmed their belief in the cause of liberty—a reason for which they were willing to risk everything, knowing that together, they were a formidable force in the pursuit of independence. Their actions, now etched in the annals of history, were a testament to the indomitable spirit of the American Revolution.

As dawn's early light washed over Philadelphia, marking another day in the heart of a burgeoning nation, the streets hummed with an undercurrent of anticipation and resolve. Though significant, the recent victory was one step in the long march toward independence. Margaret Hale and James Bradford, each carrying the weight of their roles within the rebellion, found themselves increasingly bound by a shared determination to see their cause through to the end.

Margaret, whose leadership had become indispensable, worked tirelessly. Her strategies and efforts were now more crucial than ever. The rebel cause gained momentum with each successful operation, as did the dangers they faced. Her life was a constant balance between the fervor of rebellion and the quiet moments of doubt and resolve that came with the territory.

Having fully embraced his role within the rebel ranks, James faced his own challenges. His former identity as a British officer was a shadow that followed him, a reminder of the world he had left behind. Yet, in the company of Margaret and the other rebels, he found a sense of belonging and purpose that the red coat had never provided. His transition from soldier to spy, enemy to ally, was complete.

Their next challenge loomed on the horizon, a mission that would require all their cunning and courage. A British stronghold, rumored to hold vital information and supplies, had been identified as their next target. The risks were immense, but the rewards, should they succeed, could change the war's course.

Under the cloak of night, Margaret, James, and a handpicked team of rebels made their way toward the stronghold. The air was tense, each step measured, as they navigated the silent streets. Their plan was bold, perhaps too bold, but desperation and the hunger for freedom drove them forward.

The assault was a whirlwind of chaos and precision. Margaret led from the front, her determination unyielding, while James, with his intimate knowledge of British tactics, proved invaluable. The stronghold, caught off guard, was quickly overrun, its secrets laid bare before the rebels.

As they made their way back through the darkened streets of Philadelphia, the stronghold's documents in hand, the weight of their victory and the cost it had exacted hung heavily over them. The night had taken its toll, with losses on both sides, but the spark of hope, of potential victory, burned brighter than ever.

In the aftermath, as the city awoke to the news of the daring raid, Margaret and James found themselves as leaders within the rebellion and as symbols of the fight for freedom. Their actions, once hidden in the shadows, were now celebrated, their names whispered with reverence and hope.

As the survivors surveyed the battlefield, the cost of their victory was etched in the snow-stained red and the faces of those who would not return. Margaret and James, standing amid the remnants of the battle, shared a look that spoke volumes. Their victory had been hard-won, but the spark they had helped ignite was now a flame that would not be extinguished. The journey toward liberty was ongoing, with the final outcome still uncertain. Still, at that moment, they knew they had altered its course. Together, they had faced the might of an empire and emerged victorious. The future was uncertain and perilous, but there was hope as long as they stood united. Hope for victory, freedom, and the birth of a nation built on the ideals they held dear.

In the heart of the revolution, amid the turmoil and the triumphs, Margaret and James's bond, forged in the fires of rebellion, stood as a testament to the enduring power of unity and conviction. Intertwined with the fate of a nation striving to break free from tyranny, their story continued to unfold, a narrative of courage, loyalty, and the unyielding pursuit of liberty.

In the following weeks, the impact of their successful raid on the British stronghold reverberated through the ranks of the rebellion and across the occupied city. The documents seized in the operation unveiled critical intelligence, opening new avenues for sabotage against the British and bolstering the Continental Army's strategic planning. Yet, Margaret and James's victory was bittersweet, tempered by the losses of brave comrades and the ever-looming shadow of retribution.

The duo worked closer than ever, their partnership becoming a cornerstone of the rebellion's efforts. James utilized his knowledge of British military tactics to help plan operations that exploited the enemy's weaknesses. On the other hand, Margaret played a key role in transmitting these plans to the various rebel cells in the city and beyond, thanks to her extensive network of spies and messengers. James utilized his knowledge of British military tactics to help plan operations that exploited the enemy's weaknesses. On the other hand, Margaret played a key role in transmitting these plans to the various rebel cells in the city and beyond, thanks to her extensive network of spies and messengers.

Their shared successes, however, did not go unnoticed by the British. Increased scrutiny and pressure from loyalist spies made their operations more perilous. Once familiar and navigable, the streets of Philadelphia now felt like a maze of potential traps and betrayals. During this time of heightened tension, Margaret received word of a British plot that threatened to crush the rebellion's spirit once and for all.

A large-scale operation was in the works, designed to cut off supply lines to the Continental Army and isolate Philadelphia from its surrounding support. The intelligence came from a trusted source, but acting on it would require everything the rebels had. Margaret and James understood the gravity of the situation; failure could mean the end of the rebellion's hope for independence.

They gathered a council of the rebellion's leaders with little time and high stakes to devise a countermeasure. It was a testament to their leadership and strategic minds that, despite the odds, a plan began to take shape. A daring counterattack aimed at not only thwarting the British operation but also capturing vital supplies and ammunition for the Continental Army.

The night before the counterattack, Margaret and James were restless. They knew the risks involved and understood the price of failure, yet the resolve in their hearts was unyielding. They met under the cover of darkness, not as leaders or strategists but as two souls united in a common cause. Their conversation was low, filled with the unspoken understanding that the morrow's battle might demand the ultimate sacrifice.

As dawn broke, painting the sky with streaks of crimson and gold, Margaret and James led their contingent into position. The air was charged with anticipation, every soldier aware of the day's significance. The battle, when it came, was fierce and unforgiving. Rebel and British forces clashed in a maelstrom of musket fire and desperate courage.

Through the chaos, Margaret and James fought side by side, and their actions were a seamless dance of mutual trust and shared determination. The counterattack, bold and unexpected, turned the tide. British forces, taken by surprise, faltered and retreated, leaving behind the supplies the rebels desperately needed.

In the aftermath of the battle, as the dust settled and the full extent of their victory became apparent, Margaret and James shared a moment of quiet triumph. The supplies they had captured would sustain the Continental Army through the coming months, and the victory had breathed new life into the rebellion's cause.

Their journey, fraught with danger and marked by moments of despair and triumph, had become more than a shared fight for freedom. It was a testament to the strength found in unity, the resilience of the human spirit, and the power of unwavering conviction. As they looked toward the uncertain future, Margaret and James knew that whatever challenges lay ahead, they would face them together, for the dream of liberty that had brought them together was now their shared destiny.

As spring turned to summer in Philadelphia, the air thick with the promise and peril of revolution, Margaret Hale was drawn deeper into the clandestine world of espionage. Her network, a web of shadows and whispers, had caught the attention of none other than General George Washington himself. Recognizing her talents and the potential for further intelligence operations, Washington brought Margaret into the fold of the Culper Spy Ring. This move would change the course of her involvement in the war.

Margaret's first meeting with members of the Culper Ring was shrouded in secrecy, taking place under the cover of night in a nondescript tavern. The air was tense as she was introduced to her new compatriots, each aware of their covert work's risks and rewards. Among them was a figure known only as Agent 355, a woman whose reputation for gathering vital intelligence was legendary within the ring. Margaret felt an immediate sense of camaraderie with her, a bond forged in the fire of shared purpose.

James, meanwhile, faced his own challenges. His decision to align with the rebels had placed him in a precarious position. Still, his determination to aid the cause had only strengthened. When Margaret shared news of her involvement with the Culper Ring, James saw an opportunity for their efforts to have an even more significant impact. Together, they devised a plan to feed false information to the British, using James's position to their advantage.

Their plan was risky, requiring precise timing and absolute trust in each other and their fellow spies. James's role was to subtly influence British plans, leading them into a trap the rebels could exploit. Margaret, with the help of Agent 355 and the Culper Ring, would ensure that the intelligence they needed to act was gathered and communicated with utmost secrecy.

The operation was a testament to the power of espionage in the war for independence. As British forces marched into the trap, confident in their superiority, they found themselves ambushed by the Continental Army, waiting in prepared positions. The victory was a turning point, a blow to British morale, and a boost to the rebel cause.

In the aftermath, Margaret and James's roles in the operation were celebrated in hushed tones among the rebellion's ranks. Their success had proven the invaluable role of espionage in the fight for freedom, and their partnership had become a cornerstone of the intelligence efforts.

Yet, with success came increased danger. After the British's humiliating defeat, they redoubled their efforts to root out spies. Margaret and James knew the days ahead would be fraught with new challenges. Still, they also knew that their work in the shadows was crucial to the hope of victory.

Their tale, intertwined with the destiny of the newborn United States, continued to unfurl. It was a story of bravery, cleverness, and determined dedication to the cause of freedom. In the world of espionage, where loyalty was both weapon and shield, Margaret and James stood as beacons of hope, their efforts a silent testament to the unseen battles that helped shape the course of history.

CHAPTER 7

𝔖hadows and 𝔖ecrets

With the arrival of spring, the vibrant streets of Philadelphia concealed a pulsating network of spies and informants, all operating under the shroud of secrecy. Margaret Hale, a beacon of bravery, was at the heart of this clandestine world, newly initiated into the Culper Spy Ring, whose efforts had become invaluable to the revolutionary cause. Alongside her, James Bradford, a testament to the power of transformation, had transitioned from a British officer to a rebel ally, placing him in a unique position to aid their cause from within enemy lines.

Their latest triumph, a testament to the power of intelligence and guile, had not only dealt a significant blow to the British forces but had also solidified Margaret and James's roles as key players in the shadow war that complemented the open battles of the revolution. Yet, with their success came heightened scrutiny, making their every move a high-stakes gamble against the ever-present threat of discovery.

Margaret's integration into the Culper Spy Ring introduced her to a new realm of resistance, where messages were hidden in plain sight, and trust was the most precious and perilous commodity. Under the guidance of Agent 355, whose identity remained a closely guarded secret, Margaret learned to decipher the subtle codes and signals that carried vital intelligence across enemy lines. Her natural aptitude for the work quickly made her an indispensable member of the ring, her contributions marked by a blend of boldness and cunning.

James, navigating the dualities of his existence, found himself torn between the camaraderie of his fellow officers and his commitment to the rebel cause. His role as a conduit of misinformation to the British and a gatherer of crucial intelligence for the rebels was fraught with danger. Yet, it was a role he embraced with a sense of purpose he'd never known, driven by the conviction that the future they were fighting for—a future of freedom and justice—was worth every risk.

As the narrative of Chapter 5 unfolds, Margaret and James embark on a mission that would push the limits of their courage and ingenuity. A British fort, rumored to hold a cache of documents that could expose the entire network of rebel spies, becomes their next target. The operation, filled with peril and uncertainty, demands them to infiltrate the heart of enemy territory, which requires both stealth and skill and an unshakeable trust in each other.

Philadelphia lay cloaked in darkness on the night of the operation, the moon a mere sliver in the sky. Margaret and James, accompanied by a small team of trusted rebels, silently approached the fort, each step taking them deeper into the lion's den. The tension was palpable, a tangible thread connecting them all, each aware of the price of failure.

Inside the fort, the air was thick with the scent of candle wax and the low murmur of British soldiers unaware of the danger lurking in their midst. Margaret and James moved like shadows, their movements synchronized, until at last, they found what they had come for—the documents that held the fate of their comrades in their hands.

The return journey was a race against the coming dawn, a desperate bid to return to the safety of their hidden world before their absence was noted. As they emerged from the darkness into the first light of day, the documents secured, they knew that their mission had not only changed the course of the war but also secured a future for their cause. Their actions, though hidden in the shadows, had a profound impact on the larger narrative of the revolution.

As Margaret delves deeper into the shadows of the Culper Spy Ring and her partnership with James deepens, their shared fight for freedom takes a new turn. Each successful mission and every piece of intelligence gathered not only brings them closer to their ultimate goal but also marks a significant step in their personal growth. The challenges they face are many, but so are the moments of triumph; each step forward is a testament to their courage and unwavering commitment to see the dawn of a free nation.

Their bond, forged in the quiet moments between whispers of rebellion and acts of daring, becomes their anchor. Margaret and James, once unlikely allies, now stand together as pillars of a cause greater than themselves. Through the lens of their experiences, the story weaves a rich tapestry of the human spirit's resilience and the unyielding pursuit of liberty. The challenges they face are many, but so are the moments of triumph; each step forward is a testament to their courage and unwavering commitment to see the dawn of a free nation.

As the narrative unfolds, it's clear that their journey is emblematic of the larger struggle for independence—a saga of hope, sacrifice, and the relentless quest for a future where freedom is more than just a dream. In the heart of the revolution, amid the echoes of loyalty and the whispers of spies, Margaret and James's story continues, a vivid reminder of the power of unity and the enduring fight for justice and liberty.

In the burgeoning heart of the revolution, as Philadelphia bristled under the weight of occupation and the fervent whisper of rebellion, Margaret Hale and James Bradford found themselves increasingly enmeshed in a world of shadows and secrets. Chapter 5 opens as they navigate the dangerous tightrope of their double lives, their every action cloaked in the necessity of secrecy.

Now a pivotal figure in the Culper Spy Ring, Margaret orchestrated her network with a deft hand. Her days were consumed with covert meetings, the decoding of messages, and the meticulous planning of intelligence operations. Each piece of information gathered was a thread in the larger tapestry of the rebellion, and Margaret wove them together with precision and care. Her resolve was unyielding, yet the weight of her responsibility pressed heavily upon her, a constant companion amidst the clandestine dance of espionage.

James' allegiance irrevocably shifted, and he played his part with courage and apprehension. His position within the British ranks afforded him access to critical intelligence, but it also placed him under the scrutinous gaze of those who might detect his duplicity. Each piece of information he passed to Margaret and her network was a gamble, a balance between the potential benefit to the rebellion and the risk of discovery. Though brief and shrouded in the secrecy of night, their meetings became their lifeline, a moment of connection amid tumult.

As autumn painted the city in hues of gold and crimson, a new threat emerged from the shadows. A cunning and relentless British intelligence officer arrived in Philadelphia with a single task: to dismantle the spy networks aiding the American cause. This new adversary was unlike any they had faced before; his methods were sophisticated and brutal.

Margaret and James, aware of the looming threat, understood that the stakes had never been higher. The loss of their network would endanger their lives and spell disaster for the rebellion. They were forced to innovate, to find new ways of communicating and operating that would keep them one step ahead of their pursuer.

In the night's depths, they met secretly to devise a plan. Using a complex system of coded messages and dead drops, they sought to mislead their new foe, to draw him into a maze of misinformation and false leads. It was a game of cat and mouse, played in the shadows of a city divided by war.

Their strategy was not without risks. Each message sent, and each piece of false intelligence planted could potentially lead the British officer directly to their door. Yet, in the face of such danger, Margaret and James found strength in their shared cause and each other. Their bond, forged in the secrecy of their work and the shared peril of their mission, became their beacon of hope.

As Margaret and James delve deeper into the clandestine world of espionage, their roles become ever more critical in the intricate dance of shadows and secrets that defines the struggle for American independence. As they navigate the treacherous waters of espionage, they discover that the secrets they keep are the key to their survival and the foundation of their burgeoning love. Amidst the backdrop of a city at war, their story is a testament to the power of trust, the value of sacrifice, and the indomitable spirit of those who fight for freedom.

In the dense network of allies and enemies that crisscross the burgeoning nation, Margaret's expertise and James's strategic insights have become invaluable. Once confined to the dimly lit backrooms of sympathetic taverns, their efforts now stretch across the colonies, weaving a delicate web of intelligence that could tip the scales of war.

With the Culper Ring's backing, Margaret has honed her cryptography skills, turning intercepted messages into open books that lay bare British intentions. Her nights are spent bent over coded dispatches, the candlelight casting long shadows as she deciphers the secrets they contain. Each breakthrough brings a mix of triumph and burden—the knowledge gained is crucial, yet it paints a target on her back, making her a marked woman in the eyes of the enemy.

James, navigating the dual identity that his life has become, uses his position to subtly mislead and manipulate British efforts. His days are a careful performance, each interaction measured to avoid arousing suspicion while gathering information that could prove decisive. The weight of his deception is a constant companion, a reminder of the fine line he walks between heroism and betrayal.

Together, they orchestrate a daring operation to intercept a British courier carrying plans that could lead to the capture of a key rebel stronghold. The mission is dangerous, requiring them to enter territory crawling with enemy patrols. Under the cover of darkness, they move with a silence born of necessity, their paths lit only by the moon's soft glow.

The operation's success hinges on their ability to remain unseen, to become mere shadows among the secrets they seek to uncover. As they close in on their target, the tension mounts, each heartbeat a thunderous echo in the stillness of the night. Their pursuit leads them through the wilderness, a silent ballet of stealth and precision.

When they finally confront the courier, they do so with the swift decisiveness that has become their hallmark. The documents they secure not only thwart the immediate threat but also reveal a larger strategy at play—a British plan to turn the tide of the war with a series of coordinated strikes.

Armed with this knowledge, Margaret and James return to their network, the weight of their discovery pressing upon them. The information they've obtained could save countless lives and shape the course of the conflict, but leveraging it comes with its own set of risks. They must move quickly, disseminating the intelligence to the right hands while evading the ever-watchful eyes of the British spies.

As they debrief with their closest allies in the aftermath of their mission, there's a palpable sense of urgency. Plans are set into motion, and messages are sent flying across the colonies to warn of the impending British maneuvers. Margaret and James, at the center of this whirlwind of activity, find a moment of quiet amidst the chaos.

Low and intense conversation reflects the trust and respect they've built. They understand the stakes are higher than ever, that the shadows they've navigated together have grown deeper. Yet, at this moment, they also recognize the strength they've drawn from one another, the bond forged in secrecy and solidified in the shared pursuit of a cause greater than themselves.

As the first light of dawn breaks over the horizon, signaling the start of a new day, Margaret and James stand ready to face whatever challenges come their way. They are united not just by the secrets they keep but by the shared vision of a future forged in the flames of revolution—a future where freedom is the birthright of all.

The revelation of the British plans alters the Continental Army's strategic landscape and elevates Margaret and James's standing within the rebel ranks. Their successful operation has saved the rebellion from a potentially devastating blow, yet with their success comes an increased danger. The British, aware that a leak has compromised their strategy, double down on their efforts to root out spies within Philadelphia.

Amidst this heightened scrutiny, Margaret takes steps to further secure her network, implementing more sophisticated codes and dead drops. Her leadership and quick thinking become beacons of hope for the rebellion, inspiring those around her to greater acts of courage and ingenuity.

James finds himself increasingly precarious, balancing his roles with even greater care. Bradford's contributions to the rebels have become more daring, driven by the knowledge that his actions directly impact the war's outcome. Yet, every move he makes is shadowed by the risk of discovery, each day potentially his last as a double agent.

As autumn approaches, bringing with it the chill of oncoming winter, the rebellion faces new challenges. Supplies are low, and the Continental Army's morale wavers under the strain of a prolonged conflict. Within this crucible, Margaret and James are tasked with their most critical mission yet: securing a shipment of French arms and ammunition destined for the British forces.

The operation is ambitious, requiring coordination across multiple rebel cells and precise timing to intercept the shipment before it reaches British hands. Margaret and James, drawing upon their considerable experience, plan the operation with meticulous detail, aware that the mission's success could turn the tide of the war in favor of the rebels.

The night of the operation is fraught with tension. Margaret, James, and their team move through the darkness, guided by the stars and the urgency of their mission. Their approach is silent, a ghostly procession through the woodlands that border the route of the British shipment.

The ambush, when it comes, is swift and decisive. The rebels strike with the element of surprise firmly on their side, overwhelming the British escort and securing the shipment with minimal casualties. The victory is a testament to the rebels' growing prowess in warfare, a sign that the tide of the conflict may be turning.

In the aftermath of the operation, as they oversee the distribution of seized arms and ammunition to the Continental Army, Margaret and James share a moment of quiet reflection. They have come far from their initial encounters, growing in their roles within the rebellion and their understanding and trust in each other.

The war, however, is far from over. New challenges loom, and the British will not likely underestimate the rebels again. Yet, for now, Margaret and James allow themselves a brief respite, a moment to savor the victory and the knowledge that they have once again altered the course of the conflict.

Their journey together, marked by danger, intrigue, and the shared dream of liberty, continues to unfold. Each mission strengthens their bond, becoming a force in its own right. In the shadowy world of espionage and warfare, they have become beacons of light, their story a testament to the power of unity and the unrelenting pursuit of freedom.

As the embers of their latest victory began to cool in the crisp night air, Margaret and James stood side by side, their silhouettes cast against the backdrop of a war-torn Philadelphia. The weight of their recent success was palpable, not just in the physical spoils of their daring raid but in the knowledge that each victory brought them one step closer to their ultimate goal: freedom.

However, This moment of triumph was tempered by the knowledge of the path ahead. The war was a crucible, testing the mettle of all who dared dream of independence. For Margaret and James, their journey through the shadows of espionage and the glaring light of battle had forged an unbreakable bond, a testament to the strength found in unity.

Yet, even as they prepared to face the challenges of tomorrow, there was an unspoken acknowledgment between them of the fragile nature of their endeavor. The fight for liberty was fraught with peril, a constant dance with danger that promised no guarantees. But in this uncertainty, there was also a profound sense of purpose. They had seen firsthand the impact of their actions on the course of the rebellion, a ripple effect that extended far beyond their own lives.

As they turned back towards the heart of the city, the first light of dawn began to break over the horizon, casting the world in a new light. It was a reminder that, even in the darkest of times, there was always the promise of a new day. And with this new day came the opportunity to continue their fight, to stand up for the ideals they believed in, and to forge ahead in the pursuit of a future defined by freedom.

The saga of their lives, unfolding amidst the turmoil and camaraderie of rebellion, was far from reaching its denouement. Margaret and James, through every shadowed operation and shared moment of triumph, were not just fighting for the cause of liberty—they were crafting a legacy. This legacy, born from a blend of deep affection and steadfast commitment, became a beacon for those navigating the stormy seas of revolution after them.

As the first rays of dawn pierced the night, casting a gentle light over a city caught in the grip of transformation, they stood together, gazing into the horizon. United in the face of unknown challenges, they bravely forged ahead. Their journey was a testament to the belief that beyond the strife and sacrifice lay a future where freedom and justice were not mere aspirations but tangible realities for all.

Chapter 8

The Spark Ignites

As the rebellion's influence spread like wildfire across the colonies, Margaret and James found themselves at the heart of a rapidly changing battlefield. The victories they had achieved were not without cost, but the hope they sparked ignited a fervor among the people that could not be easily extinguished.

The British, sensing the shift in momentum, redoubled their efforts, launching a series of campaigns designed to crush the burgeoning spirit of independence once and for all. It was against this backdrop that Margaret and James were tasked with their most daring mission yet—a covert operation that, if successful, could turn the tide of the war in favor of the Continental Army.

The plan was to intercept a British dispatch containing the locations of their ammunition stores. If the rebels could seize these supplies, they would not only deprive the British forces of crucial resources but also bolster their own dwindling stocks.

Margaret's network, now more extensive and efficient than ever, sprang into action, gathering intelligence on the dispatch's route. James, using his knowledge of British military protocols, helped devise a plan to ambush the convoy carrying the dispatch. It was a risky endeavor, requiring precision timing and absolute secrecy.

The night before the operation, Margaret and James reviewed their plans one final time. The air between them crackled with the tension of the impending mission, but there was also a sense of deep trust, a recognition of how far they had come together.

Under the cover of darkness, they set out with a small, handpicked team. The route was treacherous, winding through dense forests that offered cover but also concealed dangers. Every shadow could be an enemy, every sound a signal of discovery.

As they neared the ambush site, the gravity of their task settled over them like a shroud. Success would mean a significant victory for the rebellion, but failure could spell disaster for them all. They moved forward with a silent determination, each step bringing them closer to the moment that would define their fate.

The ambush was a blur of motion and whispered commands. The rebels struck with the element of surprise firmly on their side, overwhelming the British convoy before they could mount a defense. The dispatch was seized, its contents more valuable than they had dared hope.

As they made their way back to their encampment, the first light of dawn began to streak the sky, painting the world in hues of victory and relief. They had achieved the impossible, securing a lifeline for the rebellion and striking a blow against the British that would resonate throughout the colonies.

In the aftermath of the operation, as the news of their success spread, Margaret and James stood together, not just as co-conspirators in the fight for freedom but as symbols of the hope and resilience that fueled the rebellion. The spark they had ignited, through courage, determination, and an unbreakable bond, promised to blaze a trail toward independence, lighting the way for all who followed in their footsteps.

In the aftermath of their audacious operation, the encampment buzzed with a renewed energy, the rebels' spirits lifted by the tangible evidence of their impact against the British forces. This victory, secured through the cunning and bravery of Margaret, James, and their team, reverberated far beyond the immediate gains of ammunition and intelligence. It was a declaration of their resolve, a testament to the power of collective action in the face of overwhelming odds.

The success of the mission bolstered the morale of the Continental Army and provided a much-needed advantage in the ongoing struggle. Yet, for Margaret and James, the triumph was personal. It was a reflection of their growth, not only as leaders within the rebellion but as partners in a cause that had grown larger than either of them could have imagined.

As they returned to the heart of the encampment, the first rays of dawn casting a soft light over the scene, they allowed themselves a moment of quiet reflection. The path that had led them here was marked by challenges and sacrifices, by losses that weighed heavily on their souls. Yet, in each other, they found an unwavering source of strength and determination. Together, they had faced the darkness and emerged victorious, their bond deepened by the trials they had overcome.

The victory, however, was not without its consequences. The British, stung by the loss and the audacity of the rebel's strike, intensified their efforts to quell the uprising. The stakes were higher than over, and the shadow of conflict loomed large over the colonies. Margaret and James knew that the days ahead would demand even more from them, that the road to freedom was fraught with danger and uncertainty.

In the quiet hours of the early morning, as the camp around them stirred to life, Margaret and James shared a resolve to continue their fight. They understood the importance of their next steps, the need for caution and strategy as they navigated the increasingly complex landscape of war. Their mission had ignited a spark, a beacon of hope for the rebellion, but the flames of freedom required constant tending.

As they prepared for what lay ahead, Margaret and James were not just strategists or soldiers; they were symbols of the resilience and courage that defined the revolutionary spirit. Their story, intertwined with the fate of a nation striving for independence, continued to unfold. With each challenge they faced, each victory they secured, they wrote their own chapter in the annals of history, a legacy of defiance and determination that would echo through the ages.

The spark they had ignited was now a flame, burning brightly in the hearts of all who dared to dream of liberty. And as they looked toward the horizon, toward the battles yet to come, Margaret and James stood ready, united in purpose and spirit, their eyes fixed on the promise of a future forged in the fires of revolution.

The promise of the future, however, remained entangled in the immediacy of war's demands. The victory they had just secured was a step forward, but both Margaret and James were acutely aware that each step was matched by the enemy's countermove. The war was a chess game played on a grand scale, and they were both pawns and players in the struggle for independence.

As autumn approached, bringing with it the chill of impending winter, the realities of war pressed heavily upon the Continental Army and the civilian population alike. Supplies were scarce, and the cold brought new challenges to an already beleaguered force. Yet, amid these hardships, the spirit of rebellion, the spark that Margaret and James had helped to ignite, continued to burn fiercely.

In the following weeks, Margaret's network managed to uncover a British plan that threatened to sever the supply lines vital to the Continental Army's survival through the winter. The intelligence pointed to a convoy carrying supplies from the Caribbean, intended to resupply British forces stationed in the colonies. The success of their previous operation had proven the value of such information; now, they faced the challenge of intercepting this new target.

Margaret and James, understanding the significance of this mission, began to plan their interception with meticulous care. The operation would require them to venture closer to enemy lines than ever before, a dangerous gambit that left no room for error. Their strategy hinged on the element of surprise and the cover of the thick forests that bordered the British route.

The night before the operation, the camp was a hive of quiet activity. Margaret and James moved among their fellow rebels, offering words of encouragement and finalizing the details of their plan. There was a palpable sense of camaraderie among them, a shared resolve that transcended the fear of what the morrow might bring.

Under the cloak of darkness, they set out, a determined band of rebels united in their quest for freedom. The march was silent, each step taking them deeper into enemy territory and closer to the confrontation that awaited. Margaret and James, leading the way, felt the weight of their responsibility keenly. The lives of their comrades, the future of the rebellion, hung in the balance.

The ambush, when it came, was swift and brutal. The rebels struck with precision, overwhelming the British convoy and securing the supplies that were so desperately needed.

The victory was a testament to their planning, their bravery, and the indomitable will of those who fought for independence.

As they returned to camp with their spoils, the first light of dawn breaking over the horizon, Margaret and James shared a moment of triumph. The operation had been a success, but more than that, it had shown the British that the will of the rebels could not be easily broken. The spark they had ignited, fueled by victories such as these, was now a beacon of hope for all who yearned for freedom.

The war was far from over, and they knew that darker days lay ahead. But for now, Margaret and James stood together, their faith in their cause, and in each other, unshaken. They had faced the darkness and emerged victorious, a symbol of the resilience and courage that would one day lead to the birth of a nation.

As the news of their successful raid spread throughout the rebel ranks and beyond, Margaret and James became symbols of hope and defiance, their names whispered in awe among those who dreamed of liberty. The tangible impact of their actions, securing vital supplies for the Continental Army, galvanized the resolve of their compatriots, proving that even in the darkest times, a determined few could make a difference.

In the heart of the encampment, amidst the celebratory air, there was also a palpable sense of urgency. The British, they knew, would not take this affront lightly. Retaliation was imminent, and the rebels needed to be prepared for the storm that was sure to come. It was within this climate of anticipation and resolve that Margaret and James began planning their next move.

The intelligence network that Margaret had so meticulously built became more crucial than ever. Every scrap of information, every whispered rumor, could hold the key to the rebels' survival and their next victory. James, with his unique insights into British strategies and weaknesses, worked closely with Margaret to identify potential targets and opportunities for disruption.

As the war dragged on, the lines between friend and foe became increasingly blurred. The harsh realities of conflict brought betrayals, but also unexpected alliances. It was during one such operation, aimed at uncovering a British spy within their midst, that Margaret and James encountered an unlikely ally—a British officer disillusioned with the war and sympathetic to the American cause.

This officer, risking his own life, provided them with information that could turn the tide of an upcoming battle. The decision to trust him was not made lightly, but in war, as in life, sometimes the greatest risks yield the greatest rewards. This new alliance, forged in the shadows of espionage, proved to be instrumental in the days that followed.

With winter setting in, and the British forces emboldened by reinforcements, the rebels faced their most challenging hour. A major offensive was planned by the British, aimed at crushing the rebellion once and for all. The intelligence provided by their new ally painted a grim picture, but also offered a glimmer of hope—a vulnerability in the British defenses that the rebels could exploit.

The battle that ensued was among the fiercest of the war. Margaret, James, and their fellow rebels fought with a desperation born of knowing this might be their last stand. The snow-covered fields became a tableau of chaos and courage, the air filled with the sounds of musket fire and the cries of the fallen.

In the end, it was the rebels' indomitable spirit, coupled with the strategic advantage their espionage had afforded them, that carried the day. The British were repelled, their offensive thwarted, and the tide of the war began to turn.

As the survivors surveyed the battlefield, the cost of their victory was etched in the snow-stained red and the faces of those who would not return. Margaret and James, standing amid the remnants of the battle, shared a look that spoke volumes. Their victory had been hard-won, but the spark they had helped ignite was now a flame that would not be extinguished.

The war was far from over, but in that moment, they knew they had altered its course. Together, they had faced the might of an empire and emerged victorious. The path ahead was uncertain, fraught with danger and hardship, but as long as they stood together, there was hope. Hope for victory, hope for freedom, and hope for the birth of a nation built on the ideals they held dear.

In the wake of their hard-fought triumph, the encampment was alive with a mix of relief and somber reflection. The rebels had managed to secure a much-needed victory, yet the cost was palpable in the eyes of those who had survived. Margaret and James, their spirits buoyed by the success of their mission, also felt the weight of responsibility heavier upon them than ever before. They had become beacons of hope in the fight for independence, leaders who others looked to in their darkest hours.

As the news of their victory spread, it ignited a flame of resistance across the colonies. Stories of their daring and determination were shared in hushed tones, rallying more to the cause and strengthening the resolve of those already committed to the fight. Yet, with this increased support came increased attention from the British forces, who were now more determined than ever to crush the rebellion.

The British response was swift and merciless, a series of

raids and counterstrikes designed to break the spirits of the American fighters and reclaim the momentum. Margaret and James found themselves once again at the forefront of the conflict, tasked with outmaneuvering an enemy that was becoming increasingly desperate and dangerous.

In response, they planned a series of guerrilla attacks, leveraging their intimate knowledge of the local terrain and the support of the local populace. These skirmishes were designed not only to disrupt British operations but also to keep their forces spread thin and on edge. Each successful raid added to the legend of the rebellion, but also to the bounty placed on their heads.

Despite the ever-present danger, Margaret and James carved moments of solace within the chaos. Their bond, forged in the crucible of war, had grown into something profound—a source of strength and comfort amid the uncertainty. They knew that each day could be their last, yet this knowledge only deepened their connection, their commitment to each other and to the cause they fought for.

As winter approached, bringing with it the harsh realities of campaigning in the cold, the Continental Army faced its greatest test yet. Supplies were running low, and the morale of the troops wavered in the face of the relentless British onslaught. It was during these bleak times that Margaret and James undertook a daring mission to secure additional supplies from a hidden cache known only to a few within the rebellion.

The mission was fraught with peril, a treacherous journey through enemy-occupied territory in the dead of winter. Yet, the prospect of securing a lifeline for their fellow soldiers spurred them on. They traveled under the cover of darkness, evading British patrols and navigating the treacherous landscape with a combination of luck and skill.

Their return, laden with supplies, was met with cheers and tears alike. It was a much-needed victory, a ray of hope in the depths of winter. For Margaret and James, it was a reaffirmation of their commitment to the cause, a reminder of the difference they could make.

The war continued, its outcome uncertain, but in the hearts of those who fought for freedom, the spark ignited by Margaret and James's actions had become an unquenchable flame. Their story, a testament to the power of courage and conviction, inspired all who heard it to press on, to fight for the dawn of a new nation forged from the ideals of liberty and justice.

As Chapter 6 drew to a close, Margaret and James stood together, not just as leaders or lovers, but as symbols of the enduring hope that freedom might one day reign across the land. The path ahead was fraught with challenges, but they faced it as they had everything else—together, with unwavering resolve and an unbreakable bond.

As the last light of day faded into the evening, casting long shadows across the rebel encampment, Margaret and James stood side by side, watching the campfires spring to life. The air was filled with the quiet murmur of voices, the crackle of firewood, and the distant howl of the winter wind. Around them, the men and women of the rebellion shared stories of the day's endeavors, their laughter and camaraderie a stark contrast to the cold and uncertainty that lay beyond the camp's fragile borders.

In this moment, amidst the flickering flames and shared glances, Margaret and James found a profound sense of belonging. They had come through the fire of conflict, bearing the scars of battle and the weight of leadership, yet they remained undaunted. Their love, a beacon in the tumult of war, had grown stronger with each trial, a testament to the enduring power of human connection in the face of adversity.

Together, they had inspired a wave of resistance that rippled across the colonies, igniting the hearts and minds of those who yearned for freedom. Their victories, though hard-won, had proven that even in the darkest of times, hope could thrive, and courage could turn the tide of history.

As they turned their gaze toward the stars, Margaret and James made a silent vow. They would continue to fight, not just for the dream of independence, but for the promise of a future where their love could flourish in peace. They knew the road ahead would be fraught with challenges, but they also knew they would face them together, with the strength of their convictions and the unity of their spirits.

As they turned their gaze toward the stars, Margaret and James made a silent vow. They would continue to fight, not just for the dream of independence, but for the promise of a future where their love could flourish in peace. They knew the road ahead would be fraught with challenges, but they also knew they would face them together, with the strength of their convictions and the unity of their spirits. Amidst the flickering flames and shared glances, they found a profound sense of belonging and purpose. Together, they had inspired a wave of resistance that rippled across the colonies, igniting the hearts and minds of those who yearned for freedom. Their love, a beacon in the tumult of war, had grown stronger with each trial, proving that even in the darkest times, hope could thrive, and courage could turn the tide of history.

CHAPTER 9

Shadows and Whispers

In the wake of their daring victory, the revolutionaries' encampment buzzed with a mix of celebration and solemn reflection. Their recent operation not only secured vital supplies for the Continental Army but also significantly harmed British morale. Yet, the triumph was shadowed by the cost at which it came, highlighting that the conflict was evolving into a war fought not just on open fields but in the clandestine world of espionage and whispers.

The spread of news about the skirmish meant that both the revolutionaries and the British forces found themselves increasingly reliant on their networks of spies and informants. The British, stung by their loss and aware that their plans had been compromised, intensified their efforts to penetrate the rebel ranks, dispatching agents to disrupt and gather intelligence.

Amidst this tense backdrop, Margaret's significance within the rebellion's spy network grew ever more critical. Her adeptness at deciphering messages and orchestrating the movements of their informants rendered her an indispensable asset. However, with recognition came danger, drawing the watchful eyes of British counterintelligence closer to her actions.

Within this charged atmosphere, James was entrusted with a mission fraught with peril, one that would challenge his convictions and blur the lines between ally and enemy. Tasked with infiltrating a loyalist cell plotting against the revolutionaries, James navigated a precarious path, immersing himself in the ranks of those loyal to the Crown to uncover their schemes. This deep dive into espionage forced him to grapple with questions of loyalty and identity.

As these events unfolded, a cryptic message arrived for Margaret, shrouded in secrecy and delivered by a trusted courier. Encoded in a cipher known only to a select few within the rebellion, it hinted at a betrayal capable of undoing all they had achieved. The message's contents were elusive, yet its warning was unmistakable: a traitor was among them, a hidden threat poised to strike at the rebellion's heart.

This ominous revelation sent shockwaves of suspicion through the revolutionary ranks, casting shadows of doubt where trust once prevailed. Margaret found herself navigating a storm, charged with the daunting task of identifying the traitor before their actions could inflict irrevocable damage.

The intrigue and peril of intelligence work took center stage, casting a complex web of alliances and deceptions. James's journey into the heart of enemy territory tested his beliefs, confronting him with the realities of his dual existence as both a soldier and a spy. Concurrently, Margaret's quest to decipher the cryptic warning and expose the internal adversary underscored the fragile nature of their struggle for independence.

Suspense and intrigue deepened, emphasizing the crucial role espionage played in shaping the revolution's course. In this shadowed conflict, information wielded the power of both shield and sword, becoming as vital to the cause as any weapon. As the narrative progressed, the fate of the rebellion teetered on a knife-edge, sharpened by secrets and the threat of betrayal.

As the revolutionary camp wrestled with the implications of

the cryptic message and the potential for betrayal within their ranks, the atmosphere became one of heightened vigilance. Margaret, despite the swirling suspicions, focused her efforts on deciphering the message's true meaning, understanding that the survival of their cause might well depend on her ability to unravel the mystery it contained.

Meanwhile, James's mission behind enemy lines continued to test his resolve. His interactions with the loyalists, while necessary for his cover, forced him to confront the complexities of his identity and allegiance. Each piece of information he gathered was a double-edged sword, valuable to the rebellion but at the cost of deepening his entanglement in a web of deceit.

The tension within the camp and James's precarious situation underscored a broader truth: in wars of independence, battles are not only fought on the fields but also in the minds and hearts of those involved. The revolutionaries' struggle against British rule was as much about winning the war of information and perception as it was about military victories.

Margaret's breakthrough came one chilly evening as she finally cracked the code of the cryptic message. The revelation was shocking—a planned betrayal by a high-ranking officer within the Continental Army, set to occur during a crucial battle that could determine the fate of the rebellion. The officer, swayed by British promises or disillusioned with the revolutionary cause, posed a threat that could undo all they had fought for.

Armed with this knowledge, Margaret and James faced a daunting task: they needed to expose the traitor without alerting them or causing panic within their ranks. Their plan required precision and discretion, leveraging their network of spies and the trust they had built among the revolutionaries to gather incontrovertible evidence of the planned betrayal.

As they set their plan into motion, the stakes could not

have been higher. The success of their operation would not only secure the rebellion's immediate future but also reinforce the integrity and unity of the revolutionary cause. Failure, however, was not an option they could afford to consider, for it would mean not just personal loss but potentially the collapse of the rebellion itself.

The night before the battle, as the camp lay quiet under a blanket of stars, Margaret and James shared a moment of quiet determination. They knew the dawn would bring challenges that would test their courage, their loyalty, and the very fabric of their cause. Yet, in the face of uncertainty, their resolve remained unshaken.

Together, they had navigated the shadows and whispers that permeated the Revolutionary War, their bond strengthened by the trials they had faced. As they prepared to confront the traitor and safeguard their cause, they were reminded of the enduring power of belief in the face of adversity—the belief in the cause of freedom, in the bonds that united them, and in the hope of a future born from the ashes of revolution.

The dawn of the battle would prove to be a turning point, not just for Margaret and James but for the entire revolutionary movement. In the fight for independence, every whisper of treason and every shadow of doubt served to remind them that their greatest strength lay in their unity and in the unwavering conviction that freedom was a cause worth fighting for, no matter the cost.

As the first light of dawn broke over the encampment, casting a pale glow on the faces of those who had dedicated their lives to the cause of freedom, the air was thick with anticipation. The day ahead would not only see a crucial battle but also the culmination of Margaret and James's efforts to root out the traitor within their ranks. The information Margaret had deciphered was a stark reminder of the war's stakes, not just on the battlefield but within the very soul of the rebellion.

The battle, expected to be fierce, was to take place on a field that had seen its share of bloodshed. The Continental Army, bolstered by the recent influx of supplies thanks to Margaret and James's daring operations, was in a better position than ever to face the British forces. Yet, the shadow of internal betrayal loomed large, threatening to undermine their efforts before they even began.

Margaret and James worked through the night, coordinating with trusted leaders to subtly monitor the suspected traitor's movements and communications. Their plan was meticulously crafted to avoid arousing suspicion, using a series of coded messages and signals to keep each other informed. The tension was palpable, as the success of their mission hinged on precise execution and the hope that they were not too late to prevent the betrayal.

As the battle commenced, the roar of cannons and the clash of steel filled the air, a chaotic symphony that underscored the brutality of war. Amidst the smoke and confusion, James kept a watchful eye on the suspect, ready to act at a moment's notice. Margaret, though not on the front lines, remained in constant communication with her network, her focus razor-sharp as she awaited the signal that would confirm their suspicions.

The moment of truth came amidst the battle's fever pitch when a carefully orchestrated series of events led to the traitor revealing their intentions. James, with the support of a few loyal comrades, was able to intercept and detain the traitor before their plans could come to fruition. The betrayal was thwarted, and the unity of the rebel forces was preserved by the narrowest of margins.

In the aftermath of the battle, as the dust settled and the cost of their victory became apparent, the revelation of the traitor's identity sent shockwaves through the Continental Army. Margaret, James, and their allies' swift action was lauded as a decisive factor in the day's success, reinforcing the importance of vigilance and unity in the face of adversity.

The victory on the battlefield and the foiling of the betrayal served as a powerful reminder of the rebellion's resilience. Margaret and James, their bond forged in the fires of conflict and strengthened by their shared commitment to the cause, emerged from the day's events with a renewed sense of purpose. They had faced one of the greatest challenges to their cause and had prevailed, not just through martial prowess but through the strength of their convictions and the depth of their trust in one another.

As they looked out over the camp, witnessing the mingled expressions of relief and sorrow on the faces of their fellow revolutionaries, they understood that the fight for independence was far from over. There would be more battles, more challenges to face, and more shadows to navigate. Yet, in this moment of quiet reflection, Margaret and James knew that together, they were ready to face whatever the future held, united by a cause that was greater than themselves. This cause promised not just freedom for their nation but a legacy of hope and courage for generations to come.

Their victory, though hard-won, was a testament to the resilience and determination of the Continental Army and its leaders. The foiled betrayal, while a stark reminder of the internal threats that could unravel their efforts, also served to galvanize the troops. The unity and trust within the ranks were strengthened as the soldiers realized that their cause was protected not only by their readiness to fight external foes but also by their vigilance against treachery from within.

In the days that followed, as the army regrouped and tended to the wounded, Margaret and James took stock of their situation. They had emerged successful from one of their most perilous challenges yet, but the victory had brought new responsibilities. Their roles as key figures in the intelligence network and as trusted advisors to the rebellion's leadership were now more crucial than ever. They were aware that their actions, moving forward, would have significant implications for the course of the war.

The revelation of the traitor's identity and the successful defense against the British offensive had ripple effects beyond the battlefield. Word of the incident spread throughout the colonies, bolstering support for the rebellion and attracting new recruits inspired by the courage and cunning of the Continental Army. The narrative of unity overcoming division, of the underdog standing firm against a seemingly invincible enemy, resonated deeply with the American populace.

Margaret, with her network of spies and informants, found herself at the center of an ever-expanding web of intelligence that stretched across the colonies. The information she gathered and analyzed was vital in planning the rebellion's next moves, predicting British strategies, and preventing further attempts at sabotage. Her role demanded a delicate balance between bold action and cautious strategy, a challenge she met with unwavering dedication.

James, for his part, continued to undertake missions that blurred the lines between espionage and direct combat. His dual identity as a soldier and a spy allowed him to navigate the dangerous waters of war with a unique perspective. Each mission deepened his understanding of the complexities of loyalty and duty, shaping him into a leader whose actions were guided by both intellect and instinct.

As autumn turned to winter, the rebellion faced the challenges of the harsh season. Yet, the cold could not dampen the spirits of those who had committed themselves to the cause of freedom. The successes of the past months had proven that their efforts were not in vain and that the dream of independence was within reach.

Margaret and James, standing together as the snow began to fall, knew that the road ahead was fraught with uncertainty. Yet, they also knew that they had each other, a bond forged in the heat of battle and strengthened by shared ideals. They looked toward the future with a sense of hope, aware that their journey was part of a larger story unfolding across the newborn nation.

As the year drew to a close, the Continental Army and its leaders prepared for the next phase of the conflict, fortified by the knowledge that their cause was just and their resolve unbreakable. The war for independence would continue, but Margaret and James, and all those who stood with them, were ready to face whatever challenges lay ahead, driven by the belief that freedom was a right worth fighting for, no matter the cost.

The encampment, blanketed under the fresh snow, seemed at peace from a distance, but beneath the serene white landscape, the hearts and minds of the revolutionaries burned with a fervent resolve. The winter months, traditionally a time for armies to rest and regroup, were instead used by Margaret, James, and their compatriots to strengthen their position, both strategically and in terms of morale.

Margaret's network expanded, now reaching into the heart of British-held territories, bringing back not just military intelligence but also news of the civilian sentiment towards the British crown and the growing support for the revolutionary cause. This information proved invaluable, painting a broader picture of the conflict that went beyond troop movements and supply lines, capturing the hearts and minds of the people they were fighting to free.

James, embracing his role as a bridge between the covert world of espionage and the overt operations of the Continental Army, found himself increasingly involved in planning sessions with the rebellion's military leaders. His insights, drawn from his unique vantage point, helped shape the strategies that would be employed in the spring campaigns. The respect he garnered from both the soldiers and the strategists was a testament to the crucial role he played.

As the winter wore on, an audacious plan began to take shape. Drawing on the intelligence gathered by Margaret's spies and leveraging the strategic acumen of the army's commanders, the revolutionaries prepared to launch a surprise offensive against the British forces. This operation, aimed at a critical British stronghold, promised to shift the balance of power in favor of the Continental Army.

The preparation for this assault was meticulous, with every detail scrutinized and every contingency planned for. Margaret and James, working tirelessly alongside their fellow revolutionaries, were at the forefront of these efforts. The trust and camaraderie among the rebels were stronger than ever, forged in the shared belief in their cause and the trials they had endured together.

As the winter's chill began to recede, giving way to the first hints of spring, the mood in the encampment shifted from one of preparation to anticipation. The revolutionaries knew that the coming battle would be a turning point in the war, a chance to demonstrate their strength and resolve.

The night before the assault, Margaret and James shared a quiet moment away from the hustle of the camp. They reflected on the journey that had brought them to this point, on the challenges they had faced, and the victories they had secured. They spoke of their hopes for the future, not just for themselves but for the nation they were helping to build. It was a moment of calm before the storm, a brief respite filled with the weight of all that was left unsaid.

As dawn broke and the revolutionaries set out towards their target, Margaret and James stood side by side, their determination unwavering. They knew that the day ahead would bring challenges the likes of which they had not yet faced, but they also knew that they were not alone. They were part of something larger than themselves, a movement driven by the unyielding desire for freedom and justice.

The battle that ensued would be remembered as one of the most daring and decisive of the Revolutionary War, a testament to the courage and ingenuity of those who fought for independence. At the heart of it all were Margaret and James, their actions reflecting the indomitable spirit that defined the revolutionary cause.

As the camp settled into the quiet of the night, with only the soft crackle of fires breaking the silence, Margaret and James found themselves standing at the edge of the encampment, looking out into the darkness that stretched before them. The weight of the coming day lay heavy on their shoulders, a palpable tension that was mirrored in the stillness of the world around them.

They had prepared as much as they could, laying plans with meticulous care and rallying their fellow revolutionaries with words of courage and conviction. The battle that awaited them was more than a strategic maneuver; it was a test of everything they had fought for, a chance to prove that their cause was not just a fleeting dream but a tangible reality within their grasp.

Yet, in this moment of quiet anticipation, it was not the sound of battle that filled the air but the gentle whisper of the wind through the trees, a reminder of the world beyond the war. Margaret and James turned to each other, their eyes meeting in a silent exchange of understanding and resolve. They had come so far together through challenges that would have broken lesser spirits, their bond deepening with each shared hardship and victory.

This was not just their fight; it was a fight for all who yearned for freedom, for the right to determine their own destiny. But as they stood together, hand in hand, they knew that whatever the morrow brought, they would face it together, united by a cause that was greater than themselves and a love that had become their beacon in the darkest of times.

The dawn of the battle would mark a new chapter in their journey, a moment that would test their resilience, their strategies, and the strength of their bond. Yet, as the first light of dawn began to break over the horizon, casting a soft glow on the encampment, Margaret and James faced it not with fear but with quiet determination. They were ready to stand firm, to fight for the ideals they believed in, and to carve out a future where freedom was not just a whispered dream but a lived reality.

With the breaking dawn As the camp settled into the quiet of the night, with only the soft crackle of fires breaking the silence, Margaret and James found themselves standing at the edge of the encampment, looking out into the darkness that stretched before them. The weight of the coming day lay heavy on their shoulders, a palpable tension that was mirrored in the stillness of the world around them.

They had prepared as much as they could, laying plans with meticulous care and rallying their fellow revolutionaries with words of courage and conviction. The battle that awaited them was more than a strategic maneuver; it was a test of everything they had fought for, a chance to prove that their cause was not just a fleeting dream but a tangible reality within their grasp.

Yet, in this moment of quiet anticipation, it was not the sound of battle that filled the air but the gentle whisper of the wind through the trees, a reminder of the world beyond the war. Margaret and James turned to each other, their eyes meeting in a silent exchange of understanding and resolve.

They had come so far together through challenges that would have broken lesser spirits, their bond deepening with each shared hardship and victory.

This was not just their fight; it was a fight for all who yearned for freedom, for the right to determine their own destiny. But as they stood together, hand in hand, they knew that whatever the morrow brought, they would face it together, united by a cause that was greater than themselves and a love that had become their beacon in the darkest of times.

The dawn of the battle would mark a new chapter in their journey, a moment that would test their resilience, their strategies, and the strength of their bond. Yet, as the first light of dawn began to break over the horizon, casting a soft glow on the encampment, Margaret and James faced it not with fear but with quiet determination. They were ready to stand firm, to fight for the ideals they believed in, and to carve out a future where freedom was not just a whispered dream but a lived reality.

With the breaking dawn, leaving behind the shadows and whispers of the night. Ahead lay the uncertainty and turmoil of battle but also the hope of a new beginning. For Margaret, James, and all those who stood with them, the fight for independence was far from over. Still, they were prepared to face whatever challenges lay ahead, driven by the unyielding spirit of revolution and the unbreakable bonds that held them together.

Leaving behind the shadows and whispers of the night. Ahead lay the uncertainty and turmoil of battle but also the hope of a new beginning. For Margaret, James, and all those who stood with them, the fight for independence was far from over. Still, the were prepared to face whatever challenges lay ahead, driven by the unyielding spirit of revolution and the unbreakable bonds that held them together.

CHAPTER 10

Bonds Forged in Fire

In the aftermath of a hard-won skirmish against the British, the revolutionary camp was a hive of activity and quiet reflection. The day's success had bolstered the spirits of the Continental Army, affirming the strength and determination woven into the fabric of their cause. Yet, amidst the muted celebrations, Margaret and James found themselves at a crossroads, their roles within the rebellion drawing them closer together.

A covert mission loomed on the horizon, a nocturnal endeavor designed to infiltrate a British stronghold rumored to contain strategic documents vital to the enemy's forthcoming campaigns. Margaret, with her extensive spy network, had pinpointed the location, a testament to her bravery and resourcefulness. At the same time, James, with his keen strategic mind, was instrumental in devising their approach, showcasing his courage and ingenuity. As they outlined their plan under the cloak of night, the air between them crackled with anticipation and an unspoken trust, the mission ahead promising to test the strength of their partnership like never before.

Moving with the stealth of shadows, Margaret and James led their team through the darkened landscape, their actions testament to their deep trust and synchronization. The operation unfolded with precision, their surprise assault securing the documents and ensuring their safe retreat into the night. It was a resounding success that underscored their united front's potency.

However, the true challenge emerged in the quiet aftermath as they poured over the captured documents. Among the strategic insights was a personal shock—a letter revealing secrets of Margaret's lineage, intertwining her family's legacy with the origins of the rebellion itself. The discovery was a revelation, casting her commitment to the cause in a new, profound light and burdening her with a legacy she had never known. This personal struggle, hidden beneath her brave exterior, was a testament to her resilience and dedication.

As they grappled with the implications of this newfound knowledge, the bond between Margaret and James was tested and ultimately fortified. James, a pillar of strength, stood by Margaret, offering unwavering support as she navigated the turbulent waters of her identity and duty. Their partnership, already built on mutual respect and shared convictions, grew stronger in the face of these revelations, their emotions intertwining with their shared mission.

This shared moment, hidden from the world's prying eyes, solidified their connection. Their trust in each other, forged through the trials of war and the shared secrets of their hearts, had become their greatest strength. They were more than comrades in arms; they were confidants, bound by a cause greater than themselves and a love that had blossomed in the midst of revolution. This unity and trust, shining through their partnership, was a beacon of hope in the midst of turmoil.

As the first light of dawn began to pierce the night, marking the end of their clandestine operation, Margaret and James faced the dawning day with renewed resolve. The challenges ahead were daunting, the path fraught with danger and uncertainty. Yet, in each other, they had found a beacon of hope and strength, a promise that together, they could face whatever trials lay ahead in their fight for freedom and a future forged from the flames of rebellion.

Their return to camp was met with relief and eager anticipation. The documents they had secured under the cover of darkness held the potential to shift the strategic balance of the war. Yet, as Margaret and James shared their findings with the leaders of the rebellion, the weight of Margaret's personal revelation hung heavily between them. The knowledge of her family's deep-rooted connection to the cause added a layer of complexity to her role in the struggle for independence, intertwining her personal destiny with the fate of the revolution, and potentially altering the course of history.

In the days that followed, as the camp absorbed the impact of the intelligence gathered Margaret and James found themselves at the heart of the plan for the next phase of the rebellion. Their recent success had not only proven their capabilities but also deepened the trust and reliance placed upon them by their fellow revolutionaries. Together, they worked tirelessly, mapping out strategies and leveraging the insights from the stolen documents to anticipate the British forces' next moves, their leadership guiding the rebellion towards a brighter future.

Amidst this flurry of activity, Margaret and James's connection continued to evolve. The shared intensity of their mission, coupled with the revelations about Margaret's heritage, had drawn them closer, their relationship becoming an anchor in the tumultuous sea of war. They found solace in each other's company, a respite from the demands of leadership and the constant threat of danger surrounding them.

As the rebellion prepared for its next major offensive, Margaret and James's partnership became emblematic of the larger fight for freedom. Their ability to navigate the challenges of war, both on the battlefield and within their hearts, inspired those around them. The strength of their bond, forged in the fire of shared trials and tribulations, stood as a testament to the power of unity and commitment in the face of adversity.

The revelation of Margaret's lineage also sparked conversations within the camp about the nature of legacy and the ties that bind the present to the past. For many, it served as a reminder that the fight for independence was rooted in a deep history of struggle and sacrifice, a legacy that each of them was now a part of. It reinforced the notion that their actions were not just for the here and now but for future generations who would inherit the freedoms for which they fought so valiantly.

As their lives continued to unfold amidst the backdrop of revolution, Margaret and James stood ready to face whatever challenges lay ahead, their resolve unshaken. With each step forward, they carved out their place in history, not just as leaders or lovers but as symbols of the enduring quest for liberty. The bonds they had forged in the fire of conflict were not only between each other but with the cause they served, a cause that promised to reshape the world and leave a lasting legacy of hope and freedom.

The anticipation for the upcoming offensive grew each day, mirroring the rising tension within the camp. Yet, amidst the strategic preparations and drills, an undercurrent of unity and determination pulsed stronger than ever before. Inspired by the leadership and courage of figures like Margaret and James, the rebels rallied with a renewed sense of purpose. They were not just fighting for the abstract idea of freedom anymore; they were fighting for the tangible future that Margaret and James's partnership represented—a future where liberty and justice were realities for all.

As the day of the offensive approached, Margaret and James took a moment to reflect on the journey that had brought them to this point. They stood together on the eve of battle, looking out over the camp with a sense of quiet pride. Around them, the signs of preparation were everywhere, but in this moment, there was peace. They understood the risks of the morrow, the possibility that not all who stood ready to fight would see the dawn of the next day. Yet, their resolve only strengthened in the face of these daunting prospects.

The night was spent in whispered conversations and shared plans, with Margaret and James finalizing the details of their strategy. Their professional and personal connection had become the cornerstone of their effectiveness as leaders. They complemented each other perfectly, James's tactical genius meshing seamlessly with Margaret's unparalleled skill in intelligence and espionage. Together, they were a formidable force, one that the British would soon come to reckon with.

When the battle commenced, it was with a fury that took the British forces by surprise. The rebels, armed with the intelligence Margaret had uncovered and the strategies she and James had devised, struck with precision and determination. The fight was fierce and uncertain for long periods. Still, the revolutionaries fought with the passion and tenacity that only true belief in a cause can inspire.

In the thick of the battle, Margaret and James fought side by side, their partnership a beacon of hope and strength for their fellow soldiers. They moved through the chaos with a shared sense of purpose, their actions a testament to their deep trust in each other and their unwavering commitment to the cause of freedom.

As the smoke cleared and the tide of battle turned in favor of the revolutionaries, it was clear that this victory would be a defining moment in the war for independence. The rebels delivered a significant blow to the British forces and demonstrated the power of unity and shared conviction.

In the aftermath of the battle, as the camp tended to the wounded and mourned the lost, Margaret and James found solace in each other's presence. They had weathered yet another storm together, their bond strengthened by the trials they had faced. As they looked toward the future, with all its uncertainty and promise, they knew that whatever challenges lay ahead, they would face them together, united by their love and shared the dream of a free and just world.

Their story, a testament to the enduring spirit of revolution, continued to unfold. It was a narrative of courage, love, and the unshakeable belief in the possibility of a better tomorrow.

In the wake of their triumph, the revolutionary camp buzzed with somber reflection and a renewed sense of purpose. The victory had been significant, yet it came at a cost, reminding everyone involved of the high stakes of their struggle. Margaret and James, pivotal in orchestrating the successful offensive, found themselves not just as leaders within the rebellion but as symbols of hope and resilience.

The days following the battle were marked by strategic meetings and planning sessions. The success had opened new possibilities for the rebellion, creating opportunities to press their advantage. Yet, it was clear that the British would retaliate with increased fervor. Margaret and James, aware of the challenges ahead, worked diligently to prepare their forces for what was to come.

Margaret's role within the camp had evolved significantly. Her ability to gather and interpret intelligence had always been invaluable. Still, with the revelation of her family's historic ties to the cause, she felt a deeper connection to the fight. This unexpected legacy gave her a new perspective on her role in the rebellion. She delved into her tasks with renewed vigor, determined to honor the legacy left by her ancestors.

James, too, found new meaning in their shared efforts.

The revelation about Margaret's lineage and their successful collaboration on the battlefield deepened his respect and admiration for her. Their personal and professional partnership had become a cornerstone of their lives, a source of strength and comfort amid the chaos of war.

As they worked together to strengthen the rebellion's position, their plans for the next offensive began to take shape. They knew that to maintain the momentum, they would need to outmaneuver the British with coordinated strikes, targeting their supply lines and communication networks. The ambitious strategy required precise execution and unwavering courage from all involved.

Amidst the planning, a courier arrived with news that would test their resolve again. A British force, larger than any they had faced before, was amassing nearby, planning to crush the rebellion in a decisive blow. The information, confirmed by Margaret's network, set the camp into a flurry of activity. There was no time to waste; the next battle was upon them.

The gravity of the situation brought Margaret and James even closer. They spent long hours poring over maps and intelligence reports, their minds working together to devise a plan that could turn the tide in their favor. Their connection, forged in the heat of battle and the quiet moments in between, became an unspoken language of glances and gestures, each understanding the other's thoughts and fears without words.

As the day of the battle drew near, Margaret and James gathered their closest advisors and comrades to lay out their strategy. The plan was daring, leveraging their knowledge of the terrain and the element of surprise to their advantage. They would divide their forces, striking simultaneously at multiple points to disorient the British and disrupt their advance.

The night before the battle, the camp was a place of quiet determination. Soldiers checked their equipment and shared quiet words with their comrades. At the same time, leaders like Margaret and James moved among them, offering words of encouragement and solidarity. The unity was palpable, a shared conviction that they were fighting for something greater than themselves.

Margaret and James, finding a moment of solitude, looked out over the camp, their thoughts turning to the future. They knew the morrow would bring challenges unlike any they had faced, but they also knew that together, they could face anything. The bonds they had forged in the fire of rebellion were unbreakable, a testament to their shared commitment to the cause and each other.

The revolutionaries stood ready as dawn broke, casting a golden light over the encampment. The battle ahead would be a defining moment in their fight for independence, a chance to prove that their bonds, forged in the fire of shared struggles and victories, were strong enough to withstand the might of an empire.

The story of Margaret and James, intertwined with the fate of the rebellion, continued to unfold, a narrative of courage, love, and the unyielding pursuit of freedom. In the face of adversity, they stood together, their partnership a beacon of hope for all who dreamed of a better tomorrow, free from the chains of tyranny.

As the first light of dawn illuminated the encampment, casting long shadows and painting the sky with hues of orange and pink, Margaret and James stood at the forefront of the assembled forces. The air was charged with anticipation, a palpable tension that spoke of the gravity of the day ahead. Today, the rebellion would face its largest battle yet and seek to solidify its place in the struggle for independence.

The plan they had devised was bold, perhaps the most audacious yet. It relied on speed, surprise, and the indomitable will of those who fought for a cause greater than themselves. Margaret and James had spent countless hours in preparation, knowing that the success of this day could very well turn the tide of the war in their favor.

As the troops began their march towards the battlefield, Margaret and James exchanged a look of quiet resolve. This was the moment they had been working towards, culminating all their efforts. They moved with their comrades, a unified front against the looming threat of the British forces. Their hearts were heavy with the knowledge of the dangers they faced but also buoyed by the hope that this day could mark a decisive victory for the rebellion.

The battle that unfolded was fierce and unforgiving. The revolutionaries, empowered by their convictions and the strategic genius of their leaders, engaged the British with a ferocity that belied their numbers. Margaret and James were everywhere at once, rallying their troops, directing maneuvers, and fighting with a courage that inspired all who saw them.

Amidst the chaos of battle, their plan began to take effect. The British, caught off guard by the multipronged assault and the ferocity of the rebel attack, found themselves on the back foot. Slowly, through sheer determination and the sacrifices of many brave souls, the tide began to turn.

As the sun reached its zenith, casting no shadows on the battlefield, a signal flare soared into the sky, marking the retreat of the British forces. It was a moment of triumph, hard-earned and paid for with the lives of countless comrades. The battlefield, a testament to the horrors of war, was also a monument to their resilience and determination.

In the aftermath, as the revolutionaries tended to the wounded and gathered their dead, Margaret and James found a moment of peace amidst the devastation. They had achieved the impossible, delivering a blow to the British that would resonate throughout the colonies. This victory was theirs, a testament to their leadership, vision, and unbreakable bond.

But even as they celebrated their success, they knew the war was far from over. There would be more battles, more challenges to face, and more sacrifices to be made. Yet, in this moment of victory, they allowed themselves to believe in a future where their dreams of freedom and independence could become a reality.

Their journey together, a story of love and war, of sacrifice and triumph, continued to unfold against the backdrop of a nation fighting for its very soul. With each step forward, Margaret and James carved out their legacy, not just as leaders of a rebellion but as harbingers of a new dawn for their people. The bonds they had forged in the fire of conflict were unbreakable, a beacon of hope in the long night of war, guiding the way towards freedom and a better tomorrow.

As the first rays of dawn cut through the darkness, casting a soft light across the encampment, Margaret and James stood among their fellow revolutionaries, a palpable sense of unity binding them together. They were a mosaic of determination and hope, each individual a vital thread in the fabric of the rebellion. The upcoming battle was not just a confrontation with the enemy; it was a testament to their shared struggle, a fight for the very soul of their burgeoning nation.

The plan laid out the night before was bold, perhaps the most audacious they had ever conceived. Yet, as Margaret looked into the faces of those around her, she saw not fear but resolve. James, feeling the weight of the moment, squeezed her hand in silent support. They had faced adversity together before, each challenge forging them stronger, and this time would be no different.

As the camp stirred to life, preparations for the battle were made in earnest. Swords were sharpened, muskets loaded, and hearts steeled against the uncertainty of the outcome. Margaret and James, moving through the ranks, offered words of encouragement, their presence a comforting assurance that their leadership was not just born of necessity but of genuine care and commitment to their cause.

The moment of departure arrived, a collective breath held as the revolutionaries readied themselves to march into the unknown. Margaret and James, leading the way, felt the weight of their responsibility. They were not just fighting for freedom from tyranny but for the future of a nation yet to be born. The legacy of their actions, intertwined with the fate of countless others, would echo through history, a reminder of liberty's cost.

As they stepped forward, the first light of dawn illuminating their path, a sense of solemnity fell over the group. This battle, like those that came before and those that would follow, was a step on the long road to independence. Yet, with each step, they carried the hopes and dreams of their compatriots, a burden made lighter by their shared resolve.

The chapter of their lives that unfolded on the battlefield that day would be remembered not just for the clash of arms but for the bonds of fellowship and purpose that sustained them. Margaret and James, side by side, faced the horizon with a quiet determination. The challenges ahead were formidable, but together, they were invincible. Theirs was a partnership forged in the fires of revolution, a symbol of the enduring power of unity and belief in the face of adversity.

As they marched forward, the sun rose higher, casting a golden glow over the landscape. It was a new day, full of unknowns, but one thing was certain: Margaret and James, and all those who stood with them, were ready to shape their destiny, to fight for a future where freedom and justice were not just ideals but realities. The battle ahead would be fierce, but it was a necessary step on the path to independence, a path they walked together, fortified by the bonds forged in the fire of their shared commitment to the cause.

With this resolve, they stepped into the light of the new dawn, their hearts beating as one with the rhythm of revolution, their eyes fixed on the promise of a free and just world that lay just beyond the horizon.

CHAPTER **11**

The Siege of Resolve

As dawn broke over the revolutionary camp, the air was thick with anticipation. The siege that lay ahead was not just a military challenge; it was a test of the revolutionaries' resolve, a confrontation that would demand every ounce of their strength, cunning, and unity. The encampment, usually a hub of activity and planning, was somber as soldiers and leaders alike prepared for the coming conflict.

Margaret and James, having played crucial roles in the rebellion's successes thus far, were acutely aware of the stakes. The British forces, determined to quash the burgeoning revolution, had fortified their position, making the siege a daunting task. Yet, the revolutionaries had something their adversaries lacked: a cause worth fighting for and a bond forged in the fire of shared conviction.

The morning was spent in final preparations. Margaret reviewed the intelligence gathered on the British defenses, her mind racing to find any advantage they could exploit. James, meanwhile, drilled the soldiers, his voice steady and encouraging, a beacon of leadership in the uncertain hours before battle.

As they reconvened to discuss their strategy, the depth of

their partnership was evident. They approached the challenge with a blend of Margaret's analytical prowess and James's tactical ingenuity, devising a plan that leveraged their forces' strengths and unique capabilities. Their plan was daring, a multifaceted assault designed to penetrate the British defenses and break the siege.

The hours passed, and as the sun reached its zenith, the revolutionaries took their positions. The silence that fell over the camp was a stark contrast to the turmoil that raged within each of them. Margaret and James shared a moment, a final affirmation of their trust and commitment, before giving the signal to begin the assault.

The battle that ensued was fierce, a maelstrom of chaos and resolve. The revolutionaries, driven by the dream of freedom, fought with a tenacity that startled their foes. Margaret and James, at the heart of the fray, exemplified the spirit of their cause, inspiring those around them with their courage and determination.

As the siege wore on, the revolutionaries' resolve was tested like never before. The British defenses were formidable, and the cost of the battle was high. Yet, amidst the smoke and the clamor, a breakthrough was achieved. The revolutionaries, through a combination of strategy, bravery, and sheer will, began to turn the tide.

When it came, the fall of the British stronghold was not just a military victory; it was a symbol of the revolutionaries' unwavering resolve. The siege, a crucible of their determination, had galvanized their movement, proving that their cause was not just viable but victorious.

In the aftermath, as the revolutionaries took stock of their win and mourned their losses, Margaret and James stood together amidst the ruins. The siege had been a trial by fire, one that had tested their leadership, their strategy, and their faith in each other and their cause. Yet, they emerged from the battle not just as victors but as embodiments of the resolve that had carried them through.

The Siege of Resolve, as it would come to be known, was a turning point in the revolution. It demonstrated the power of unity and conviction, serving as a beacon of hope and a call to arms for those still uncertain of the rebellion's chances. For Margaret, James, and all who fought beside them, it was a reaffirmation of their commitment to the fight for freedom—a fight they were now more certain than ever could be won.

As they looked towards the horizon, weary but undefeated, they knew that the path ahead would be fraught with more challenges. But the siege had proven that no obstacle was insurmountable when faced with resolve and united in purpose. The battle for independence was far from over, but the spirit of the revolution, the unbreakable bond between its defenders, had never been stronger.

As dawn's first light crept over the encampment, Margaret and James stood overlooking the preparations, the weight of the upcoming siege palpable in the air around them.

"Are the men ready?" Margaret asked, her voice steady despite the turmoil brewing within.

James turned to her, his gaze resolute. "As ready as they'll ever be. Your intelligence has given us the edge we needed. Now, it's up to us to make it count."

A brief smile crossed Margaret's face, a testament to the trust and camaraderie they had built. "Then let's not waste the opportunity," she replied. "Every advantage counts today."

Their conversation was interrupted by the arrival of Lieutenant Harris, a trusted ally. "The British fortifications are stronger than we anticipated," he reported, concern etching his features. "But your plan... it's bold. It might just work."

James clapped Harris on the shoulder, a gesture of reassurance. "Boldness is what will win us this day. Fearlessness in the face of the impossible."

As they moved through the camp, Margaret and James engaged with their fellow revolutionaries, offering words of encouragement and solidarity. Their interactions were brief but meaningful, each exchange reinforcing the bonds that held them together.

"You've got this, Thomas," James said to a young soldier, nerves apparent in his stance. "Remember, it's not the size of the dog in the fight, but the size of the fight in the dog."

Margaret, overhearing the exchange, added, "And remember why we're fighting. For freedom, for our future."

The soldier nodded, visibly bolstered by their words. "For freedom," he echoed, a newfound determination in his voice.

As the hour of the assault approached, Margaret and James gathered their leaders for one final briefing. The room was charged with anticipation, every individual aware of the role they were about to play.

"Today, we fight not just for the land beneath our feet but for the very ideals that define us," Margaret began, her voice cutting through the tension. "We fight for freedom, for the right to shape our destiny. And we fight together as one."

James stepped forward, laying out the strategy with clarity and conviction. "Our unity is our strength. The British expect us to falter, to break under their might. But today, we'll show them what we're made of. Today, we stand as one, unbreakable."

Nods of agreement and murmurs of assent filled the room, the collective resolve of the group palpable. They were ready, each person prepared to play their part in the history about to unfold.

As they filed out of the tent, Margaret caught James's eye, and a silent exchange of trust and acknowledgment passed between them. This battle would test them in ways they had yet to imagine, but together, they were unstoppable.

The Siege of Resolve was more than a confrontation; it was a declaration of the revolutionaries' unyielding spirit. It was a battle fought as much with words and convictions as with swords and muskets. As Margaret and James led their forces into the fray, their voices united with those of their comrades, a chorus of defiance and determination that would echo through the ages.

As the revolutionaries advanced, the battlefield became a cacophony of shouts, gunfire, and clashing steel. Amidst the chaos, Margaret and James found themselves at the forefront, their leadership roles never more critical. They moved with purpose, their actions coordinated as if by an unspoken understanding honed through countless hours of planning and shared experiences.

In a lull between the volleys of musket fire, Margaret turned to James, her voice cutting through the din. "We need to rally the eastern flank; they're starting to falter," she shouted, her gaze fixed on a segment of their line that was dangerously close to breaking.

James nodded, understanding immediately. "I'll take the lead. Follow with reinforcements!" he called back before sprinting towards the embattled flank, his presence alone enough to bolster the spirits of the weary soldiers.

Margaret watched him go, a mix of pride and concern

etching her features. She quickly organized a group of reserves, leading them to support James and the eastern flank. Together, they pushed back against the British forces, a testament to their ability to inspire and lead by example.

As the day wore on, the tide of battle began to turn. The revolutionaries, fueled by their leaders' courage and the righteousness of their cause, fought with renewed vigor. The British, surprised by the ferocity and resilience of their opponents, started to give ground.

In the aftermath of the conflict, as the sun dipped below the horizon, painting the sky in hues of orange and red, Margaret and James regrouped with their forces. The battlefield was a grim sight, a stark reminder of the cost of freedom. Yet, amidst the sorrow, there was also a sense of accomplishment. They had held their ground, defying the odds and proving the mettle of the revolutionary spirit.

James, his face smeared with soot and sweat, turned to Margaret, a weary smile on his lips. "We did it," he said, the weight of their victory and the losses they had incurred reflected in his eyes.

Margaret nodded, her emotions a whirlwind of relief, exhaustion, and resolve. "We did," she agreed, her voice steady. But this is just the beginning. We've shown them what we're capable of, and we'll need to be ready for their response."

As they stood together, surveying the aftermath, their bond was palpable. They had faced one of the greatest challenges of the rebellion head-on, their leadership pivotal in the day's success. The siege had not just been a test of military strength but of their resolve, their ability to lead, and the depth of their commitment to the cause.

The night fell quiet around them, the sounds of the battlefield fading into a solemn silence. The Siege of Resolve, as it would come to be known, was a turning point, not just in the strategic sense but in the hearts and minds of all who fought. It was a declaration that the fight for independence was alive and more potent than ever, driven by leaders who were not just commanders but symbols of hope.

Margaret and James, their partnership strengthened in the fire of conflict, looked towards the future with a clear vision. The road ahead was fraught with challenges, but together, they were ready to face them, to continue the fight for freedom, and to forge a legacy that would inspire generations to come.

Through it all, the bond between Margaret and James only deepened their partnership, which was a cornerstone of the rebellion's continued success. They had become more than just leaders; they were symbols of the resilience and determination that fueled the fight for independence. Their efforts to expand their network brought fresh recruits and much-needed supplies, while the daring raid to disrupt the British supply lines further cemented their standing in the war.

As the Siege of Resolve receded into memory, it stood not just as a pivotal victory but as a turning point in the war and in the hearts of those who fought it. Margaret and James, at the heart of this transformation, looked to the future with a renewed sense of purpose. The path to freedom was long and fraught with peril, but they were ready to face it head-on, together, fortified by the bonds forged in the fire of their shared resolve.

Their leadership, tested in the crucible of battle, had proven decisive, not only in military terms but in strengthening the morale and unity of the rebellion. Every victory, every sacrifice, brought them closer to their goal, weaving their individual stories into the larger tapestry of the revolution.

In the quiet moments between strategies and skirmishes, Margaret and James found strength in each other's company.

Their conversations once focused solely on tactics and plans, but they began to touch upon dreams of peace and visions of the nation they were fighting to build. These dreams, once distant, seemed increasingly within reach with each passing day.

The rebellion, bolstered by their victories and the growing support among the colonies, prepared for the next phase of the conflict with a sense of optimism. Margaret and James, leading from the front, inspired those around them with their dedication and vision. The challenges ahead remained daunting, but the foundation they had built—a foundation of trust, strategic acumen, and unwavering commitment to the cause—promised to sustain them through the trials to come.

As dawn broke on a new day, the camp stirred to life, a community bound by a common cause and led by two individuals who had transcended their roles as mere soldiers in the fight for independence. Margaret and James stood ready, their resolve unshaken, their spirits unbroken, poised to continue the fight for freedom, justice, and the birth of a new nation.

In the days following the successful mission, the camp settled into a routine, and the atmosphere was one of cautious optimism. The recent victories had bolstered the revolutionaries' morale, but both Margaret and James knew the importance of maintaining momentum. Their thoughts were already turning towards the next strategic moves, and they understood that the fight for freedom was a marathon, not a sprint.

One evening, as they pored over maps and reports in their tent, the flicker of the lantern casting shadows on their determined faces, a new challenge presented itself. A scout rushed in, breathless with news that British reinforcements were moving closer, a force larger and more formidable than any they had faced before.

Margaret's gaze met James's, a silent communication

passing between them. "We'll need to be smarter, not just braver," she said, her mind racing with possibilities. "If we can't outfight them, we'll outthink them."

James nodded, his expression grim but resolute. "Let's call a council. We need every mind on this, every idea that can give us an edge."

The council meeting was a fervent brainstorming session, with Margaret and James leading the discussion. Ideas flew back and forth, from ambushes to sabotage; each proposal weighed for its merits and risks. It was in these heated debates that the true strength of their leadership shone through—not just in their ability to strategize but in their capacity to inspire and unite their followers around a common goal.

A plan began to take shape, one that would require precision and daring in equal measure. They would use the terrain to their advantage, luring the British into a narrow pass where their numbers would be less overwhelming. Simultaneously, a small team would infiltrate the enemy camp, aiming to disrupt their supply lines and create chaos from within.

Margaret turned to James as the council dispersed, a determined glint in her eye. "This could change the tide of the war," she said, the weight of the moment not lost on either of them.

James reached for her hand, squeezing it gently. "We'll make it work. Together, we've overcome worse odds."

The days leading up to the operation were a blur of activity. Margaret coordinated with her network of spies to gather intelligence on the British movements while James trained the troops for the upcoming confrontation. Their efforts were a testament to their shared commitment to the cause, a dance of preparation and anticipation that drew them ever closer.

As the night of the operation approached, the camp was alive with a tense energy. Margaret and James shared a quiet moment alone, reflecting on the journey that had brought them here. "No matter what happens," James said, his voice steady, "know that I couldn't have asked for a better partner in this fight."

Margaret smiled, her heart full despite the uncertainty of the morrow. "Nor I. Together, we're making history."

The operation would be a decisive moment in the rebellion, a daring endeavor that could shift the balance of power. As Margaret and James stepped out into the cool night air, their resolve was clear. They were ready to face whatever challenges lay ahead, united in purpose and strengthened by the bond they shared. The fight for freedom continued with each victory, a step closer to the dream of a nation forged in the fires of revolution.

As the final rays of the setting sun dipped below the horizon, casting long shadows across the revolutionary camp, a palpable sense of anticipation hung in the air. The plans had been laid, the roles assigned, and now, as night enveloped the world in a cool embrace, Margaret and James stood together amidst their fellow revolutionaries on the cusp of undertaking one of the most audacious operations yet.

The camp, usually a buzz of activity, was eerily silent, the quietude a testament to the gravity of the impending mission. Soldiers and strategists alike shared knowing glances, their usual banter replaced by a focused determination. It was a moment that seemed to suspend time, each person lost in their thoughts, reflecting on the journey that had brought them here and the battles yet to fight.

Margaret, her eyes scanning the faces of those she had come to know as family, felt a surge of pride. Together, they had faced adversity, celebrated victories, and mourned losses. The rebellion had grown from a scattered group of dissidents into a formidable force united by a shared dream of freedom. And at the heart of it all were she and James, whose partnership had become the beacon of hope and leadership the rebellion needed.

James, catching Margaret's gaze, offered a reassuring smile. Despite the uncertainty of what lay ahead, their confidence in each other and in their cause was unwavering. "No matter what happens tonight," he said, his voice steady and sure, "we stand together. For freedom, for our future."

Margaret nodded, her resolve firm. "Together," she echoed, the word a promise, a vow that extended beyond the confines of the camp to every soul yearning for liberty.

As they turned to face the darkness, ready to embark on their mission, the camp came to life once more, not with words but with action. Quiet farewells were exchanged, weapons checked and rechecked, and final preparations made. The air was charged with a sense of purpose, the kind that forges legends and alters the course of history.

And then, with a final look back at the camp that had become their home, Margaret and James stepped into the night, leading their team into the unknown. The operation that lay ahead was fraught with danger. Still, it was also an opportunity—an opportunity to strike a decisive blow against tyranny, to demonstrate the strength and cunning of the rebellion, and to move one step closer to the dream that had ignited the flame of revolution.

As they disappeared into the shadows, the camp behind them whispered prayers and hopes for their safe return. The chapter of their struggle was far from over, but this night, this moment would be remembered as a testament to their courage, their resilience, and their unbreakable bond. The fight for freedom continued, each step forward a testament to the unyielding spirit of those who dare to dream of a better world.

And so, under the cover of darkness, Margaret, James, and their band of revolutionaries ventured forth, their hearts alight with the fire of liberty, their resolve as strong as the bonds that united them. The night ahead would be long, and its challenges many, but they faced it together, driven by the hope of dawn on the horizon—a dawn of a nation conceived in liberty and dedicated to the pursuit of justice for all.

CHAPTER 12

The Price of Liberty

As dawn broke over the encampment, the air was thick with anticipation and the grim knowledge of the day ahead. Under Margaret and James's unwavering leadership, the revolutionaries prepared as best they could, fully aware that the confrontation looming on the horizon would be unlike any they had faced before. It was not just a battle for territory but a fight for the very soul of their burgeoning nation, a testament to the unwavering bravery and determination they were willing to exhibit for the cause of liberty.

The British forces, emboldened by reinforcements, advanced with a confidence that belied the ferocity of the resistance they would encounter. The rebels, though outnumbered, were driven by a fierce determination, their resolve steeled by the knowledge of what was at stake.

As the two sides clashed, the battlefield became a maelstrom of chaos and valor. Margaret and James, not just leaders but also [specific relationship], led their forces with a bravery that inspired those around them. Yet, even as they fought with all their might, the brutal reality of war spared no one. Amidst the clamor and smoke, a beloved figure, a close friend who had stood with them through thick and thin, fell.

The loss was a blow that reverberated through the ranks of the revolutionaries, a stark reminder of the price of their struggle. Margaret and James felt the weight of the sacrifice deeply, the grief a heavy chain around their hearts. Yet, even in the face of such sorrow, they found strength in each other, their shared loss forging an unbreakable bond. The revolutionaries, too, were deeply affected, their spirits dampened but their resolve strengthened.

In the quiet moments after the battle, as they gathered to honor the memory of their fallen comrade, the camp was united in a profound sense of grief and resolve. The loss of their friend was not just a personal tragedy but a symbol of the sacrifices made by all who dared to dream of freedom, a shared grief that bound them together in their common cause.

With their hands clasped, Margaret and James stood as pillars of strength for their people. Their grief was palpable, yet so was their determination to continue the fight. They understood that the path to liberty was paved with such sacrifices, each loss a reminder of the stakes of their rebellion.

As they looked out over the camp, the faces of their fellow revolutionaries alight with the flames of the memorial fires, Margaret and James made a silent vow. They would carry on, not just for those who had fallen, but for all who yearned for a future free from tyranny. The battle had taken much from them, but it had also reinforced their unwavering commitment to the cause, each other, and the dream of a nation born from the ashes of conflict, a commitment that would see them through the darkest of times.

The night closed in, a blanket of stars watching over the encampment. The revolutionaries found a moment of unity in the shared silence, a collective strength drawn from their shared losses and hopes. The fight for freedom would continue, its cost ever-present in their hearts. Still, so too would the unyielding spirit of those who fought for a better tomorrow.

The aftermath of the battle was a [specific description of the scene], a stark reminder of the immediate and long-term effects of the conflict.

In the dim light of dawn, Margaret and James surveyed the encampment, the quiet before the storm hanging heavy in the air. Soldiers moved like shadows among the tents, their silhouettes etching a stark contrast against the morning light. Today, they knew, would test them all—not just as soldiers of a cause but as human beings bound to the harsh realities of war. The air was thick with a mix of [specific emotions], a testament to the psychological toll of the impending battle.

"Margaret," James began, his voice low, the map in his hands creased from use, "the British forces are advancing faster than we anticipated. We need to adjust our strategy."

Margaret nodded, her mind racing through scenarios. "Let's reinforce our eastern flank. That's where they'll hit us hardest. We can use the terrain to our advantage, funnel them into a narrower path."

As they discussed, a young runner approached hesitation in his steps. "Excuse me," he interrupted, "but Thomas—he's asking for you. Says it's urgent."

Margaret glanced at James before they both hastened towards Thomas's tent, concern quickening their steps. Thomas, a steadfast friend and a key strategist in their ranks, rarely used the word 'urgent' lightly.

Inside the tent, Thomas's expression was grave. "The scouts just came back. There's a British regiment, larger than any we've seen, moving this way. We have a few hours, at most."

The news settled like a stone in Margaret's stomach. "How many are we talking about?"

"Enough to overwhelm us if we don't act swiftly," Thomas replied, his gaze steady.

James leaned over the makeshift table, spreading the map out. "Then we don't give them the chance. We strike first, hit them where they least expect it."

Margaret's strategic mind kicked into gear. "A surprise attack could work, but it's risky. We'll need every advantage we can get. Thomas, gather the captains. We'll need to move fast."

The council of war was a flurry of activity, ideas clashing and merging in a desperate bid to form a plan that could turn the tide. Margaret stood at the forefront, her leadership and unwavering determination never more critical. "We fight not just for the land beneath our feet," she reminded them, "but for the future we believe in. Today, more than ever, we need to stand together. We are not just soldiers, but [specific term], and we will not be defeated."

The plan was daring—a preemptive strike at dawn, utilizing the cover of the misty morning to surprise the advancing British forces. James and Thomas would lead the main assault, while Margaret coordinated a secondary force to cut off any retreat.

As the commanders dispersed to ready their troops, Margaret pulled James aside. "Be careful," she implored, the unspoken fears for his safety evident in her eyes.

James clasped her hand, his resolve clear. "Always. You do the same. We'll get through this, together."

When it came, the battle was a cacophony of noise, smoke, and confusion. Margaret and James fought with a desperate ferocity, their forces pushing against the British with all the might of their convictions behind them. Yet, war cared little for bravery or belief. Amidst the fray, a beloved figure, fighting valiantly by Margaret's side, fell—a blow that would leave scars far more profound than any sword could wield. The scene was a [specific description of the battlefield], a testament to the chaos and danger of war.

As the smoke cleared and the cost of their daring became apparent in the aftermath, Margaret and James found themselves amidst a battlefield that was both a testament to their resolve and a graveyard of their hopes. The victory was theirs, but the taste was bitter with loss.

Gathering the remnants of their forces, they returned to camp, the silence among them a stark contrast to the battle's roar. There, in the quiet that followed, they came together, not just as leaders but as comrades in grief, sharing the burden of loss and the unspoken vow to honor the sacrifice of those who had fallen.

In the flickering light of the campfires, Margaret and James shared a moment of profound connection, their shared grief a bond that transcended words. There had never been a more bitter price for freedom. Yet, they found the fortitude to face each new day with a shared determination to keep fighting for the sake of those who had died and the future they had always imagined.

In the burgeoning light of dawn, the camp was alive with a tense energy as soldiers and strategists alike readied themselves for the confrontation that lay ahead. Margaret moved among the ranks, her presence a reassuring beacon to the anxious faces she passed. Beside her, James issued orders with calm authority, his demeanor instilling confidence in their troops.

The pair made their way to the command tent, where a map of the surrounding area lay spread across a makeshift table dotted with markers representing both their forces and the advancing British. The air was thick with anticipation, each breath silently acknowledging the day's weight.

"Margaret," James said, his finger tracing a path through a densely wooded area on the map, "if we can lead them here, the terrain works in our favor. It's narrow, limits their numbers."

Margaret leaned over the map, considering. "And if we position archers here," she pointed to a ridge overlooking the path, "and here, we can catch them in a crossfire."

Their strategy session was interrupted by a runner, who burst into the tent, his chest heaving. "The British... they're moving faster than expected. They'll be upon us within the hour."

The news hit like a cold wave, rushing them into immediate action. Margaret and James exchanged a look, a silent agreement passing between them. There was no more time for planning; now was the moment to act.

"Sound the alarm," Margaret commanded, her voice cutting through the morning's quiet. "Get everyone to their positions. This is it."

As the camp sprung into action, James turned to Margaret. "We knew this day would come. I can't imagine facing it with anyone but you."

Margaret nodded, her resolve firm. "Together, we've weathered worse. Today will be no different."

They parted ways then, each to lead their respective charges. The air filled with the sounds of preparation: the clanking of armor, the murmur of prayers, and the steady beat of boots on the earth as soldiers took their positions.

Margaret found herself at the head of a column, her heart

steady despite the adrenaline coursing through her veins. She raised her sword, her voice carrying over the assembled troops. "Today, we fight not just for our lives, but for the future of our nation. Stand strong, stand together. For liberty!"

Her words were met with a resounding cheer, a unified cry that echoed through the trees and across the fields.

As the British forces came into view, a sea of red uniforms and gleaming bayonets, the air became charged with the imminent clash. James, leading a flank, caught Margaret's eye across the distance, a shared moment of determination amidst the chaos.

The battle erupted with fury, the sound of musket fire and clashing swords filling the air. Margaret fought with grace and ferocity that inspired those around her, her every move driven by her belief in their cause.

But war, in its indiscriminate cruelty, spared no one. Amidst the fray, a figure dear to both Margaret and James fell, their sacrifice a stark testament to the battle's brutality. The loss was a gut-wrenching blow; their names whispered like a benediction, a promise to remember and honor their fight.

As the dust settled and the sounds of battle faded, Margaret and James found themselves side by side once more, surveying the aftermath. The victory was theirs, but the joy of it was overshadowed by the cost. Together, they mourned, their shared grief a testament to the bonds formed in the heat of battle, bonds that were both a source of strength and a painful reminder of all that had been lost.

Margaret and James's connection deepened in the quiet that followed amidst the weary troops and the somber task of tending to the wounded and fallen. They stood together, not just as leaders but as pillars of a cause that had demanded everything from them. Their resolve, forged in the crucible of loss and sacrifice, was unbroken, a beacon for all who looked to them for guidance and hope.

They knew the fight for liberty was far from over. But at that moment, amidst the pain and loss, they found solace in their unity, a reminder that they were not alone in their struggle. Together, they faced the dawn of a new day, their hearts heavy but their spirits undeterred, ready to continue fighting for a future where freedom was more than a dream.

In the aftermath of the battle, the camp was a tableau of triumph shadowed by loss. The victory had been hard-won, the cost etched in the faces of Margaret, James, and every soul who had stood in defiance against the encroaching British forces. As they moved among the ranks, their presence offered solace to the weary and heartbroken, their words a balm to those who had witnessed too much.

Margaret paused beside a young soldier, his arm bandaged, his eyes hollow with the sights of war. "You fought bravely today," she said, her voice soft yet carrying the weight of her position. "Your courage has not gone unnoticed."

The soldier looked up, a flicker of pride igniting in his gaze. "We fight for freedom, ma'am. For a future where such battles are but memories."

James, overhearing, joined them. "And fight we will, until that day comes." His affirmation was more than a promise; it was a vow, a shared mission that bound them all.

As evening fell, Margaret and James found themselves at the edge of the camp, looking out over the land that had borne witness to their struggle. The setting sun cast long shadows, turning the battlefield into a landscape of somber beauty.

"It never gets easier, does it?" James broke the silence, his voice heavy with the day's toll.

Margaret shook her head, her eyes not leaving the horizon. "No. But our resolve must never waver. Not when so much is at stake."

They stood silently, the weight of leadership and the pain of loss a shared burden. Yet, in this moment of quiet reflection, there was also an unspoken understanding, a recognition of the strength they drew from one another.

"Today, we mourn," Margaret finally said, facing James. "But tomorrow, we continue the fight—for those we've lost, those who still stand, and for the generations yet to come."

James nodded, his resolve mirroring hers. "Together, Margaret. Always."

The urgency in Thomas's voice was evident as he reported, "The British are regrouping," interrupting their conversation. "We've won the battle, but the war is far from over."

Margaret and James exchanged a determined look, the fire of their commitment undimmed by the prospect of continued conflict. "Then we prepare," Margaret stated, her voice laced with command. "We've shown them our strength today. We'll show them our resilience tomorrow."

As they returned to the heart of the camp, the flames of the campfires casting a warm glow against the gathering dusk, their thoughts were with their people. The night would be spent planning, reinforcing their defenses, and readying their strategies for the challenges ahead.

For all its weariness, the camp was alive with a sense of purpose. The soldiers, the strategists, and the leaders shared a bond forged in the heat of battle. This bond was as much about the fight for independence as it was about belief in a cause greater than themselves.

Margaret and James, at the center of this unified spirit, were not just leaders but symbols of the resilience and hope that drove the rebellion forward. Their actions, sacrifices, and unwavering commitment to the cause were the heart of the struggle for liberty. They were a beacon for all who dared dream of a future free from tyranny.

The challenge ahead was evident as they met with their top advisors to strategize the next steps. But so, too, was their determination to overcome it, to forge ahead in the face of adversity, united by a shared vision of liberty and justice. The future had many unknowns, but one thing was sure: they would fight, stand united, and pay whatever it took for liberty.

As the last light of day faded into the embrace of twilight, the camp settled into a somber quietude, the kind of silence that speaks volumes. Around the campfires, the glow illuminated the faces of those who had fought, those who had lost, and those who dared to hope amidst the shadows of war. Margaret and James, their figures silhouetted against the flickering light, stood a moment longer at the edge of the camp, their thoughts a shared reflection on the day's trials and triumphs.

The battle had taken its toll, not just in the lives lost but in the reminder of the high stakes of their struggle for freedom. Yet, as they turned to look back at the faces of their comrades—their fellow revolutionaries who had become like family—their spirits were buoyed by the indomitable will that pulsed through the camp. Everyone there, from the youngest runner to the most seasoned soldier, was united by a common cause: the pursuit of liberty. This dream was worth every hardship and every sacrifice.

Margaret broke the silence, her voice steady and infused with a resolve that mirrored the flames before them. "Today, we have paid a heavy price. But let this victory remind us why we fight, not just for the land we stand on, but for the future we build together."

James nodded, his gaze meeting those of their followers. "Our journey is far from over, and there will be more challenges ahead. But together, we are unbreakable. We draw strength from each other, from our shared losses and our united hopes."

They joined their comrades around the fire, the warmth a small comfort against the chill of the night. Stories were shared, memories of the fallen honored, and vows renewed. At this moment, they were not just a band of rebels but architects of a future yet to be realized, warriors for a cause that transcended the individual.

As the night deepened, Margaret and James, surrounded by their faithful companions, looked up at the stars. The constellations, ancient and unyielding, bore witness to their resolve. They knew the road ahead would be perilous, but the fire that burned within them—a fire kindled by the dream of liberty—would light their way through the darkest of times.

The chapter of their struggle closed with the night, but the flame of their resolve burned ever brighter. For Margaret, James, and all who stood with them, the fight for freedom was more than a battle against tyranny; it was a covenant with the future, a promise to forge a nation where liberty and justice were not just ideals but realities for all.

In the quiet solidarity of that night, under the watchful gaze of the stars, they found not just the courage to continue but the assurance that their cause was just, their spirits unbroken. Together, they faced the dawn of a new day, ready to write the next chapter in their quest for liberty, guided by the unwavering flame of their shared conviction.

CHAPTER **13**

Shadows and Ashes

In the cool embrace of dawn, with the camp still shrouded in the remnants of night's shadow, Margaret, the leader of the rebellion, and James, her trusted advisor, convened a council with their most trusted advisors. The air was thick with the anticipation of decisions that could alter the course of their struggle. Despite the recent victory, the weight of loss lingered, a somber reminder of the cost that came with each hard-won battle.

Margaret initiated the discussion, her voice resolute despite the fatigue that edged her features. "The British are regrouping faster than we anticipated. We've intercepted dispatches that suggest a counterattack is imminent."

James, standing beside her, unfolded a map across the table. "Our scouts have confirmed movement to the north. If we don't act now, we risk being outflanked."

The room hummed with the murmur of strategy and concern, each leader contributing insights and suggestions. The air was heavy with the scent of [specific scent], a reminder of the long hours they had spent in this room. Amidst these moments, it was clear that their collective determination was made up of individual courage.

133

A figure at the back of the tent stepped forward, her presence commanding attention despite her youth. Anna, a brilliant strategist who had risen quickly through the ranks, pointed to a narrow pass on the map. "If we can lead them here, we can use the terrain to our advantage. It's risky, but it might be our best chance to diminish their numbers."

Margaret and James exchanged a glance, a silent conversation passing between them. "Prepare your units," Margaret instructed, her decision clear. "We move at dusk. Anna, your plan will lead us tonight."

As the council disbanded, James lingered, his gaze fixed on the map. "Margaret, are you certain about this? It's a bold move," he voiced his concern, his voice tinged with worry.

Margaret met his gaze, her determination unwavering. "It's precisely because it's bold that we have a chance. We've always known this fight wouldn't be won by playing it safe."

The day wore on, a tense prelude to the night's endeavor. Margaret and James spent the hours in preparation, rallying their forces and reinforcing the sense of unity that had become their greatest strength. Amidst the clatter of weapons and the steady march of feet, their voices rose, not just as commanders but as leaders who shared the burden of every life under their command, fostering a sense of belonging and camaraderie.

As dusk fell, casting long shadows across the camp, the rebels moved out, a silent procession of shadows and resolve. The narrow pass loomed ahead, its darkness a mirror to the uncertainty of their path. Yet, in the hearts of Margaret, James, and every soul who marched with them, there was a light that no darkness could diminish—the light of hope, of belief in a cause greater than themselves. Their footsteps echoed in the silence, a steady rhythm that spoke of their determination and courage.

The ambush was set with meticulous care, and every rebel knew their role. Margaret and James, at the forefront of the operation, waited under the trees, the tension a tangible presence among them.

The first signs of the British forces came as a low rumble, the march of feet, and the clank of armor growing louder with each passing moment. Margaret's hand found James's in the darkness, a brief touch that spoke volumes of the trust and shared destiny that bound them.

The battle raged, a tempest of steel and fire, and when the dawn broke, it revealed a scene of stark contrasts-victory and loss, shadows and ashes. The rebels had prevailed, their bravery shining through the darkness. Margaret and James fought side by side, their leadership inspiring their forces to fight with a courage that defied their numbers.

The battle raged, a tempest of steel and fire, and when the dawn broke, it revealed a scene of stark contrasts—victory and loss, shadows and ashes. The rebels had prevailed, but the cost was etched in the weary lines of their faces and the silence that fell upon the pass. Margaret and James, their hearts heavy with the weight of the fallen, could not help but feel a mix of relief and sorrow. Each victory was a step closer to their goal, but it came at a high price.

As they tended to the wounded and honored the fallen in the aftermath, Margaret and James found solace in knowing their fight was not in vain. Each sacrifice, each moment of courage, brought them closer to the dream of a free nation. They had lost [specific number or names of comrades], each one a dear friend and a brave soul. Their absence was a painful reminder of the price they were paying for freedom.

The day ended not with triumph but with a quiet reflection on the costs of liberty. Amidst the shadows and ashes, Margaret and James stood together, their resolve as strong as ever.

They knew the road ahead would be fraught with more challenges. Still, they faced it as they always had—united with the unwavering belief that freedom was a cause worth fighting for, a cause that resonated deeply with every soul in the rebellion, no matter the cost.

In the quiet aftermath of the battle, as the sun climbed higher, casting light upon the stark reality of the night's events, Margaret and James began the solemn task of recovery and reflection amidst the remnants of their forces. The victory had been theirs, but the landscape told its own story of sacrifice and loss, a tangible reminder of the cost of their cause.

Gathered around a small fire, the leaders of the rebellion, weary and somber, shared a moment of silence for those they had lost. It was a necessary pause, a chance to honor the bravery and sacrifice of their fallen comrades before the mantle of leadership demanded their focus once more.

"We can't let their sacrifices be in vain," James finally broke the silence, his voice carrying a mix of resolve and sorrow. "We need to strengthen our position, ensure this victory turns the tide in our favor."

Margaret nodded, her expression somber yet determined. "We'll need to send word to our allies, rally more support. The British will come at us with everything they have after this."

The discussion turned to logistics and the need for reinforcements and supplies. Still, an underlying current of grief could not be ignored. Each decision was weighted with the memory of the night before, each strategy a testament to the ongoing struggle for freedom and survival.

As the meeting dispersed, Margaret looked over the camp, her thoughts heavy. Thomas approached, but his usual confidence was now tempered by the events of the battle.

"Margaret, we've intercepted another set of dispatches," he said, handing her a small bundle of papers. "It seems the British are not as scattered as we hoped. They're planning a counteroffensive, and soon."

Margaret scanned the documents, her mind racing through scenarios and countermeasures. "We'll need to be ready," she said, the weight of command settling upon her shoulders again. "Gather the captains. We have work to do."

But it was not just the threat of the British that occupied her thoughts. Among the papers was a letter, a personal correspondence from a British officer that spoke of the war's toll on the battlefield and the hearts and minds of those who fought. It was a poignant reminder that their enemies were not so different from themselves, each soldier a person with their own hopes and fears.

"James," Margaret said later as they stood alone, the letter in her hand. "This war... it's changing us. I fear for what we might become if it drags on much longer."

James took the letter, reading it in the dimming light. "We fight to end this war, Margaret. To build a world where such conflicts are a thing of the past. But we must never lose sight of our humanity, of the reasons why we fight."

Their conversation then turned to the future and the nation they hoped to build after the conflict. It was a future filled with uncertainty but also with hope—a hope that their sacrifices would lead to a lasting peace, to a freedom that would endure for generations to come.

As the day turned into night, Margaret and James stood united by their resolve, with campfires flickering like beacons in the darkness. The path ahead was fraught with danger, but they faced it as they always had—together, with the courage of their convictions and the unshakable belief that the cause of liberty was worth any price.

The war was far from over, and the shadows of conflict stretched long across the land. But in the hearts of Margaret, James, and all who stood with them, the flames of hope burned bright, casting light into the darkness and forging a path toward a future forged in the ideals of freedom and justice for all.

In the hushed aftermath of the battle, as the first light of dawn began to lift the shadows from the field, Margaret and James, accompanied by their weary but resilient band of rebels, surveyed the cost of their audacity. The air was thick with the scent of spent gunpowder and the earthy tang of blood-soaked soil, a stark testament to the night's ferocity.

"We held them," James murmured, his voice a mix of relief and sorrow as he stepped over the remnants of the conflict. "But at what cost?"

Margaret's gaze lingered on the faces of the fallen, each a story cut tragically short. "Every life given was a sacrifice for our cause," she replied, her voice steady but her eyes betraying the weight of her grief. "We owe it to them to keep fighting, to make sure their sacrifices were not in vain."

As they moved among their people, offering comfort and commendation, a young soldier approached, her expression somber yet resolute. "Commander," she addressed Margaret, "we've captured a British officer. He might have information."

Margaret nodded, her mind shifting to the strategic implications. "Take us to him."

The captured officer, a young man with the proud bearing of the British military, was held in a makeshift brig. Despite his predicament, his demeanor was defiant.

James, ever the tactician, began the interrogation. "Your forces were caught off guard. Tell us, what are your commanders planning next?"

The officer met James's gaze with a cool, measured look. "Do you think me so easily broken? I'll not betray my comrades."

Margaret stepped forward, her approach softer, more probing. "It's not about betrayal. It's about ending this conflict with as few lives lost as possible. Help us understand, and perhaps we can find a way to peace."

A flicker of uncertainty crossed the officer's face, a crack in his resolve that Margaret quickly noted. Yet, an urgent message arrived before he could reply, drawing their attention away.

Thomas burst into the room, his face etched with concern. "We've spotted another British unit, larger than the last. They're moving fast, likely seeking retribution for tonight's loss."

The news hit like a cold wave, forcing Margaret and James to quickly recalibrate their plans. The captured officer, momentarily forgotten, watched as they transitioned into leaders of war once more, their resolve unshaken by the looming threat.

Margaret turned to the officer, and her decision was made. "You'll be treated fairly and returned to your people. We seek no further bloodshed."

As they prepared to face this new challenge, Margaret and James gathered their commanders, faces lit by torches, a beacon of determination amidst the uncertainty.

"We'll meet them head-on," James declared, his voice

ringing with command. "But we'll do it on our terms, using the knowledge we've gained to outmaneuver them."

Standing beside him, Margaret added, "This is more than a battle for territory; it's a fight for the heart of our nation. Remember who we are and what we stand for."

The resolve in her voice galvanized those around her, a rallying cry that steeled them for the confrontation ahead. As they dispersed to ready their forces, Margaret and James's bond stood as a pillar of strength, their shared leadership a guiding light in the tumult of revolution.

As they readied themselves for what was to come in the quiet before the storm, Margaret and James shared a moment of reflection. "No matter what happens," James said, his hand finding Margaret's, "we stand together."

Margaret squeezed his hand in return, a silent vow of unity and purpose. "Together," she affirmed, her gaze fixed on the horizon, where the first signs of the approaching British forces could be seen. "For liberty, for our future."

The stage was set for a confrontation that would test their resolve, strategies, and the fabric of their burgeoning nation. But in the hearts of Margaret, James, and all who stood with them, the flame of rebellion burned brighter than ever, a beacon against the shadows and ashes of war.

As the early warnings of the approaching British forces reached the rebel camp, a sense of urgency swept through the ranks. Margaret and James, with the weight of command resting heavily upon them, marshaled their forces with a calm efficiency that belied their racing hearts.

In the hush of the pre-dawn hours, they met once more in the strategy tent, poring over maps illuminated by the flickering light of lanterns. Anna, who had repeatedly proven her mettle, joined them, and her keen insight into enemy movements was invaluable.

"We have to use the terrain to our advantage," Anna suggested, pointing to a series of ridges that could cover their archers. "If we can draw them into the valley, their numbers won't count for as much."

James nodded in agreement. "It's our best shot. We'll need to be quick and precise. A well-timed volley could turn the tide in our favor."

Margaret, who had been listening intently, finally spoke. "Let's make sure our communication lines are secure. We can't afford any missteps. James, take a contingent of our best marksmen to the ridges. Anna and I will lead the main force into the valley."

Their plan was daring, a high-stakes gamble that relied on precision and the element of surprise. As they dispersed to set their plan into motion, the camp buzzed with activity, the air charged with anticipation and the unspoken fears of what the day might bring.

James, leading his group to the ridges, moved with purpose, his mind focused on the task at hand. The weight of responsibility for the lives of his men was a familiar burden, one he bore with a solemn dignity.

Meanwhile, Margaret and Anna coordinated the positioning of their forces in the valley, ensuring that every soldier knew their role in the upcoming confrontation. The first light of dawn was just beginning to touch the sky, casting a pale glow over the scene of impending battle.

As the British forces appeared on the horizon, a sea of red moving steadily towards them, Margaret raised her hand, signaling her troops to hold their positions. The tension was palpable, the valley's silence a stark contrast to the thunderous march of their adversaries.

Then, with a nod from Margaret, the valley erupted into chaos. Arrows rained down from the ridges, finding their marks with deadly precision, while the rebels in the valley charged with a ferocious cry that echoed off the hills.

The battle was fierce, a whirlwind of steel and determination. Margaret and Anna fought side by side, their swords a blur as they parried and struck with a grace born of necessity. All around them, their comrades battled with the desperation of those fighting for everything they held dear.

In the midst of the fray, a shout from the ridge caught Margaret's attention. Squinting against the light, she saw James directing his marksmen, their arrows a deadly shower upon the British ranks. His presence, steadfast and commanding, filled her with fierce pride and deep affection.

The battle raged on, the outcome hanging in the balance until, at last, the British lines began to falter. Pressed on all sides and harried by the relentless assault from above, their formation broke, retreating in disarray.

As the last of the enemy forces vanished from sight, Margaret, James, and their rebels let out a ragged cheer, the sound mingling with the sighs of relief and the mourning of losses yet to be counted. They had won the day, but the victory was bittersweet, the cost written in the shadows and ashes of the battlefield.

Gathering their wounded, the rebels took stock of their triumph and losses. Margaret and James found each other in the aftermath, their eyes meeting in a silent exchange that spoke volumes. They had weathered another storm together, strengthening their bond in the crucible of conflict.

Yet, even as they took a moment to breathe, mourn, and celebrate, the knowledge that the war was far from over lingered in the air. The shadows of the day's battle may have passed, but the ashes of the conflict would mark their path forward, a constant reminder of the price of liberty.

In the days ahead, they would need to regroup, heal, and plan their next move. But for now, they stood together amidst the remnants of the day's struggle, united in their resolve and commitment to the cause that had brought them together. The fight for freedom would continue, each victory a step towards the dream of a nation forged from the fires of rebellion, a dream that Margaret and James were determined to make a reality.

As the night deepened around the rebel camp, a quiet resolve settled over Margaret and James, standing together amidst the flickering campfires. Their shared gaze upon the gathered fighters reflected a silent promise, a commitment to the cause that had bound them together in this struggle for freedom.

"We've weathered this day," Margaret said, her voice a beacon of strength in the enveloping darkness. "Our journey is far from over, but together, we have the power to change the course of our future."

Looking out over the men and women who had put their faith in them, James felt a surge of pride. "Each challenge we face," he responded, "only strengthens our resolve. We fight for a cause greater than ourselves. For freedom. For a tomorrow filled with hope."

Though softly spoken, their words carried through the camp, inspiring a renewed sense of purpose among their followers. In the quiet before the dawn, there was a palpable sense of unity, a collective belief in the righteousness of their cause.

Margaret turned her attention back to the map before them, tracing potential strategies with a steady hand. "Tomorrow, we plan our next move. The British will not expect us to strike so soon. It's time we take the fight to them, on our terms."

James nodded in agreement, his strategic mind already considering the possibilities. "We'll need to be swift and decisive. Let's gather the commanders at first light. We have a narrow window of opportunity, and we must seize it."

As they prepared for the rest that would fortify them for the days ahead, the camp buzzed with quiet activity. The rebels, each lost in their thoughts or tending to their duties, were united by a common thread of determination and hope. The battles fought were not just for the land they stood on but for the ideals that sparked the flame of rebellion.

In the shared moments of planning and reflection, Margaret and James found not just the strategy for their next encounter but a deeper connection forged in the fires of conflict and the shared dream of a better tomorrow. Their leadership, a blend of courage, wisdom, and unwavering determination, was the beacon that guided their people through the darkness.

As the first light of dawn began to pierce the night sky, casting a soft glow over the encampment, the rebels readied themselves for the challenges ahead. The fight for freedom was an ongoing battle, marked by both loss and triumph. Still, in the hearts of Margaret, James, and all who stood with them, the flame of liberty burned ever bright, illuminating the path toward the dawn of a new day.

CHAPTER 14

Bonds Forged in Battle

Under the cloak of predawn darkness, the rebel camp stirred with a quiet urgency. Margaret and James, their faces illuminated by the soft glow of a lantern, poured over maps and dispatches in their tent, the weight of leadership etched into their expressions. The recent victories had given them precious momentum, but both knew the war was far from over.

"We need to consolidate our forces," Margaret said, tracing a line along a river that snaked through the territory. "If we can secure the bridges here and here, it will give us a strategic advantage, cutting off the British supply lines."

James nodded, his mind racing through the logistics. "Agreed. But we'll need to move quickly. The British won't expect an offensive so soon after our last engagement. Surprise will be on our side."

Their planning was interrupted by a soft knock on the tent flap. Thomas entered a grim set to his jaw. "There's been a development," he announced, his voice tight with concern. "A group of our scouts encountered a British patrol near the eastern ridge. There was a skirmish."

Margaret straightened, her focus sharpening. "Casualties?"

"Minimal, thankfully," Thomas replied. "But one of our own was taken. They're holding him at a garrison nearby."

A tense silence enveloped the tent. The captured scout was one of their best, a young man whose loyalty and courage had proven invaluable time and again.

James broke the silence, his determination clear. "We mount a rescue. Tonight."

Margaret met his gaze, her resolve mirroring his. "We'll need a small team. Stealth is paramount."

The decision made, they moved into action, selecting a handful of their most skilled fighters for the mission. Among them was Anna, whose strategic mind and bravery had earned her a place at their side.

As night deepened, the rescue team gathered at the edge of the camp, shrouded in the shadows of the forest. Margaret addressed them, her voice low but fierce. "Remember, our goal is to retrieve our man and get out without alerting the entire garrison. Speed and silence are your allies."

James added, "Watch each other's backs. We leave no one behind."

The team moved out, melting into the darkness like wraiths. The journey to the British garrison was fraught with danger. Every rustle of leaves and snap of twigs is a potential alarm. Yet, under Margaret and James's leadership, they advanced with a precision that spoke of their training and unity.

Upon reaching the garrison, they found it less fortified than expected, the British seemingly confident in their remote location. Using the cover of darkness, they infiltrated the holding area, neutralizing guards with swift, silent efficiency.

The rescue was executed flawlessly, the scout retrieved from his cell, bewildered but unharmed. As they made their way back to the camp, the first light of dawn began to touch the sky, painting the world in hues of gold and blue.

Their return was met with quiet relief and celebration, the camp embracing their returned comrade like a lost brother found. The success of the mission was a testament not just to their skill and bravery, but to the bonds forged in the crucible of battle- -bonds that held them together, stronger and more resolute than ever.

In the aftermath, as the camp settled once more, Margaret and James shared a moment of quiet reflection. The rescue, while a small victory in the grand scheme of the war, was a poignant reminder of what they were fighting for: not just for land or power, but for each other, for the idea of a community and nation built on the principles of freedom and solidarity.

Their gaze turned to the horizon, where the rising sun heralded the promise of a new day. With each challenge they faced, each battle they fought, the dream of liberty grew clearer, fueled by the courage and sacrifice of those who dared to stand with them. The road ahead was uncertain, but one thing was clear: together, they were forging a future worth fighting for, a future where the bonds of battle were the foundation of their strength and unity.

As the camp awoke to the full light of day, murmurs of the night's daring rescue rippled through the ranks, bolstering the morale of the rebels. The successful return of their comrade was not just a victory; it was a declaration of their resolve, a demonstration of the lengths to which they would go for one another.

Margaret and James, having debriefed with the rescue team, now turned their attention to the broader implications of their actions. They convened with their advisors, and the air in the tent charged with a renewed sense of purpose.

"The rescue last night sent a clear message to the British," James began, his voice firm. "We're not just a ragtag band of rebels; we're a force to be reckoned with."

Margaret nodded, her mind already on the next steps. "And we must capitalize on this momentum. The securing of the bridges, as we planned, becomes even more crucial now. We strike while the iron is hot, disrupt their supply lines, and give ourselves a strategic advantage."

Anna, who had been instrumental in the rescue, spoke up. "The garrison was less guarded than we expected. It's possible they're concentrating their forces elsewhere, maybe preparing for a larger offensive."

Her insight sparked a flurry of strategic planning, maps, and reports scattered across the table as they plotted their next move. The atmosphere was electric, a dynamic blend of strategy and camaraderie that had become the hallmark of their leadership.

As the meeting drew to a close, Margaret addressed her leaders with a clarity that cut through the complexity of their situation. "This war is fought on many fronts, but at its heart, it's about the bonds we forge—in battle, in loss, and in victory. It's those bonds that will see us through to the end."

Later, as Margaret and James walked through the camp, their presence among the rebels was a tangible reminder of the leadership that had guided them through so many trials. Soldiers nodded their respect, and the two leaders took the time to speak with their people, sharing words of encouragement and gratitude.

Their walk took them to the outskirts of the camp, where

the rescued scout, now recovered from his ordeal, awaited them. His gratitude was palpable, his voice steady but filled with emotion. "I owe you my life. I... we all would follow you to the ends of the earth."

Margaret placed a hand on his shoulder, her gaze encompassing the camp and all it represented. "We're in this together. It's not just about following—it's about standing side by side, fighting for the future we believe in."

As the day waned, plans for the assault on the bridges were finalized, each leader and soldier aware of the stakes. The evening brought a sense of unity, a shared meal where laughter and stories flowed freely, a brief respite from the weight of their cause.

Yet, even in these moments of lightness, the resolve that bound them was ever-present, a steady undercurrent that spoke of battles fought and those yet to come. Margaret and James, at the heart of this gathering, were not just commanders but symbols of the hope and determination that drove the rebellion forward.

The night fell, and with it, a quiet determination settled over the camp. Tomorrow would bring new challenges, but for tonight, they found strength in their bonds, in the knowledge that they faced the dawn not as individuals but as a united front, ready to forge ahead in their quest for liberty.

Their shared experiences in combat shaped the story of their fight, which is a moving tribute to the strength of togetherness and the determination of individuals who give their lives for a cause bigger than themselves.

Under the canvas of stars, the rebel camp was a hive of whispered strategy and quiet camaraderie. Margaret and James, having spent the day in the company of their soldiers, now found themselves seated by a modest fire, with Anna and Thomas joining them. The flickering flames cast a warm glow on their faces, softening the harsh lines drawn by days of relentless planning and combat.

"We've proven our strength, not just in the field, but in the spirit of our people," Margaret reflected, her gaze flitting across the camp where small groups gathered, sharing stories and sustenance. "The bridges are our next objective. Securing them will not only cripple the British supply lines but also bolster our position significantly."

James nodded, his eyes on the map sprawled between them. "The element of surprise has served us well so far. We strike at dawn, fast and hard. Anna, your insight into the British patrols has been invaluable. We'll need your eyes on this again."

Anna, whose keen strategies had saved many lives, leaned in. "I've already sent scouts to monitor their movements. We'll know their patterns by nightfall. This," she tapped a finger on the map, "is where we hit them hardest."

Thomas, ever the voice of cautious wisdom, chimed in, "And we mustn't underestimate their response. The British will retaliate, and we need to be prepared for that. Our defenses must be as strong as our offense."

The conversation flowed seamlessly from tactics to logistics, each leader contributing their expertise, their unity a testament to the bonds forged in the heart of rebellion. It was during these moments, in the quiet before the storm, that the true depth of their commitment to each other and their cause was most palpable.

As the meeting drew to a close, Margaret stood, her gaze sweeping over her trusted commanders. "Tonight, we rest. Tomorrow, we fight—not just for the bridges, but for every soul yearning for freedom. Our resolve is our weapon, and it is unbreakable."

The group disbanded, each to their own preparations, leaving Margaret and James by the dying fire. In the silence that followed, the weight of leadership lay heavy upon them, yet it was a burden they bore willingly, strengthened by their shared purpose.

James broke the quiet, "You know, Margaret, there was a time I doubted we could ever make a difference. But standing here, with you, with all of them," he gestured to the camp, "I've never been more certain of our path."

Margaret met his gaze, a soft smile playing on her lips. "We're writing history, James. And it's not just the battles that define us, but the moments between—the laughter, the tears, and the unwavering belief in a cause greater than ourselves."

Together, they watched the embers fade, the darkness around them not just a veil for the night but a canvas for the dawn of a new day. A day that would bring its own challenges, its own battles. But for now, in this moment of calm, they found solace in the bonds they shared, bonds not easily broken, forged in the fires of battle and the quiet resolve of shared dreams.

The night deepened, wrapping the camp in a blanket of anticipation and resolve. Tomorrow's battle loomed large, but so too did the hope for what each victory brought them closer to achieving—a free nation born from the ashes of conflict and the unyielding spirit of those who dared to dream of liberty.

As the first light of dawn tinged the sky with shades of pink and gold, the camp stirred into action, the air charged with a palpable sense of purpose. Margaret and James, alongside Anna and Thomas, moved through the ranks, their presence bolstering the spirits of their comrades as they prepared for the day's crucial endeavor.

"Remember, speed and silence," James reminded a group of soldiers, adjusting the grip on his own weapon. "We strike swiftly, secure the bridges, and retreat before they can mount a counteroffensive."

Margaret, standing atop a small rise, addressed a larger assembly, her voice cutting through the morning chill. "Today's action is pivotal. The bridges represent more than just strategic points; they symbolize the connections we're fighting to establish—a united front against tyranny. Let's show them the strength of our resolve."

Nods of agreement and determined shouts met her words, the rebels rallying around the cause with renewed vigor.

As the attack groups formed up, Anna approached Margaret and James, a map in hand. "The scouts report minimal activity along the river. It seems we've caught them off guard, but we should expect reinforcements once they realize what we're attempting."

Thomas, overhearing, joined the huddle, his brow furrowed. "We'll need to be quick, then. Establish control and fortify our position as much as possible before they can respond."

The plan was set, and the groups dispersed, melting into the forest with practiced stealth. Margaret and James, leading one of the assault teams, shared a brief look—a silent exchange of trust and shared determination—before plunging into the shadowy underbrush.

The journey to the bridges was tense, every rustle of leaves and snap of twigs underfoot echoing like thunder in their ears. Yet, under Margaret and James's leadership, the rebels moved with cohesion and discipline that spoke of their deep bond and mutual respect.

Reaching the first bridge without detection, they found

it lightly guarded, the British seemingly unaware of the impending threat. With a swift, coordinated assault, they overpowered the guards, securing the bridge with minimal resistance.

"Secure the perimeter," James ordered, his eyes scanning the horizon for any sign of British reinforcements. "We don't have much time."

Margaret, meanwhile, worked alongside her team to fortify their new position, setting up defenses that would hold long enough for them to achieve their objective. "Every moment counts," she reminded her team. "Let's make sure this victory can stand against whatever they throw at us next."

The operation was a testament to their planning and the unshakeable will of the rebels. As reports came in of similar successes at the other targeted bridges, a wave of cautious optimism swept through Margaret and James's ranks.

Yet, their celebration was cut short by the distant sound of bugles—the call to arms from a British battalion roused to action by the sudden threat to their supply lines.

"They're coming," Anna reported, joining Margaret and James at the forefront of the defense. "But we're ready for them."

As the British forces emerged from the forest, the rebels braced for the onslaught, their resolve hardened by the knowledge of what was at stake. The battle that ensued was fierce, a chaotic symphony of steel and gunfire that tested the limits of their courage and ingenuity.

Margaret and James fought side by side, their leadership a beacon in the tumult. With every command and countermove, they demonstrated the depth of their commitment to the cause and to each other, their partnership a force to be reckoned with.

The bonds forged in battle were their greatest strength, the trust and unity among the rebels a counterpoint to the division and tyranny they opposed. As the conflict raged, it became clear that these bonds were not easily broken—that together, they were more than a match for the challenges before them.

In the heart of the struggle, amidst the shadows and ashes of war, the rebels found not just the will to fight but the hope for a future shaped by their shared vision of freedom and justice. The battle for the bridges was more than a tactical victory; it was a declaration of their unyielding spirit, a testament to the bonds forged in the heat of battle.

As the night deepened around the rebel camp, a palpable sense of unity and determination settled over those gathered. The fire had dwindled to embers, casting a soft glow that barely pierced the darkness, mirroring the quiet resolve in each heart and soul present. Margaret and James, their plans laid and their spirits buoyed by the solidarity of their comrades, stood up from their place by the fire, their silhouettes blending into the night.

The camp, alive with the whispered conversations of those who had come to call this rebellion their home, began to quiet as soldiers and strategists alike sought rest in preparation for the dawn. The air was thick with the promise of action, the anticipation of what the morning would bring—a crucial strike that could shift the tide in their favor.

Margaret, her gaze sweeping over the camp one last time before retiring, felt the weight of leadership and the warmth of belonging. This band of rebels, this family forged in the crucible of conflict, was ready to stand against the might of an empire united by a shared dream of freedom.

James, walking beside her, shared a quiet confidence. "Tomorrow, we show the world the strength of our resolve," he said, his voice low but filled with an unwavering belief in their cause and in the people who fought for it.

Together, they stepped into the quiet of their tent, the fabric walls a thin barrier against the chill of the night but a sanctuary for two hearts beating as one. Outside, the camp slept, the rebels resting under the watchful eyes of sentries, the silence a testament to the calm before the storm.

In these hours before dawn, the rebellion was a breath held tight, a force gathered in anticipation of the moment it would burst forth. The strategies laid out, the bonds fortified, and the resolve steeled—each element was a thread in the tapestry of their cause, woven tightly to withstand the trials of the day ahead.

As the first light of dawn began to seep into the sky, painting the horizon with hues of gold and crimson, it heralded not just a new day but the next chapter in their fight for liberty. The rebels would wake to face their challenges head-on, guided by the bonds forged in battle and the shared vision that had brought them together.

In this moment of quiet before the battle, the camp was a symbol of hope, a beacon for all who yearned for freedom. As the light grew stronger, so did the determination of those ready to fight for a future where liberty was not just a dream but a reality forged in the bonds of battle.

CHAPTER 15

Echoes of War

As the first light of dawn crept over the horizon, casting a pale glow over the rebel encampment, Margaret stood atop a small rise, her heart pounding with a mix of anticipation and anxiety. The land that had become both their battlefield and home was quiet, the silence of the morning punctuated only by the distant calls of waking birds and the soft rustle of leaves in the gentle morning breeze. Beside her, James joined, his face a mirror of her emotions, sharing in the moment of calm before the day's demands pressed in.

"The British will be regrouping after our last engagement," James said, his voice low, reflecting the strategic mindset that had served them well thus far. We need to anticipate their next move."

Margaret nodded, her eyes scanning the landscape as she considered their options. "Our victory at the bridges has given us a strategic advantage, but it won't hold them off for long. We need to fortify our position, make sure we're ready when they strike again."

The sound of approaching footsteps turned their attention to Anna, who came with a sense of urgency. In her hand, she held a cluster of dispatches, the early morning light glinting off the seal of their makeshift intelligence network.

"We've intercepted messages," Anna announced as she reached them, her voice tinged with urgency. "The British are planning a significant offensive, sooner than we expected. They're not just aiming to reclaim lost ground; they want to end this rebellion once and for all. We must act swiftly."

The gravity of the news hung heavily in the air, a stark reminder of the ever-present threat looming over their fight for freedom, intensifying the sense of urgency and the high stakes of their battle.

"We'll need to call a council," Margaret decided swiftly, the leader in her rising to meet the challenge head-on. "Gather everyone. We have little time to prepare, and every moment counts."

As they returned to the camp's heart, the day began to come alive around them. Rebels stirred from their makeshift shelters, the clatter of morning routines blending with the murmur of voices as news of the impending council spread.

The air was thick with tension in the council tent as Margaret, James, Anna, and their advisors convened; the intercepted dispatches laid bare before them. The room was a blend of determination and concern as they poured over the messages, plotting their course of action.

"Our defenses are strong, but we can't underestimate the British forces," James stated, his gaze locked on the map before them. "We need to be strategic, use our knowledge of the land to our advantage."

Her mind racing through possibilities, Margaret added, "And we need to protect the civilians. Their safety is paramount. Evacuations need to be planned for those in the direct path of the offensive."

The discussion evolved into a flurry of planning, each leader contributing their expertise to form a cohesive strategy. Amidst the talk of logistics and tactics, the underlying current of unity and resolve was palpable, a testament to the unbreakable bonds forged in the heat of shared struggle.

As the council adjourned, with tasks delegated and plans set into motion, Margaret and James shared a moment of quiet resolve. The echo of war was a constant in their lives, a reminder of the sacrifices and ones still to come. Yet, in each other, they found the strength to face the uncertainty ahead, their commitment to the cause and each other unwavering.

The camp was a hive of activity, with every member of the rebellion contributing to the preparations for the impending British offensive. In every action, in every determined face, the echoes of war rang loud, a call to arms that was met with the unwavering courage and resilience of those who fought not just for their own freedom, but for the future of a nation yet to be born.

The camp was a hive of activity, with every rebellion member contributing to the preparations for the impending British offensive. Amid the hustle, Margaret made her way to the medical tents, where the healers and medics worked tirelessly to prepare for the casualties that war inevitably brought.

"Let's ensure we have enough supplies," Margaret instructed Sarah, a skilled nurse who had become indispensable to the rebel forces. "And set up triage stations at these points," she added, pointing to strategic locations on a map of the camp.

Sarah nodded, her face set in a mask of determined professionalism. "We'll be ready, Margaret. We've trained for this."

Margaret's next stop was the armory, where James oversaw the distribution of weapons and ammunition. The air was thick with the scent of metal and oil, the sound of metal on metal echoing as swords were sharpened and muskets cleaned.

"How are we on supplies?" Margaret asked, her gaze sweeping over the organized chaos.

James looked up a trace of concern in his eyes. "We're managing, but we could always use more. The last raid helped, but if this offensive is as big as we think, we'll need to be judicious with our resources."

Margaret placed a reassuring hand on his arm. "We've faced worse odds. We'll make do, we always do."

Their conversation was cut short by Thomas's arrival, who came bearing news from the scouts: "The British forces are moving faster than anticipated. They could be upon us by nightfall."

The urgency of the situation was not lost on any of them. Margaret turned to address the assembled leaders and soldiers. "This is it," she began, her voice carrying over the din. "We knew this day would come. We've prepared for it, trained for it. Remember, we're not just fighting for survival, but for the very ideals that brought us together. Stand strong, fight with honor, and we will prevail."

Her words seemed to galvanize the troops, and there was a visible shift in their demeanor as they readied themselves for battle. James, standing beside Margaret, nodded in gratitude. "No matter what happens, I'm proud to stand with you," he said, his voice steady.

Margaret offered him a small, determined smile. "And I with you. Together, we'll see this through."

As the day wore on, the tension in the camp grew palpable, the air charged with the anticipation of the coming conflict. Margaret and James spent the remaining hours before the British arrived with their soldiers, offering encouragement, checking on defenses, and ensuring that their plan was executed flawlessly.

The sun began its descent, painting the sky in hues of fire and blood, an ominous backdrop to the battle that loomed. The rebels took their positions, and the camp's silence was a stark contrast to the turmoil that churned within each of them.

Margaret and James found a moment of quiet amidst the chaos. Standing together at the edge of the camp, they watched as the first signs of the British forces appeared on the horizon.

"This is it," James said, his hand finding Margaret's.

"Yes," Margaret replied, her grip firm. "But remember, whatever happens, we fight as one. For freedom, for our future."

As the British forces drew nearer, the echo of war rang out, a clarion call that was met with the resolute hearts and ready arms of those who had chosen to stand against tyranny. The battle that would unfold under the setting sun would be remembered not just for the clash of arms, but for the spirit of a people united in the pursuit of liberty—a spirit that would endure, no matter the cost.

As the British forces advanced, a sea of red uniforms and glinting bayonets under the fading light, the rebels braced for impact. The air was thick with tension, the silence before the storm stretching thin across the lines of determined faces.

Margaret and James stood at the forefront, their presence a beacon of strength for their followers. "Remember, hold the line until the signal, then push forward. We have the advantage of the terrain," Margaret called out, her voice cutting through the quiet with clarity and command.

Beside her, James surveyed the approaching enemy, calculating the moments until their paths would collide. "Stay sharp," he added, his tone steady. "Trust in each other, trust in our cause."

The initial clash was thunderous, the sound of metal on metal, cries of battle, and the roar of gunfire filling the air. Margaret found herself in the thick of the fight, her sword a blur as she parried and struck with lethal precision. Around her, the rebels fought with a ferocity born of desperation and belief in their cause; their actions synchronized in a dance of chaos and determination.

James, leading a contingent to flank the British forces, moved with purpose, his strategies playing out with each step taken. The surprise of their maneuver took the British off guard, their formation faltering under the unexpected assault.

In the midst of the turmoil, Anna directed a group of archers, their arrows raining down upon the enemy from a hidden vantage point. Her commands were calm and precise, each shot contributing to the disarray among the British ranks.

As the battle raged, Thomas rallied the rebels, his voice a rallying cry that spurred them on even as fatigue set in. "For freedom!" he shouted, his words echoing across the battlefield, a reminder of what they were fighting for.

The tide of the battle shifted and turned, moments of triumph shadowed by loss. Margaret felt the sting of a blade graze her arm, a sharp reminder of the stakes at play. Yet, she pressed on, her resolve unbroken, her actions inspiring those around her.

James, encountering a British officer in the melee, engaged in a duel that was both brutal and balletic. Their swords clashed a test of skill and will that ended with the officer yielding, taken aback by the determination in James's eyes. "Why do you fight so hard for a cause that seems lost?" the officer gasped, defeated.

James's response was simple, yet it held the weight of their entire struggle. "Because it's right. Because even the smallest chance at freedom is worth fighting for."

As dusk turned to night, the battle reached its crescendo. Margaret, spotting an opening in the British lines, seized the moment. "Now!" she cried, signaling the rebels to push forward with renewed vigor.

The final push was a blur of action and adrenaline, the rebels breaking through the British defenses with a combination of strategy and sheer will. When the dust settled, the field was theirs, the British forces retreating into the night, a testament to the resilience and unity of the rebels.

Breathing heavily, Margaret and James regrouped, their eyes meeting in the aftermath. Around them, their people celebrated, though the cost of their victory was not forgotten. The echoes of war rang in their ears, a solemn reminder of the sacrifices made and the battles yet to come.

Yet, in this moment of victory, there was also hope. Hope that their fight for liberty, for a future forged in the fires of rebellion, was not in vain. Together, they faced the challenges ahead, united by the bonds forged in battle, their resolve echoing through the annals of history as a beacon of courage and determination.

The horizon darkened with the advancing British forces, their march a dull thunder rolling over the land. Margaret and James watched, their expressions set in grim determination. Around them, the rebel forces stood ready, a patchwork of resolve woven from their shared convictions and battles fought side by side.

"We hold them at the ridge," James whispered to Margaret, his gaze never leaving the approaching army. "The cannons are in position; when they're in range, we give the signal."

Margaret nodded, her attention split between the battlefield and her people. "And if they break through?" she asked, the possibility hanging between them like a specter.

"We fall back to the secondary line," James responded, his voice steady. "But we won't let it come to that. We have the advantage."

Their whispered strategy was interrupted by a runner, a young boy no more than sixteen, who approached breathlessly. "The eastern flank reports movement, commanders. Looks like they're trying to outflank us."

Margaret's eyes flashed with the strategic acumen that had led them this far. "Signal the flank. Tell them to hold their positions. We can't afford to stretch our lines too thin."

James gave a quick nod to the runner, who dashed off to relay the orders. Turning to Margaret, he said, "This is it, the moment we've prepared for. No matter what happens, know that—"

"—we stand together," Margaret finished for him, a fierce pride shining in her eyes. "Always."

As the British forces neared, the tension among the rebels reached its peak. Then, with a nod from James, the air erupted with the roar of cannons, the first volley tearing into the twilight. The battle for the ridge had begun.

The rebels fought with a desperation born of the knowledge that this ground could not be lost. Margaret and James moved among their forces, their presence a rallying cry that spurred their fighters on. The British, undeterred by the initial resistance, pressed forward, their numbers and discipline a formidable tide.

But the rebels held fast, their defense bolstered by the

strategic placement of their forces and the impassioned fervor with which they fought. For every advance the British made, they were met with a wall of determination, the rebels yielding nothing without a fierce contest.

In the midst of the chaos, Anna led a contingent in a daring sortie, exploiting a weakness in the British flank. Her success provided a brief respite, a momentary shift in the battle's momentum that allowed the rebels to regroup and push back with renewed vigor.

As night fell, the battlefield became a blur of shadows and flashes of gunfire, the din of battle a constant roar. Margaret and James, side by side, fought with a synergy that inspired those around them, their leadership the beacon that guided their forces through the darkness.

In a lull, as both sides momentarily withdrew to reassess, Margaret and James met in the quiet of the forest behind the ridge, the sounds of battle a distant rumble.

"We've held them," James said, his voice rough with exhaustion and smoke. "But they'll regroup. We need to be ready."

Margaret, her face smeared with dirt and blood, nodded. "We will be. Tonight, we've proven that we're more than just a thorn in their side. We're a force to be reckoned with."

Their eyes met, a silent vow passing between them. They would see this through, together, fighting for every dawn that promised freedom.

As they returned to their positions, readying themselves for the battle to resume, the echoes of war rang through the night, a testament to the resilience and courage of those who fought not for glory but for the hope of a better world.

The battle resumed with a ferocity that matched the

desperation of its participants. The British, regrouped and reinforced, launched a renewed assault on the ridge, their numbers seemingly endless in the dim light of the early night. The rebels, weary but resolute, met their advance with a steadfast defense, each soldier fighting with the knowledge that the survival of their cause hung in the balance.

In the thick of the fray, Margaret found herself shoulder to shoulder with her fellow fighters, her sword a blur as she parried and struck with a dancer's grace and a warrior's ferocity. James, not far from her side, directed their forces with shouts that cut through the cacophony, his pistol firing in a steady rhythm.

A sudden movement to her left caught Margaret's attention—a group of British soldiers had found a weak point in their line and were pushing through. "To me!" she cried, rallying a contingent of rebels to her side. Together, they surged towards the breach, Margaret leading the charge with a rallying cry that echoed off the ridge.

The skirmish was intense, a chaotic dance of steel and gunfire. But under Margaret's lead, the rebels managed to repel the advance, sealing the breach and driving the British back once more.

Breathing heavily, Margaret scanned the battlefield, taking stock of the situation. The British forces, though still formidable, showed signs of weariness, their movements less coordinated, their attacks less synchronized.

James joined her, his expression grim but determined. "We're holding them, but we can't keep this up indefinitely. We need to force a retreat."

Margaret nodded, her mind racing through their options. "If we can push them back to the river, the terrain will work against them. It's our best chance to break their assault."

James agreed, and together, they quickly formulated a plan. Rallying their forces for a concerted push, they aimed to exploit the British's momentary disarray.

The counterattack was a gamble, but it was one born of necessity. With a fierce cry, Margaret and James led their troops forward, the rebels channeling their fatigue and fear into a final, desperate effort.

The British, caught off guard by the sudden aggression, faltered. The rebels, sensing the shift, redoubled their efforts, their cries filling the night as they drove their adversaries back, step by grueling step.

As the British forces neared the river, their retreat became a rout, the once-disciplined soldiers scrambling to escape the relentless pursuit of the rebels.

Finally, as the first hints of dawn began to lighten the eastern sky, the British withdrew across the river, leaving the ridge— and the night's hard-won victory—in the hands of the rebels.

Exhausted but elated, the rebels regrouped on the ridge, the sense of relief palpable in the air. Margaret and James, standing amidst their victorious but battered forces, allowed themselves a moment of quiet satisfaction.

"We've won the night," James said, his voice carrying over the assembled fighters, "but this war is far from over. We must remain vigilant, ready to defend our freedom with the same courage you've all shown today."

Margaret stepped forward, her gaze sweeping over the faces of her comrades, each one a testament to the cost of their struggle. "This victory is yours, each and every one of you. Together, we've proven that our cause is just, our resolve unbreakable. Let this dawn mark not just a victory, but a promise of the future we're fighting to create."

As the sun rose, casting its light over a battlefield strewn with the echoes of war, the rebels took a moment to honor those they had lost, their voices rising in a song of remembrance and hope. The battle had ended, but their fight for liberty, for a nation born from the ashes of conflict, was just beginning.

As the first rays of dawn stretched across the sky, painting the battlefield in hues of gold and crimson, the rebels gathered to tend to their wounded and honor the memory of those who had fallen. The air, though heavy with the scent of gunpowder and loss, also carried a note of solemn victory. Margaret and James moved among their people, offering words of comfort and gratitude, their presence a steady beacon of hope in the aftermath of conflict.

In the quiet that followed the battle's clamor, plans were already taking shape for the future. The victory at the ridge was a significant milestone, yet both leaders knew the path ahead would be fraught with further challenges. They convened with their closest advisors, and their maps and strategies spread before them, not just as tools of war but as blueprints for the nation they aspired to build.

"The British will think twice before underestimating us again," James remarked, his eyes scanning the terrain on the map. "But we must stay vigilant. They will regroup, and we must be prepared to meet them, not just with strength, but with the conviction of our cause."

Margaret, her thoughts aligned with his, added, "Our victory today has given us more than just strategic advantage. It has woven us tighter together, our resolve fortified by shared purpose. We'll need every ounce of that unity in the days to come."

As the day wore on, the camp buzzed with activity, the rebels repairing and rebuilding, their spirits buoyed by the recent victory but tempered by the knowledge of the long road ahead. Stories of bravery and sacrifice from the night's battle were shared, each tale a thread in the fabric of their burgeoning legend.

As evening approached, Margaret and James found a moment of respite, looking out over the camp, their hearts full of both pride and sorrow. The setting sun cast long shadows, the light flickering over the faces of those they led, each one a mirror of resilience and hope.

"We move forward, together," Margaret said, her voice a soft but unwavering promise to those who had placed their trust in her leadership. "Not just for those we've lost, but for those who stand with us now, and for those who will join us in the days to come. This is our covenant, forged in the heat of battle and the quiet of our resolve."

James stood beside her, his presence a testament to their shared journey. "To liberty," he said, the words not just a toast but a vow.

The camp settled into a rhythm of preparation and rest, the rebels drawing strength from their leaders and from one another. As night fell, the stars overhead bore witness to their resolve, the echoes of war a reminder of the price of freedom and the bonds that had been strengthened in its pursuit.

In the quiet of the night, Margaret and James turned their gaze to the horizon, where the challenges of tomorrow awaited. But they, and the rebels they led, would face them as they had faced everything else: together, united by a common cause and the unbreakable bonds forged in the heat of battle. The story of their fight for liberty was far from over, but they were ready for whatever lay ahead, their spirits unyielded, their determination unquenched.

CHAPTER 16

The Fog of War

In the early hours of the morning, with the mist still clinging to the ground and the air thick with the anticipation of what the day might bring, Margaret and James convened with their closest advisors in the heart of the rebel camp. The remnants of last night's victory had been cleared away, but the cost of their success lay heavy on their hearts.

"The British will be reeling from their defeat, but they won't be deterred," James started, his voice carrying a mix of fatigue and determination. "We need to be prepared for their next move. They'll come at us harder and more cunningly than before."

Margaret nodded, her eyes scanning the maps spread out before them. "We've proven we can stand our ground, but we can't afford to get complacent. Our scouts report increased activity to the north. It could be they're planning to flank us through the forest."

Anna, who had been poring over the intercepted dispatches, looked up. "There's more. Our spies in the city have uncovered plans for a supply convoy headed towards the British camp tomorrow at dawn. It's a chance to cut them off, weaken their position."

The room hummed with the weight of the decision. Attacking the convoy would stretch their resources thin, but the opportunity was too great to pass up.

"We'll need to divide our forces," Margaret concluded, her strategy clear. "A smaller contingent to intercept the convoy, while the rest of us fortify our position here. We can't let them catch us off-guard."

Thomas, ever the voice of caution, interjected, "We should consider the fog. It's been heavy these past mornings. It could cover our movements, but it could just as easily conceal theirs."

Margaret considered this, the corners of her mouth turning up slightly. "Then we use it to our advantage. We move under the cover of the fog, silent and swift. It's a risk, but it's one we're trained for."

The group around her nodded, the resolve in the room palpable. They were a unit bound by shared battles and the belief in the cause they fought for.

As the meeting adjourned, Margaret pulled James aside. "Be careful," she said, her voice softer now, the commander giving way to the person beneath. "We can't afford to lose you."

James offered her a small, reassuring smile. "I could say the same to you. We'll get through this, Margaret. Together."

With their plans set, the rebels moved with efficiency, the camp soon bustling with preparation. Weapons were checked, provisions packed, and farewells exchanged with a solemnity born of knowing the dangers that lay ahead.

In the pre-dawn light, as the mist began to roll in from the fields, Margaret stood watching her fighters ready themselves. This was the fog of war, both literal and metaphorical, where clarity was elusive, and the line between friend and foe could blur. Yet, amidst the uncertainty, one thing remained clear: their resolve to fight for freedom, for a future where such battles were no longer necessary.

As the first light of dawn broke over the horizon, piercing the fog with fingers of gold, the rebels moved out, disappearing into the mist like ghosts. The day ahead would be fraught with challenges, but they faced it as they had all others: united, with hearts full of hope and minds set on victory.

The fog lay thick upon the ground as Margaret's contingent, a select group of her most skilled fighters, moved silently towards their objective. The world around them was muffled, sounds dampened, and distances obscured by the dense mist. It was a world rendered in shades of gray, where shapes loomed suddenly from the fog only to dissolve back into the mist just as quickly.

Anna, moving with the quiet confidence of one well-versed in covert operations, gestured for the group to halt. "We're close," she whispered, her eyes scanning the fog-shrouded path ahead. "The convoy should be passing through this valley within the hour. We'll set up here, use the fog as cover."

The rebels quickly but quietly set to work, their movements practiced and precise. Ambush points were established, weapons readied, and the tension of waiting settled over them like another layer of fog.

James, leading another group tasked with fortifying their main position, worked with equal urgency. The fog, while a boon to Margaret and her team, added an element of unpredictability to their defenses. Orders were given in hushed tones, barricades strengthened, and lookouts positioned at key points, their eyes straining through the mist for any sign of an advance.

As the sun climbed higher, its rays began to pierce the fog, thinning it in places but leaving pockets of dense mist that continued to shroud the valley. It was in one such pocket that Margaret's team lay in wait, the silence around them heavy with anticipation.

Suddenly, the muffled sound of wagon wheels and the low murmur of voices broke the silence. The British convoy, a line of supply wagons guarded by red-coated soldiers, emerged from the fog, oblivious to the danger that awaited them.

Margaret exchanged a look with Anna, a nod passing between them. This was the moment. As the lead wagon drew level with their position, the rebels struck. The quiet of the morning was shattered by the roar of gunfire and the clash of steel on steel, the ambush executed with devastating efficiency.

Back at the main camp, James and his defenders heard the distant echoes of the battle, a stark reminder of the cost of their struggle. They remained vigilant, their focus on the forest that bordered their camp, where the fog still lingered, thick and impenetrable.

The battle at the convoy was swift and fierce. Margaret's fighters, leveraging the element of surprise and their intimate knowledge of the terrain, quickly overwhelmed the British soldiers. The wagons, laden with supplies critical to the British effort, secured a significant blow to the enemy's capabilities.

As the fog began to lift, revealing the chaos of the ambushed convoy, Margaret surveyed the scene. Her expression was one of grim satisfaction mixed with sorrow for the inevitable losses of war. "Secure the supplies," she ordered her team. "Treat the wounded, no matter their uniform. We're not like them."

The return to camp was marked by an eerie silence, the fog now burned away by the unforgiving light of day. The victory at the convoy was a hard-won success, but the knowledge of the British retaliation hung over them like a shadow.

James met Margaret upon her return, relief evident in his gaze. "A successful mission," he said, clasping her arm in a gesture of solidarity and support.

Margaret nodded, her eyes weary but resolute. "Yes, but this is just the beginning. The fog may have lifted, but the path ahead remains clouded. We must stay vigilant, ready for whatever comes next."

Together, they turned to face the camp, where their people were already busy preparing for the next challenge. In the aftermath of the fog of war, their resolve was only strengthened; their bonds only deepened. They stood on the brink of the unknown, but they stood together, united in their fight for freedom and the dawn of a new day.

As the rebels integrated the captured supplies into their reserves, the atmosphere in the camp shifted subtly from one of wary anticipation to cautious optimism. The success of the morning's raid had provided not only much-needed resources but also a tangible boost to morale. However, Margaret and James knew that this victory, significant though it might be, was merely a precursor to the larger conflict that loomed on the horizon.

In the relative calm that followed the return to camp, they gathered their leadership once again to assess their situation and plan their next move. The map of the region lay spread out before them, dotted with markers and annotations that represented potential strategies and threats.

"The British won't take this lightly," Thomas remarked, his finger tracing a route on the map that the enemy might use for their counterattack. "We've struck a significant blow, but we should expect a swift response."

Margaret leaned over the map, her eyes sharp. "Then we'll use this time to strengthen our defenses. We've seen today that the fog can be an ally, but we should not rely solely on it for cover."

Anna, who had been quiet, spoke up. "There's also the matter of the local populace. The convoy's capture won't go unnoticed. We should prepare for an influx of refugees or those seeking to join our cause."

Her point was met with nods of agreement. The rebellion, though primarily a military effort, had become a beacon for those disillusioned with British rule. Each victory against the oppressors swelled their ranks with new recruits eager to contribute to the cause of liberty.

James, considering their limited resources and the necessity of maintaining a mobile and effective fighting force, added, "We'll need to organize a system for integrating new recruits quickly—training them, equipping them. Every hand will be needed in the days to come."

As the meeting drew to a close, the leaders dispersed, each to their respective duties, leaving Margaret and James alone with their thoughts. The brief respite allowed them a moment to reflect on the path that had led them here, to the heart of a rebellion that had grown beyond their wildest dreams.

"We're making a difference, Margaret," James said, breaking the silence. "Every day, we're one step closer to our goal."

Margaret looked out over the camp, where men and women worked side by side, united by a common cause. "Yes, we are. But the cost..." Her voice trailed off, a somber note in the midst of their achievements.

James took her hand, his grip firm. "The cost is high, but the cause is just. We fight for freedom, for a future where our children won't have to."

Their shared resolve, tempered by the trials they had faced and strengthened by the bonds they had forged, was a testament to the spirit of the rebellion. As they turned their attention back to the camp, to the people who looked to them for leadership, they did so with a renewed sense of purpose.

The fog of war, with all its uncertainty and peril, lingered. Yet, within the camp, clarity prevailed—the clarity of their mission, of their commitment to each other, and of the future they were determined to build. There were many challenges ahead, but together, they faced them as a united front, ready to weather the storms and emerge victorious in the pursuit of liberty.

The day waned as preparations across the camp intensified, underpinned by the knowledge that time was a luxury they could not afford. The rebels worked with a sense of urgency, fortifying positions, training newly arrived volunteers, and distributing the recently acquired supplies. Margaret and James, ever present among their people, offered guidance and encouragement, their leadership a steady beacon in the tumult of war.

As the sun dipped below the horizon, painting the sky in hues of crimson and gold, a sense of solemnity settled over the camp. The beauty of the dusk belied the tension that gripped every heart, a stark reminder of the contrast between the world they fought for and the reality of their struggle.

In the growing twilight, a council of war convened once more, this time under the open sky. The leaders of the rebellion gathered around a flickering fire and discussed the intelligence gathered throughout the day. Scouts reported increased British activity to the north, a likely indication of the impending counterattack.

"We must assume they'll strike at first light," Margaret said, her voice cutting through the crackle of the fire. "Our scouts will continue to monitor their movements, but we should prepare for an engagement sooner rather than later."

James, examining a makeshift map scratched in the dirt, pointed to a series of natural chokepoints. "If we can funnel them through here, we can mitigate their numerical advantage. It'll give our forces a fighting chance to hold them off."

Anna chimed in, her strategic mind analyzing every angle. "And if we can harass their flanks as they advance, it might slow them down enough for us to exploit any weaknesses."

The discussion continued, each leader contributing their insights until a plan began to take shape—a strategy that relied on their intimate knowledge of the terrain and the unyielding spirit of their forces.

As the meeting drew to a close, the camp around them quieted, the rebels seeking rest in the hours before the storm. Margaret, James, Anna, and Thomas lingered by the dying fire, the weight of the coming day heavy upon them.

"It won't be easy," Thomas said, his usual optimism tempered by the gravity of their situation. "But I believe in this cause. I believe in us."

Margaret looked at each of her companions and her friends, seeing in their faces the same determination that fueled her own resolve. "We've come so far," she reflected. "Not just in miles, but in the hearts we've touched, the lives we've changed. Whatever tomorrow brings, we've already made a difference."

James nodded, his gaze meeting Margaret's. "Together, we've built something that will outlast us all. No matter what happens, that's something to be proud of."

The group disbanded, each to their own thoughts and preparations, but united by a common purpose. The camp settled into a tense silence, the rebels stealing what rest they could before dawn.

As the first light of morning began to seep into the sky, turning the fog into a gossamer veil that shrouded the camp, the rebels awoke to face the day. They gathered their weapons, donned their armor, and looked to Margaret and James, who stood ready to lead them once more into the fog of war.

With a quiet determination, the rebels moved out, disappearing into the mist as they took their positions. The air was charged with anticipation, every heart beating in unison, every breath a testament to their courage and their commitment to the cause.

As the sun rose, piercing the fog and casting long shadows across the land, the echoes of war grew louder, a reminder of the battles fought and those yet to come. But amidst the uncertainty, one thing remained clear: they were ready. Ready to fight, to stand together, and to face whatever challenges lay ahead in the pursuit of liberty.

As the first rays of the sun broke through the morning fog, casting a soft light over the landscape, the rebels braced for the imminent clash. The silence of the early dawn, a stark contrast to the turmoil that lay ahead, was soon shattered by the distant sound of marching feet and the clanging of armor. The British forces, emerging from the mist-like specters of war, advanced with a determination that matched their numbers.

Margaret and James, standing at the forefront of their assembled forces, exchanged a glance that spoke volumes. It was a look of shared resolve, an unspoken acknowledgment of the path they had chosen together. They turned to face their comrades, their presence a rallying point for the men and women who had chosen to stand with them against tyranny.

"This is the moment we've prepared for," Margaret called

out, her voice carrying across the ranks, imbued with the strength of her conviction. "Remember why we fight. For freedom, for our future!"

James stepped forward, his gaze sweeping over the faces of the rebels, each one a testament to the courage and sacrifice that had brought them to this point. "Together, we have faced adversity and emerged stronger. Today, we stand united, not just as fighters, but as a symbol of hope. Let's show them what we're made of!"

The battle cry that rose from the rebels was a sound born of defiance and unity, echoing off the hills and into the heart of the advancing British forces. As the two sides collided, the clash of steel and the roar of gunfire filled the air, a chaotic symphony that marked the beginning of the battle.

Margaret and James fought side by side, their leadership inspiring those around them to feats of bravery and resilience. The fog of war, both literal and metaphorical, swirled around them, obscuring friend from foe, but their focus remained unwavering.

The conflict raged on, a test of wills and strategies, each side pushing and pulling in a deadly dance. But through the smoke and chaos, the rebels held their ground, their determination fueled by the knowledge that they fought for a cause greater than themselves.

As the day wore on, the tide of battle began to turn. The British, unprepared for the ferocity and resolve of the rebels, found themselves outmaneuvered and outmatched. Slowly, inexorably, they were forced to retreat, leaving the field in the hands of those they had sought to subdue.

In the aftermath of the battle, as the last of the mist dissipated under the afternoon sun, the rebels took stock of their victory. It was a moment of triumph tempered by the cost at which it had come. Friends and comrades lay among the fallen, a solemn reminder of the price of freedom.

Margaret and James, their faces marked by the smoke and toil of battle, stood together amidst their people. Their victory was not just a military success but a reaffirmation of their cause, a testament to the strength of their bonds and the righteousness of their struggle.

As they began the somber task of tending to the wounded and honoring the fallen, the echoes of war faded, replaced by a quiet determination. The battle was over, but their fight for liberty was far from finished. With each victory, they moved closer to their goal, each challenge faced together forging the bonds that held them stronger.

The day ended not with celebrations of victory but with a reflective acknowledgment of the journey ahead. For Margaret, James, and all who stood with them, the path forward was clear. They would continue to fight, to stand against oppression, and to strive for a future where freedom was more than a dream—it was a reality forged in the heart of battle, in the unity of their cause, and in the unwavering belief in the justice of their cause.

CHAPTER 17

Aftermath

In the quiet aftermath of the battle, the first light of dawn cast a soft glow over the camp, revealing the toll the night had taken. Margaret and James moved through the camp with solemn grace, their presence a comforting assurance to their weary fighters. They stopped to offer words of gratitude, their hands resting on the shoulders of those who had stood bravely in defense of their cause.

The camp buzzed with the subdued sounds of recovery. Healers, their hands steady and hearts resolute, tended to the wounded, stitching wounds and offering solace to the battle-weary fighters. Smoldering fires were reignited, around which small groups huddled, engaging in quiet conversations that wove a tapestry of resilience and shared purpose.

Margaret paused beside a young soldier, her gaze filled with understanding as she took in the sight of his bandaged arm. "You fought well," she said, her voice a gentle reassurance in the morning stillness. "Your courage under fire has not gone unnoticed."

The soldier looked up, his eyes filled with a mix of exhaustion and determination. "I only did what was necessary, ma'am. For freedom... for our future." His voice quivered, the weight of the battle etching a deep mark on his young soul, a mark that would never fade.

James worked methodically to distribute supplies salvaged from the battlefield. Each resource was a precious commodity vital to their continued resistance. His focus shifted as Margaret approached, a silent exchange passing between them—a shared acknowledgment of the weight of their responsibilities.

A messenger, his breath ragged from his hasty journey, arrived bearing news of British movements in the vicinity. The information he brought was a stark reminder that their struggle was far from over. The brief respite they now experienced was just the calm before the storm of war descended upon them once more, its path uncertain and its outcome unknown.

In the council that followed, tensions surfaced as strategies were debated. The path forward was fraught with uncertainty, each option carrying its own set of risks. Margaret listened to her advisors, weighing their counsel with the gravity it deserved. It was a delicate balance, steering the course of their rebellion towards victory without incurring losses they could ill afford.

As the meeting dispersed, James lingered. "We'll need to be ready," he said, his tone resolute. Margaret nodded, her resolve mirrored in her steady gaze.

The discovery of a fallen comrade's memento amidst the detritus of battle brought a poignant moment of reflection. Margaret held the small, personal item—a locket, its surface dulled by dirt and wear. It was a tangible connection to the cost of their fight, a reminder of the personal stories intertwined with the cause they championed, a cause that demanded such high sacrifices.

The day culminated in a memorial for the fallen, the camp

gathering as one to honor those who had made the ultimate sacrifice. Margaret stood before her people, her voice steady as she spoke of loss, of courage, and of the unyielding hope that drove them forward.

"We remember them not as soldiers fallen in battle, but as heroes who have lit the path to freedom with their bravery," she proclaimed. "Their sacrifice lays the foundation of the future we strive to build—one where such sacrifices are no longer necessary."

Her words, heartfelt and resonant, served not only as a tribute but as a unifying call. In the faces of those gathered, Margaret saw the reflection of her own determination. They were bound together, not just by the battles they had fought, but by the vision of the future they fought for—a future bought with the currency of their courage and sealed with the promise of freedom.

As night fell, the camp settled into a watchful quiet, the stars overhead a silent testament to the enduring spirit of those who dared to dream of liberty. In the aftermath of war, amidst the echoes of loss and victory, the rebels found strength in their unity, their resolve undimmed by the challenges that lay ahead.

In the aftermath of their hard-fought victory, the rebel camp was a tableau of resilience and sorrow. As the first light of dawn crept over the horizon, Margaret and James made their way through the camp, their presence a comforting reminder of the leadership that had steered them through the darkness.

The air was filled with the sounds of the morning after battle: the soft murmur of voices offering consolation, the clink of tools as soldiers repaired defenses, and the distant cries of those tending to the wounded. The smell of smoke still lingered, a ghost of the previous day's conflict.

Margaret stopped beside a young soldier who sat apart from the others, his gaze lost in the distance, his hands trembling slightly. She knelt beside him, her voice gentle. "You fought bravely yesterday," she said. The soldier looked up, his eyes meeting hers, and in them, she saw the weight of what he had experienced.

"It was my first battle," he admitted, his voice barely above a whisper. "I never knew... I couldn't have imagined..."

Margaret placed a hand on his shoulder, offering a silent strength. "The cost of freedom is high," she acknowledged. "But remember, we fight not for the love of battle, but for the promise of peace. For a future where such sacrifices are no longer necessary."

James, meanwhile, was a few paces ahead, organizing a group of rebels tasked with reinforcing the camp's perimeter. His orders were clear and precise, reflecting the tactical acumen that had become his hallmark. Yet, even as he worked, his thoughts were with Margaret and the weight she bore. Their shared glances were a silent exchange of support and understanding.

The morning's work was interrupted by the arrival of a messenger, breathless and covered in dust. "British forces," he gasped, "moving to the east. Larger numbers than we've seen before."

The news spread quickly, casting a shadow over the camp. Margaret and James convened an impromptu meeting with their advisors, and the map of the surrounding area was laid out before them. The debate was intense, with each leader voicing their thoughts on how best to respond.

"We can't meet them head-on," Anna argued, her finger tracing potential paths of retreat and guerrilla tactics on the map. "We need to use our knowledge of the terrain to our advantage."

Margaret listened, her mind weighing each option. "We'll divide our forces," she decided. "Harass their flanks and slow their advance. We need to buy time to regroup and plan our next move."

As the meeting dispersed, Margaret found herself standing alone at the edge of the camp, looking out towards the east. The rising sun painted the sky in brilliant hues of orange and pink, a stark contrast to the turmoil that lay ahead.

James joined her, his presence a steady comfort. "We've faced worse odds," he said, his voice firm with conviction.

Margaret nodded, her resolve hardening. "We have. And we'll face this together, as we always have."

Their shared determination was a beacon for the rebels, who set about their tasks with renewed vigor, fortified by the knowledge that their leaders stood with them, unwavering in the face of uncertainty.

As the day unfolded, not in the quiet of defeat but amid the clamor of readiness, the camp buzzed with activity. Preparations for the impending challenge were underway, fueled by the steadfast resolve of those who had chosen the path of resistance. In the wake of the battle, the uncertainty of the next engagement hung like a fog over the camp. Yet, beneath this veil of uncertainty, the spirit of the rebellion burned brightly. Their determination, far from being diminished by the specter of a larger conflict on the horizon, was only galvanized. United by a common dream of freedom and guided by leaders who stood firm in the face of adversity, their resolve remained unshaken, a testament to the enduring strength of those committed to carving out a brighter future from the shadows of war.

As the morning progressed into a bustling hive of strategy and steel, Margaret and James, along with their closest advisors, moved among the rebels with a purpose that was infectious. Each task, from the sharpening of swords to the bandaging of wounds, was carried out with a precision that spoke to the rebels' growing experience and unity.

In one corner of the camp, Anna led a group of scouts, poring over maps and marking potential routes for reconnaissance. "We need eyes on their movements at all times," she instructed, her voice carrying the authority of someone who had navigated countless dangers. "Use the terrain to your advantage, and remember, information is as valuable as any weapon we wield."

Elsewhere, Thomas was overseeing the training of new recruits, a mix of seasoned fighters and those new to the cause. The air was filled with the sounds of wooden swords clashing and the occasional bark of laughter. Despite the gravity of their situation, there was a sense of camaraderie that bound the group together, a shared recognition of the stakes at play.

James, after conferring with a group of engineers about fortifications, found himself standing beside Margaret, watching the camp's activities unfold. "They're ready," he observed, not just referring to their physical preparations but to the resolve etched on every face.

Margaret nodded, her gaze sweeping over her people. "They are. It's remarkable, seeing how far we've come. This...," she gestured to the camp, "is more than just a gathering of rebels. It's a testament to what people can achieve when they're driven by a shared purpose."

Their conversation was momentarily interrupted by the return of a scout, her appearance prompting immediate attention. "The British are advancing more cautiously than expected," she reported. "It seems yesterday's actions have given them pause."

"This could work to our advantage," Margaret mused, the wheels of strategy already turning. "We'll use this time to strengthen our position further. Let's make sure when they do decide to move, we're ready to meet them on our terms."

The day wore on, each hour a step closer to the inevitable clash, yet within the camp, a sense of purpose prevailed over the anxiety of anticipation. Margaret, James, and their advisors worked tirelessly, not just as leaders but as part of a larger whole, each contribution pivotal to the rebellion's strength.

As dusk embraced the encampment, casting long shadows between the makeshift tents, Margaret's steps were measured and deliberate. The recent skirmish had taken its toll, not just on lives but on the weary spirits of those who survived. She could see the weight of the day etched in the faces of her compatriots, their usual resolve tempered by the harsh reality of their struggle. Yet, in their somber silence, there was a palpable sense of determination, a shared understanding that their fight was far from over.

Margaret paused beside a small fire where a group of young rebels gathered, their eyes reflecting the flames that danced before them. They looked up as she approached, their expressions mixing admiration and solemnity. She offered them a gentle smile, sitting among them on the cold ground. "Today, we faced the harsh truths of our endeavor," she began, her voice soft yet carrying the weight of leadership. "We've lost friends, brothers, and sisters in arms. But their sacrifice will not be in vain. Our cause is just, and our resolve is unbreakable."

The group listened intently, hanging on to her every word as if drawing strength from her presence. One young rebel, a boy not yet out of his teens, spoke up, his voice hesitant. "Miss Hale, how do you keep fighting, knowing the odds we face?" His earnest and raw question echoed the unspoken fears of many around the fire.

Margaret looked at him, her gaze unwavering. "Because I must," she replied with quiet conviction. "Because the future we dream of—a future where freedom and justice prevail—is worth every hardship. We fight not just for ourselves but for those who will come after us. And in each other, in our unity, we find the courage to continue."

The conversation that followed was a mixture of reflections and resolutions. Margaret listened more than she spoke, allowing each rebel to voice their fears and their hopes. It was a cathartic exchange that fortified their bond and reignited the embers of determination smoldering within.

As the night deepened, Margaret rose, excusing herself from the gathering. She walked to the edge of the camp, where the forest met the clearing, and gazed up at the stars. The constellations, unchanged despite the turmoil on the ground, offered a sense of permanence, a reminder of the world beyond their immediate struggles. It was here, in the quiet solitude, that she allowed herself a moment of vulnerability, a brief respite from the weight of leadership.

The sound of approaching footsteps broke her contemplation. Turning, she saw James making his way toward her, his silhouette outlined by the campfires behind him. "I thought I might find you here," he said, coming to stand beside her. "It's one of the few places you allow yourself to just be, Margaret, not the leader, not the spy—just you."

Margaret offered a small, wistful smile. "Sometimes, I fear I've forgotten who 'just me' is," she confessed, her voice barely above a whisper.

James took her hand, his grasp warm and reassuring. "She's someone extraordinary," he said, looking into her eyes. "Someone who inspires us all to keep fighting, even when the darkness seems insurmountable."

They stood together in silence, finding comfort in each other's presence. The challenges ahead were daunting, the path fraught with danger, but in that moment, they were reminded of the personal stakes that underscored their shared mission. The fight for freedom, for a nation born from the ashes of rebellion, was also a fight for the right to love, dream, and forge a future defined by their ideals.

As they returned to the camp, hand in hand, the night no longer seemed as oppressive. The watchful quiet of the rebels, each lost in their thoughts, now felt like a collective breath before the plunge—a gathering of strength for the trials ahead. Margaret knew the road to liberty was long and filled with hardship, but she also knew they would face it together, united by a cause that transcended the sum of their individual fears and hopes.

Dawn was still hours away, but within the camp, a new day was already beginning—a day of planning, preparation, and undying hope. For Margaret, James, and their band of rebels, the fight for freedom—for the very soul of their nascent nation—was far from over. But they faced the future as one, their resolve unshaken, their spirits unbroken.

As the first light of dawn crept over the horizon, painting the sky in hues of orange and pink, the rebel camp stirred to life. The air, crisp and cool, carried with it the promise of a new beginning, a reminder that with each day came another opportunity to edge closer to their goal of liberty. Margaret, already awake and contemplating the day's strategies, watched her fellow rebels as they prepared for the morning's tasks. Their routines, though born of necessity, had become a testament to their resilience, a daily recommitment to their cause.

James joined her, a map in hand, his expression focused. "We've received word," he began, spreading the map on a nearby tree stump. "There's a British convoy, heavily guarded, moving supplies through the valley. It's a risk, but if we can intercept it..."

Margaret leaned over the map, her mind racing through the possibilities, the dangers. "It could provide us with the ammunition we need, and more importantly, deprive the British of crucial resources," she mused, her finger tracing the route. "We'll need a solid plan. Ambushes are tricky, and the terrain there..." Her voice trailed off as she assessed the topography, already visualizing the ambush.

The morning council convened, with Margaret and James presenting their proposal. The debate was intense, each leader weighing in with their concerns and suggestions. The risks were significant, but the potential rewards were too great to ignore. In the end, the decision was made: the ambush would proceed.

Preparations began in earnest, with Margaret overseeing the logistics and James coordinating the scouting parties. The atmosphere in the camp was one of focused determination, each rebel aware of the stakes. They moved with a quiet efficiency, honed through months of struggle, their actions guided by a shared vision of victory.

As the rebels set out, Margaret at their head, the sun climbed higher, its rays cutting through the thin mist that had settled over the valley. The march was silent, each step taking them deeper into enemy territory. Margaret could feel the tension among her troops, a tangible current of apprehension and resolve. She offered words of encouragement, her confidence unwavering, her belief in their cause unshakeable.

The ambush site was chosen with care, a narrow pass where the dense forest hugged the road. The rebels concealed themselves among the trees and underbrush, their weapons ready, their hearts pounding. Margaret took her position, her gaze fixed on the road, waiting for the signal.

When the British convoy appeared, snaking its way along the road, the rebels held their breath. At Margaret's signal, a flurry of arrows and musket balls tore through the air, catching the British off guard. The ambush was swift, brutal, and effective. In the chaos, Margaret led her fighters with a calm ferocity, directing their efforts and exploiting every advantage.

The battle was over quickly; the British convoy was overwhelmed, and its supplies were seized. The rebels worked quickly to secure their prize, aware that more British troops could arrive at any moment. As they retreated to the safety of their camp, the weight of their success settled over Margaret. They had achieved a significant victory, but she knew it was but one battle in a much larger war.

Back at camp, the mood was one of cautious celebration. The supplies they had captured would sustain them for the coming weeks, and the victory had bolstered their morale. Margaret allowed herself a moment of pride, watching her fellow rebels, their faces alight with triumph and relief. Yet, her thoughts were already turning to their next move, to the challenges that lay ahead.

James found her as the celebrations continued, his smile reflecting the day's success. "We did well today," he said, his hand finding hers.

Margaret nodded, her eyes meeting his. "We did," she agreed, "but tomorrow, we plan. The road to freedom is long, and today was just one step."

Together, they turned back to the camp, to their people, ready to face whatever the future held. The new day had brought them victory, but Margaret knew that each day was another step in their journey toward independence. The fight for liberty was far from over, but she also knew that, together, they were unstoppable.

As the night fell on the rebel camp, the day's excitement gradually subsided into a contemplative quiet. The rebels gathered around fires, their faces illuminated by the flickering light, sharing stories of the day's battle and remembering those who could no longer join them. The air was filled with a mixture of exhaustion and elation, the kind that only comes after a hard-won victory that had demanded every ounce of their courage and cunning.

Margaret stood at the edge of the encampment, watching over her people with a leader's vigilance and a comrade's affection. Today, they had struck a significant blow against the British, securing not just vital supplies but also the momentum to push forward. Yet, the victory was tinged with the somber understanding that their struggle was far from over, each triumph inching them closer to their ultimate goal but also reminding them of the cost.

James approached her, his presence a steady comfort. "You should rest," he suggested, concern evident in his voice. "You've carried us through today with unwavering strength. Let us take the watch tonight."

Margaret considered his words, feeling the weight of the day settle into her bones. She knew the importance of rest, of conserving one's strength for the battles ahead. Yet, the responsibility she felt for her fellow rebels, for the cause they all fought for, made it hard to step back, even for a night.

"Very well," she finally conceded, her gaze sweeping over the camp one last time before turning to join James. "But we all stand watch, together. This fight is ours, shared equally among us."

Together, they walked back towards the heart of the camp, their steps light despite the fatigue that clung to them. Around them, the rebels began to settle, the conversations dimming as the night deepened. In the quiet that followed, there was a sense of unity and purpose, a collective resolve to continue their fight for freedom, no matter what challenges lay ahead.

Margaret and James found a quiet spot near one of the fires, the warmth a small comfort against the night's chill. They sat, shoulder to shoulder, the events of the day replaying in their minds. In the silence, there was a mutual understanding of the sacrifices they had made and the ones still to come.

As the embers glowed in the darkness, Margaret looked up at the stars, their light undiminished by the fires below. They were a reminder of the world beyond their immediate struggle, a world they were fighting to change. For a moment, she allowed herself to dream of peace, of a time when their swords could be beaten into plowshares and freedom was a reality for all.

"On the rebel camp, a small island of resistance in the vast darkness, its inhabitants are united by a common cause and a shared hope for the future. Tomorrow will bring new challenges, but for tonight, they rest. Their spirits are uplifted by the day's victory and the knowledge that they are not alone in their fight."

CHAPTER 18

Crossroads

In a secluded glen, where the dense canopy above whispered ancient secrets and the air was filled with wildflowers, the rebels, resilient in the face of war, found themselves a slice of tranquility amidst the turmoil. Here, they laid down their arms, if only for a moment, allowing the soothing balm of nature to tend to their weary spirits.

Margaret and James, the stalwart leaders of the rebel group, sought solace in each other's company away from the prying eyes of their encampment. Seated by the bank of a babbling brook, they indulged in the luxury of unhurried conversation, a rare reprieve from the demands of command.

Their dialogue, like the stream before them, meandered. It touched upon fears and dreams with a raw honesty that the chaos of rebellion seldom afforded. In these moments of vulnerability, their bond, built on shared struggles and aspirations, deepened. They found in each other not just a comrade but a confidant, a beacon of hope in the long shadow of conflict.

The respite was shattered by the sudden arrival of a young scout, his face etched with the urgency of his tidings. The British, it seemed, weary from the persistent thorn of resistance pricking at their side, had extended an olive branch—a proposition for parley.

193

The news sent a ripple of surprise through the rebel ranks. An offer of negotiation from an empire known for its iron fist over its outstretched hand was unexpected, to say the least. It posed a conundrum steeped in both opportunity and risk, igniting a fervor of debate among the rebels.

Gathered around a fire that evening, the leaders of the rebellion, with Margaret and James at the helm, weighed their options. The glow of the flames cast long shadows as they deliberated the merits and perils of accepting the British offer. To engage in dialogue could pave the path to peace, yet the specter of treachery loomed large, a reminder of the high stakes at play.

Margaret, ever the strategist, argued for cautious engagement, seeing in the proposal a chance to glean insight into British intentions and perhaps secure a more favorable position for their cause. "This could be our chance," she posited, her voice firm with conviction, "to end this conflict on our terms."

James, tempered by his knowledge of British tactics and the duplicities of war, counseled vigilance. "We must tread carefully," he warned, "for the British are no strangers to the art of deception. Our resolve has been our shield; let it not now become our downfall."

The discussion stretched into the night, each leader voicing their piece, their faces flickering in the firelight. In the end, a consensus emerged, a testament to their unity and shared purpose, born of a resolve to seek an end to the bloodshed, yet tempered by the wisdom to guard against folly. They would meet the British, but on their terms, prepared for all eventualities.

As the meeting disbanded, Margaret and James lingered by the dying fire, the weight of their decision heavy on their shoulders. They had chosen a path fraught with unknowns, but it was a path they would walk together, their faith in each other unshaken.

The dawn of the next day brought with it a sense of uneasy anticipation. The rebels busied themselves with preparations, their movements deliberate, their conversations hushed. Margaret and James, at the center of this maelstrom of activity, stood as pillars of calm, their resolve a beacon for their followers.

As they set out for the appointed place of parley, the forest seemed to hold its breath, the usual chorus of birdsong silenced by the gravity of the moment. Ahead lay a meeting that could alter the course of their struggle, a crossroads between continued conflict and the elusive promise of peace.

Margaret, James, and their group of rebels stand at a pivotal juncture, their courage shining through as they face the unknown. They have chosen an uncharted path with an uncertain outcome, but they take a step forward into the unknown together, united in their shared dream of a future free from oppression and full of freedom.

As they marched towards the rendezvous point, the dense canopy above gradually gave way to a clearing bathed in the soft light of morning. The appointed place for parley was an ancient oak, its sprawling branches a testament to the passage of time, standing solitary in the midst of the open field. It was here, under the watchful gaze of nature, that the destinies of many would converge, poised on the thin edge between war and peace.

Margaret and James, flanked by a select contingent of their most trusted comrades, approached the oak with measured steps. Their eyes scanned the horizon, vigilant for any hint of treachery. Only the gentle sway of grass in the morning breeze filled the still field.

From the opposite direction, a small British delegation made its way forward, their red coats stark against the green of the field. At their head was a man of imposing stature, his uniform adorned with the insignia of high rank. His gaze, as he surveyed the approaching rebels, was one of grudging respect.

The two groups met beneath the ancient oak, the air between them charged with the tension of countless battles, the ground beneath their feet a silent witness to the bloodshed of their conflict. For a long moment, no one spoke, the weight of the moment pressing down upon them all.

Finally, Margaret stepped forward, her posture commanding, her voice steady. "You have requested this parley," she began, her eyes locked on the British commander. "We are here to listen but know this: our resolve is as strong as ever. We seek peace, but not at the cost of our freedom."

The British commander, a seasoned veteran named Colonel Grey, nodded slowly. "I understand your position, Miss Hale," he replied, his voice betraying a hint of admiration. We, too, seek an end to this conflict, though our visions for the future may differ. Perhaps, however, there is common ground to be found."

The discussions that followed were cautious, each side carefully navigating the delicate dance of diplomacy. Proposals were made and countered, and terms debated and revised. Through it all, Margaret and James stood united, their presence a silent reminder of the sacrifices their people had made, of the ideals they fought to uphold.

As the sun climbed higher, marking the passage of time, a tentative agreement began to take shape. It was far from perfect, a delicate compromise that left neither side wholly satisfied. Yet it was a start, a flicker of hope in the long darkness of war.

When the parley finally concluded, the delegations retreated, leaving Margaret and James alone beneath the ancient oak.

They exchanged looks, a complex tapestry of emotions reflected in their eyes—relief, uncertainty, but above all, determination.

"We've taken the first step," James said, breaking the silence. "It may lead to peace, or it may be but a brief respite. Either way, we'll face what comes together."

Margaret nodded, her gaze turning to the horizon, where the future lay shrouded in the mists of possibility. "Together," she echoed, her hand finding James's. "No matter what lies ahead, we'll meet it as we always have: united in purpose, unwavering in our pursuit of freedom."

With that, they turned back toward their camp, towards the uncertain path that lay ahead. The parley under the ancient oak was but a chapter in the larger story of their rebellion, a story still being written in the hearts and deeds of those who dared dream of a better world.

As they disappeared into the forest, the ancient oak stood silent, a sentinel at the crossroads of history, its branches whispering of the fragile hope for peace in a land torn by war.

As Margaret and James made their way back through the dense forest, the weight of the morning's parley sat heavily upon them. They had negotiated with the enemy, a notion that would have seemed inconceivable when they first took up arms. Yet, the war had taught them that the path to freedom was not a straight line but a winding road fraught with difficult decisions and unlikely alliances.

Their return to the rebel camp was met with anxious faces and a flurry of whispered questions. The rebels, a tight-knit band forged in the heat of battle, looked to Margaret and James for direction, their eyes reflecting a mix of hope and apprehension.

Margaret addressed the gathering, her voice carrying over

the assembled crowd, steady and reassuring. "We've spoken with the British under a flag of truce," she began, pausing to let her words sink in. "It was a discussion born of necessity, a chance to seek an end to the bloodshed that has cost us so dearly."

She went on to explain the tentative agreement reached, careful to temper expectations. "This is but the first step on a long road. There are no guarantees, but we owe it to ourselves, and to those we've lost, to explore every avenue towards peace."

The reaction was mixed; relief and hope clashed with skepticism and a sense of betrayal. James stepped forward, lending his support. "We haven't forgotten our cause or the sacrifices that have brought us here. This decision wasn't made lightly. But war," he paused, his gaze sweeping over the faces before him, "war should always be the last resort, not a state we cling to out of pride or fear."

The words hung in the air, a challenge to their collective resolve. In the silence that followed, the rebels looked to one another, finding unity in their shared longing for peace and the trust they placed in Margaret and James.

As discussions continued into the evening, the campfire's glow illuminating determined faces, a plan began to take shape. They would proceed cautiously, preparing for the possibility of peace while remaining vigilant against the threat of betrayal. Scouts were dispatched to monitor British movements, while envoys were selected to continue the negotiations, their every step watched over by the keen eyes of the rebellion.

In the days that followed, the rebel camp was a hive of activity. Preparations were made for a potential ceasefire, even as training and patrols continued unabated. Through it all, Margaret and James worked tirelessly, their leadership a beacon guiding the rebels through uncertain waters.

Then, word arrived that the British were calling for another meeting, this time to discuss the terms of the ceasefire in detail. It was a sign that the negotiations were being taken seriously, that the possibility of peace was within reach.

Margaret and James set out once more, accompanied by a small retinue of trusted advisors. The meeting place was the same ancient oak, now a symbol of the fragile hope that had blossomed between two weary adversaries.

The negotiations were long and fraught with tension, both sides keenly aware of what was at stake. Yet, as the sun dipped below the horizon, a breakthrough was reached. Terms were agreed upon, and promises were made. It was a ceasefire, fragile and tentative, but it was a start.

As they made their way back to the camp, Margaret and James allowed themselves a moment of cautious optimism. The war was far from over, and the road ahead promised new challenges, but they had achieved something remarkable—a chance for peace.

The rebel camp welcomed them back with open arms, their return a sign that the tide was turning. That night, as they gathered around the campfire, there was a sense of celebration in the air, tempered by the knowledge of the long journey still ahead.

Margaret looked around at the faces illuminated by the firelight, each one a story of resilience and hope. "This ceasefire," she said, her voice filled with quiet determination, "is our chance to build the future we've been fighting for. It won't be easy, but nothing worth having ever is. Together, we'll face whatever comes, united in our dream of freedom."

And at that moment, under the canopy of stars, the rebels felt the weight of their struggle lighten. They were fighters, yes, but more than that, they were builders of a vision that had sustained them through the darkest of times. With Margaret and James leading the way, they looked towards the dawn, ready to forge their destiny together.

The chapter closed not with an end but with a beginning, the promise of peace a beacon guiding them towards a horizon filled with the light of newfound hope.

As Margaret and James made their way back through the dense forest, the weight of the morning's parley sat heavily upon them. They had negotiated with the enemy, a notion that would have seemed inconceivable when they first took up arms. Yet, the war had taught them that the path to freedom was not a straight line but a winding road fraught with difficult decisions and unlikely alliances.

Their return to the rebel camp was met with anxious faces and a flurry of whispered questions. The rebels, a tight-knit band forged in the heat of battle, looked to Margaret and James for direction, their eyes reflecting a mix of hope and apprehension.

Margaret addressed the gathering, her voice carrying over the assembled crowd, steady and reassuring. "We've spoken with the British under a flag of truce," she began, pausing to let her words sink in. "It was a discussion born of necessity, a chance to seek an end to the bloodshed that has cost us so dearly."

She went on to explain the tentative agreement reached, careful to temper expectations. "This is but the first step on a long road. There are no guarantees, but we owe it to ourselves, and to those we've lost, to explore every avenue towards peace."

The reaction was mixed; relief and hope clashed with skepticism and a sense of betrayal. James stepped forward, lending his support. "We haven't forgotten our cause or the sacrifices that have brought us here. This decision wasn't made lightly. But war," he paused, his gaze sweeping over the faces before him, "war should always be the last resort, not a state we cling to out of pride or fear."

The words hung in the air, a challenge to their collective resolve. In the silence that followed, the rebels looked to one another, finding unity in their shared longing for peace and the trust they placed in Margaret and James.

As discussions continued into the evening, the campfire's glow illuminating determined faces, a plan began to take shape. They would proceed cautiously, preparing for the possibility of peace while remaining vigilant against the threat of betrayal. Scouts were dispatched to monitor British movements, while envoys were selected to continue the negotiations, their every step watched over by the keen eyes of the rebellion.

In the days that followed, the rebel camp was a hive of activity. Preparations were made for a potential ceasefire, even as training and patrols continued unabated. Through it all, Margaret and James worked tirelessly, their leadership a beacon guiding the rebels through uncertain waters.

Then, word arrived that the British were calling for another meeting, this time to discuss the terms of the ceasefire in detail. It was a sign that the negotiations were being taken seriously, that the possibility of peace was within reach.

Margaret and James set out once more, accompanied by a small retinue of trusted advisors. The meeting place was the same ancient oak, now a symbol of the fragile hope that had blossomed between two weary adversaries.

The negotiations were long and fraught with tension, both sides keenly aware of what was at stake. Yet, as the sun dipped below the horizon, a breakthrough was reached.

Terms were agreed upon, and promises were made. It was a ceasefire, fragile and tentative, but it was a start.

As they made their way back to the camp, Margaret and James allowed themselves a moment of cautious optimism. The war was far from over, and the road ahead promised new challenges, but they had achieved something remarkable—a chance for peace.

The rebel camp welcomed them back with open arms, their return a sign that the tide was turning. That night, as they gathered around the campfire, there was a sense of celebration in the air, tempered by the knowledge of the long journey still ahead.

Margaret looked around at the faces illuminated by the firelight, each one a story of resilience and hope. "This ceasefire," she said, her voice filled with quiet determination, "is our chance to build the future we've been fighting for. It won't be easy, but nothing worth having ever is. Together, we'll face whatever comes, united in our dream of freedom."

The evening air was alive with the crackle of the campfire and the murmur of voices, a symphony of cautious optimism and renewed determination. Around the fire, rebels exchanged stories and plans, the glow of the flames reflecting off their faces, casting them in a light of resolve and unity. Margaret and James stood slightly apart, their presence a silent pillar of strength for those they led.

Margaret's gaze swept across the camp, taking in the faces of her fellow rebels, each one a testament to the resilience of the human spirit. She felt a surge of pride for how far they had come, for the battles they had faced together, and for the unwavering belief in the cause that united them. Turning to James, she saw the same resolve mirrored in his eyes, a shared conviction that they were on the cusp of something monumental.

"This ceasefire," she reiterated, her voice carrying over the assembly, "is not just a pause in the fighting. It's an opportunity for us to strengthen our position, to gather our resources, and to plan our next steps. We've been given a chance to breathe, to prepare for what comes next. We must use this time wisely."

James nodded, stepping forward to add his voice to hers. "Let's not forget," he began, his tone imbued with the gravity of experience, "that the path to freedom is often paved with trials. This ceasefire may test our patience and our resolve, but it also offers us a glimpse of the peace we fight for. Let's hold fast to our vision, to the dream of a nation built on the principles of liberty and justice for all."

The rebels listened intently, their faces a tapestry of emotions—hope, determination, and the scars of battles past. In the flickering firelight, they found a moment of unity, a collective breath before diving back into the fray.

As the meeting dispersed, Margaret and James remained, lost in thought as the fire dwindled to embers. The night enveloped the camp in a cloak of stillness, broken only by the occasional crackle of wood and the distant hoot of an owl. The peace was a bittersweet respite, a reminder of what they fought for and the cost of such a fight.

In the days that followed, the camp was a whirlwind of activity. Scouts were dispatched to keep a watchful eye on British movements, supplies were stockpiled, and strategies devised for the myriad possibilities that lay ahead. Through it all, Margaret and James were a constant presence, guiding, planning, and preparing their people for the challenges of the days to come.

Yet, amidst the bustle of preparation, there were moments of quiet reflection, of shared glances between Margaret and James that spoke volumes. They were leaders, yes, but they were also individuals, each carrying the weight of their choices and the hopes of their people.

One evening, as the sun dipped below the horizon, casting long shadows through the trees, Margaret found James standing at the edge of the camp, looking out into the forest. She joined him, following his gaze into the dense thicket where the mysteries of the future seemed to dwell.

"We stand on the brink of a new chapter," she said softly, her voice a blend of hope and apprehension.

James turned to her, his hand finding hers in the dim light. "Together, we'll write that chapter," he replied, his voice steady. "For our people, for the future we believe in."

Their eyes met, and in that moment, the uncertainty of the future seemed less daunting. They were together, united by a cause greater than themselves and bolstered by the support of those who believed in the dream of freedom.

The night grew deep, the stars wheeling overhead in their silent dance. Margaret and James returned to the heart of the camp, to their people, ready to face whatever the morrow would bring. The ceasefire was a gift, but it was also a challenge—a test of their resolve, their leadership, and their vision for a free and just nation.

And so, as a new day dawned, the rebels rose, not just as fighters but as architects of the future they yearned to see. Under the leadership of Margaret and James, they would navigate the uncertain waters of ceasefire, forging ahead with unwavering determination. The road ahead was uncharted, fraught with peril, but they would walk it together, shoulder to shoulder, with their eyes fixed on the horizon and their hearts alight with the flame of liberty.

Chapter 19

The Turning Tide

The dawn broke with a crimson hue, painting the sky with the colors of fire and promise. The air was crisp and cool, carrying the scent of dew and anticipation. As the first light of morning pierced the veil of night, the rebel camp stirred to life, its inhabitants moving with a sense of urgency and renewed purpose. The ceasefire had granted them a precious respite, but it was the calm before the storm, a temporary peace in the shadow of an impending clash, that would determine the fate of their struggle.

Margaret, a seasoned warrior and strategist, stood at the edge of the camp, watching the sunrise with a contemplative gaze. The days following the ceasefire had been a whirlwind of activity, each moment spent fortifying their position, strategizing, and preparing for the inevitable resumption of hostilities. Yet, in the quiet solitude of dawn, she allowed herself to reflect on the journey that had brought them to this point, on the sacrifices made and the lives altered forever by the crucible of rebellion. James, a trusted advisor and skilled tactician, joined her, his presence a silent support.

James joined her, his presence a silent testament to their shared vision. Together, they watched the day awaken, aware that the turning tide awaited their command, ready to surge forward at their united behest. The air between them was charged with the anticipation of what was to come, with the knowledge that the decisions they made in the coming days would shape the course of history.

"We've done everything we can to prepare," James said, breaking the silence. "Our scouts report that the British are mobilizing. They'll test the terms of the ceasefire, see if we've grown complacent."

Margaret nodded, her resolve steeling. "Let them come," she replied, her voice firm. "We'll show them that our resolve has only strengthened, that we stand united in the face of their aggression. This ceasefire has been a gift, not of peace, but of time—time we've used to our advantage."

As they returned to the heart of the camp, the mood was one of determined anticipation. The rebels, their faces etched with determination and weariness, moved with an efficiency born of necessity. Weapons were checked and rechecked, supplies were distributed, and positions were reinforced. Margaret and James, their eyes filled with a mix of hope and anxiety, directed their forces with a calm authority, their leadership the keystone of the rebellion's resilience.

The message came at midday, a runner breathless with urgency. The British, in a bold move to shatter the fragile peace, were advancing in force, their intention clear: to crush the rebellion in a decisive strike.

The news quickly circulated throughout the camp, spreading like wildfire. Igniting a fierce determination in the hearts of the rebels. This was the moment they had been preparing for, the battle that would define their cause. Margaret rallied her troops, her words cutting through the tension like a beacon of hope. Her voice, filled with a mix of determination and fear, echoed across the camp, stirring the hearts of the rebels and fueling their resolve.

"Today, we stand at the turning tide," she proclaimed, her gaze sweeping over the assembled ranks. "The enemy seeks to end our fight for freedom with a single blow. But they underestimate us. They underestimate our courage, our unity, and our will to persevere. Today, we fight not just for our lives, but for the future of our nation! For years, we have endured their oppression, their disregard for our rights and our dignity. Today, we rise up, united in our determination to reclaim what is rightfully ours."

Cheers rose from the rebels, a thunderous affirmation of their readiness to face the coming storm. James, standing beside Margaret, offered a nod of solidarity. Together, they led their forces out of the camp into the open fields where the British army awaited.

The battle that ensued was fierce, a maelstrom of steel and fire that tested the limits of their endurance and their commitment to the cause. Margaret and James fought side by side, their presence on the front lines a rallying cry for their troops, who met the British onslaught with unyielding resistance. The rebels' hearts pounded with a mix of fear and determination, their every move a testament to their courage and their belief in their cause.

As the sun began its descent, casting long shadows across the battlefield, the tide of the conflict shifted. The rebels, fueled by their indomitable spirit, pushed forward, driving the British back with a ferocity that belied their numbers. Inch by inch, they reclaimed the ground that had been contested with such cost, their victory a testament to their determination and their sacrifice.

When, at last, the fighting ceased, the rebels stood triumphant, the British forces in full retreat. The battlefield, a testament to their struggle, bore witness to their indomitable spirit and their unwavering bravery.

Margaret and James surveyed the scene, their hearts heavy with the price of their triumph but buoyed by the knowledge that they had turned the tide. They had faced the might of an empire and emerged stronger, united by their shared dream of liberty.

As they returned to the camp, the rebels greeted them with cheers and tears, a celebration of their victory and a mourning for those who would not return. The night was filled with the songs of freedom and the stories of the day's battle, a reaffirmation of their cause and their commitment to see it through, no matter the cost. Margaret and James, their hearts heavy with the price of their triumph, joined in the celebration, their spirits buoyed by the knowledge that they had turned the tide. They had faced the might of an empire and emerged stronger, united by their shared dream of liberty.

The dawn broke with a crimson hue, painting the sky with the colors of fire and promise. As the first light of morning pierced the veil of night, the rebel camp stirred to life, its inhabitants moving with a sense of urgency and renewed purpose. The ceasefire had granted them a precious respite, but it was the calm before the storm, a temporary peace in the shadow of an impending clash, that would determine the fate of their struggle.

Margaret stood at the edge of the camp, watching the sunrise with a contemplative gaze. The days following the ceasefire had been a whirlwind of activity, each moment spent fortifying their position, strategizing, and preparing for the inevitable resumption of hostilities. Yet, in the quiet solitude of dawn, she allowed herself to reflect on the journey that had brought them to this point, on the sacrifices made and the lives altered forever by the crucible of rebellion.

James joined her, his presence a silent support. Together, they watched the day awaken, aware that the turning tide awaited their command, ready to surge forward at their behest.

The air between them was charged with the anticipation of what was to come, with the knowledge that the decisions they made in the coming days would shape the course of history.

"We've done everything we can to prepare," James said, breaking the silence. "Our scouts report that the British are mobilizing. They'll test the terms of the ceasefire, see if we've grown complacent."

Margaret nodded, her resolve steeling. "Let them come," she replied, her voice firm. "We'll show them that our resolve has only strengthened, that we stand united in the face of their aggression. This ceasefire has been a gift, not of peace, but of time—time we've used to our advantage."

As they returned to the heart of the camp, the mood was one of determined anticipation. The rebels, seasoned by battle and bonded by their shared cause, moved with an efficiency born of necessity. Weapons were checked and rechecked, supplies were distributed, and positions were reinforced. Margaret and James, at the center of this flurry of activity, directed their forces with a calm authority, their leadership the keystone of the rebellion's resilience.

The message came at midday, a runner breathless with urgency. The British, in a bold move to shatter the fragile peace, were advancing in force, their intention clear: to crush the rebellion in a decisive strike.

The news spread through the camp like wildfire, igniting a fierce determination in the hearts of the rebels. This was the moment they had been preparing for, the battle that would define their cause. Margaret rallied her troops, her words cutting through the tension like a beacon of hope.

"Today, we stand at the turning tide," she proclaimed, her gaze sweeping over the assembled ranks. "The enemy seeks to end our fight for freedom with a single blow. But they underestimate us. They underestimate our courage, our unity, and our will to persevere. Today, we fight not just for our lives, but for the future of our nation!"

Cheers rose from the rebels, a thunderous affirmation of their readiness to face the coming storm. James, standing beside Margaret, offered a nod of solidarity. Together, they led their forces out of the camp into the open fields where the British army awaited.

The battle that ensued was fierce, a maelstrom of steel and fire that tested the limits of their endurance and their commitment to the cause. Margaret and James fought side by side, their presence on the front lines a rallying cry for their troops, who met the British onslaught with unyielding resistance.

As the sun began its descent, casting long shadows across the battlefield, the tide of the conflict shifted. The rebels, fueled by their indomitable spirit, pushed forward, driving the British back with a ferocity that belied their numbers. Inch by inch, they reclaimed the ground that had been contested with such cost, their victory a testament to their determination and their sacrifice.

When, at last, the fighting ceased, the rebels stood victorious, the British forces in retreat. The battlefield, a testament to their struggle, bore witness to their resolve and their bravery.

Margaret and James surveyed the scene, their hearts heavy with the price of their triumph but buoyed by the knowledge that they had turned the tide. They had faced the might of an empire and emerged stronger, united by their shared dream of liberty.

As they returned to the camp, the rebels greeted them with cheers and tears, a celebration of their victory and mourning for those who would not return. The night was filled with the songs of freedom and the stories of the day's battle, a reaffirmation of their cause and their commitment to see it through, no matter the cost. Margaret and James, their hearts heavy with the price of their triumph, joined in the celebration, their spirits buoyed by the knowledge that they had turned the tide. They had faced the might of an empire and emerged stronger, united by their shared dream of liberty.

The rebels, under the leadership of Margaret and James, had faced their greatest challenge yet and emerged victorious. But the war was far from over, and the victory, while significant, was but one battle in a larger war that stretched beyond the horizon. As the celebration waned and the campfires dimmed to glowing embers, the leaders of the rebellion convened in a solemn gathering. The air was thick with the weight of responsibility as they acknowledged the cost of their triumph and contemplated the path that lay ahead.

Margaret, her face illuminated by the flickering light, spoke first. "Today, we've proven our strength and our resolve. But this victory, hard-won as it was, will only incite further challenges. The British will come at us with renewed vigor, seeking to quash the hope we've ignited."

James, standing by her side, added, "We must use this momentum to our advantage. Strengthen our alliances, gather resources, and expand our ranks. Our cause has never been more just, nor more urgent. We fight not only for our freedom but for the very soul of our nation."

The discussion that followed was marked by a pragmatic determination. Plans were drawn for the immediate fortification of their position, for outreach to sympathetic factions, and for a series of swift, targeted strikes designed to keep the British off balance. The air was charged with a sense of purpose, each leader contributing their expertise, united by a common goal.

In the days that followed, the camp was a hive of activity. Margaret and James, their partnership strengthened by shared victories and losses, worked tirelessly. They met with scouts, poring over maps to identify strategic targets and with envoys to secure the supplies and alliances necessary for the continued fight. Every decision was weighed against the backdrop of the broader struggle, every action a step towards the realization of their vision for a free and independent nation.

As they prepared for the next phase of the conflict, a sense of camaraderie permeated the camp. The rebels, inspired by the leadership of Margaret and James and galvanized by their recent victory, trained with a fervor that spoke of their deep commitment to the cause. Stories of the battle were shared, not just as tales of valor, but as lessons for the fights to come.

One evening, as the sun set, painting the sky in shades of gold and crimson, Margaret found herself standing on the outskirts of the camp, her gaze fixed on the horizon. James joined her, his presence a silent comfort. Together, they stood in quiet reflection, aware of the long road ahead but bolstered by the knowledge that they did not walk it alone.

"It's a beautiful world we're fighting for," Margaret mused, her voice tinged with weary hope.

James nodded, his arm coming to rest around her shoulders. "A world worth every sacrifice. We've come far, Margaret, but I believe the hardest battles are yet to come."

"We'll face them," Margaret affirmed, her eyes meeting his. "Together. For freedom, for justice, and for the future of our nation."

They turned back to the camp, to their people, who looked to them for leadership and hope. In the faces of the rebels, in the strength of their resolve, Margaret and James saw the reflection of their own determination. The tide had indeed turned, but it was only the beginning of the tempest that would test their courage, their unity, and their dreams of liberty.

In the days that ensued, the rebellion moved like a shadow across the land, striking swiftly and fading back into the wilderness. Each action was a statement of their defiance, a declaration that they would not be subdued. And as the news of their exploits spread, so too did the legend of their leaders, Margaret and James, whose names became symbols of hope for the oppressed and beacons of fear for their oppressors.

The start of a greater fight for the freedom of a nation had only just begun. Margaret and James were well aware of the difficulties that lay ahead of them, but they also understood that their cause was greater than themselves. It was a cause born out of the people's desire for freedom, sustained by the sacrifices made by those who dared to dream of a brighter future. As they braced themselves for the challenges that lay ahead, they remained resolute in their determination to achieve their ultimate goal.

The next day dawned with a hush over the camp as if the very land itself was holding its breath, anticipating the rebels' next move. The recent victories and skirmishes had infused the rebels with a cautious optimism, but Margaret and James knew that each day could bring new challenges, each victory could be met with retaliation. The British, their pride stung, would be regrouping, planning. The ceasefire had ended, and the war for independence was entering a critical phase.

As the camp stirred to life, Margaret convened with her advisors at first light, their figures silhouetted against the awakening sky. The map of the region was spread out before them on a makeshift table, dotted with markers indicating British positions, potential targets, and areas of strategic importance. The air was crisp, carrying the scent of pine and the undercurrent of resolve that had come to define the rebel encampment.

"Scouts report increased activity at Fort Harrison," reported one of the advisors, pointing to a spot on the map. "It seems the British are fortifying their defenses, possibly in preparation for a counterattack."

Margaret considered this, her gaze fixed on the map. "Then we must act swiftly. Fort Harrison controls the supply route to the south. If we could take it, or even disrupt its operations, it would be a significant blow to the British supply chain."

James, who had been quietly listening, spoke up. "It's a well-defended position. Any direct attack would be costly." His experience as a former British officer lent weight to his words. "However, if we could outmaneuver them, strike where they least expect it..."

A plan began to take shape, one that relied on speed, surprise, and the intimate knowledge of the land that the rebels possessed. It was a daring strategy, requiring precise execution and a bit of luck. But the rebels had come to thrive on the edge of possibility, their successes built on the foundation of audacity and belief in their cause.

Throughout the day, preparations were made. Small teams were assembled, each with specific roles in the upcoming operation. Margaret and James oversaw the planning, and their leadership was a steady hand in guiding the rebels' efforts. There was a palpable tension in the air, a mix of anticipation and the weight of responsibility that came with command.

As night fell, the rebel camp was a hive of quiet activity. The operation would begin under the cover of darkness, leveraging the night as an ally. Margaret and James, clad in dark cloaks, moved among their troops, offering words of encouragement, their presence a reassurance in the face of the unknown.

Then, with a nod from Margaret, the rebels set out, melting into the shadows, their movements a whisper against the backdrop of the forest. James took a moment to look back at the camp, its fires dimmed to avoid drawing attention, before following his comrades into the night.

The march to Fort Harrison was tense, each step carrying them closer to confrontation. Yet, the rebels moved with a purpose, driven by the vision of freedom that had sparked their rebellion, now burning brighter with each victory.

As they neared the fort, the plan was set into motion. Diversions drew the attention of the British sentries, creating an opening for Margaret, James, and their team to infiltrate the fort's defenses. The element of surprise was on their side, and for a few critical moments, the night erupted into chaos.

The battle for Fort Harrison was fierce, the outcome uncertain until the final moments. But as the first light of dawn broke over the battlefield, it revealed the rebels victorious, the fort's flag replaced with their own—a symbol of their resilience, their determination, and the turning tide of the war.

Exhausted but elated, Margaret and James surveyed the captured fort, aware of the significance of their victory. This was more than a strategic win; it was a declaration that the rebels were a force to be reckoned with and that their dream of independence was within reach.

As the sun rose, casting long shadows across the fort's grounds, the rebels gathered, looking towards Margaret and James for what came next. In the light of the new day, with the captured fort standing as a testament to their efforts, they knew the road ahead would be fraught with challenges. But for now, they allowed themselves a moment of triumph, a brief pause to savor the victory and to gather strength for the battles to come.

As the sun ascended, its rays illuminating Fort Harrison now under rebel control, the air was charged with a sense of accomplishment and anticipation of the journey ahead. This victory was not just a testament to their tactical prowess but also a symbol of their growing strength and unity. The rebels gathered in the fort's shadow and looked to Margaret and James, their faces alight with the promise of what they could achieve together. In this moment of triumph, they found not just satisfaction but also the resolve to press on, knowing well the path ahead was lined with both trials and possibilities. This phase in their struggle concluded with a hard-earned victory, but the next phase of their fight for independence had just begun. The story of their rebellion, vibrant and unwavering, was ready to unfold further, pushing them into uncharted territories, both literally and figuratively, as they continued their quest for freedom and the right to define their own destiny.

Chapter **20**

𝕾𝔥𝔞𝔡𝔬𝔴𝔰 𝔞𝔫𝔡 𝔚𝔥𝔦𝔰𝔭𝔢𝔯𝔰

In the aftermath of their victory at Fort Harrison, the rebel camp was alive with a quiet buzz, a mix of relief, and the tension of anticipation for what was yet to come. While the battle had been a significant triumph, it was the shadows cast by their success that now occupied Margaret and James. The British would not take this defeat lightly, and the rebels knew that the response would be swift and, likely, ruthless.

As dawn broke, casting a soft light through the trees surrounding their encampment, Margaret and James met in the relative privacy of the forest's edge. Their conversation was hushed, underscored by the seriousness of their situation.

"We've struck a blow, yes, but now we must be prepared for the backlash," Margaret said, her eyes scanning the dense woods as if expecting an enemy to emerge at any moment. "Our scouts report increased British patrols in the area. It's only a matter of time before they attempt to retaliate."

James nodded, his expression grim. "We've also heard whispers among the locals. The British are recruiting more than just soldiers; they're enlisting spies to infiltrate our ranks, sow discord among our allies."

The revelation was a chilling one, underscoring the complex web of warfare that extended beyond the battlefield. It wasn't just a fight of arms but of information, loyalty, and betrayal. The shadows they now faced were not just the physical cover of their forested haven but the creeping doubt and suspicion that could unravel their cause from within.

Determined to confront this new threat head-on, Margaret and James devised a plan. They would tighten security around the camp, implementing stricter protocols for communication and meetings. Additionally, they would establish a counterintelligence network, using their own whispers to spread disinformation, confuse the British efforts, and root out any spies who managed to infiltrate their ranks.

The days that followed were a testament to the resilience and adaptability of the rebel forces. Margaret and James worked tirelessly, coordinating with their lieutenants to enforce the new security measures and train selected rebels in the art of espionage. The camp, once a place of open camaraderie, took on a more guarded atmosphere, a necessary evolution in the face of the unseen threats that surrounded them.

Yet, it was within this climate of caution that a new kind of unity was forged. The rebels, understanding the gravity of the risks they faced, drew closer, their resolve hardened by the knowledge that their fight was as much against the shadows as it was against the redcoats.

One evening, as a cool mist descended upon the camp, Margaret received word of a captured British scout found lurking too close for comfort. The man, young and visibly terrified, was brought before her and James for interrogation. His eyes darted between his captors, the fear evident in his gaze.

Margaret addressed him firmly but without malice. "Who sent you?" she asked, her voice steady.

The scout, after a moment's hesitation, spoke of a British commander determined to crush the rebellion, of plans to dismantle the rebel networks through deceit and espionage. His words, while not entirely unexpected, confirmed the dangerous game of cat and mouse into which both sides had entered.

James, leaning in, added a layer of intimidation to the interrogation. "And if we were to let you go, to send a message to your commander, what would you tell him?"

The question hung in the air, charged with potential. The scout, understanding the precariousness of his position, offered information about British movements in exchange for his life—a proposal that, after careful consideration, Margaret and James decided to accept. They would release him, but not before feeding him carefully crafted falsehoods to take back to his superiors.

As the scout disappeared into the night, a small figure of deceit sent to mislead the enemy, Margaret, and James shared a look of determination. They were playing a dangerous game, one that required cunning and caution in equal measure. But it was a game they were prepared to win, for the stakes were nothing less than the freedom of their people and the future of their nation.

As the mist of dawn dissipated, revealing the dense forest that enveloped the rebel camp, Margaret and James convened an emergency meeting with their most trusted advisors and commanders. The information gleaned from the British scout had provided them with a dual advantage: insight into the enemy's intentions and the opportunity to feed them misinformation. However, the true challenge lies in leveraging this advantage without exposing themselves to further risk.

"The British believe they can undermine our efforts with spies and deception," Margaret began, her voice firm, echoing through the makeshift meeting hall. "We'll turn their strategy against them. We'll feed them shadows and whispers, false trails that lead nowhere."

James, standing beside her, unrolled a map across the table. "We've identified several key locations where we can stage mock operations, drawing their forces away from our true objectives." He pointed to a series of marked spots, each representing a potential diversion. "Simultaneously, we'll launch a series of raids on their supply lines. With their attention divided, we can strike where they're weakest."

The plan was ambitious, requiring precise timing and flawless execution. It also demanded a level of secrecy and trust among the rebels that had become increasingly difficult to maintain in the face of the enemy's espionage efforts. Yet, the consensus among the group was clear: the risk was worth the potential reward. With a renewed sense of purpose, they set to work, each member of the leadership team tasked with a crucial part of the operation.

Over the following days, the rebel camp buzzed with a quiet intensity. Small units were dispatched under the cover of night, their movements a closely guarded secret. Meanwhile, Margaret and James worked to reinforce the resolve of their forces, reminding them of the stakes of their struggle.

The first of their staged operations went off without a hitch, drawing a sizable British contingent to the west, where they found nothing but empty forest and the echoes of their own footsteps. Encouraged by this success, the rebels pressed on, launching hit-and-run attacks on British supply caravans and outposts, each strike further sowing confusion and frustration among their adversaries.

However, it was the raid on a British armory that marked the turning point. Led by James, the rebels managed to seize a significant cache of weapons and ammunition, dealing a crippling blow to the British logistical chain in the region. More importantly, it demonstrated the rebels' ability to outthink and outmaneuver their opponents, bolstering morale and cementing their reputation as a formidable force.

As news of their successes spread, the camp's atmosphere shifted from one of cautious optimism to one of jubilant defiance. Margaret, witnessing the transformation, knew that they had not only secured a series of tactical victories but had also struck a vital blow to the enemy's confidence.

Yet, even as they celebrated, she remained acutely aware of the challenges that lay ahead. The British would not be easily deterred, and the game of shadows and whispers was far from over. The war for independence was a marathon, not a sprint, and each victory brought with it the promise of retaliation.

One evening, as she and James stood once again at the edge of the camp, looking out into the twilight forest, she spoke her thoughts aloud. "We've shown them our strength, our resilience. But we must remain vigilant. The British will adapt, and so must we."

James nodded, his expression one of quiet determination. "Let them come. We'll be ready. Together, we've built something that can withstand any storm. This is our moment, Margaret. The tide is turning in our favor."

In the wake of their strategic victories, the rebels' spirits were high, yet both Margaret and James knew the importance of maintaining their momentum. With the British momentarily off balance, they had a critical window of opportunity to further their cause. Yet, they also recognized the necessity of caution; overextension now could lead to vulnerability later.

Margaret convened a strategy session under the canopy of ancient trees, the dappled sunlight casting patterns on her determined face as she addressed her inner circle. "Our recent successes have given us an edge, but we must not become complacent. We must think ahead, anticipate the British response, and prepare accordingly."

James, who had been reviewing reports from their scouts, added, "Intelligence suggests the British are gathering forces for a significant counteroffensive. We've managed to disrupt their plans, but they're adapting quickly. We need to be one step ahead."

The meeting evolved into a brainstorming session, with leaders proposing various tactics and strategies to capitalize on their current advantage. Ideas ranged from further diversions to solidifying alliances with neighboring factions that had remained neutral or even slightly hostile due to the uncertainty of the rebellion's prospects.

As dusk approached, a plan began to take form. It was daring and potentially transformative for the rebellion, but it would require every ounce of their cunning and bravery. They would launch a two-pronged operation: while continuing their campaign of misinformation to keep the British forces dispersed and confused, they would also reach out to other oppressed groups, offering a united front against their common enemy. This would not only expand their base of support but also stretch the British forces even thinner, making it harder for them to mount an effective counterattack.

Margaret tasked her most trusted envoys with the delicate mission of forging these new alliances. "We share a common cause," she reminded them. "Freedom from tyranny, a chance to live our lives on our own terms. Let's extend our hand in solidarity."

Meanwhile, James focused on fortifying their defenses and preparing for the expected British onslaught. He organized drills and training sessions, ensuring that every rebel was ready for the fight to come. He also oversaw the creation of hidden caches of supplies throughout the forest, ensuring that they could sustain a protracted conflict if necessary.

The rebels moved with a sense of purpose, buoyed by their leaders' confidence and the tangible sense of progress towards their goals. The camp, once a place of hushed conversations and wary glances, now buzzed with activity and optimism.

However, amidst the preparations, a lone figure approached the camp under the cover of night. It was a deserter from the British army, weary of the endless conflict and disillusioned by the promises of his commanders. He sought asylum with the rebels, offering valuable intelligence on the British plans in exchange for safety.

Margaret and James met with the deserter in a secluded clearing, listening intently as he shared details of the British strategy, including the locations of vulnerable supply lines and the identity of key commanders. This information was a boon to the rebellion, providing them with the means to further disrupt British operations.

As the deserter was led away to be debriefed further, Margaret turned to James, a thoughtful expression on her face. "This war... it's changing us all, isn't it? Enemies become allies, the oppressed find their strength. We're not just fighting for freedom from the British. We're fighting for the soul of our land, for the right to define our own destiny."

James nodded, his eyes reflecting the flickering light of the nearby campfires. "And we'll keep fighting, together. Every victory, every alliance we forge, brings us closer to that dream."

As the night grew darker, the camp became more active and alert. The rebels were preparing themselves for the silent battle for justice and freedom, each passing whisper of the wind and shadow cast by the moonlight reminding them of their purpose.

As they prepared for the days ahead, Margaret and James stood united, not just as leaders, but as symbols of the resilience and hope that fueled their rebellion. The road ahead was uncertain, fraught with danger and betrayal, but they faced it together, their resolve unshaken, their spirits undimmed by the darkness that surrounded them. Their struggle had only just begun.

As dawn crept over the horizon, painting the sky with hues of pink and gold, the rebel camp stirred into action. The day ahead promised new challenges but also new opportunities for Margaret, James, and their growing band of rebels. With the intelligence provided by the British deserter, they had a critical advantage, but leveraging it would require precision and audacity.

Margaret, standing at the center of the camp, addressed her assembled commanders, her voice clear and commanding. "Today, we strike at the heart of the British supply chain. Our goal is not just to disrupt their operations, but to send a message: we are not merely surviving; we are thriving, growing stronger with each passing day."

James, overseeing the preparation of their strike teams, added, "Remember, speed and stealth are our greatest allies. Hit hard, hit fast, and vanish before they can mount a counteroffensive. We are the shadows that haunt their dreams, the whispers that unsettle their ranks."

The operation was ambitious, targeting multiple sites simultaneously to maximize the impact while minimizing the risk to any single rebel unit. Teams were dispatched with specific targets: a munitions depot, a supply convoy route, and a communications outpost. Each strike was timed to coincide with the others, creating a symphony of disruption that would resonate far beyond the immediate targets.

As the teams moved out, the camp fell into a tense silence, the weight of anticipation heavy in the air. Margaret and James retreated to their command tent, pouring over maps and reports, ready to adapt their strategy as the situation evolved.

The first reports came in just before noon, a mixture of triumph and setback. The munitions depot had been destroyed, its loss a significant blow to the British logistical capabilities. However, the team targeting the supply convoy encountered unexpected resistance, resulting in a fierce skirmish. Quick thinking and the rebels' intimate knowledge of the terrain allowed them to disengage with minimal casualties, but the convoy remained largely intact.

The communications outpost, meanwhile, had been taken without a single shot fired, the rebels using the element of surprise to their full advantage. With the outpost in their control, even temporarily, they had a window to intercept and confuse British communications, adding another layer of chaos to their day's work.

As the sun began to set, painting the sky with fiery streaks, the strike teams returned to the camp, weary but buoyed by their successes. Margaret and James greeted each team personally, offering praise and consolation where needed, ensuring that every rebel knew their value to the cause.

That evening, as the camp gathered around the fire, the mood was one of quiet reflection. The day's actions had demonstrated the rebels' growing strength and sophistication, but the cost had been real. Margaret addressed her people, her voice resonant with pride and sorrow.

"Today, we proved once again that we are a force to be

reckoned with. We have shown our enemy, and ourselves, what we are capable of. But let us also remember those who sacrificed, who put themselves in harm's way for the sake of our shared dream."

James stood beside her, his gaze sweeping over the assembled faces, each one marked by the trials of their struggle. "Our fight is far from over. There will be more challenges, more battles. But as long as we stand together, as long as we fight with one heart and one purpose, there is nothing we cannot achieve."

The night deepened around them, the fire casting long shadows across the camp. Yet, in the faces of the rebels, there was a light that no darkness could dim—a light of hope, of determination, of an unbreakable will to forge their own destiny.

Chapter 18: Shadows and Whispers evolved from a tale of covert operations and strategic victories to a deeper narrative of resilience, unity, and the indomitable spirit of those who fight for freedom. As Margaret and James looked towards the future, they knew the road ahead would be fraught with adversity. Yet, they also knew that their cause was just, their resolve unyielding, and their conviction that freedom was within their grasp stronger than ever.

The struggle had indeed just begun, but in the hearts of the rebels, the flame of liberty burned bright, a beacon guiding them through the shadows and whispers of the uncertain path ahead.

As the fire dwindled to embers and the night wrapped the rebel camp in a cool embrace, Margaret stood before her people, the day's trials etched in the lines of her face, but her eyes alight with an unwavering resolve. James, ever her steadfast companion in leadership, stood by her side, his gaze sweeping over the assembled rebels with pride and a touch of solemnity.

"Today, we have proven once more that we are a force to be reckoned with," Margaret began, her voice carrying through the silent camp. "We struck at the heart of the enemy, not just with our weapons but with our spirit. We have faced loss, yes, but in our fight, we have gained something far greater. We have forged a unity that no adversary can break."

The rebels gathered around and listened intently, drawing strength from her words. They had felt the weight of the day's battles and had mourned the loss of comrades, yet in their hearts burned a fire that no hardship could extinguish.

James stepped forward, his voice joining Margaret's in the night air. "Our struggle is far from over. The enemy will come at us with renewed vengeance, but they will find us ready. We will adapt, as we always have. We will meet their swords with our shields, their deceit with our resolve."

A murmur of agreement rose from the rebels, a unified declaration of their continued commitment to the cause. In their leaders, they saw the embodiment of their aspirations, the beacon guiding them through the darkest nights.

Margaret and James shared a glance, a silent acknowledgment of the path that lay ahead. It would be fraught with danger, paved with sacrifice, but it was a path they would walk together, shoulder to shoulder with those who had chosen to follow them.

As the meeting dispersed, the rebels finding solace in their shared purpose, Margaret took a moment to gaze up at the stars. They shimmered brightly, timeless sentinels in the vast expanse of the night sky. "For freedom," she whispered, a vow that carried on the wind, a promise to those who had fallen and those who still stood.

James joined her, his presence a comforting certainty. "For freedom," he echoed, his voice a testament to the journey they had undertaken, to the battles fought and those yet to come.

The chapter of Shadows and Whispers drew to a close not with the silence of defeat but with the whispers of defiance, the shadows cast by their fire a testament to their resilience. The rebels, under the leadership of Margaret and James, faced the future not as a looming specter but as a challenge to be met with courage and determination.

As dawn broke on the horizon, heralding the start of a new day, it found the camp not weary and beaten but fortified by their victories, however small, and united in their cause. The fight for freedom, for the right to determine their own destiny, continued, each day a step on the long road to liberty.

CHAPTER **21**

The Eve of Reckoning

As dawn painted the sky in shades of amber and crimson, the rebel camp awoke to a palpable sense of anticipation. Today marked the eve of their most ambitious operation yet, a coordinated strike designed to sever the British command's head from its body. The success of their previous endeavors had paved the way for this moment, but the weight of expectation hung heavy in the air.

Margaret stood before the map table, her advisors gathered around. The plan before them was the culmination of weeks of preparation, a daring gamble that could turn the tide of the war in their favor. Yet, as she looked into the faces of her trusted comrades, she knew that the true strength of their rebellion lay not in plans or strategies but in the hearts of those who fought for freedom.

James, sensing the unspoken tension, broke the silence. "We've come far on the back of our unity and resolve. Let's not forget, it's our belief in each other, in our cause, that has brought us to this point. No matter what tomorrow brings, that belief will see us through."

Margaret nodded, her gaze meeting each of her advisors in turn. "James is right. Tomorrow, we strike not just as soldiers, but as bearers of hope for all who suffer under tyranny. Our actions will echo far beyond these woods, a call to arms for the oppressed and a warning to the oppressors."

The meeting dispersed, and Margaret found herself walking alongside James through the camp. They passed by rebels preparing weapons, tending to the wounded, and strengthening their resolve with quiet moments of reflection.

"Remember our first days?" James asked a wistful note in his voice. "Back when our biggest concern was surviving the night?"

Margaret smiled, the memories flooding back. "We've come a long way from hiding in the shadows, fearing every rustle in the woods. Now, we're the ones keeping the British awake at night."

Their path took them to a clearing where a group of young rebels sat, listening intently to an older soldier recounting tales of battles past. Noticing Margaret and James, he called out, "Commander, care to share a word of wisdom on the eve of our great endeavor?"

Margaret approached, the eager faces turning towards her. She sat down among them, her expression serious but kind. "Tomorrow, we make history," she began, her voice steady and sure. "But it's important to remember why we fight. We fight for those who can't, for the future we believe in. Courage isn't the absence of fear; it's the resolve to face it head-on. Remember, no matter what happens, we stand together."

The rebels nodded, their spirits lifted by her words. James joined in, "And keep in mind, every one of you plays a crucial role. From the scouts to the medics, each contribution moves us closer to our goal. Tomorrow, we fight as one."

As night fell, the camp was alive with a quiet energy. Margaret and James retired to their tent, the weight of the coming day pressing upon them. Yet, in their shared silence, there was a bond of unspoken understanding and mutual respect that had been forged in the heat of battle and solidified in moments of victory and loss.

James broke the silence, his voice soft in the darkness. "No matter what tomorrow brings, I want you to know—I couldn't have asked for a braver or more dedicated partner in this fight."

Margaret reached out, finding his hand in the dim light. "And I, you. Together, we've built something that will outlast us both, a beacon of hope in the darkness. Let's give them a dawn they'll never forget."

The Eve of Reckoning was upon them, a chapter yet unwritten, but in the hearts of Margaret, James, and their fellow rebels, the resolve to fight for freedom, to turn the tide of history, burned brighter than ever. Tomorrow's battle would be their greatest challenge yet, but it was a challenge they would face together, united in purpose and unyielding in their quest for liberty.

As dawn broke on the day that would come to be known as "The Eve of Reckoning," the first rays of sunlight pierced through the darkness, casting long shadows over the encampment where Margaret, James, and their fellow rebels gathered. The air was charged with anticipation and the weight of what was to come. Around them, the sounds of preparation filled the morning air—metal clinking, horses neighing, and the subdued murmur of voices reciting silent prayers for the day ahead.

Margaret stood beside James, her gaze fixed on the horizon where the battle would unfold. In her heart, a mix of fear and fierce determination. She had come a long way from the shadows of espionage to stand openly in the field of battle, yet her resolve had never been stronger. "This is the day we've been fighting for," she said quietly, her voice steady despite the tumult of emotions within.

James looked down at her, seeing not just the spy or the woman he had come to love but a symbol of the revolution itself—brave, unyielding, and boundlessly hopeful. "Together, we've changed the course of this war," he replied, his hand finding hers, their fingers intertwining. "Today, we'll change the future."

Around them, their comrades-in-arms shared final words of encouragement and solidarity. There was no mistaking the gravity of the day, for on their shoulders rested the hopes of a nation yearning to breathe free. The strategies devised in secrecy, the alliances forged in the face of adversity, and the sacrifices made along the way—all led to this moment.

As the army began to move out, Margaret and James joined the ranks, their hearts beating as one with the drums that sounded the march. They knew the battle ahead would be fierce, that not all who marched beside them would return. But in this moment of reckoning, they found strength in their unity, in the shared vision of liberty that had brought them together against all odds.

The battlefield awaited, a vast expanse where the future of the Continental Army and the dream of an independent nation would be contested. Margaret and James, side by side, stepped forward into the dawn, ready to face whatever the day brought. For in their hearts burned the unquenchable flame of freedom, a light that no darkness could dim. Today, history would remember the courage of those who dared to fight, sacrifice, and dream of a world remade in the image of liberty.

The Eve of Reckoning was upon them, but they were ready.

As the dawn gave way to the full light of day, the battlefield lay stretched out before them, an expanse of land that would soon bear witness to the resolve and bravery of those fighting for a cause greater than themselves. Margaret and James, at the forefront of the Continental Army, could see the British forces assembling in the distance, a sea of red uniforms against the green backdrop, stark and foreboding.

The air was tense with the anticipation of the imminent clash, the silence of the morning broken only by the occasional snort of a horse or the rustle of leaves in the gentle morning breeze. The rebels stood ready, a mosaic of determination and fear, understanding the magnitude of the battle ahead.

General Washington rode along the ranks, his presence a steady calm in the storm of emotions. His eyes met Margaret's and James's, a silent nod conveying his trust and confidence in them. It was a moment of unspoken communication, a reassurance that their leadership and courage were instrumental in the day's strategy.

As the order to advance was given, Margaret felt a surge of adrenaline. She gripped her musket tighter, the weapon familiar in her hands despite the tremor of anticipation. Beside her, James checked the pistol at his belt, his expression focused, resolute. They had faced danger before, but never like this, never so exposed and with so much at stake.

The battlefield came alive with the sounds of war as the two forces collided. Cannon fire roared, shaking the ground beneath their feet as musket volleys exchanged their deadly greetings. Smoke filled the air, obscuring vision and turning the morning into a hazy twilight.

Margaret and James moved as one, their training and instincts guiding them through the chaos. They fought not just with weapons but with their hearts, with every strike a blow for freedom, every maneuver a dance of defiance against tyranny.

As the battle raged, Margaret found herself separated from James in the confusion of smoke and combat. A surge of fear gripped her heart, not for her own life, but for his. They had promised to face this challenge together, and the thought of losing him now, amidst the tumult of war, was unbearable.

Pushing through the fear, Margaret redoubled her efforts, her aim true as she took down enemy soldiers threatening to breach their lines. Around her, the tide of battle ebbed and flowed, a relentless struggle for every inch of ground, for every moment of survival.

Then, as if guided by fate, she and James found each other again amidst the chaos. Back to back, they stood, a testament to their unbreakable bond, fighting off the encroaching British forces with a ferocity born of their shared conviction.

The battle reached its zenith, the outcome hanging in the balance when a decisive charge led by General Washington himself turned the tide. Margaret and James joined the surge, their spirits lifted by the sight of their leader at the helm, his presence igniting a renewed vigor in the Continental forces.

As the British lines began to falter, a cheer went up among the American ranks, a sound that carried over the battlefield, a harbinger of victory. Margaret and James, through the smoke and din of war, shared a look of relief and triumph, knowing that their contributions had helped secure this moment of success.

The battle of "The Eve of Reckoning" would be remembered as a turning point, a testament to the bravery and sacrifice of those who fought. As the sun set on the battlefield, casting long shadows over the land they had fought to claim, Margaret and James stood together, weary but undefeated, their hearts full with the knowledge that they had played their part in the fight for liberty.

Their journey was far from over; the war would rage on, but this victory was a beacon of hope, a sign that their dreams of freedom and a new nation might one day be realized. Together, they looked toward the future, ready to face whatever challenges lay ahead, united in purpose and unyielding in their quest for liberty.

After the victory of "The Eve of Reckoning," the Continental Army continued its relentless push towards liberty, engaging in numerous skirmishes that tested the resolve and fortitude of its fighters. Among these was a minor but pivotal confrontation at Brandywine Creek, an event that would not only challenge Margaret and James but also solidify their roles within the army and the rebellion.

In the thick of a fog-laden morning, word reached the rebel camp of a British contingent moving to secure a strategic ford along Brandywine Creek, a move that would enable them to flank the Continental forces. Recognizing the urgency of the situation, General Washington tasked a small detachment, including Margaret and James, to intercept and delay the British, buying time for the main army to reposition.

Margaret and James, leading a group of seasoned rebels, moved swiftly through the dense woodland that bordered Brandywine Creek. The element of surprise was crucial, and under the cloak of mist, they positioned themselves along the high ground overlooking the Ford.

As the British troops emerged from the treeline, confident in their numbers and the element of surprise, they were met with a volley of musket fire from Margaret, James, and their contingent. The skirmish erupted into chaos, the sounds of gunfire and clashing steel echoing through the woods as both sides engaged in a fierce struggle for control.

Margaret, ever the strategist, directed her forces with precision, her commands cutting through the din of battle.

James, for his part, fought with a ferocity that belied his former allegiance, his actions driven by a deep-seated belief in the cause for which they battled.

The skirmish at Brandywine Creek was intense but brief, and the rebels' determination and tactical advantage forced the British to withdraw, so their plans were thwarted. Margaret and James, amidst the adrenaline and aftermath, shared a moment of quiet acknowledgment of their victory, aware that their success was but a small step in the long march toward independence.

However, the battle was not without cost. Among the wounded was a young rebel soldier whom Margaret had trained, his injury a stark reminder of the personal toll of their fight for freedom. As James helped tend to the injured, Margaret's resolve hardened. Each battle, each skirmish, was a testament to their cause's righteousness and the sacrifices it demanded.

The skirmish at Brandywine Creek, though minor in the grand scheme of the war, was a defining moment for Margaret and James. It showcased their leadership, courage, and unwavering commitment to the fight for liberty. As they returned to camp with their contingent, the respect and admiration of their fellow soldiers were palpable, a recognition of their contributions to the rebellion's cause.

In the quiet that followed, as they prepared for the battles yet to come, Margaret and James knew that each skirmish, each confrontation, brought them one step closer to the realization of their dream—a free and independent nation. And in this knowledge, they found the strength to press on, united in purpose and spirit.

In the shadowed predawn light, Margaret and James, along with a handpicked group of Continental soldiers, moved silently towards Brandywine Creek. Their mission was clear yet fraught with danger: to halt the advance of a British detachment long enough for the main Continental forces to reposition. The weight of their task was palpable in the cool morning air, a silent testament to the sacrifices demanded by the fight for freedom.

As they neared the creek, the soft murmur of the flowing water was a stark contrast to the thundering pulse in Margaret's ears. Beside her, James scanned the tree line, his experience as a former British officer providing invaluable insight into the enemy's likely approach. Together, they represented a bridge between worlds—Margaret with her keen intelligence network and James with his strategic military knowledge.

The first rays of dawn broke over the horizon, casting a golden light on the creek. It was then that the British forces appeared, seemingly confident in their numbers and the element of surprise. Little did they know, Margaret, James, and their contingent lay in wait, shadows among the trees ready to defend their nascent nation.

With a nod from Margaret, the ambush was sprung. The silence of the morning shattered as muskets roared to life, the rebels unleashing a devastating volley into the unsuspecting British ranks. James directed their fire with precision, ensuring each shot served to sow maximum confusion and chaos among the enemy.

The British, taken aback by the ferocity and determination of the Continental forces, attempted to regroup and return fire. But Margaret and James, understanding the stakes, pressed their advantage. They moved through the skirmish with a grace born of desperation, their actions not just a fight for survival but a declaration of their unyielding pursuit of liberty.

As the battle raged, Margaret found herself face to face with a British soldier, his bayonet aimed at her heart. In that moment, time seemed to slow, the sounds of battle fading into a distant echo. All that mattered was the man before her, the embodiment of the tyranny they sought to overthrow. With a swift move, she parried his thrust and countered, her resolve as sharp as the blade in her hand.

The skirmish at Brandywine Creek, though brief, was intense. When the smoke cleared, the British were in retreat, their plans thwarted by the bravery and strategic cunning of a few determined rebels. Margaret, James, and their comrades had secured a vital victory, not through overwhelming force but through the strength of their conviction and their willingness to stand against the odds.

In the aftermath, as they surveyed the battlefield, the cost of their victory was apparent. Wounded soldiers lay on both sides, a sobering reminder of the war's toll. Yet, in this moment of triumph, Margaret and James shared a profound connection, recognizing the depth of their commitment to the cause and each other.

As they returned to camp, the skirmish at Brandywine Creek became a symbol of their fight—a testament to the power of unity and the enduring spirit of those who dared to dream of freedom. It was a moment of valor, a chapter in the larger story of the revolution that would be told and retold, a reminder that even the smallest battles can turn the tide of history.

As the last echoes of the skirmish at Brandywine Creek faded into the quiet of the forest, Margaret and James stood amid their fellow soldiers, their gazes lingering on the horizon where the retreating British forces had disappeared. The victory was theirs, hard-earned and fraught with sacrifice, yet in their hearts, they knew the battle for freedom was far from over.

Around them, the Continental Army began the solemn task of tending to the wounded and paying respects to the fallen. The air was filled with a mingling sense of triumph and mourning, a testament to the complex tapestry of war. Margaret's thoughts turned to those who had given everything for the cause, their names forever etched in the memory of those who continued the fight. Beside her, James shared a silent vow, a promise made to the comrades they had lost: their sacrifices would not be in vain.

As they prepared to leave the battlefield, Margaret and James shared a quiet moment of reflection. The skirmish at Brandywine Creek had tested their resolve, reaffirmed their commitment to the revolution, and reminded them of the unbreakable bond they shared. Together, they had faced the might of an empire and emerged victorious, a beacon of hope in the darkest of times.

With the dawn of a new day, they turned their eyes toward the future, toward the next chapter in their fight for liberty. The road ahead was filled with challenges, but Margaret and James faced them with unwavering determination. They were united in their cause and strengthened by the victories, big and small, that lay behind them.

Their struggle continues, a narrative woven from the threads of courage, sacrifice, and an enduring quest for freedom. As the pages turn, the saga of Margaret, James, and the Continental Army unfolds, a tale of resilience in the face of adversity and the indomitable spirit of a nation fighting for its birthright.

CHAPTER **22**

𝕭attle 𝕷ines

The morning sun rose over the encampment, casting long shadows that seemed to stretch with anticipation toward the unknown day ahead. The air was crisp, charged with a tension that spoke of the significant confrontations to come. Today, Margaret and James, two brave souls, would face one of their most formidable challenges yet, their courage a beacon of inspiration for their fellow patriots.

General Washington summoned his officers for a final briefing in the quiet that preceded the storm. Among them, Margaret and James stood, their presence a testament to their vital roles within the Continental Army's ranks. The General's eyes swept over his trusted commanders, pausing on Margaret and James, his gaze imbued with a mix of gratitude and solemnity.

"We stand on the precipice of history," Washington began, his voice steady, imbuing courage into the hearts of those gathered. "The enemy advances, but in our unity, we find our strength. Today, we fight not just for our freedom but for the future of a nation yet unborn."

As the assembly dispersed, Margaret turned to James, her determination mirrored in his eyes. "No matter what happens today, know that I..." Her voice trailed off, the words unspoken yet understood between them. They had both lost loved ones to the war, seen their homes destroyed, and yet, they continued to fight. Their shared experiences and the bond they had formed in the face of adversity were what kept them going.

James nodded, reaching for her hand, a silent vow passing between them. "Together, until the end," he affirmed before they parted ways to join their units.

The battle lines were drawn, a stark demarcation across the landscape that would soon become a tumultuous sea of men, muskets, and the fervent desire for liberty. Margaret took her position, her spyglass trained on the advancing British lines, while James coordinated the Continental forces, his strategic acumen more crucial than ever.

As the first shots rang out, the battle erupted into a cacophony of sound and fury. Margaret, utilizing her intelligence network, relayed crucial information that allowed the Continental forces to counter the British maneuvers effectively. James, leading a battalion, moved with precision, and his every decision was aimed at protecting his men and securing an advantage. He ordered his troops to form a defensive line, using the natural terrain to their advantage, and to hold their fire until the enemy was within range. This strategy allowed them to conserve ammunition and inflict maximum damage on the advancing British forces.

The conflict surged like a living entity, ebbing and flowing with the fortunes of war. Amidst the chaos, Margaret and James fought with a fervor born of their shared convictions, their actions a beacon to those around them.

As the day wore on, the battle reached its zenith. A critical breach in the British lines presented itself, a moment of opportunity that could turn the tide definitively in their favor. Recognizing the moment, General Washington ordered a daring assault, with Margaret and James at the heart of the charge.

The push was grueling, a test of every ounce of their resolve and training. Side by side, they breached the enemy lines, their comrades rallying behind them, driving the British forces back in a decisive rout.

As the dust settled and the reality of their victory sank in, Margaret and James found themselves on the battlefield's scarred landscape, the setting sun casting long shadows over the victorious but weary Continental forces.

"We did it," Margaret whispered, allowing herself a moment of relief amidst the remnants of the fray.

"We did," James agreed, his arm finding its way around her shoulders, pulling her close. "But this victory is not just ours; it belongs to every man who fought, to every sacrifice made for the dream of a nation founded on the principles of freedom and justice."

As they stood together, looking out over the field, the weight of their journey, from the first sparks of rebellion to this moment of triumph, was palpable. They had faced adversity, witnessed the cost of freedom, and fought relentlessly for a cause greater than themselves.

The battle lines had been drawn, and they had emerged victorious, a testament to their unwavering spirit and determination. The war for independence was far from over, but at this moment, the promise of a new dawn for America seemed closer than ever, a dream within reach, forged in the fires of revolution and the unbreakable spirit of those who dared to fight for it. This victory, however small, was a significant step towards that dream.

As they prepared for the council, the significance of their

next actions weighed heavily upon them. The path to freedom was indeed paved with nights like these—filled with quiet reflection, shared dreams, and the relentless pursuit of a vision that was both fragile and necessary.

Margaret and James, standing side by side, faced the flickering light of the campfire, their silhouettes casting long shadows into the night. The air was thick with anticipation, the quiet before the storm of battle that awaited them. Their journey, marked by victories and losses, had brought them to this moment, a testament to their commitment to the cause and to each other.

"We stand ready," James said quietly, his voice carrying a determination that matched the resolve in Margaret's eyes.

"For freedom," Margaret responded, her gaze steady on the horizon that held both promise and peril.

As they turned towards the tent where the council of war awaited, their steps were firm, their spirits unbroken. The night air carried their whispered vows to fight, to strive, and to never yield until the dream of liberty became the reality of a nation reborn.

Under cover of night, with the campfires dwindling to embers, Margaret found herself walking along the periphery of the encampment, her thoughts as tumultuous as the war-torn landscape around her. Each step seemed to echo with the weight of the battles fought and those looming on the horizon. The victory today was a testament to their resolve, yet the cost of freedom was etched deeply in the faces of every soldier she passed. She couldn't help but wonder how many more would have to pay that price before the war was over.

James, meanwhile, engaged in a quiet discussion with a group of young soldiers, their faces alight with the fervor of the cause and the naivety of youth. He shared tales of strategy and survival, each story a lesson in leadership and the harsh realities of war. Yet, even as he spoke, his gaze often drifted to Margaret, their shared experiences forming an unspoken bond that had become the cornerstone of their strength.

As dawn approached, whispers of the enemy's movements began to circulate among the camp. Scouts reported a significant mobilization to the north, suggesting a forthcoming engagement that could prove to be the turning point of the war. With this news, the atmosphere within the camp shifted, a tangible tension replacing the brief respite of victory.

Margaret, upon hearing these reports, immediately sought out James. Together, they joined General Washington's council, a gathering of minds tasked with anticipating the enemy's next move. The council debated strategies into the early hours, the map before them a complex web of possibilities and perils. Margaret, with her intricate knowledge of enemy tactics, and James, with his tactical expertise, contributed insights that shaped the course of their deliberation.

The decision was made to advance at first light, to meet the enemy in a bid to control the narrative of the war. The stakes were higher than ever, a fact not lost on any in attendance. As the council disbanded, the weight of the impending battle settled heavily on Margaret and James.

In the quiet before dawn, as the camp stirred to life around them, Margaret and James shared a moment of solitude. They reflected on the journey that had brought them here, on the ideals that had sustained them, and on the uncertain future they were fighting to secure. It was a moment of profound connection, a reaffirmation of their commitment to the cause and to each other.

With the first light of dawn, the army mobilized, the air thick with determination and the solemn acknowledgment of the challenge ahead. Margaret and James, standing among their fellow soldiers, felt the unity of purpose that bound them. They were ready to face whatever the day brought, to fight for the ideals of liberty and justice that had ignited the flame of rebellion.

As dawn's first light broke over the horizon, marking the onset of a day destined to be etched in history, Margaret and James, alongside their compatriots, stepped forward into the fray. This moment, poised on the edge of conflict, was a culmination of their courage, sacrifices, and the shared resolve that had bound them together. The chapter they were living through, though merely one passage in the broader saga of their fight for freedom, emerged as a defining ordeal in their relentless pursuit of a dream—a dream of liberty and justice for a nation striving to claim its place in the annals of history.

As the early mists of dawn began to lift, revealing the expanse of no-man's land that lay between the Continental forces and the British lines, a palpable tension gripped the hearts of all who stood ready to fight. The previous victories, the skirmishes and battles fought, had all led to this moment—a confrontation that promised to be pivotal in the struggle for independence.

Margaret, her eyes scanning the horizon, could see the movement of the British troops, their formations a stark reminder of the formidable enemy they faced. Beside her, James reviewed the plans once more, his mind racing through scenarios, each decision weighed against the backdrop of their collective hope for victory.

The signal to advance was given, and the Continental Army moved as one, a sea of determination set against the dawn. Margaret and James found themselves in the vanguard, their roles critical in the initial push. They had discussed their strategies the night before, knowing full well the importance of their actions in the coming hours.

As they approached the British lines, the first shots rang out, a harrowing melody that would soon crescendo into a full symphony of war. Margaret, with her rifle in hand, moved with purpose, each shot aimed with precision, her mind clear despite the chaos that erupted around them.

James, leading a contingent of soldiers, maneuvered through the battlefield with a tactical acumen that had been honed through countless engagements. His voice, steady and commanding, offered guidance and reassurance to his men, even as they faced the enemy's relentless onslaught.

The battle raged, a tumultuous clash of wills and weaponry, with both sides vying for dominance. Amidst the turmoil, Margaret and James found themselves back-to-back, fighting off a British charge that threatened to overwhelm their position. In that moment, their bond, forged in the fires of conflict, became their strength, each protecting the other, their resolve unyielding.

It was then, in the heart of battle, that an opportunity presented itself—a weakness in the British formation, a chance to turn the tide. With a quick exchange of glances, Margaret and James understood what had to be done. Rallying their comrades, they led a daring assault, breaking through the enemy lines and sowing confusion in their ranks.

The Continental forces, seizing upon the opening created by Margaret and James, surged forward, their spirits lifted by the sight of their compatriots breaking through. The battle, which had seemed so evenly matched, began to tip in their favor, the momentum shifting with each passing moment.

As the sun climbed higher, illuminating the battlefield with its unforgiving light, the outcome became clear. The

British, unable to regroup and counter the unexpected ferocity of the Continental Army, began a tactical withdrawal, their movements harried by the relentless pursuit of freedom's champions.

When the dust of battle settled, Margaret and James stood amidst their fellow soldiers, the field before them a testament to the day's hard-fought victory. They were weary and bruised but unbroken, their spirits buoyed by the knowledge that their actions had contributed to a significant turning point in the war.

The victory at "Battle Lines" would be remembered not just as a military triumph but as a moment of unity and courage, a point in history where the dream of independence, so fiercely defended, became a tangible reality on the horizon.

As the battlefield fell silent, save for the soft moans of the wounded and the distant cries of victory, Margaret and James took a moment to survey the land that had witnessed such ferocity. The victory was theirs, but it had not come without cost. The ground was littered with the remnants of the battle, a stark reminder of the price of freedom.

In the aftermath, as the Continental Army began the somber task of tending to the injured and honoring the fallen, Margaret and James joined their efforts. Each soldier they helped, each comrade they laid to rest, served as a poignant reminder of the sacrifices made for the cause of liberty. It was a moment of collective mourning and reflection, a time to grieve and to remember.

Yet, amidst the sorrow, there was a sense of hope—an understanding that their victory at "Battle Lines" was a significant stride towards the independence they so desperately sought. General Washington, addressing his weary but victorious troops, spoke words of gratitude and encouragement, his voice resonating with the weight of their shared experiences.

"Today, we have proven once again that our resolve is stronger than the mightiest of armies. Our victory is a testament to the courage and the spirit of every man and woman who stands for freedom. Let us remember those we have lost, not as a toll of war, but as heroes who have paved the way for a future free from tyranny."

As the General's speech echoed across the encampment, Margaret and James found solace in each other's presence. They had been through the unimaginable together, their bond strengthened by the trials of war. In the quiet of the evening, as the campfires flickered to life, they shared a moment of peace, a rare reprieve in the relentless tide of conflict.

However, the war was far from over. The victory at "Battle Lines" was but a chapter in the ongoing struggle for independence. As they looked towards the days ahead, Margaret and James knew that they would face more challenges, more battles, and more moments of uncertainty.

But for now, they allowed themselves to savor the victory, to cherish the quiet before the storm of war descended once more. They sat side by side, watching the night sky, the stars above a testament to the enduring hope that guided them. They spoke of dreams for the future—a future where their sacrifices would be remembered, where their fight for freedom would culminate in the birth of a nation.

As the night deepened, Margaret and James, along with their fellow soldiers, prepared for the journey ahead. The path to independence was a long and arduous one, but they were ready to face it head-on, united by a common cause and a shared vision of liberty.

The battle lines had been drawn, and they had emerged victorious, but the war for freedom raged on. Together, they would continue to fight, strive, and hope until the dream of a free and independent America was realized.

As dawn broke on the camp, the light of the new day brought with it a renewed sense of purpose. The victory at "Battle Lines" had bolstered the spirits of the Continental Army, infusing them with a belief in the possibility of triumph despite the odds stacked against them. Margaret and James, their resolve unshaken, prepared for the continuation of their journey, knowing well that the road to independence was fraught with challenges yet unseen.

The days that followed were a mix of preparation and anticipation. Word of their victory had spread, igniting a flame of hope across the colonies. Reinforcements, albeit few, began to arrive, each new soldier a valuable addition to their ranks. Margaret took charge of training the newcomers, and her expertise in espionage and tactics made her an invaluable asset to the cause.

James, on the other hand, found himself engrossed in strategy meetings with General Washington and his aides. The victory, while significant, was but a single battle in a much larger war. The British, they knew, would not be deterred easily. The intelligence reports that Margaret managed to procure through her network were critical in planning their next moves. The information painted a picture of an enemy regrouping with plans to strike back with renewed vigor.

In the midst of strategizing and preparation, Margaret and James found moments of solace in each other's company. Their shared experiences on the battlefield had forged a bond that was unbreakable. In the quiet of the evening, they would walk along the perimeter of the camp, sharing their hopes and fears for the future. It was during one of these walks that they encountered a young soldier, no more than sixteen, sitting alone, staring into the fire.

The boy, Thomas, had joined the army fueled by the fervor of patriotism but was now grappling with the realities of war.

The stories of valor and freedom he had heard were far removed from the death and destruction he had witnessed. Margaret and James sat with him, sharing their own doubts and fears but also speaking of the importance of their fight, the belief in the cause of liberty that made every sacrifice worthwhile.

Their words seemed to comfort Thomas, offering him a glimpse of the bigger picture, the reason why they all fought so valiantly. This moment with Thomas was a reminder for Margaret and James of the impact of their actions, not just on the battlefield but on the hearts and minds of those who looked up to them.

As news of the British movements reached the camp, the brief period of respite came to an end. The enemy was advancing towards a critical stronghold, one that held not just strategic value but also symbolized the spirit of the revolution. The defense of this stronghold would be their next great challenge, a battle that would require all their cunning, bravery, and resolve.

The night before the march, the camp was abuzz with activity. Soldiers checked their equipment, letters were written to loved ones, and prayers were whispered into the night. Margaret and James, standing before the assembled troops, felt the weight of responsibility on their shoulders. They were not just soldiers; they were symbols of the fight for freedom, embodiments of the hope that drove the Continental Army forward.

As they set out at dawn, the silhouette of the army stretched across the horizon, a testament to their unwavering commitment to the cause. Margaret and James led their troops with a determination that belied the uncertainty of the outcome. They knew that the coming battle would be a defining moment in their fight for independence, a test of their will against the might of an empire.

The march was long and arduous, but the resolve of the Continental Army was unyielding. As they neared the battlefield, the reality of the imminent conflict set in. This was not just another skirmish; it was a battle for the soul of a nation, a fight for the very ideals that had ignited the flame of revolution.

As the first light of dawn pierced the horizon, casting long shadows over the landscape, the Continental Army stood ready. Margaret and James, their faces set with determination, looked out over the ranks of soldiers who had become more than just comrades-in-arms; they were family, united by a common cause that transcended individual desires.

The air was thick with anticipation, each breath a silent pledge to the ideals for which they were willing to lay down their lives. The upcoming battle loomed large in their minds, a decisive confrontation that could very well dictate the future course of the American Revolution. Yet, amidst the uncertainty, there was a palpable sense of hope, a belief in the righteousness of their cause that fortified their spirits.

Margaret turned to James, her gaze conveying a world of emotions. "No matter what happens," she said, her voice steady, "we stand together, for freedom, for justice, and for the dream of a nation conceived in liberty."

James nodded, taking her hand in his. "Together," he affirmed, the word a vow that bound them to each other and to the cause they were about to fight for. They turned their eyes forward, facing the challenges that awaited with unwavering courage and a shared resolve.

As the army began its march towards destiny, the chapter of "Battle Lines" drew to a close, leaving the echoes of their determination to resonate in the hearts of all who shared in their struggle. The battle ahead would test their resolve, challenge their convictions, and demand sacrifices they were all prepared to make.

For Margaret, James, and the Continental Army, the fight for independence was more than a military campaign; it was a testament to the enduring spirit of freedom, a battle waged in the name of all those who dared to dream of a better world.

CHAPTER 23

New Beginnings

The dawn of the day after the battle greeted the Continental Army with an almost surreal silence. The tumult and clamor of war had given way to a calm that spread across the encampment like a soothing balm. Yet, beneath this veneer of peace, there was an undercurrent of activity and anticipation. The victory at the battle had opened a new chapter in their fight for freedom, filled with possibilities and the daunting task of forging ahead.

Margaret walked among the rows of tents, her steps unhurried but purposeful. The relief of victory was palpable, yet so was the cost. She stopped to offer words of comfort to the wounded, her presence a beacon of hope and strength. Her role had evolved beyond that of a spy; she had become a symbol of resilience, embodying the spirit of the revolution.

James, too, was in the midst of reflection and action. The strategic victory had affirmed his place as a leader within the army, but it had also underscored the immense responsibilities that came with it. As he conferred with General Washington and other officers, planning the next steps in their campaign, he was acutely aware of the weight of his decisions and their impact on the lives of his men.

In their quiet moments together, Margaret and James

spoke of the future. The victory had shifted the tide of the war, opening the door to new strategies and alliances. There was talk of a declaration, a formal statement of independence that would announce to the world their intentions and their right to freedom. The prospect was both exhilarating and daunting; it would undoubtedly draw more attention and possibly ire from their adversaries.

As the days passed, the army began the process of recovery and preparation. Supplies were gathered, strategies were devised, and the troops were trained with renewed vigor. The encampment buzzed with the energy of anticipation, a shared sense of purpose uniting them all.

Amidst this flurry of activity, Margaret received news that would once again change the course of her journey. A missive from her network of spies hinted at crucial intelligence that could further their cause, necessitating a journey into enemy territory. The risks were immense, but the potential rewards were too significant to ignore.

James, faced with the prospect of Margaret's departure, felt a surge of conflict. The thought of her in danger was unbearable, yet he understood the necessity of her mission. Their farewell was a mixture of fear and resolve, a promise to return to each other no matter what.

As Margaret set out on her mission, James turned his focus to the tasks at hand, leading his men in reinforcing their positions and planning for the inevitable counterattacks. Yet, his thoughts often drifted to Margaret, her safety a constant concern.

The Continental Army, strengthened by their victory, faces the future with determination, even as they contend with the challenges of sustaining their momentum. For Margaret and James, the victory marks both an endpoint and a new beginning, their paths diverging yet intertwined by their shared commitment to the cause and to each other.

Margaret's decision to venture into enemy territory was met with a mix of admiration and concern among her peers. The night before her departure, she and James found themselves seated by a dwindling campfire, a small circle of trusted comrades gathered around them.

"Margaret," began James, his voice tinged with worry, "this mission... it's unlike any you've undertaken before. The risks—"

Margaret interrupted, her gaze steady. "I know the risks, James. But think of what we stand to gain. This intelligence could change everything for us."

One of their comrades, a young lieutenant named Samuel, chimed in, "But is it worth the risk to you, Margaret? To all of us who rely on you?"

Margaret smiled gently at Samuel's concern. "Every mission we undertake is a risk. But it's for our cause—for freedom. And if my actions can further that cause, then it's a risk I'm willing to take."

James looked into the fire, struggling with his emotions. "Just promise me you'll be careful."

"I promise," Margaret replied, reaching out to squeeze his hand. "And I'll be back before you know it."

The group fell into a contemplative silence, each lost in their thoughts about the uncertain days ahead. After a moment, Margaret stood, her posture resolute. "Let's not dwell on what may come. Tonight, let's just be here, together, as friends fighting for a common dream."

Her words lifted the somber mood, and the evening progressed with tales of past exploits, shared laughter, and quiet moments of reflection. It was a much-needed respite, a reminder of the bonds that held them together amidst the turmoil of war.

The following morning, as the camp stirred to life, Margaret prepared to depart. She was dressed in a simple traveler's cloak, a nondescript appearance that belied the significance of her mission. James accompanied her to the edge of the encampment, where a horse awaited.

"Remember, keep to the shadows, avoid the main roads, and trust no one," James advised, his voice low.

Margaret nodded. "I have your lessons etched in my mind, James. I'll be cautious."

They shared a long look, words unnecessary at the moment. Then, with a final embrace, Margaret mounted her horse and set off, disappearing into the morning mist.

James watched until she was out of sight, a sense of foreboding tightening in his chest. Turning back to the camp, he was met by General Washington, who had come to see Margaret off.

"She's a remarkable woman," Washington remarked, clapping James on the shoulder. "Her courage does her credit, as it does all of us."

James nodded pride and fear mingling in his heart. "She is, sir. And she'll succeed. We must make sure we're ready to act on the intelligence she brings back."

"Indeed," Washington agreed, his gaze following the path Margaret had taken. "Let us prepare, then. The next battle will not wait, and we must be ready to seize the opportunity she affords us."

As they walked back to the heart of the camp, the plans for the coming days began to take shape, a strategy forming that would capitalize on Margaret's mission. The war was far from over, but each step forward was a step closer to victory, each sacrifice a testament to the unyielding spirit of those who fought for freedom.

As the morning mist dissipated, signaling Margaret's journey into the heart of enemy territory, James found himself before the troops, ready to address the men and women who had become not just his soldiers but his extended family. Their faces, marked by the trials of war yet alight with determination, turned towards him, awaiting his words.

"Today," James began, his voice carrying across the assembled ranks, "we find ourselves at a crossroads. The path ahead is fraught with danger, but it is also brimming with hope. Margaret's mission is a beacon of that hope. Her courage serves as a reminder of what we are fighting for—not just for land, but for the very ideals that make us who we are."

A murmur of agreement rippled through the crowd, the mention of Margaret's name bringing a collective sense of pride.

"Let us use this time wisely," James continued, his gaze sweeping over his audience. "Train harder, plan smarter, and when the time comes, fight with all the strength and heart you possess. Our enemy may have numbers, but we have something far stronger—we have a cause worth fighting for."

The camp erupted into a chorus of cheers, the soldiers' spirits lifted by James's words. In that moment, they were united, a single entity bound by a shared vision of freedom.

As the day wore on, James threw himself into the

preparations, his mind constantly drifting to Margaret. Each report that came in, each piece of intelligence gathered, was a step closer to understanding the enemy's next move and, consequently, a step closer to ensuring Margaret's safe return.

Meanwhile, Margaret navigated the perilous landscape with the skill of a seasoned spy. Disguised as a simple traveler, she used her wits and her intimate knowledge of the land to avoid British patrols. Her heart was set on her mission, but part of her mind lingered back on James and the army, hoping that her efforts would indeed turn the tide in their favor.

One evening, as she made camp in a secluded grove, Margaret allowed herself a moment to reflect. Drawing a small, well-worn journal from her pack, she penned her thoughts and fears, her hopes for the future, and her unwavering belief in their cause. It was a small comfort, a way to feel connected to James and her comrades even as she ventured deeper into enemy lines.

Back at the camp, a council of war convened under the cover of night. James, alongside General Washington and the other officers, pored over maps and reports, their strategies becoming ever more refined with each piece of information that trickled in.

"It's clear," General Washington observed, pointing to a marked location on the map, "that our next move must be bold. The British expect us to be licking our wounds, to be on the defensive. We will use that to our advantage."

James nodded, his thoughts aligning with the General's. "A surprise attack," he suggested, "targeting their supply lines. It would cripple their advance and give us the upper hand."

The plan was daring and fraught with risk, but it was precisely the kind of strategy that could change the course of the war. As the meeting adjourned, James felt a renewed sense of purpose. The coming battle would be critical, and everything hinged on the success of Margaret's mission and their ability to capitalize on the intelligence she gathered.

In the days that followed, the camp was a hive of activity. Soldiers trained with renewed vigor, supplies were stockpiled, and every possible outcome was meticulously planned for. The anticipation of the coming confrontation was palpable, a tangible energy that fueled their preparations.

As night fell on the eve of their planned offensive, James found himself looking up at the stars, wondering about Margaret. In the vastness of the night sky, he found a semblance of peace, a reminder of the enduring nature of their struggle and the hope that, against all odds, they would emerge victorious.

In the tense quiet before dawn, with the stars still holding court in the sky, the camp was alive with a quiet energy. Soldiers checked their gear, whispered plans were exchanged, and everyone prepared for the action to come. Amid this bustle, James found himself standing alone for a moment, looking eastward, where the first hints of light promised a new day and, with it, a new challenge.

His thoughts were interrupted by the approach of Elizabeth, a young messenger who had become indispensable to their operations. Her face, usually bright with youthful optimism, was etched with concern.

"James," she began, her voice low, "there's word from Margaret."

James's heart skipped. "What news? Is she—"

"She's completed her mission," Elizabeth hurried to assure him, seeing the worry etch deeper into his features. "But she's encountered trouble on her return. British patrols have increased. She's laying low but needs extraction sooner than planned."

Without hesitation, James's mind shifted into action. "Gather a small team. We'll head out at first light. Elizabeth, you know the land better than anyone; you'll guide us."

Elizabeth nodded, determination setting in. "We'll bring her back, James."

As they prepared to depart, General Washington approached, having been informed of the situation. "Your loyalty speaks well of you, James. But remember, the success of our coming engagement relies on the intelligence Margaret carries. Be swift, but be cautious."

James met the General's gaze, the weight of his responsibility grounding him. "We'll return with the information, sir. And with Margaret."

The rescue party moved out as the camp behind them stirred to life, unaware of the silent shadows slipping through the trees at the break of dawn.

Meanwhile, Margaret, hidden in a dense thicket, watched the road for signs of the enemy. She had been moving under the cover of darkness, avoiding the paths and places she knew would be watched. The mission's success was a small beacon of hope, but she was not out of danger yet. Every rustle in the underbrush felt like a discovery, every distant footstep a threat.

Her thoughts drifted to James and the others, their faces a comforting presence in her mind. She allowed herself a moment to imagine their reunion, drawing strength from the thought. But as the sky lightened, Margaret shook off her reverie, focusing on the task at hand—survival.

Back with James and his team, Elizabeth led them through lesser-known paths, her knowledge of the land an invaluable asset. They moved quickly, aware that time was of the essence.

As they neared Margaret's last known location, the tension among them grew. Every sense was heightened, every shadow a potential enemy. But they were not untested in the arts of stealth and combat; each member of the team had been chosen for their skills and their resolve.

Finally, after hours of tense navigation, they found Margaret. The relief on both sides was palpable, but there was little time for reunions. Quickly, they shared the intelligence Margaret had gathered, the pieces of the puzzle falling into place to reveal the larger picture of the enemy's intentions.

With no time to waste, they retraced their steps, and the precious information Margaret carried now became the key to the upcoming battle. Their return to camp was a mix of urgency and caution, every step bringing them closer to their comrades and the confrontation that awaited.

Upon their return, the camp was a flurry of activity, the imminent offensive palpable in the air. General Washington welcomed them back, his nod to Margaret both a greeting and an acknowledgment of her bravery.

With the intelligence integrated into their plans, the Continental Army was now positioned to strike a significant blow against the British, their strategy informed by the risks Margaret had taken and the swift action of James and his team.

As they prepared for the battle, James and Margaret stood together for a moment, their shared experiences a bond that no war could sever. They were soldiers in a fight for freedom, but in each other, they had found something just as vital—a reason to hope, a reason to fight on.

As the night settled over the Continental Army's camp, a quiet reflection took hold among the troops and their leaders. Margaret's successful return and the critical intelligence she brought back had ignited a spark of optimism in the hearts of all who heard. Yet, this was a moment balanced between the joy of reunion and the sobering realities of the challenges that lay ahead.

James, after ensuring Margaret had received the care and rest she needed, found himself wandering to the outskirts of the camp. There, looking out into the darkness, he contemplated the path that had led them here—the sacrifices made, the victories won, and the losses mourned. The war had changed them all, forging bonds of friendship and love in the crucible of conflict, shaping their lives in ways none could have anticipated.

Margaret, meanwhile, sat alone in her tent, the maps and missives that detailed their next moves spread out before her. The weight of her journey weighed heavily on her, a testament to her courage and the trust placed in her by her comrades. Yet, there was also a sense of accomplishment, a knowledge that her actions had the power to alter the course of the war.

It was General Washington who brought them back together, summoning his officers for a brief meeting under the stars. His gaze lingered on Margaret and James, acknowledging their contributions with a nod of respect. "This victory," he said, addressing the group, "is a testament to the strength of our cause and the valor of our soldiers. But let us not forget the battles that lie ahead. We must remain vigilant, prepared, and united."

His words were a reminder of the long road still to travel, the continued fight for freedom that would demand their utmost dedication and sacrifice. Yet, within his message lay an undercurrent of hope—the belief that their cause was just and that they would emerge victorious.

As the meeting disbanded, James and Margaret found themselves side by side once more, their thoughts turning to the future. "This war has taken so much from us," Margaret said quietly, her voice steady despite the emotion that threatened to overwhelm her.

James took her hand, his grip firm and reassuring. "But it has also shown us what we're capable of—fighting for what we believe in, standing up against tyranny. No matter what comes, we face it together."

Their shared resolve, in the face of all they had endured and the battles yet to come, was a beacon of light in the uncertainty of war. As they returned to their duties, preparing for the next day's challenges, they carried with them the knowledge that their journey was far from over.

During the trying times of a nation fighting for its birthright, Margaret and James stood as symbols of hope and perseverance. Their story is intertwined with the fate of the Continental Army and is a testament to the enduring spirit of those who dare to dream of freedom.

CHAPTER **24**

The Fabric of Society

The camp was abuzz with activity, the air charged with anticipation as the Continental Army readied itself for what was to come. Amidst the clatter of weapons and the murmur of voices, General Washington convened a final council with his officers. The intelligence brought back by Margaret had revealed a vulnerability in the British defenses, one that they were now poised to exploit.

James, now back at Margaret's side, participated in the discussions, offering insights and suggestions. The plan was bold, requiring precise coordination and timing, but the stakes were too high for any hesitation. As the meeting concluded, there was a palpable sense of unity and resolve among the officers. This battle was their chance to change the course of the war.

Margaret, for her part, was preparing in her own way. The information she had risked so much to obtain was about to be put to the test, and the weight of it rested heavily on her shoulders. She moved through the camp, checking on the preparations and offering words of encouragement to the soldiers. Her presence was a reminder of what they were fighting for—not just the strategic objectives but the very essence of freedom and independence.

As the army set out, James and Margaret found themselves

riding side by side. Their conversation turned to the future, to what peace might look like and the world they hoped to build from the ashes of war. It was a future uncertain yet filled with potential, a dream that sustained them through the darkest of times.

The battlefield awaited, a sprawling expanse that would soon become a testament to their courage and determination. As the two forces collided, the air was filled with the sound of gunfire, the clash of steel, and the cries of men. Margaret, using her sharp intellect and knowledge of the terrain, directed small units with precision, disrupting the British lines and sowing chaos.

James, leading a contingent of his own, fought with a fierceness that belied a strategic mind, always aware of the bigger picture and the objectives they sought to achieve. Together, they were a formidable force, their actions inspiring those around them to fight with renewed vigor.

The battle raged on, the outcome hanging in the balance until, slowly, the tide began to turn. The British, caught off-guard by the audacity and determination of the Continental Army, found themselves retreating, their lines breaking under the relentless assault.

As the sun began to set, casting long shadows over the field, it became clear that the day was theirs. It was a victory hard-won, with losses on both sides, but it was also a turning point. For the first time, the dream of independence seemed not just a distant hope but a tangible possibility.

The aftermath of the battle was a time for reflection and mourning, for honoring those who had fallen and caring for the wounded. But it was also a time for celebration, for recognizing the courage and sacrifice that had led to this moment.

As they gathered around campfires that evening, the

soldiers of the Continental Army shared stories and songs, their voices mingling with the crackling of the flames. Margaret and James, sitting together, allowed themselves a moment of quiet satisfaction. They had played their part in this historic victory, but they knew the war was far from over.

Looking up at the stars, they made a silent vow to continue the fight, to persevere until the dream of a free and independent nation became a reality. The tide had turned, but the journey ahead was still long and fraught with challenges.

The dawn of a pivotal day broke over the Continental camp, casting long shadows and a golden hue over the faces of those who had risen early. The air was thick with anticipation, each soldier aware of the importance of the battle ahead. General Washington's words from the night before lingered in their minds, a call to arms that was both a reminder of their duty and a testament to their shared resolve.

Margaret, having provided the intelligence that would guide their strategy, worked closely with the officers to finalize the plans. Her insight into the enemy's movements and weaknesses had proven invaluable, shaping their approach and tactics. As she moved through the camp, her presence bolstered the spirits of the soldiers, and her bravery and determination were a tangible reminder of what they were fighting for.

James, leading a contingent tasked with a critical flank maneuver, reviewed the maps one last time. His troops, seasoned and ready, looked to him for leadership—a role he had grown into over the course of the war. "Today, we turn the tide," he addressed his men, his voice firm. "We fight not just for victory, but for the future of our nation. Follow me, and fight with all your might."

As the army moved out, the quiet of the morning was soon shattered by the sounds of march and preparation. The battlefield, a vast expanse of open land bordered by dense woods, awaited them, the site of what would be remembered as a defining moment in their struggle for independence.

The British forces, confident in their strength and numbers, were taken aback by the ferocity and cunning of the Continental Army's assault. The battle, intense and unforgiving, raged on, a chaotic dance of strategy, bravery, and desperation.

Margaret, positioned at a vantage point, relayed crucial information back to the field commanders, her eyes never leaving the fray. The weight of her responsibility was a heavy burden, but one she bore with unwavering commitment.

James, in the thick of the battle, led his men with valor, their flank maneuver catching the British off-guard and turning the tide in their favor. The clash of swords, the roar of muskets, and the cries of men filled the air, a cacophony that was both harrowing and exhilarating.

As the sun reached its zenith, the tide of battle shifted unmistakably in favor of the Continental Army. The British, overwhelmed and outmaneuvered, began a disorganized retreat, their ranks broken and spirits dampened.

The victory, when it came, was both exhilarating and sobering. The field, marked by the scars of battle, bore witness to the cost of their triumph. Soldiers, friends, and brothers in arms were lost, but their sacrifice had not been in vain.

In the aftermath, as the army gathered to tend to the wounded and honor the fallen, there was a sense of unity and strength that pervaded the camp. This battle, this victory, had proven that their cause was just, their resolve unbreakable.

General Washington, addressing his troops in the wake of their success, spoke of pride and gratitude. "Today, you have all shown the courage and determination that defines us as a people fighting for our freedom. This victory is ours, but let us not forget those who laid down their lives so that we might stand here today. We honor them best by continuing our fight, by remaining steadfast in our pursuit of liberty."

As the camp settled into the evening, Margaret and James found a moment of quiet together, their thoughts on the day's events and the path ahead. "Today, we made history," Margaret said, a sense of awe in her voice.

James nodded, looking out over the camp where soldiers were sharing meals and stories. "We did. And we'll do it again, as many times as it takes, until we're free."

The victory is a significant milestone in their journey, but the war for independence is far from over. The path ahead will be fraught with challenges, but the Continental Army, strengthened by their triumphs and united in their cause, is ready to face whatever comes next with determination and hope.

As the night deepened, casting the Continental camp into a mosaic of shadow and firelight, the soldiers, still buoyed by the day's victory, gathered in small groups, sharing tales of bravery and loss. Among them, Margaret and James moved like spirits of the revolution, their presence a testament to the leadership and courage that had become synonymous with their names.

In a quieter part of the camp, away from the celebrations, General Washington convened an impromptu council with his closest advisors under the canopy of stars. The victory had shifted the strategic landscape, presenting new opportunities and challenges. Margaret and James invited to join this select gathering, listened intently as Washington outlined his vision for the coming weeks.

"The British will be reeling from this defeat," Washington began, his voice carrying the weight of experience. "But they will not be deterred for long. We must use this moment to our advantage, to strike where they least expect and to fortify our positions."

Margaret, her mind always working, saw the wisdom in Washington's words. "We have an opportunity to expand our intelligence network. The more we know about their movements, the better we can anticipate their strategies."

James, focusing on the tactical implications, added, "And our men need to be ready. This victory gives us momentum, but our training cannot lapse. We must be prepared for whatever comes next."

Washington nodded, pleased with their insights. "Indeed. This victory is a testament to your bravery and dedication. Let us ensure it is not a fleeting success, but a cornerstone upon which we build our path to independence."

As the meeting disbanded, Margaret and James found themselves alone, the weight of the coming days heavy on their minds. They walked together in silence, each lost in thought until they reached the edge of the camp, where the darkness of the forest met the light of the fires.

"It feels like the world is on the brink of change," Margaret whispered, looking up at the stars that seemed to watch over them. James took her hand, his grip firm and reassuring.

"It is," he agreed. "And we're a part of that change. Tomorrow, we'll begin planning in earnest. But tonight, let's just be here, together."

Their shared moment of peace was a rare luxury amidst the turmoil of war. Around them, the camp carried on, but for Margaret and James, time seemed to stand still. They knew the road ahead would be fraught with danger and uncertainty, but as long as they stood together, they believed there was no obstacle they couldn't overcome.

The next morning brought with it the harsh light of reality. Reports arrived of British movements to the south, a clear indication that the enemy was regrouping for another push. The Continental Army, bolstered by their recent victory, responded with a renewed focus on preparation.

Margaret, taking her leave to coordinate with her network of spies, felt the familiar thrill of purpose. Each piece of information she gathered was a thread in the larger tapestry of their struggle for freedom. James, watching her depart, felt a pang of worry but also pride. Her bravery and intelligence had become indispensable to their cause.

As he turned to join his men for training, James knew that the coming battle would test them in ways they had not yet imagined. But he also knew that they were not the same army that had begun this fight. They had grown stronger, more cohesive, forged in the fire of shared adversity and triumph.

As dawn broke, casting a new light over the encampment, the day's urgency began to unfold. Reports of British movements to the south had arrived, signaling a regrouping of their forces and a looming threat that could not be ignored. The Continental Army, still riding the high of their recent victory, found themselves once again facing the stark realities of war.

Margaret, with her resolve as strong as ever, prepared to venture out to gather intelligence. Each piece of information she could uncover was a crucial piece of the puzzle in their fight for freedom. James, though always concerned for her safety, could not help but feel a swell of pride for the role she played in their cause.

Training sessions resumed with renewed vigor, the soldiers' movements sharp and focused. James, leading his men, felt the weight of responsibility on his shoulders. They were not just fighting for territory; they were fighting for the very ideals of liberty and justice.

As Margaret disappeared into the horizon, her silhouette merging with the morning mist, and James returned to his drills, the narrative of their struggle continued to unfold. It was a tale marked by resilience, a deep-seated love for their homeland, and an unyielding pursuit of freedom.

The war had brought them together, forging bonds of friendship, loyalty, and love in the crucible of conflict. Their journey was emblematic of the larger fight, a microcosm of the revolution itself—a battle not only for independence but for the soul of a nation yet to be born.

The Continental Army, strengthened by their victories and tempered by their losses, marched forward. With each step, they carried the hopes and dreams of a people yearning to breathe free, their spirits buoyed by the belief that, against all odds, they would emerge victorious.

As the new day dawned, breaking over the horizon with promises and challenges anew, the Continental Army, buoyed by their recent victory but keenly aware of the trials ahead, began their meticulous preparations. Chapter 23, "In the Shadow of Victory," opens with the camp stirring to life, the air filled with a blend of determination and the lingering tension of anticipation.

Margaret, having returned with critical intelligence and now playing a pivotal role in strategizing the next moves, found herself in deep consultation with General Washington and his advisors. Her insights, hard-earned and fraught with peril, offered them an edge—a way to outmaneuver an enemy still reeling yet dangerously capable.

James, meanwhile, focused on rallying his troops, instilling in them the discipline and resolve that the coming days would demand. Their recent success had proven their mettle, yet complacency was the enemy of victory. "Let our triumph fuel your courage, not your recklessness," he admonished, his voice carrying the weight of responsibility.

The day was spent in a flurry of activity; weapons were checked and rechecked, supplies were distributed, and plans were laid out with precision. The camp, a hive of shared purpose, echoed with the sounds of preparation—a symphony of readiness for the battle they knew was on the horizon.

As the evening approached, Margaret and James stole a moment away from the demands of leadership and strategy. They found themselves on the outskirts of the camp, where the bustle of activity gave way to the quiet of the forest. It was a moment of reprieve, a chance to breathe and to be reminded of the world beyond the war.

"The trees don't know of our struggles," Margaret observed, her gaze tracing the silhouette of the forest against the twilight sky. "They stand tall, indifferent to our battles, our victories."

James looked at her, a soft smile playing on his lips. "Perhaps there's a lesson in that for us. To stand tall, regardless of the storm."

Their conversation meandered from the philosophical to the personal, each sharing their hopes for the future—a future both uncertain and bright with the promise of freedom. It was a future they were fighting to secure, not just for themselves but for generations yet unborn.

As they returned to the camp, the night had fully descended, wrapping the world in a blanket of stars. The campfires flickered like beacons, guiding them back to their duties, to their roles in this historic endeavor.

The night before the next engagement passed with a palpable sense of expectancy. Soldiers whispered their fears and dreams into the darkness, finding comfort in the camaraderie that had become their most steadfast ally.

Margaret and James, back among their comrades, felt the

weight of the coming day. They knew that battles were not just fought on the fields but in the hearts of those who dared to dream of a better world. As they lay down to rest, the stars overhead bore witness to their resolve, to their enduring hope.

Morning broke with the roar of cannons, the clash of steel, and the cries of the brave. The battle, when it came, was fierce, a testament to the tenacity of the Continental Army and the strategic brilliance born of necessity and courage.

Margaret, amidst the chaos, moved with purpose; her actions were a dance of survival and defiance. James, leading his men into the heart of the fray, fought with a valor that inspired those around him.

As the dust settled and silence reclaimed the battlefield, the Continental Army emerged victorious once again. But this victory, like those before it, bore the cost of sacrifice—a reminder of the price of freedom.

In the aftermath, as they tended to the wounded and mourned the fallen, Margaret and James stood together, their hands clasped in a silent vow to continue the fight, honor the sacrifices made, and never lose sight of the dream that had brought them together.

As the dusk settled into a serene night, wrapping the weary but victorious Continental Army in a cloak of hard-won peace, the campfires flickered like stars come down to earth, mirroring the celestial bodies that watched over them from above. Around these fires, the soldiers, Margaret and James among them, found solace in shared silence and occasional whispered conversations—a momentary respite from the relentless march of war.

The battles fought had been many, each victory a step closer to the dream that united them, each loss a stark reminder of the cost of their pursuit. In this quiet hour, as they tended to their wounds—both visible and invisible—they were reminded of the delicate balance between the joy of triumph and the sorrow of sacrifice.

Margaret and James, their bond forged in the crucible of conflict and cemented by shared ideals, stood slightly apart from the others, their gaze shared between the flickering flames and the vast, indomitable night sky. At this moment, free from the immediacies of strategy and survival, they allowed themselves to dream of a future forged by their sacrifices, a future where liberty was not just an ideal but a reality.

"Today, we fought not just for the land beneath our feet but for the very soul of our nation," James whispered, his voice barely rising above the crackle of the fire.

Margaret nodded, her eyes reflecting the firelight and something more—a flame of resolve that not even the darkest nights could extinguish. "And we will continue to fight, for as long as it takes, for everyone who stands with us now and for those who can only dream of standing free."

As they turned their eyes back to the campfire, joining in the silent camaraderie that enveloped the camp, they knew that the path ahead was fraught with more battles and more decisions that would test their resolve and their hearts. But at this moment, under the watchful gaze of the stars, they also knew that they were not alone. They were part of something greater—a cause that transcended the individual and bound them all together in a shared destiny.

With the coming of dawn, the camp would stir to life once more, the march would continue, and the fight would go on. But for now, in the shadow of victory, they found strength in each other and in the shared belief that freedom—a dream so dearly fought for—was within their grasp.

Chapter **25**

Trials of Leadership

As dawn breaks over a camp marked by the wear of battle and the tension of anticipation, the Continental Army, under the leadership of General Washington and buoyed by the recent successes spearheaded by Margaret and James, finds itself at a critical juncture. The air is thick with the promise of forthcoming battles and the responsibility that leadership entails in such turbulent times.

Margaret, having become an indispensable asset to the army's intelligence efforts, faces new challenges that test her cunning and resolve. The missions ahead require not only stealth and information gathering but also a deeper understanding of the enemy's psychology. Each piece of intelligence she uncovers could tilt the scale in favor of the revolution, yet the dangers she must navigate become increasingly perilous.

James, recognized for his bravery and strategic mind, is tasked with leading a battalion in a crucial forthcoming engagement. The weight of responsibility rests heavily on his shoulders; each decision he makes affects not only the outcome of battles but the lives of the men under his command. His leadership is characterized by a blend of courage and compassion, inspiring loyalty and bravery among his troops.

In the quiet hours before the camp awakes, General Washington calls Margaret and James to his tent. The general, a figure of stoic determination, shares his strategic vision for the upcoming campaigns. "The war," he begins, "is not just fought on the battlefields but in the hearts and minds of our soldiers and our supporters. Your roles are pivotal not just for your skills but for the leadership you exemplify."

Margaret listens intently, aware of the gravity of her assignments and the trust placed in her. The silent nod she shares with James speaks volumes of their mutual respect and the unspoken promises to safeguard each other's backs.

James, with a firm voice, assures the general, "We understand the stakes, sir. We will not let you—or our cause—down." His resolve is a beacon for those who look up to him, a testament to the kind of leader who not only commands but inspires.

As they leave the general's tent, the camp begins to stir, signaling the start of another day's preparations. Soldiers mend their gear, officers pore over maps, and messengers dart back and forth with reports and orders. Amidst this activity, Margaret and James share a moment of quiet resolve, understanding the challenges that lie ahead.

Margaret, cloaked in the predawn light, embarks on a mission to penetrate deeper into enemy territory. Her journey is solitary but vital, a delicate balance between secrecy and discovery that could change the course of the war.

James, rallying his battalion, instills in them a sense of purpose and urgency. "Remember," he tells them, "we fight for more than victory; we fight for our future, for a nation built on the principles we hold dear."

As the chapter unfolds, Margaret's and James's paths diverge, each embroiled in their own trials of leadership.

Margaret's intelligence-gathering efforts unveil a potential turning point in the war, while James's leadership on the battlefield faces the ultimate test in a daring confrontation with British forces.

Their trials are not just physical but emotional, testing their convictions, their courage, and their ability to lead in the face of overwhelming odds. Yet, through these trials, their leadership evolves, forged in the fire of conflict and shaped by the unwavering belief in their cause.

Margaret's solo mission deep into enemy lines was fraught with risk. Slipping through the shadows, her heart raced with every step. The intelligence she sought—plans for the British army's next major offensive—was critical. Each piece of information she gathered, each risk she took, brought the revolution closer to victory. Yet, the deeper into enemy territory she ventured, the more she realized the enormity of her task. It wasn't just about gathering intelligence; it was about understanding the enemy, predicting their moves, and staying one step ahead. The mission tested not only her skills as a spy but her resolve as a leader committed to the cause of freedom.

Meanwhile, James faced his own set of challenges. Leading his battalion into a crucial engagement, he felt the weight of each decision. The night before the battle, he walked among his troops, sharing words of encouragement, understanding that morale could be as decisive as muskets in the outcomes of battles. "We're not just fighting against an army," he reminded them. "We're fighting for the idea of what our nation can become. Trust in each other, in our cause, and in yourselves." His words, imbued with a genuine belief in their shared purpose, served to strengthen the bonds among the soldiers, reinforcing their commitment to the fight.

The day of the engagement dawned clear and cold. Margaret, having successfully infiltrated the British camp, discovered critical intelligence that could alter the course of the upcoming battle. Meanwhile, James, positioned with his battalion at a strategic vantage point, awaited the signal to advance.

As the battle commenced, the chaos of war enveloped them. James, amidst the smoke and din of conflict, led his troops with a calm determination, his strategic decisions turning the tide in several key moments. Margaret, her mission accomplished, made her harrowing escape from the enemy camp, the precious intelligence in her possession a beacon of hope.

Their trials on this day were emblematic of the larger struggle for independence. Margaret's daring infiltration and James's leadership on the battlefield were but two threads in the rich tapestry of the revolution. Each victory, each setback, was a lesson in the art of leadership, teaching them that true leadership was not just about command and control but about inspiration, sacrifice, and the courage to make difficult decisions in the service of a greater good.

As they reunited in the aftermath, their shared experiences serving to deepen their bond, Margaret and James understood that their trials had honed their abilities, shaping them into the leaders the revolution required. They also realized that their successes were not theirs alone but belonged to every soldier who fought, every spy who risked everything for the cause, and every supporter who dreamed of a free nation.

"The war is far from over," General Washington reminded them when they presented their reports. "But your actions today have brought us one step closer to victory. Your leadership, your courage, and your unwavering dedication to our cause will be remembered."

As they prepared for the challenges ahead, Margaret and James knew that their trials of leadership were far from over. But they also knew that together, with the trust and support of their comrades, they could face whatever the future held. The path to independence was long and uncertain, yet it was made surer by the conviction and leadership of those willing to fight for the dream of a nation founded on the principles of freedom and justice.

The victory, while significant, was but a precursor to the challenges that lay ahead. In the wake of their successful engagement and the vital intelligence Margaret had risked so much to obtain, the Continental Army found itself at a pivotal crossroads. The information Margaret provided unveiled a British strategy that, if executed, could potentially cripple the revolutionary efforts.

Gathered around a dimly lit table strewn with maps and dispatches, the leadership council, with General Washington at its head, weighed their options. The air was thick with the smoke of candles and the heavy responsibility that rested on their shoulders. It was here, in the quiet before the storm of decisions to be made, that Margaret and James's contributions were once again brought to the forefront.

"Your intelligence has given us a fighting chance," General Washington began, his gaze sweeping over those assembled. "But it's more than just a chance to engage the enemy; it's an opportunity to change the course of this war."

Margaret, feeling the weight of her next words, spoke up. "The British plan relies heavily on their supply lines. If we can disrupt those, we not only weaken their position but also bolster our own."

James, his strategic mind already turning over the possibilities, added, "We have allies who can aid in this effort. If we coordinate our attacks, we can stretch their forces thin, making it harder for them to mount a consolidated offensive."

The discussion that followed was a testament to the

collaborative spirit that had come to define the Continental Army's leadership. Plans were drawn, roles assigned, and contingencies considered. Margaret and James, once again, found themselves at the heart of the strategy, their insights and leadership crucial to the endeavor at hand.

As the council disbanded, preparing to put their plans into motion, General Washington pulled Margaret and James aside. "Your bravery and leadership have not gone unnoticed," he said, a note of deep respect in his voice. "The road ahead is fraught with uncertainty, but I am confident in our cause, especially with individuals like you leading the charge."

The subsequent days were a blur of activity. Margaret coordinated with spy networks and local militias, her efforts aimed at undermining the British supply lines. James, leading a contingent of soldiers, prepared for a series of swift, strategic strikes designed to disrupt and demoralize the enemy.

Their actions, carried out under the cover of darkness and with the precision of a well-oiled machine, began to turn the tide. Supply depots were raided, convoys ambushed, and critical bridges destroyed. The British, caught off-guard by the ferocity and coordination of the attacks, found themselves scrambling to respond.

In the midst of this campaign, Margaret and James's leadership styles evolved. Margaret's approach, rooted in empathy and understanding, inspired loyalty and courage among those she worked with. James, his confidence bolstered by their successes, led with a clarity of purpose that galvanized his troops.

Their victories, however, were not without cost. Each engagement brought with it the risk of capture or death. The stakes were made all too real when a trusted member of their spy network was discovered and executed. The loss was a stark reminder of the dangers they faced, a sobering moment that tempered their resolve.

Yet, even in the face of such adversity, Margaret and James pressed on, driven by the belief in their cause and the knowledge that their leadership could make a difference. They understood that the fight for independence was more than just a series of battles; it was a struggle for the soul of a nation.

As the campaign to disrupt the British supply lines gained momentum, Margaret and James found themselves not at the end of their trials but deep in the crucible of leadership. The victories they had secured were significant, yet each success unveiled new layers of complexity in the war for independence. They stood now, not on the precipice of conclusion, but at the threshold of deeper involvement and greater challenges.

In the aftermath of a particularly daring raid that had left a key British supply depot in flames, Margaret and James convened with their closest advisors under the cover of an ancient oak, its branches a testament to endurance. The air was crisp, carrying the scent of autumn and the distant echoes of battle.

"We've struck a blow," James acknowledged, scanning the faces of those gathered, "but we must be wary. The British will retaliate, and we need to be prepared."

Margaret, her gaze fixed on a map strewn across the makeshift table, added, "Our intelligence suggests they're planning to concentrate their forces here," her finger tapping a location near a critical crossroad. "If they succeed, our recent gains could be jeopardized."

The discussion that ensued was a blend of strategy and speculation. Ideas were exchanged, plans formed and reformed. It was leadership by council, with Margaret and James at the helm, guiding the conversation with insights born of their experiences on the front lines and behind enemy lines.

"The next few days will be critical," Margaret concluded, her voice imbued with a mix of resolve and caution. "We need to reinforce our positions, gather more intelligence, and, most importantly, keep our troops motivated."

James, turning to address a young lieutenant whose bravery had been proven in the recent raid, said, "Gather your men. We'll need to move quickly to fortify our defenses. And send word to our allies; we'll need every available hand."

As the meeting dispersed, Margaret and James remained, their conversation turning to the personal toll of their leadership roles. "Do you ever wonder," Margaret began, her voice softer now, "if the choices we're making are the right ones?"

James considered her question, the weight of command visible in his furrowed brow. "Every day," he admitted. "But I also know that we're fighting for something bigger than ourselves. Doubt is a part of leadership, Margaret. It keeps us grounded, makes us consider our actions more carefully."

Margaret nodded, taking solace in his words. "It's the hope for a free future that keeps me going," she said. "That, and knowing I don't face these trials alone."

Their moment of reflection was brief, however, as a scout arrived, breathless with news. A British contingent, larger than any they had faced before, was advancing towards their position. The information galvanized them into action, their thoughts of doubt and reflection replaced by the immediate need to respond.

As they mobilized their forces, Margaret and James exemplified the essence of leadership in times of crisis. They issued orders with clarity and conviction, ensuring their troops were positioned to meet the oncoming threat. Their presence on the field, standing shoulder to shoulder with those they led, served as a powerful testament to their commitment to the cause.

The battle that ensued was fierce, a maelstrom of strategy and valor. Margaret and James, through their leadership, steered their forces through the chaos, their actions decisive in the face of overwhelming odds. As the dust settled and the British were repelled, their leadership had not only secured another victory but had also deepened the resolve of their troops, reinforcing the belief in the possibility of victory against a formidable foe.

As they surveyed the aftermath, the costs and triumphs of their leadership laid bare, Margaret and James understood that their journey was far from over. The trials they had faced had prepared them for the road ahead, a road marked by uncertainty but paved with the promise of freedom.

In the quiet aftermath of their hard-won victory, as they tended to the wounded and mourned the fallen, Margaret and James found themselves at the heart of a makeshift camp that had become a beacon of hope and resilience. The battle, though victorious, had extracted a heavy toll, and the air was thick with a mixture of relief and sorrow. Around them, the soldiers, their faces smeared with dirt and sweat, shared stories of narrow escapes and acts of bravery, their voices a testament to the human spirit's indomitable will.

Margaret, moving among the rows of injured, offered words of comfort and gratitude. Her presence was a calming force, her leadership extending beyond tactics and strategy to the very soul of their cause. "Your courage has not gone unnoticed," she would say, kneeling beside a young soldier whose eyes spoke of terror and pride. "You've fought not just for the land beneath our feet, but for the ideals that make it worth fighting for."

James, meanwhile, stood at the edge of the camp, his gaze lost in the distance. The battle had proven their mettle, but he knew that the war was far from over. The British would regroup, and new challenges would arise. His thoughts were interrupted by the approach of a seasoned sergeant, his uniform bearing the scars of countless skirmishes.

"Sir, the men are ready to follow you into hell itself if need be," the sergeant said, his voice gruff with respect. "Your leadership today has shown us what we're capable of."

James nodded, his heart heavy with the responsibility that those words carried. "Thank them for me, Sergeant. And tell them to rest now. We'll need all our strength for the days to come."

As dusk fell and the campfires began to flicker to life, Margaret and James convened a council of their closest advisors and lieutenants. The glow of the flames cast long shadows as they discussed their next moves, their faces etched with determination and fatigue. The victory had given them a strategic advantage, but they needed to capitalize on it quickly.

"We need to send word to General Washington," James began, his voice cutting through the crackle of the fire. "The intelligence we've gathered could turn the tide of this war."

Margaret, unfolding a map, pointed to a series of strategic locations. "And we must continue to disrupt their supply lines. Our spies have identified two more depots vulnerable to attack."

The meeting stretched into the night, plans forming like pieces of a puzzle coming together. Their strategy was bold, a series of coordinated strikes designed to weaken the British hold on the region. Yet, as they plotted and planned, there was an unspoken understanding that the real battle was still ahead.

In the days that followed, Margaret and James led their forces with a renewed sense of purpose. Each raid, each skirmish, brought them closer to their goal, but also deeper into the heart of enemy territory. The risks were greater, but so were the rewards.

Margaret's network of spies and informants became the lifeblood of their operations, her ability to gather and interpret intelligence proving invaluable. James, for his part, honed his skills as a tactician, his strategies becoming more daring and innovative.

Their leadership, once tested in the fires of battle, now flourished, becoming a guiding light for their troops and a symbol of hope for the revolution. They were more than commanders; they were visionaries, their eyes fixed on the horizon, on the promise of a free and independent nation.

Yet, as "Trials of Leadership" drew to a close, Margaret and James understood that the true test of their leadership was not in the victories they achieved but in the challenges they overcame together. Their journey had taught them that leadership was not a position but a choice, a commitment to stand for something greater than themselves.

C HAPTER **26**

Legacy of War

In the nascent light of dawn, which painted the recovering landscape in hues of hope and somber reflection, the remnants of the Continental Army and the newly freed civilians gathered around a field that had been transformed overnight. Where once there had been the scars of encampments and the turmoil of preparation now stood a solemn monument—a testament to the fallen, crafted from the very land they had fought to liberate.

Margaret walked alongside James through the crowd, their steps measured, their hearts heavy with the gravity of the ceremony about to unfold. Around them, murmurs of anticipation and grief mingled in the crisp morning air, a communal breath of a nation reborn through sacrifice.

As they approached the monument, a simple obelisk of stone inscribed with the names of the fallen, they found General Washington already there, his presence a steadfast beacon as always. He greeted them with a nod, the lines on his face telling stories of battles both won and lost.

"Margaret, James," Washington began, his voice carrying a depth of emotion rarely displayed. "Today, we bear witness to the cost of our freedom. It is a day for remembrance, for honor, and for solemn gratitude."

Margaret stepped forward, her gaze sweeping over the assembled crowd. "These names," she gestured towards the obelisk, "represent the best of us. They fought not for glory, but for a belief in something greater than themselves. It is our duty to ensure their sacrifices were not in vain."

A hush fell over the gathering as James took his place beside her. "Let this monument serve as a reminder," he added, his voice firm, "of the price of freedom. A reminder that peace is not simply the absence of war, but a legacy we must continually strive to uphold."

The ceremony continued, with each name read aloud, followed by a moment of silence. The emotional weight of the event was palpable, and tears and solemn nods were a shared language of grief and respect.

After the formalities concluded, the crowd began to disperse, leaving Margaret, James, and Washington in a reflective silence. It was then that a young boy, no older than ten, approached, his eyes wide with a mixture of awe and sorrow.

"Sir, ma'am," he addressed them, his voice wavering. "My father's name is on that stone. He told me, if anything should happen, to find you. To tell you he believed in what we were fighting for."

Margaret knelt down, bringing herself to eye level with the boy. "Your father was a hero," she said softly, her hand reaching out to gently squeeze his shoulder. "And we will do everything in our power to honor his belief."

James added, "He fought for a future where all might live in freedom and peace. It's a promise we intend to keep—not just in memory of your father but for all those we've lost."

The boy nodded, a determined glint in his eyes. "Then I

want to help, too. I want to make sure my father's fight wasn't for nothing."

General Washington placed a hand on the boy's other shoulder, a smile breaking through his solemn demeanor. "And help you shall, young man. The road ahead will need all of us, working together to heal the wounds of war and to build the nation your father dreamed of."

As they stood there, united by the shared commitment to the legacy left by the fallen, Margaret and James understood that their roles had evolved. From soldiers to leaders, they were now guardians of a new dawn, tasked with guiding the fledgling nation through its infancy, nurturing the seeds of unity, forgiveness, and reconciliation.

As the assembly dispersed, leaving in its wake a silence that spoke volumes, Margaret, James, and General Washington remained. They watched as the young boy, a living embodiment of the war's legacy, walked away with determination in his small frame back to his mother, waiting at the edge of the crowd. It was a poignant reminder of their responsibility not just to the past but to the future.

General Washington turned to them, his expression thoughtful. "This war has asked much of us all," he mused, his gaze lingering on the monument. "But it is in peace that our true test begins. We must forge a nation that honors the sacrifices made in its name."

Margaret nodded, her mind already racing with the enormity of the task ahead. "The war has left deep wounds, not just on the land, but in the hearts and minds of its people. Healing them will require more than just time."

James looked toward the horizon, where the first light of day was giving way to the warmth of the morning sun. "And yet, it is a task we must undertake. For the sake of those who fell, and for those who survived, we owe it to them to build something lasting and just."

Their conversation was interrupted by the arrival of a figure from the edge of the encampment—a man known to them both but one whose allegiance had once stood in stark opposition to their cause. Captain Edward Harrington, a British officer who had found himself questioning the very principles he had fought for, approached with a hesitant determination.

Margaret and James exchanged a glance, understanding the significance of his presence. Harrington stopped before them, his posture rigid, yet his eyes betrayed a vulnerability rare in a man of his rank.

"I come before you, not as an enemy, but in search of forgiveness," Harrington began, his voice steady but low. "The war has ended, but its shadows linger in my heart. I seek to make amends, to contribute to the healing of a nation divided."

General Washington regarded him for a moment, a silent assessment that felt like an eternity. Then, extending his hand, he bridged the gap that uniforms and flags had once imposed. "Your courage, Captain Harrington, is a testament to the possibility of reconciliation. It is in forgiveness that we find our path forward."

Margaret stepped forward, her leadership instincts guiding her. "Let us work together, then. There are many who need our help—soldiers and civilians alike, who bear the scars of war. Your efforts in aiding them could be the first step towards healing the rifts that have torn our land apart."

James offered a nod of agreement. "And it is only together, setting aside past grievances, that we can hope to build a future worthy of those we've lost."

As they spoke, a small group gathered, drawn by the sight

of former foes in earnest conversation. It was a powerful image, one that spoke of the possibilities that lay in the wake of the conflict—a nation not defined by its battles but by its capacity for forgiveness, unity, and collective healing.

In the days following, Margaret, James, and Harrington dedicated themselves to the task of healing. They visited the wounded, both in body and spirit, offering support and solidarity. They helped rebuild homes and lives torn asunder by the war, their efforts a beacon of hope in a landscape still shadowed by loss.

Their journey was not without its challenges. Skepticism and old hatred lingered, reminders of the divisions that the war had wrought. But in each act of kindness, in every gesture of forgiveness, Margaret and James saw the slow, steady emergence of a new nation—one built on the principles of liberty and justice for all.

The chill of the early morning air was a stark contrast to the warmth of the community gathered in the center of the town, a space that had witnessed both the ravages of war and the resilient spirit of its people. At the heart of this gathering stood Margaret, James, and a figure who had once been an adversary, Captain Harrington, united by a common purpose—to honor the memory of those lost and to foster the healing of a nation still bearing the scars of conflict.

Margaret took the lead, her voice echoing with a blend of strength and gentleness. "Today, we gather not just to remember the sacrifices made, but to affirm our commitment to healing the wounds left in their wake," she began, her gaze meeting those of the people who had come to symbolize the hope of recovery.

James stepped forward, his presence reinforcing the message of resilience. "Each day brings with it a choice—to dwell on the divisions of the past or to work towards the unity of our future. Our efforts to rebuild are as much about mending the spirit of our nation as they are about restoring its towns and fields."

The crowd listened, their faces a tapestry of shared grief and budding hope, as Captain Harrington, his uniform a reminder of the complexities of forgiveness, added his voice to the chorus. "Seeking forgiveness is the first step towards reconciliation. I stand before you as someone who has taken that step, hopeful for a future where former foes can stand together in peace."

Their words set the tone for the day's events, which unfolded as a series of heartfelt tributes and collaborative endeavors. The ceremony to honor the fallen was poignant, with each name read aloud serving as a solemn reminder of the cost of freedom. Yet, it was the unveiling of a community project, a garden of remembrance and renewal, that marked a pivotal moment in the chapter.

Margaret and James, alongside volunteers from every walk of life, including soldiers from both sides of the conflict, worked side by side to plant trees and flowers—a living memorial to those lost and a symbol of the community's commitment to moving forward.

As they worked, conversations sparked, bridging gaps between individuals who had once viewed each other through the lens of enmity. These interactions, simple yet profound, wove a narrative of reconciliation, demonstrating Margaret and James's belief in the power of understanding and forgiveness.

The project culminated in a gathering in the garden, where stories of loss were shared, not just as tales of sorrow but as reminders of the resilience and courage that defined their shared experience. Margaret, observing the mingling of former adversaries and newfound friends, felt a surge of hope.

"This garden," she addressed the crowd, "is a testament to what we can achieve together. It's a place of healing, a space where we can reflect on our past and nurture our hopes for the future."

James, standing beside her, nodded. "Let it also be a place where we teach our children the value of peace, the importance of forgiveness, and the strength found in unity."

As the sun dipped below the horizon, casting a soft glow over the garden, the community stood together, a mosaic of individuals bound by a shared journey of healing and reconciliation. The day's events, though rooted in the solemn memory of loss, had planted seeds of hope and understanding, fostering a sense of collective purpose.

As the day's events drew to a close, the garden they had nurtured together stood as a vivid symbol of their collective journey from conflict to reconciliation. It wasn't merely the planting of trees and flowers that mattered, but the mingling of souls once divided by war, now united in peace. Margaret and James, through their actions and leadership, had illuminated a path forward for their community, demonstrating that healing was possible when hearts and hands worked together. Their vision for a future built on understanding and forgiveness was taking root, not just in the physical landscape but in the hearts of all who participated. The seeds of hope and unity they planted promised to grow into a legacy of peace, a living memorial to the resilience of the human spirit in the aftermath of strife.

As the day's events drew to a close, the garden they had nurtured together stood as a vivid symbol of their collective journey from conflict to reconciliation. It wasn't merely the planting of trees and flowers that mattered, but the mingling of souls once divided by war, now united in peace. Margaret and James, through their actions and leadership, had illuminated a path forward for their community, demonstrating that healing was possible when hearts and hands worked together. Their vision for a future built on understanding and forgiveness was taking root, not just in the physical landscape but in the hearts of all who participated. The seeds of hope and unity they planted promised to grow into a legacy of peace, a living memorial to the resilience of the human spirit in the aftermath of strife.

As the last rays of the setting sun bathed the garden in a warm, golden light, Margaret found herself standing beside the newly planted oak tree, its young branches reaching toward the sky. James joined her, and together, they admired the work of their community—a tangible manifestation of their shared hope for the future.

"It's beautiful, isn't it?" Margaret remarked, her gaze fixed on the garden. "It's more than I imagined. A place of remembrance, yes, but also of renewal."

James nodded, his eyes reflecting the colors of the dusk. "It's a testament to what we can achieve when we come together. Not just as soldiers, but as builders of peace."

Their contemplation was interrupted by the approach of Captain Harrington, his stride hesitant yet determined. Stopping a respectful distance away, he cleared his throat, drawing their attention.

"I wanted to thank you," he began, addressing Margaret and James with a sincerity that bridged the gap of former enmities. "For allowing me to be a part of this. For showing me that forgiveness isn't just a word, but an action."

Margaret turned to him, offering a smile that spoke volumes of her acceptance. "Your help today, and your willingness to seek reconciliation, speaks more to your character than any past actions. We're honored to have you with us."

James extended his hand to Harrington, a gesture that symbolized far more than a simple thanks. "We're all architects of the future now. Your contributions today are part of the foundation we're building on."

Harrington accepted the handshake, the significance of the moment not lost on him. "I'm committed to being a part of that future, to help mend what's been broken. It's the least I can do, in memory of those we've lost and for those we can still save."

As they stood together, the divisions of the past seemed to dissolve, overshadowed by the collective effort to forge a path toward healing and unity. The garden around them, with its mix of flowers and trees, served as a vivid reminder of their interconnected fates—diverse yet unified, separate yet together.

Margaret looked around at the faces still lingering in the garden, their expressions a mix of reflection and resolve. "Let's gather everyone," she suggested. "I think it's time we shared our hopes for this place, for our community, out loud. Together."

As the small crowd reconvened, Margaret, James, and Harrington were among them, and each person was invited to share a thought, a hope, or a dream for the future. The exercise, simple in its execution, became a powerful act of collective envisioning—a mosaic of individual aspirations forming a shared vision for tomorrow.

In the cool embrace of the evening, as stories and dreams were shared under the canopy of the night sky, the Legacy of War chapter evolved into something more—a narrative of hope, community resilience, and the enduring human capacity for forgiveness and growth.

As the circle of townsfolk, soldiers, and former adversaries shared their hopes and dreams under the starlit sky, a profound sense of community spirit enveloped the garden. Each voice that rose in the night air, each story of loss and hope, wove a stronger bond among them, transcending past divisions.

In the midst of this communal sharing, a figure detached from the shadows at the garden's edge, moving slowly towards the gathering. It was Anna, a nurse who had served tirelessly at the field hospitals, her hands healing the wounds of war while her heart bore its unseen scars. Her approach was tentative yet determined as if she carried a message too important to remain unspoken.

Margaret noticed her first, inviting her into the circle with a gentle nod. "Anna has been with us through some of our darkest times," she introduced herself to the gathering, her voice warm and respectful. "Her courage and compassion have brought many of our soldiers back from the brink. Anna, would you share with us?"

Encouraged by Margaret's introduction, Anna took a deep breath, finding her voice amidst the sea of attentive faces. "In the hospitals, I saw the cost of this war up close—the pain, the loss, the sacrifices made. But I also witnessed incredible acts of bravery and kindness," she began, her voice steady and clear. "Healing is more than tending to physical wounds; it's about mending the spirit, about finding hope amidst despair."

She paused, her gaze sweeping over the assembled crowd, making a silent connection with each person. "This garden, this gathering, it's a symbol of what we can achieve together. Let's continue to support one another, to listen and to share, to heal not just as individuals, but as a community."

Her words resonated deeply, stirring the hearts of all present. James, moved by Anna's testimony, added, "Our journey of healing is just beginning. This garden will grow and change, just as we will. Let it be a place where we can come to remember, to reflect, and to renew our commitment to each other and to our future."

The gathering concluded with a communal pledge, led by Margaret, to nurture the garden as a living monument to their shared experiences and hopes. Together, they envisioned it flourishing—a vibrant testament to resilience, a sanctuary of peace and healing for generations to come.

As the group slowly dispersed, leaving behind the warmth of shared stories and the promise of new beginnings, Margaret, James, Harrington, and Anna remained. They stood together in silent camaraderie, united by the journey they had undertaken and the work that lay ahead.

The night sky, vast and adorned with stars, seemed to echo their resolve—a canvas of infinite possibilities, a reminder of the enduring human capacity for renewal and growth.

As the night deepened and the last of the townsfolk made their way home, leaving the garden to the quiet watch of the stars, Margaret, James, Harrington, and Anna lingered a moment longer. They stood in a silence filled with shared understanding and anticipation of the path that lay ahead—a path they had committed to walk together.

Margaret broke the silence, her voice soft yet carrying an undercurrent of resolve. "This evening, we've shared more than just hopes and memories. We've woven together the beginnings of a new tapestry, one that includes all of us, in all our diversity and strength."

James nodded, his gaze fixed on the horizon, where the first hint of dawn promised a new day. "A day we will greet not just as survivors of a war, but as architects of the peace that follows. Our work continues, but for tonight, we've laid a cornerstone of understanding and unity."

Harrington, the former adversary turned ally, felt the weight of his own journey and the transformative power of forgiveness. "I came here seeking absolution, but I've found so much more—a sense of purpose in the peace to come, and a place among those who once called me foe."

Anna, whose hands had brought healing to so many, looked at the garden around them, envisioning its growth and the healing it symbolized. "This garden will be a testament to our collective journey from the shadows of war into the light of peace. It's a legacy we all share."

Together, they made their way out of the garden, the silence a comfortable cloak around their shoulders. As they parted ways at the garden's edge, each carrying the weight of the evening's promises and the work to come, the bond forged among them was palpable—a bond of shared purpose and newfound hope.

The chapter of "Legacy of War" closed not with an ending but with the promise of a beginning. The legacy left by the fallen, honored in stone and memory, would be carried forward in the actions and hearts of those who remained. It was a legacy of resilience, compassion, and a shared commitment to building a future that honored the past while forging a path toward healing and unity.

In the quiet that followed their departure, the garden stood as a silent guardian of their promises—a beacon of hope in a world reborn from the ashes of conflict, ready to face the dawn of a new era.

CHAPTER **27**

𝔗𝔥𝔢 𝔗𝔦𝔢𝔰 𝔗𝔥𝔞𝔱 𝔅𝔦𝔫𝔡

In the heart of the burgeoning nation, a sense of anticipation vibrated through the air, as palpable as the crisp breeze that heralded the coming of spring. The town, once marred by the scars of war, now buzzed with preparations for a celebration unlike any it had seen before—a Celebration of Union. It was a day to mark not only the end of the conflict but also the forging of a new beginning, a testament to the resilience of a people united in purpose and hope.

Margaret and James found themselves at the center of this whirlwind of activity, their roles as leaders having evolved in the peacetime that followed the tumult of war. Today, however, their focus was on the celebration, a chance to honor the ties that bound them all together as a nation, as a community, and as families, both old and new.

As they walked through the town square, overseeing the final touches to the decorations, they were approached by Elizabeth, a young woman whose contributions to the war effort had not gone unnoticed. With a bright smile, she presented them with a bundle of handcrafted ribbons, each one bearing the colors of their fledgling nation.

"These are for the children," Elizabeth explained, her eyes alight with excitement. "I thought it would be a nice touch for the parade. A symbol of our Hope for the future—a future they will inherit."

Margaret accepted the bundle, touched by the gesture. "This is wonderful, Elizabeth. Thank you. It's gestures like these that remind us of the importance of today. It's not just a celebration; it's a promise to our new generation."

James nodded in agreement, his gaze following a group of children laughing as they darted between the stalls. "Let's make sure these ribbons find their way to them. It'll be a beautiful sight to see them leading the parade, our future unfurling with every step they take."

The conversation was interrupted by the arrival of Samuel, a seasoned carpenter who had been tasked with creating a new symbol for the town square—a statue representing unity and strength. With a proud smile, Samuel gestured towards the covered figure standing at the square's center.

"I've finished it," Samuel announced. "I was hoping you'd do us the honor of unveiling it during the ceremony."

Margaret exchanged a look with James, both moved by the significance of the moment. "We'd be honored, Samuel. Your work has always been a reflection of our community's heart. I'm sure this will be no different."

As the town gathered for the ceremony, the air filled with the sound of music and laughter, a vibrant backdrop to the speeches that would remind them all of the journey they had undertaken together. General Washington, his presence a bridge between the past and the present, took to the stage, his words weaving the story of their nation's birth.

"We stand here today, not as individuals, but as a testament to what unity and shared purpose can achieve," he began, his voice carrying across the square. "Today, we celebrate not only our victory in war but our commitment to peace and to each other."

Margaret and James, standing among the crowd, felt the weight of his words, a reminder of the roles they had played and the future they were helping to build.

The moment of the statue's unveiling arrived, a hush falling over the gathering as Margaret and James stepped forward, the fabric falling away to reveal Samuel's creation. The statue, a figure with arms outstretched, holding aloft a chain broken in its center, was met with gasps of awe and applause. It was a powerful symbol of their collective struggle, of bonds broken and then reforged in the fires of unity.

As the celebration continued, with the parade led by children adorned with Elizabeth's ribbons, Margaret and James found themselves reflecting on the ties that bound them all. Their thoughts were interrupted by the approach of a young couple, holding between them a small, wriggling bundle of joy—the newest member of their community.

"We wanted you to meet her," the mother said, her voice brimming with pride. "She was born on the very day the war ended. We named her Hope."

Margaret reached out to gently touch the baby's hand, but her heart was swelling. "Welcome, Hope," she whispered. "May you grow to see the dreams of today become the realities of tomorrow."

James, his eyes misty, added, "And may you always know the strength of the ties that bind us—ties of love, of community, and of a shared destiny."

As the day gave way to evening and the celebrations continued under the stars, Margaret and James knew that the journey ahead would be filled with challenges. But for today, they reveled in the joy of the moment, in the unity of their nation, and in the promise of the future—a future symbolized by the laughter of children, the solidarity of their community, and the quiet slumber of a child named Hope.

As the celebrations in Philadelphia continued, marking the dawn of peace and the forging of a new nation, Margaret and James found themselves in the company of General Washington one quiet evening. The general, who had led them through the darkest hours of the war, now carried an air of solemnity about him, a sense of profound duty fulfilled.

Washington gathered his closest companions and aides in a small, intimate setting, away from the festivities. The room was filled with those who had been instrumental in the struggle for independence, their faces illuminated by the soft glow of candlelight.

"My friends," Washington began, his voice resonant with the gravity of the moment, "as we stand on the threshold of a new era for our nation, I am reminded of the responsibilities that leadership bestows upon us. Not just to lead in times of conflict, but to know when to step aside for the greater good of the country we love."

He paused, allowing his words to settle among those present, each person hanging on to his every word.

"I have made a decision, one that I believe is in the best interest of our fledgling nation. I will soon travel to Annapolis, to the Congress, to tender my resignation as commander-in-chief of our Continental Army."

A murmur of surprise and emotion swept through the room. Margaret felt a tightness in her chest, a mix of admiration and sadness at the thought of their steadfast leader stepping down.

"Your leadership has been our guiding light, General,"

James spoke, his voice steady yet filled with emotion. "Your decision...it is a testament to the integrity and selflessness that have defined your command."

Washington nodded, acknowledging James's words. "It is my deepest Hope that this act will underscore the principles we have fought for—liberty, democracy, and the belief that no one person holds dominion over the fate of our nation. The true strength of our country lies in its people, in the rule of law, and in the peaceful transfer of power."

Margaret found her voice, though it trembled slightly with the weight of her emotions. "Your example will guide us, General, as we strive to build this nation. Your sacrifice, stepping away from power, will be remembered as one of your greatest acts of leadership."

The general looked around the room, his gaze lingering on each person. "Our journey together has been long, marked by hardship and triumph. As I prepare to take this step, I do so with the full confidence that each of you will continue to serve our nation with the same dedication and fervor that brought us to this point."

As the evening came to a close, and Washington shared his final thoughts with those who had become not just allies but family, the significance of his impending resignation became a poignant symbol of the chapter they were all about to close. It was a moment of reflection on the sacrifices made and a look forward to the legacy they would all carry forward—the promise of a nation built on the ideals of freedom and unity.

Following that profound evening with General Washington, the spirit of his words lingered in the hearts and minds of all who were present. It casts a new light on the celebrations, infusing them with a deeper sense of purpose and reflection on the responsibilities of freedom and governance.

In the days that followed, as Washington made his journey to Annapolis to formally resign his commission, the town of Philadelphia buzzed with discussions and debates about the future of their fledgling nation. Margaret and James found themselves at the center of these conversations, their roles as leaders naturally evolving to meet the new challenges of peace.

One afternoon, as they walked through the town, now vibrant with the activities of reconstruction and the joyous noise of celebration, they encountered a group of citizens gathered in the town square, animatedly discussing the news of Washington's resignation.

"Can you believe it?" one man exclaimed, his voice carrying a mix of astonishment and respect. "To walk away from power, to place such trust in the hands of the people... it's unprecedented."

Margaret and James joined the group, their presence immediately drawing attention and quieting the murmurs.

"It's a testament to his character," Margaret offered, her voice thoughtful. "And a challenge to us all—to carry forward the principles for which we fought, in how we govern, how we live, and how we relate to one another as citizens of a new nation."

James nodded in agreement, adding, "It also underscores the importance of unity and collective action. Our strength lies in our ability to come together, to debate and decide the path forward as a community, not as subjects under a crown."

The discussion that followed was lively and wide-ranging, touching on topics from governance and democracy to the everyday challenges of rebuilding a war-torn land. Margaret and James listened and contributed, their leadership roles naturally extending into facilitating these crucial conversations about the nation's future.

As the meeting dispersed, a young girl approached Margaret and James, holding up a drawing she had made—a crude but heartfelt depiction of the town square, with people of all ages and backgrounds coming together, the monument to the fallen in the background.

"I drew this," she said shyly, "to remember today. When everyone talked about what comes next, it made me feel like I'm a part of something big."

Margaret knelt to meet her eye level, taking the drawing and examining it with genuine interest. "You are a part of something big," she affirmed, her voice gentle but emphatic. "This—what you've drawn—is the essence of our new nation. It's about all of us, together, building the future."

James smiled, looking over Margaret's shoulder at the drawing. "Keep this safe," he advised the young artist. "One day, you'll look back and remember how you, too, contributed to the shaping of our nation."

Encounters like these, rich with dialogue and the sharing of ideas and hopes, became frequent in the days that followed. Margaret and James, along with other leaders and citizens, engaged in the foundational work of nation-building, guided by the principles and sacrifices of those who had fought for their independence.

The Celebration of Union, as the day came to be known, was not just a moment of commemoration but a catalyst for the ongoing process of defining and refining what their nation would stand for. It was a celebration underscored by the recognition of a new generation's role in shaping the legacy of freedom, democracy, and unity.

As the season turned, marking the first year of peace, the town found itself in a period of transformative growth, reflecting the burgeoning nation's aspirations. The Celebration of Union had ignited a collective determination to rebuild stronger than before, laying the foundations for a society rooted in the ideals for which they had fought so hard.

Amid this backdrop of renewal, Margaret and James embarked on a project that symbolized the bridging of past sacrifices with future aspirations—a community center named "Liberty Hall." Envisioned as a place of learning, dialogue, and commemoration, it would serve as a beacon of the community's resilience and unity.

On a bright morning, with the construction of Liberty Hall well underway, Margaret and James met with Elizabeth, Samuel, and Anna to discuss plans for the inaugural event. The air was filled with the sounds of construction and the palpable sense of anticipation for what this space would represent.

"We should dedicate a section of the hall to our history, to the journey we've undergone as a people," suggested Samuel, his hands animated as he spoke. "A place where the stories of the war, of our fallen heroes, and of our path to peace are preserved for future generations."

Anna, her experience in healing both physical and emotional wounds lending her a unique perspective, added, "And let's not forget a space for healing and reflection. A quiet corner where people can come to find solace and strength, surrounded by the stories of our collective resilience."

Elizabeth, who had become instrumental in educational initiatives, proposed, "What about workshops and classes? We could offer lessons in everything from reading and writing to governance and law. It's important that our freedom is underpinned by knowledge and understanding."

Margaret listened intently, her heart swelling with pride at the collaborative spirit that had taken root. "These are wonderful ideas. Liberty Hall will be more than a building;

it will be a testament to our values, a place where every member of our community, young and old, can find a way to contribute and learn."

James, ever the strategist, considered the practical aspects. "Let's also ensure we have a space for public meetings and discussions. The hall should be a forum for debate and decision-making, where every voice can be heard, and every opinion considered."

As they finalized their plans, a sense of excitement built among them. Liberty Hall was shaping up to be a cornerstone of the community's identity, embodying the principles of liberty, education, and civic engagement.

The day of the inauguration arrived with much fanfare. The townsfolk gathered, eager to witness the unveiling of a project that symbolized their collective hopes and dreams. Margaret and James stood before the entrance, the building behind them a manifestation of countless hours of labor and love.

"Today, we open the doors to Liberty Hall, not just as a structure of wood and stone, but as a home for our collective aspirations," Margaret addressed the gathering, her voice echoing in the clear morning air.

James continued, "This hall is a pledge of our commitment to each other—to nurture the ties that bind us, to honor the sacrifices that have brought us here, and to engage in the hard work of building a future worthy of those sacrifices."

With a flourish, the doors were opened, inviting the community into a space that was theirs to shape and define. Liberty Hall, in its conception and realization, was a testament to the enduring spirit of a people united in their diversity, their struggles, and their hopes for a brighter tomorrow.

As Liberty Hall began to buzz with activity, its spaces filled with eager learners, thoughtful debates, and the shared stories of a community knitting itself back together, Margaret and James turned their attention to another pressing issue—the integration of soldiers returning home from the war. Many found it difficult to adjust to a life of peace after the traumas of conflict, their needs extending beyond physical healing to encompass emotional and social reintegration.

Recognizing the gravity of this challenge, Margaret proposed the initiation of a mentorship program within Liberty Hall. "We have a wealth of experienced individuals among us, not only in matters of war but in trades, crafts, and civic duties. Pairing our veterans with mentors can help ease their transition, providing them with support, guidance, and a sense of purpose."

James, seeing the wisdom in her suggestion, began to organize a committee dedicated to this cause. They reached out to craftsmen, educators, and seasoned civic leaders, inviting them to share their knowledge and skills. The response was overwhelmingly positive, with many in the community eager to contribute to the healing process.

In one of the brightly lit rooms of Liberty Hall, a workshop on carpentry was taking place, led by Samuel. Among his attentive students was Thomas, a young soldier who had served under James. Thomas had struggled with his return to civilian life, but in the art of woodworking, he found not just a potential livelihood but a therapeutic outlet for his restless energy.

"Focus on the wood, feel its grain, imagine what it can become," Samuel instructed, guiding Thomas's hands as they worked on shaping a piece of oak. The concentration required for the task allowed Thomas a reprieve from his haunting memories, offering him moments of peace and accomplishment.

Meanwhile, Elizabeth organized a series of reading groups for children and adults alike, fostering a love for literature and learning. One afternoon, she was surprised by a visit from Captain Harrington, who expressed a desire to participate.

"I've always had a love for books," Harrington admitted, a hint of vulnerability in his voice. "Perhaps I could share some of that, help in bridging the gaps between us with stories and knowledge."

Elizabeth welcomed his involvement, recognizing the power of storytelling in healing and reconciliation. Together, they curated a selection of works that spoke of forgiveness, courage, and the common bonds of humanity.

As weeks turned into months, Liberty Hall flourished as a center of communal life, embodying the ideals and aspirations of a nation reborn from the ashes of war. Its success lay not just in the bricks and mortar that housed it but in the vibrant tapestry of lives that filled its spaces—each person a thread woven into the larger story of rebuilding and renewal.

Margaret and James, watching the community gather for a celebration of Liberty Hall's achievements, felt a profound sense of gratitude and Hope. They had witnessed the transformation of their town from a place marked by the scars of conflict to a beacon of progress and unity.

"Together, we've built something extraordinary," James remarked, his arm around Margaret as they stood among their friends and neighbors. "But this is only the beginning. The true measure of our success will be in how we continue to grow, learn, and support one another in the years to come."

Margaret nodded, her eyes reflecting the shared conviction of those gathered. "Our journey has taught us the strength of unity, the value of each voice, and the power of shared dreams. Let's carry these lessons forward, for ourselves and for the generations that will follow."

As the evening drew to a close, with the laughter and voices of Liberty Hall's celebrants echoing softly into the night, Margaret and James shared a quiet moment of reflection. Around them, the hall stood as a testament to the power of unity and the indomitable spirit of a people dedicated to forging a new path forward.

"We've come so far," Margaret said, her voice filled with a mixture of pride and wonder. "It's remarkable to see how much can be achieved when we come together, driven by a shared purpose."

James nodded, his gaze lingering on the faces of their community members as they began to make their way home. "This hall, this celebration, it's more than just a mark of what we've endured. It's a symbol of our hopes, a foundation for what we aspire to be."

Together, they watched as the last lights of Liberty Hall were extinguished, leaving the building in silhouette against the starlit sky. It was a beacon of their collective achievements and the challenges they had overcome, a reminder of the resilience and compassion that had guided them through the darkest times.

"This chapter may be closing," James mused, his hand finding Margaret's in the darkness, "but our story is far from over. There's much work to be done, many more chapters to write in the story of our nation."

Margaret squeezed his hand in agreement, her eyes on the horizon, where the first hints of dawn promised a new day. "Together, we'll continue to build, to dream, and to grow. Our legacy is just beginning."

And with that, the chapter known as "The Ties That Bind" drew to a close, not with an ending, but with the promise of new beginnings. It was a chapter that would be remembered not just for the challenges it presented, but for the enduring spirit of Hope, unity, and determination it instilled in the heart of a community ready to face whatever the future might hold.

Chapter **28**

Toward a Brighter Dawn

The early morning sun cast a gentle glow over the town, its rays like the fingers of hope reaching into every home, every heart, stirring the community from its slumber. Today was not just another day; it was the dawn of a new era, a tangible shift in the air that promised renewal and growth.

Margaret stood on her porch, watching this new world awaken. The peace they had fought for, the future they had dreamed of, was unfolding before her eyes. Yet, it was not just the peace that moved her—it was the realization of how much had been sacrificed to reach this moment and how much work lay ahead to honor those sacrifices fully.

James joined her, sharing in the silent reverence of the morning. "It feels like we're on the cusp of something profound," he remarked, his voice low, echoing Margaret's sense of anticipation and responsibility.

The sound of hurried footsteps broke their shared contemplation. Turning, they saw a young messenger, breathless and wide-eyed, approaching them with an urgency that immediately set Margaret's and James's hearts racing.

"Miss Margaret, Mr. James," the young boy gasped,

struggling for breath, "you're needed at Liberty Hall. It's... it's something you'll want to see for yourselves."

Without a moment's hesitation, they followed the messenger, curiosity and a sense of foreboding mingling in their steps. As they approached Liberty Hall, the sight that met their eyes was one they could have never anticipated.

In the center of the square, surrounded by a gathering crowd of townsfolk, stood a figure cloaked in the early morning shadows—a person they thought lost to the war, a friend whose absence had left a void in their hearts and in the fabric of their community.

Margaret's hand flew to her mouth, her eyes brimming with tears of disbelief. James stood frozen, his mind racing to comprehend the sight before him. The figure stepped forward into the light, the rising sun casting a halo around him as if welcoming a hero from the tales of old.

"It can't be..." James whispered, taking a step forward, almost afraid that the vision before him would vanish.

But it was true. Against all odds, Thomas, a young soldier who had fought alongside them and had been captured by the enemy, presumed lost to the merciless tide of war, had returned. His appearance was weary, his uniform worn, but his eyes sparkled with the indomitable spirit of survival.

The crowd erupted into cheers and tears, a tumult of emotion that echoed through the square. Margaret rushed forward, followed by James, to embrace their long-lost friend. Their reunion was a powerful testament to the resilience of the human spirit and the unbreakable bonds forged in the crucible of shared struggle.

Thomas, overcome with emotion, managed to speak, his

voice cracking, "I thought of this moment every day... of coming home. You all gave me the strength to survive, to make it back."

His words, simple yet profound, resonated with everyone present, a poignant reminder of what they had fought for and the miracles that their newfound peace could bring.

As the community gathered around Thomas, sharing in the joy of his return, stories began to flow—tales of bravery, of sacrifice, and of the unwavering hope that had sustained them through the darkest times. It was a moment of catharsis, a collective exhale after the long, held breath of war.

Margaret and James, standing amidst their friends and family, felt a surge of purpose. This reunion, this miraculous return, was a sign that their work, their fight for a better future, was far from over. It was a call to action, a reminder that every day brought with it the chance to make a difference and strengthen the ties that bound them as a community and nation.

Today, Toward a Brighter Dawn, was not just a chapter in their history; it was a living narrative of hope, resilience, and the enduring power of human connection. And as they looked into the faces of those around them, they knew that together, they could face any challenge, turn any dream into reality.

As the initial shock of Thomas's return settled into a warm glow of reunion and celebration, the townsfolk began to disperse, leaving Margaret, James, and a few close friends to welcome Thomas back properly. They gathered in a quiet corner of Liberty Hall, where the early morning light streamed through the windows, casting a serene glow over the group.

Thomas, looking around at the faces of those he considered family, began to share his story. "It was in the depths of captivity that I lost hope," he confessed, his voice steady but haunted by the memory. "But there was a moment, a single, fleeting moment, when the thought of this place, of all of you, pierced through the darkness. It became my beacon, guiding me home."

Margaret reached out, squeezing his hand in silent support. James, ever the pillar of strength, added, "Your return is a testament to the resilience of the human spirit, Thomas. It's a reminder to us all that even in our darkest hours, hope can find a way."

Their conversation turned toward the future, reflecting on the lessons learned from the war and the visions they held for the new nation. It was during this exchange that an idea began to take shape—a plan that would not only celebrate Thomas's miraculous return but also serve as a symbol of their enduring hope and unity.

"We should host a festival," Elizabeth suggested, her eyes alight with inspiration. "Not just for Thomas, but as a celebration of all we've overcome and all we aspire to be. It could be a day of remembrance, hope, and unity, bringing together every corner of our community."

The idea was met with unanimous agreement. The festival would be a reflection of their journey, a tapestry of their shared experiences woven with the threads of loss, triumph, and the unbreakable bonds of friendship.

As plans for the festival took shape, Margaret and James took a moment to step outside, seeking a breath of fresh air amidst the flurry of activity. They found themselves walking towards the garden of remembrance and renewal, where the first signs of spring were beginning to show.

"It's remarkable, isn't it?" Margaret mused, gesturing to the garden around them. "How life finds a way to push through the soil, to reach towards the light, no matter how harsh the winter."

James nodded, his gaze tracing the delicate blossoms that dared to bloom. "It's a powerful metaphor for our own journey. We've faced the winter, and now it's our time to bloom, to build the future we've dreamed of."

Their walk led them to the center of the garden, where the statue erected in memory of those lost stood as a solemn guardian. Here, they made a silent vow—to honor the sacrifices of the past by nurturing the seeds of hope and unity they had planted, ensuring that their legacy would flourish in the years to come.

The festival, they decided, would be more than just a day of celebration; it would be a declaration of their community's strength, resilience, and unwavering commitment to the ideals that had guided them through the darkest times. It would be a testament to the ties that bound them, ties forged in adversity but strengthened in love and shared purpose.

As they returned to Liberty Hall, their hearts were full, not just with the joy of Thomas's return but with the anticipation of the festival and all it represented. They were ready to face the dawn, to embrace the challenges and opportunities of building a nation grounded in the principles of freedom, equality, and justice.

The festival, they knew, would be a momentous occasion, a beacon of hope for a brighter future, a future they would build together, one day at a time.

As the riders completed their solemn procession, they were met with a profound silence from the townsfolk lining the streets. Each person, standing shoulder to shoulder, embodied the community's collective strength and resilience. As the last horse passed, this quiet homage to the past seamlessly transitioned into the present's celebration.

The first notes of hopeful melody, played by a small ensemble of musicians near Liberty Hall, marked this transition. The music, a bridge between past sorrows and future hopes, invited the day forward with a spirit of rejuvenation and joy.

Margaret stepped forward, capturing the attention of all present with her resonant voice, beginning the festival with words of remembrance, unity, and commitment to the future. "Today, we gather not just to remember the sacrifices that have brought us here but to celebrate the strength and spirit that define us as a community. Our journey has been marked by hardship, but also by incredible resilience. This festival is a declaration of our unity and our commitment to a future built on the foundations of freedom, justice, and mutual respect."

The day unfolded with an array of activities that engaged every member of the community. Children raced in games that filled the air with laughter and cheers, artisans displayed their crafts, sharing the stories behind their creations, and historians gave talks on the significance of their newfound independence, ensuring that the lessons of the past would inform the path forward.

James oversaw a series of friendly competitions, reflecting on the significance of the day. "This is about more than just the games we play today. It's about building a community where everyone has a place, where every contribution is valued. We're laying the groundwork for the society we dream of—a society where the bonds of friendship and solidarity are our greatest strength."

As the sun began to set, the community gathered around a large bonfire in the central square. Margaret and James joined hands with Thomas, Elizabeth, Samuel, Anna, and others who had been instrumental in the town's journey, forming a circle that symbolized their unbreakable bond.

Looking around at the faces illuminated by the firelight—faces marked by diversity, by stories of loss and triumph—Margaret felt a surge of gratitude. "This is the true strength of our nation. Not in the battles we've won, but in the community we've built, in the ties that bind us together."

The festival concluded with stories shared around the bonfire, tales of heroism and sacrifice, each story a thread woven into their collective memory. As the embers of the fire burned down, the townsfolk dispersed under the starlit sky, carrying with them the warmth of the community and the promise of a brighter dawn.

. As the festival's echoes waned and the night deepened, Margaret and James found themselves lingering by the dying embers of the bonfire, not yet ready to let go of the day's profound sense of community and hope. Around them, the square had emptied, leaving behind a stillness that spoke volumes of the day's significance.

"It's been a remarkable day," Margaret said, her voice low, reflecting the mix of emotions that danced within her. "Seeing everyone come together like this, it's... it reaffirms why we fought, what we envisioned."

James, looking into the flames, nodded. "It does. And yet, it's only the beginning, isn't it? Today was a celebration, but tomorrow, the real work continues. The work of building, of making all those hopes and dreams a reality."

Margaret sighed, a sound of agreement and resolve. "Yes, the real work. But after today, I feel more confident than ever that we're ready for it. The ties that bind us—they've proven to be stronger than I ever imagined."

Their conversation was gently interrupted by the approach of Elizabeth, Samuel, and Anna, who, like them, were drawn to the warmth of the fire and the company of trusted friends. Together, they formed a small circle, a microcosm of the larger community they were part of.

Elizabeth, her eyes bright with the day's memories, shared her reflections. "Today, I saw laughter where there once was sorrow, hope where there was despair. It's as if we've turned a page, started a new chapter."

Samuel, his hands still bearing the marks of his day's labor, added, "We've built more than just structures and homes in this town. We're building a legacy. One that's about more than survival—it's about thriving, about living up to the ideals we hold dear."

Anna, whose work had touched the lives of many in their community, spoke softly, "And let's not forget the healing that's begun. Today was a testament to the strength found in shared experiences, in understanding and supporting each other."

Their conversation meandered through topics of the future, of dreams for their community, and the challenges they anticipated. Yet, underlying all their discussions was a thread of unwavering optimism, fueled by the day's events and the palpable sense of unity it had fostered.

As the night gave way to the first hints of dawn, the group disbanded, each person carrying with them the warmth of the fire and the certainty that, together, they were moving toward a brighter dawn.

In the days and weeks that followed, the energy and spirit of the festival did not fade but rather infused the community with a renewed vigor. Liberty Hall buzzed with activity, becoming the heart of the town's civic life. Workshops, debates, and planning sessions became the norm, each contributing to the tapestry of their evolving society.

Margaret and James, alongside their friends and fellow citizens, were at the forefront of these efforts, guiding, facilitating, and participating in the shared task of nation-building. They encountered obstacles, of course—differences of opinion, logistical challenges, and the daunting task of reconciling their ideals with practical realities. Yet, each hurdle was met with the same collaborative spirit that had characterized the festival, a reminder of the resilience and capacity for growth that defined their community.

It became clear that the festival was not just a day of celebration but a catalyst for change, a symbol of the community's commitment to building a future that reflected the best of their shared values and aspirations. It was a chapter in their ongoing story, filled with the promise of progress, the challenges of growth, and the unshakeable belief in the power of unity and purpose.

The momentum initiated by the festival and the shared experiences of the community didn't merely carry on; it flourished. The town, once marked by the scars of a nation's birthright struggle, now thrummed with the vibrant pulse of creation and unity. From the youngest child to the oldest elder, each individual contributed to the fabric of their society, weaving threads of their own stories into the collective narrative of resilience and hope.

In this atmosphere of renewed purpose, Margaret found herself spearheading a project that was close to her heart—a library within Liberty Hall. It wasn't just to be a repository of books and knowledge but a sanctuary of learning, where the tales of their past and the dreams of their future could reside together. As she discussed the plans with James and the committee, her vision for a space that could educate and inspire future generations became a tangible goal, met with enthusiasm and support.

James, on the other hand, turned his attention to the infrastructure of their growing town. The festival highlighted the necessity of not just rebuilding but innovating. With a team of engineers and visionaries, he embarked on designing sustainable systems for water, agriculture, and trade—systems that would ensure the prosperity of their community and safeguard their independence.

As the library took shape and the infrastructure projects progressed, the townsfolk began to see the fruits of their labor and the reality of their aspirations. Liberty Hall buzzed with activity, its doors open to all who sought to learn, to debate, and to plan for the future.

One evening, as the sun set, painting the sky in brilliant hues of orange and crimson, a gathering took place in the newly completed section of Liberty Hall. The event was to celebrate the library's inauguration, but for Margaret, James, and their companions, it was a celebration of much more.

Standing before the community, Margaret felt a swell of pride. "This library," she addressed the gathered crowd, "is a beacon of our enduring commitment to knowledge, to understanding, and to each other. It stands as proof that from the ashes of conflict, we can build a legacy of peace and wisdom."

James, joining her, added, "It's through learning from our past that we can navigate our future. This library is not just a collection of books; it's a repository of our collective hopes and a guidepost for the journey ahead."

The inauguration became a night of storytelling, of sharing personal accounts of the war, of loss, of survival, and of the unbreakable spirit that had led them to this point. Each story, whether whispered among friends or declared to the assembly, added to the tapestry of their community's history, enriching the library's significance.

In the weeks that followed, the library and Liberty Hall became the heart and soul of the town, a place where the ties that bound them were continually strengthened. Workshops, lectures, and book clubs flourished, drawing in even the most isolated members of their society, knitting them closer together with each shared experience.

The narrative of "Toward a Brighter Dawn" was unfolding in real-time, with each day bringing new challenges, but also new opportunities to grow, to learn, and to strengthen the bonds of their community. The festival had been a catalyst, but it was the daily acts of courage, of compassion, and of collaboration that truly propelled them toward the brighter dawn they sought.

Margaret and James, standing together in the library one quiet morning, looked out at the town they had helped nurture. They saw not just buildings and streets but a living, breathing community—a community that had come through the fire of war to forge a future filled with promise.

Their journey was far from over, but as they turned to face the new day, they did so with the knowledge that together, they could face whatever came their way.

Margaret and James, standing together in the library, gazed out at the town that had become a testament to the strength and spirit of its people. This moment of quiet reflection underscored the journey they had undertaken together, from the ashes of war to the cusp of a new dawn.

Their community, once fractured by conflict, now stood united, a beacon of hope and a model of what could be achieved when hearts and minds worked in concert towards a common goal. The library, with its shelves filled with the wisdom of ages and the stories of their own trials and triumphs, symbolized the legacy they were building—a legacy of knowledge, understanding, and compassion.

As they turned from the window, their gaze fell on the assembled townsfolk within Liberty Hall, each individual a vital thread in the fabric of their society. The air was filled with the murmur of conversation, the laughter of children, and the shared anticipation of the future they were crafting together.

Margaret took a deep breath, feeling a profound sense of gratitude and responsibility. "Our work is far from finished," she said, her voice resonant with purpose. "But today, we stand on solid ground, ready to face whatever challenges come, to continue building a future worthy of the sacrifices made."

James nodded, his resolve mirrored in his eyes. "Together, we move toward that brighter dawn," he affirmed. "With each day, we write a new page in our story, guided by the lessons of the past and our hopes for tomorrow."

The chapter closed not with an ending but with a promise—a promise of continued growth, of dreams pursued with tenacity and courage, and of a community forever bound by the ties of shared struggle and shared triumph.

Together, they stepped forward, not just as leaders, but as partners in the unending task of nation-building, their hearts buoyed by the knowledge that with every challenge faced, they grew stronger, more united, forging a path toward a brighter dawn.

Epilogue: Reflections on a Nation Forged

Years had passed since the day Margaret and James stood in the newly built library of Liberty Hall, witnessing a town that had risen from the ashes of conflict. These years had not just seen the change of seasons and the growth of children, but a remarkable transformation of the community. The once distant dreams of unity, learning, and mutual respect had become the strong foundations of a society that now thrived.

As another day drew to a close, casting long shadows across the square that had once been the heart of their celebrations and gatherings, Margaret walked slowly towards a bench under the great oak in the center of the garden. This garden, not just a beautiful space, but a meticulously tended living memorial, was a riot of colors and scents. It stood as a testament to both the losses of the past and the hopes for the future.

Beside her walked Anna, a young woman named for the beloved friend who had seen the community through its darkest times and its brightest dawns. Anna, now a historian, had taken upon herself the crucial task of documenting their nation's journey from its tumultuous beginnings to the vibrant present, ensuring that their history would not be forgotten.

As they sat, Anna turned to Margaret, her eyes filled with the curiosity that had driven her to understand the depths of their history. "You've seen so much change," Anna began, her voice echoing awe and respect. "From the days of war to this era of peace and prosperity. What do you think has been the key to our success?"

Margaret looked out over the garden, her eyes tracing the paths wound through the flowers and trees. "Unity," she replied, her voice imbued with the weight of her experiences. "The understanding that despite our differences, we share common dreams and fears. It was the unity that saw us through the darkest times, and it's unity that has built the world you see today."

Their conversation was a bridge between generations, a passing of wisdom and responsibility. Within this reflective mood, we find a moment to pay homage to the enduring spirits of Margaret Hale and James Bradford, whose lives and legacies have woven through the very fabric of this narrative.

As the final pages of "From Rebellion to Nation: The Flame of Liberty" turn, we reach a moment of reflection and homage to the enduring spirits of Margaret Hale and James Bradford. In the tumultuous canvas of the American Revolutionary War, their stories stand as testaments to the power of courage, conviction, and the indomitable will to forge a path toward freedom. With her unwavering resolve and keen intellect, Margaret became an unsung heroine, her espionage efforts critical to the Continental Army's strategies. Her sacrifices, often borne in silence, guided the cause of liberty with a steady hand.

James Bradford, once a soldier for the Crown, found his true allegiance in the ideals of justice and freedom that the revolution embodied. His journey showcases the tumultuous path of a man torn between two worlds, ultimately choosing the side of righteousness. Together, Margaret and James embodied the revolution's core belief that one nation could emerge from the many, built on the foundations of liberty and equality.

Their names may not grace the pages of widely read history books or their faces etched into monuments, but within the heart of our story, they stand immortalized—symbols of the countless unnamed who dared to dream of a better world.

As peace settles over the newly born United States of America, we recognize Margaret Hale and James Bradford not just for their dedication and sacrifices but for their indispensable and pivotal contributions to the victory of the Continental Army. Their legacy, woven into the fabric of American independence, reminds us that history is made by the personal stories of individuals who fought, loved, and hoped for a future where freedom reigns supreme.

In honoring Margaret and James, we pay tribute to the spirit of all those who, facing the tempest of revolution, found the strength to change the course of history. Their journey from rebellion to nation stands as a beacon of liberty's flame, a light that, once kindled, burns eternally bright in the annals of time.

And so, as we close this chapter of their story, we do not say farewell but promise to carry forward the flame they have passed to us. For in their legacy lies not just the memory of past struggles but the guiding light for future generations to follow toward a brighter dawn. Their legacy is not just a memory, but a living inspiration that continues to shape our present and future.

[The End]

Historical Setting and Events Notes for "From Rebellion to Nation"

Philadelphia's Role in the Revolutionary War:

Philadelphia, a central setting in our story, was indeed the heart of revolutionary activity and intellectual exchange during the American Revolution. As the meeting place of the Continental Congress and the site where the **Declaration of Independence** was adopted on **July 4, 1776**, the city's historical significance is unparalleled. Our narrative explores Philadelphia's vibrant yet tumultuous life, reflecting its status as a crucible of American independence.

British Occupation of Philadelphia (1777-1778):

The British occupation of Philadelphia from September 1777 to June 1778 was a pivotal moment in the Revolutionary War. This event brought significant hardship to the city's residents and is depicted in our story to highlight the challenges and dangers faced by the characters, particularly those involved in espionage and the Patriot cause. The occupation ended when British forces evacuated Philadelphia in anticipation of the French fleet's arrival, a strategic turn that shaped the war's outcome.

Espionage and the Culper Spy Ring:

Espionage played a critical role in the American struggle for independence, a theme central to our narrative. The Culper Spy Ring, though not explicitly named in our story, inspired the covert activities of our protagonists. This network, established by Major Benjamin Tallmadge under orders from General George Washington in 1778, was crucial in providing intelligence on British troop movements and plans, much like the espionage endeavors undertaken by our characters.

Societal Divisions and Allegiances:

The internal conflict within American society over loyalty to the British Crown or the revolutionary cause is a key element of our story. This division tore families and communities apart, a reality that many, including our characters, navigated daily. Our narrative aims to capture the personal and societal turmoil of the era, reflecting the complex loyalties and decisions faced by those living through the revolution.

Military Strategies and Engagements:

While our story focuses more on the human and espionage aspects of the war, it unfolds against the backdrop of ongoing military engagements and the strategic maneuvers of both the Continental and British forces. The narrative alludes to broader military campaigns and the tactical challenges of the war, underscoring the constant threat and uncertainty that shaped the lives of the characters.

Continental Congress and Declaration of Independence:

The Continental Congress's role in governing the fledgling United States and its adoption of the Declaration of Independence are seminal events that loom large in the historical backdrop of our story. These events symbolize the colonies' united stand for freedom and the ideological foundation of the revolution, influencing the convictions and actions of our protagonists.

Skirmish at Brandywine Creek - A Moment of Valor:

"As we have journeyed through the pivotal moments and underlying currents that shaped the Revolutionary War, we've seen how the fabric of this historic struggle is woven with both the grandiose and the granular, the monumental battles and the quieter acts of defiance. It is within this intricate tapestry that the Skirmish at Brandywine Creek finds its place—a fictionalized yet emblematic encounter that captures the essence of individual courage and strategic acumen. While inspired by the myriad real-life skirmishes that punctuated the war, this event epitomizes the resolve and sacrifices of those who fought not just for the idea of freedom, but for its very realization. As we conclude this exploration of the historical setting and events that frame our story, let us remember that history, at its core, is made not only by the outcomes of conflict but by the spirit and actions of those who dare to challenge the status quo."

Among the many engagements that punctuated the Revolutionary War, the skirmish at Brandywine Creek stands as a testament to the valor and resilience of the Continental Army and its supporters. While fictionalized in our narrative, skirmishes like this were commonplace and crucial to the strategic positioning and morale of the American forces.

Historical Context: The actual Battle of Brandywine, which occurred on September 11, 1777, was a significant engagement between the American forces under General George Washington and the British Army led by General Sir William Howe. The battle was part of the British campaign to capture Philadelphia, the American capital at the time. Though the battle resulted in a British victory, it exemplified the determination and resilience of the American forces.

<u>*Note</u> **Fictionalized Skirmish:** In our story, the Skirmish at Brandywine Creek is a smaller, fictional engagement inspired by the many similar confrontations that occurred throughout the Revolutionary War. These skirmishes, though not as well-documented as major battles, were vital to the war effort, testing the resolve of the Continental Army and disrupting British plans.

Margaret and James's Involvement: By placing Margaret Hale and James Bradford at the heart of this fictional skirmish, we illuminate the roles played by countless unsung heroes of the Revolution. Their leadership and bravery, though fictional, represent the spirit of all those who stood up against seemingly insurmountable odds for the cause of freedom.

Impact of the Skirmish: While the skirmish at Brandywine Creek is a creation of our narrative, it serves to highlight the strategic importance of intelligence, quick thinking, and the courage of individual soldiers and small units. Such skirmishes were instrumental in keeping the British forces spread thin and on edge, contributing to the overall effort of the Continental Army.

Legacy: The fictional skirmish at Brandywine Creek, though a minor episode in the grand scheme of the war, underscores the themes of sacrifice, unity, and the pursuit of liberty that define our story. It reminds readers that history is not only made by the outcome of great battles but also shaped by the bravery of individuals in smaller moments of conflict.

Additional Elements:

- **Women's Roles in the War Effort:** The narrative acknowledges the critical roles women played, from running households in their husbands' absence to acting as messengers and spies, reflecting the broader contributions of women to the revolutionary cause.

- **The Declaration of Independence's Ideological Impact:** Beyond its adoption, the Declaration's principles of liberty and equality echo throughout the narrative, shaping characters' motivations and the societal changes they advocate for.

- **The Franco-American Alliance (1778):** This turning point in the war, securing French military support, is alluded to as a beacon of hope and strategic advantage for the American cause. It impacted the morale of the characters and altered the course of the war.

These notes aim to bridge the gap between historical events and the fictional narrative of "From Rebellion to Nation: The Flame of Liberty," providing readers with a richer understanding of the story's historical and imaginative landscape.

The Real Revolution: Historical Insights into From Rebellion to Nation

Philadelphia's Role in the Revolutionary War: Philadelphia, a central setting in our story, was indeed the heart of revolutionary activity and intellectual exchange during the American Revolution. As the meeting place of the Continental Congress and the site where the Declaration of Independence was adopted on July 4, 1776, the city's historical significance is unparalleled. Our narrative explores the vibrant yet tumultuous life in Philadelphia, reflecting its status as a crucible of American independence.

British Occupation of Philadelphia (1777-1778): The British occupation of Philadelphia from September 1777 to June 1778 was a pivotal moment in the Revolutionary War.

This event brought significant hardship to the city's residents and is depicted in our story to highlight the challenges and dangers faced by the characters, particularly those involved in espionage and the Patriot cause. The occupation ended when British forces evacuated Philadelphia in anticipation of the French fleet's arrival, a strategic turn that shaped the war's outcome.

Espionage and the Culper Spy Ring: Espionage played a critical role in the American struggle for independence, a theme central to our narrative. The Culper Spy Ring, though not explicitly named in our story, inspired the covert activities of our protagonists. This network, established by Major Benjamin Tallmadge under orders from General George Washington in 1778, was crucial in providing intelligence on British troop movements and plans, much like the espionage endeavors undertaken by our characters.

Societal Divisions and Allegiances: The internal conflict within American society over loyalty to the British Crown or the revolutionary cause is a key element of our story. This division tore families and communities apart, a reality that many, including our characters, navigated daily. Our narrative aims to capture the personal and societal turmoil of the era, reflecting the complex loyalties and decisions faced by those living through the revolution.

Military Strategies and Engagements: While our story focuses more on the human and espionage aspects of the war, it unfolds against the backdrop of ongoing military engagements and the strategic maneuvers of both the Continental and British forces. The narrative alludes to broader military campaigns and the tactical challenges of the war, underscoring the constant threat and uncertainty that shaped the lives of the characters.

Continental Congress and Declaration of Independence: The Continental Congress's role in governing the fledgling

United States and its adoption of the Declaration of Independence are seminal events that loom large in the historical backdrop of our story. These events symbolize the colonies' united stand for freedom and the ideological foundation of the revolution, influencing the convictions and actions of our protagonists.

Skirmish at Brandywine Creek: A Moment of Valor

As we have journeyed through the pivotal moments and underlying currents that shaped the Revolutionary War, we've seen how the fabric of this historic struggle is woven with both the grandiose and the granular, the monumental battles and the quieter acts of defiance. It is within this intricate tapestry that the Skirmish at Brandywine Creek finds its place—a fictionalized yet emblematic encounter that captures the essence of individual courage and strategic acumen. While inspired by the myriad real-life skirmishes that punctuated the war, this event epitomizes the resolve and sacrifices of those who fought not just for the idea of freedom, but for its very realization. As we conclude this exploration of the historical setting and events that frame our story, let us remember that history, at its core, is made not only by the outcomes of conflict but by the spirit and actions of those who dare to challenge the status quo

Among the many engagements that punctuated the Revolutionary War, the skirmish at Brandywine Creek stands as a testament to the valor and resilience of the Continental Army and its supporters. While fictionalized in our narrative, skirmishes like this were commonplace and crucial to the strategic positioning and morale of the American forces.

Historical Context: The actual Battle of Brandywine, which occurred on September 11, 1777, was a significant engagement between the American forces under General George Washington and the British Army led by General Sir William Howe. The battle was part of the British campaign to capture Philadelphia, the American capital at the time. Though the battle resulted in a British victory, it exemplified the determination and resilience of the American forces.

Fictionalized Skirmish: In our story, the Skirmish at Brandywine Creek is a smaller, fictional engagement inspired by the many similar confrontations that occurred throughout the Revolutionary War. These skirmishes, though not as well-documented as major battles, were vital to the war effort, testing the resolve of the Continental Army and disrupting British plans.

Margaret and James's Involvement: By placing Margaret Hale and James Bradford at the heart of this fictional skirmish, we illuminate the roles played by countless unsung heroes of the Revolution. Their leadership and bravery, though fictional, represent the spirit of all those who stood up against seemingly insurmountable odds for the cause of freedom.

Impact of the Skirmish: While the skirmish at Brandywine Creek is a creation of our narrative, it serves to highlight the strategic importance of intelligence, quick thinking, and the courage of individual soldiers and small units. Such skirmishes were instrumental in keeping the British forces spread thin and on edge, contributing to the overall effort of the Continental Army.

Legacy: The fictional skirmish at Brandywine Creek, though a minor episode in the grand scheme of the war, underscores the themes of sacrifice, unity, and the pursuit of liberty that define our story. It reminds readers that history is not only made by the outcome of great battles but also shaped by the bravery of individuals in smaller moments of conflict.